Penguin Books
Regent Square

Forbes Bramble was born in 1939 and is an architect by profession. As a student at University College, London, he wrote plays performed by London University, and his play *The Dice* was televised. He has written two previous novels, *Stone*, which won a Scottish Arts Council award, and *The Strange Case of Deacon Brodie*.

Forbes Bramble

Regent Square

Penguin Books

Penguin Books Ltd, Harmondsworth,
Middlesex, England
Penguin Books, 625 Madison Avenue, New York,
New York 10022, U.S.A.
Penguin Books Australia Ltd, Ringwood,
Victoria, Australia
Penguin Books Canada Ltd, 2801 John Street,
Markham, Ontario, Canada L3R 1B4
Penguin Books (N.Z.) Ltd, 182–190 Wairau Road,
Auckland 10, New Zealand

First published by Hamish Hamilton 1977

Published in Penguin Books 1980

Typeset, printed and bound in Great Britain by
Hazell Watson and Viney Ltd,
Aylesbury, Bucks
Set in Linotype Pilgrim

As by the Templar's hold you go,
The horse and lamb display'd
The emblematic figures show
The merits of their trade.
The clients may infer from thence
How just is their profession;
The lamb sets forth their innocence,
The horse their expedition.
Oh, happy Britons! happy isle!
Let foreign nations say,
Where you get justice without guile
And Law without delay.

*Anonymous nineteenth-century doggerel chalked
on the Temple doorway. The Pegasus and
the Lamb and Flag are the emblems of the
Inner Temple and the Middle Temple*

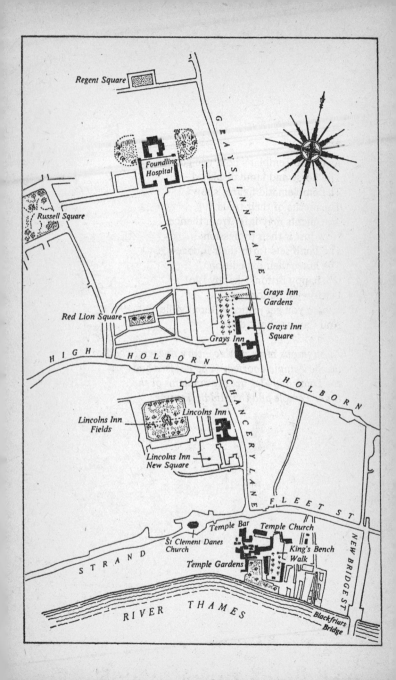

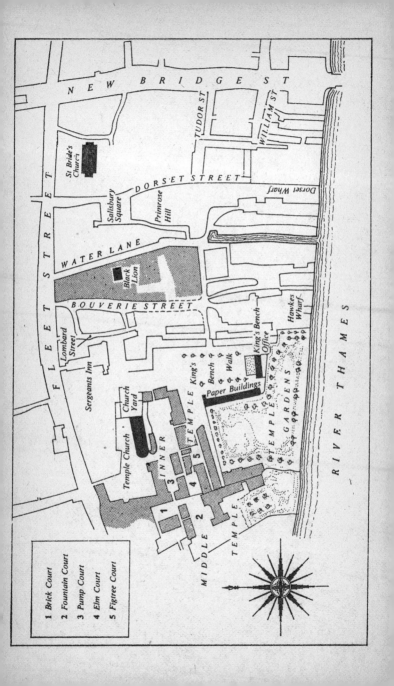

Part One 1821

When a warm sun rose drowsily from the haze of the Essex marshes, it was taken as an omen in support of the Queen by most, and in support of the King by some.

Despite the early hour, London seemed to pulsate with an air of expectation. The normal rhythms of the city were suspended. There was a buzz, a murmur no louder than the sound of traffic heard on still evenings, but it was not traffic. Few carriages passed, but those that did clipped by at a great pace, their drivers and passengers looking aloof as though about business of great purpose. Shops were already unlocked and doors thrown open, but not for trade. For the moment, at least, that was postponed.

Provincial Mail Coaches pouring into London were jammed inside and on top with tired and irritable passengers. The *Alert* and *Magnet* from Oxford, the *Phenomenon* from Norwich, *Eclipse*, *Wonder* and *Triumph* from Birmingham, all jostled and clattered into Aldersgate, Holborn or Piccadilly. The tired travellers ate hastily of cold meat and moved on, on foot.

In the poorer and meaner streets, make-shift bunting had been hung out on thin cordage, criss-crossed from upper windows and lamp-brackets. Hammersmith, Kensington, Whitechapel and Mile End had fluttering skies of ribbon torn from strips of cloth. Banners hung across the street with stitched-on lettering.

'God save the Queen.'

It was July 17, the King's coronation day.

On the Hampstead Road, where lime-white bricklayers had started early to finish off the last of a row of yellow-brick cottages, a block of stone was being set in gauged lime mortar. The stone was inscribed 'Caroline Cottages'. The builder was proud of the idea. They would sell well. His men would have the rest of the day off to get drunk.

*

In Regent Square there was no vulgar bunting, no banners or flags. In the mews behind the houses, horses clattered on cobbles and harness jingled. Horses and carriages were being brushed and polished until they shone. Hired barouches stood by the railings that surrounded the garden in the centre of the square, the horses with heads bowed and half asleep. Men in livery rubbed at bodywork and leather until black lacquer sparkled and looked wet.

The Kelleway family had decided to foregather for this occasion in their father's house in the square. From there they would proceed in two carriages to seats in a box in front of the Abbey. Caroline Kelleway, who owed her christened name to the Queen who had not been invited to be crowned, was in charge of arrangements. Although at twenty-four she was the youngest of the Kelleway children, she was the only female. It was a return to a once-familiar role in the motherless household. She had not married despite suitors and her evident good looks. Old Thomas, in a fit of belated guilt, had bought her a house in Highgate so that she might make something of her life in exchange for her stolen youth. He had installed a housekeeper, but in this had been his outrageous self. The woman was to report to him, so that Caroline might not be indiscreet without it reaching his ears. He had no thought of it as spying, but as looking after the child.

Caroline had left the house in Highgate for a week to prepare her father and family for the event. Her brother Henry and his wife Jane had arrived the evening before from their house in Kensington. They thought little of the house in Regent Square that Thomas refused to leave. It was certainly not as grand as Tavistock Square or Gower Street where lawyers lived in style. Thomas despised stucco pilasters and what he called the high and haughty rooms of the Duke of Bedford's new estates. His was a modest four storey terraced house of human proportions and simple detail. He liked its plain brick. It was close to Gray's Inn Lane which led directly to Chancery Lane and the Temple. He thought Henry guilty of ostentation and extravagance.

The atmosphere between them had not been relaxed. Now they waited for William and his wife Maria to join them for breakfast and complete the party. Caroline and Henry were united in their trepidation over this, for old Thomas openly described William as 'a natural disaster', the will of God, such as smites the soundest ship on some occasion. As a painter, William had already stood himself firmly beyond what Thomas considered to be the reasonable boundaries of human behaviour. As a painter and a Whig who had married a woman who made no secret of her views on the injustice of men to women, or indeed upon anything else, and who also wrote verse and painted, he had to be considered insane or under the power of evil influences. But while Thomas was openly hostile to them both, Caroline was concerned to keep the peace. It seemed to be another old role. She liked William, who was clever, and regarded Maria with some awe.

At this moment, Caroline was helping her father wrestle with his waistcoat buttons. Thomas was trying to keep his temper and it showed in his complexion.

'These contraptions are more suited to the criminally insane than to ordinary men!'

'You have them in the wrong buttonholes.'

'Devil take them!' he shouted angrily, tugging helplessly at the cloth. 'And what do you think they're doing downstairs?'

Caroline patiently undid the buttons and did them up again. 'Breakfast is prepared and on the sideboard. Everything is arranged and in order. The footman has checked with the coachman and the carriages will be ready. He has extra feed in the nose-bags so that they don't become restive ...'

'No, no! I mean Henry and his wife. Devil take their horses. You know I mean them. Have you observed them? He goes round my house as though it's not good enough for him. I hear they complained about their room. It is, I believe, rather too small for their tastes.'

'Father, no one said that.'

'Henry observed that he could not understand how anyone could live for long in such a limited space. His house in Kensington is a fine place no doubt, but you tell me how many usurers, banks and brokers it is cut up amongst? I should be surprised if he owns the chimney-pots.'

'Come on, Father, keep still. You mustn't work yourself up like this. You promised me before they came. Remember?'

Thomas grunted. At fifty-four, he was going to fat, but was vigorous and combative towards life in general and his sons in particular.

'Men's clothing seems to me to have been invented by the Inquisition,' he grumbled, evading the point. 'Everything constricts and we have all our ends tied in like wine-skins to prevent natural ventilation. We would be more comfortable in the old Scotch dress.' He walked uneasily to a cheval-glass, shrugging and tugging. He looked neither comfortable nor elegant. He snorted at what he saw. 'In all honesty, is that a man?'

Caroline laughed. He had in no way changed. A boy who needed a mother when his wife died. She must not dwell upon it as she was inclined to. She was being watched by him in the mirror for any sign that she was still vulnerable. She looked back at him steadily. He changed the subject.

'You know perfectly well that I'm correct. And Jane will discreetly be remarking upon the carpets, furniture, silver and crystal.'

'At least it shows they have good taste.'

'It shows they have damnably bad taste to poke at your father's possessions. Would I do it to them?'

'Yes.'

Thomas stared at her in disbelief. Caroline continued, but there was warm indulgence in her voice that betrayed what she had been to him.

'Whenever you visit them, you come back remarking that they eat and drink from nothing but the finest. You remark upon Henry's wines and Jane's jewels. Upon their curtains and linen and the livery of their servants. If I remember correctly, even upon the polish of their bell-pull. "Dee me!" you shouted to the street at large, "that pull has the polish of a communion cup!" And not satisfied with being a public embarrassment, you gave me a comprehensive lecture all the way back on the collapse of the social structure in the profession of the law, where a barrister must needs live in Kensington!'

Thomas roared with laughter, so that it seemed he might burst out of his clothing.

'I did! You're right, I did. I remember it.' He too had reverted to an earlier time and an earlier situation. Caroline sensed it with alarm and was prepared for his next words. 'You know, you are still our little mother. It takes me back, sadly, but it was not long ago.'

Caroline was quick to interrupt in defence. 'No. I am an independent woman now, as you intended, with my own house and servants. And you are an independent man.'

'Independence in a man is a virtue – when channelled and checked. It must not run riot like our French friends do. But independence in a woman should be a transitory state. That's still my hope. You know what Milton wrote,

> For contemplation he and valour formed;
> For softness she and sweet attractive grace,
> He for God only, she for God in him :
> His fair large front and eye sublime declared
> Absolute rule.'

Caroline could not answer or tell him of the resentment this provoked. She could not tell him that at this moment she believed herself to be with child by a man who had no intention of marrying, that she felt ill and afraid. It did not show yet, she was sure. She hoped she could continue to conceal her inability to eat breakfast which made her feel sick. As it might be the only meal she would get today, it was going to be an ordeal and she had to control her panic. She was determined that she would not be forced abroad with her infant. If that was what decency demanded she had no respect for it.

'Come on, Father, you'll never be ready in time.' She wanted to sit down.

'I don't care so much for George that I care if I miss his Coronation. His petty persecution of that unfortunate woman is a national disgrace. They say he's spent £25,000 on his coronation robes alone, and the whole thing is to cost a quarter of a million. I've been a Tory all my life but I would never have approved it !'

'But you would like to see Queen Caroline?'

Thomas stopped in the act of tucking in his kerchief. Caroline had only made the remark to tide over her discomfort. She must loosen her clothes. It would be hot in the box and she must not faint. Thomas turned to her and quoted the rhyme that balladeers had peddled round the country.

'Most gracious queen, we thee implore,
To go away and sin no more;
But if that effort be too great,
To go away at any rate.

'I subscribe to it. We are sunk so low that I believe the monarchy itself is in danger. If I have to, I'll tolerate a scandalous king. A scandalous king with a scandalous queen is more than should be wished on us.'

'She intends to come. Everyone is saying so.'

'With Brougham behind with a goad, lest she should take the modest part!'

Caroline picked up a silver brush and brushed down the shoulders of his coat. She was sure she could manage to eat nothing, yet must force herself to try a little buttered toast. She could break it up, and it would appear all right. She wondered where the queen's sin was when her husband hated her, and why it should be a sin for her and only a scandal for the king. Would she, this Caroline, go away and sin no more? No. Nor even go away at any rate. She wished she could escape this whole family performance. Like brother John, in Assam. The heaving of her stomach subsided with the rhythmic brushing. Thomas stopped her.

'That's enough, my dear, you look quite breathless. Burges looks after my clothes.' He took her hand and kissed it. 'And yet you still look after me, don't you?' There was a duplicity of self-interest in his voice that she could not bear. It was monstrous blackmail.

'No, Father,' she said, knowing she would hurt him, 'I look after myself now, and you must do the same.'

He dropped her hand angrily like a boy caught in the act of theft. It was neither a denial nor an acceptance of what she said, he had merely postponed the attempt. Her struggle for survival was not over yet and the gift of the house in Highgate had only been a tactical retreat.

*

Henry and Jane were hungry, and impatient at the delay. Henry prowled up and down the dining-room as though caged by its small dimensions. Jane was, as her father-in-law had guessed, examining the furnishings.

Henry, unlike his father, was tall and elegant. His broad forehead and long curved nose gave him a superficial resemblance to Wellington in his youth, which he was careful to cultivate in the style of his hair and dress. He had a habit of sticking his thumbs in his waistcoat when talking, as though addressing the bench. In some this might have appeared amusing but in Henry it seemed a needless affectation.

He dominated by pause and pose, as an actor on the stage. Around his neck he wore a pair of pince-nez on a black silk cord, which he used as objects of aggression, his eyesight being perfectly sound. Discerning judges dismissed these trappings as marks of insecurity and noted his quick intelligence. Many, however, were disposed to take him at face value. A handsome and presumptive pup, too clever by far and too mannered by a mile.

Jane was staring at a murky oil-painting, marks of asperity showing on her pretty face. She knew what judges thought. Her father Sam Leigh was Thomas's great friend and fellow barrister. They had sat at mess together before she was born.

She never appeared relaxed. Her skin was too white, almost transparent and her cheeks lacked natural colour. When she spoke, her mouth was almost immobile so that she seemed to have a porcelain head on a long porcelain neck. Her manner of moving her head had a certain awkwardness, too, that heightened this impression.

Henry stopped by the window and stared out onto the square. The sun already cast long morning shadows across the red-brown gravel of the road.

'He is keeping us waiting deliberately. He lives in this house deliberately. He can afford a better house than we can. He husbands his money like a miser and he'll plough it all into business. I could do with some help now, and he knows it.' He gestured to the modest buildings of the square. 'Who are his neighbours? Tradesmen?' His thumbs were thrust in his waistcoat. 'I'll wager there's not one person of quality lives in the entire square.'

'He says there are other barristers . . .'

Henry grunted rudely and prowled over to the sideboard where he lifted the covers to inspect the breakfast meats.

'He eats well enough.'

'That will be Caroline's doing.'

'It has her touch about it. He'll move to her house in Highgate one day, wait and see.' He strolled back to the window again, posing in the light. 'Do you know, when we were children we played in the garden in that square and sometimes we sat and ate on the grass.' He said it as though the proposition was incredible to a man now in his station. It seemed very big then, and rather grand. Poor children in rags used to come and stare at us through the railings, following every bit of food from plate to mouth with their eyes. John was always a bit of a devil; he would drop a bit of cake on the ground just out of their reach, so that all their bony arms scraped about in the earth. I remember it particularly because one of the boys had only two fingers on one hand. They used to call us "sir". "Please sir, kick it nearer!" Then John would give it to the wretch with two fingers missing. He called him "two-finger Jack". Here you are, Jack, he would say and the boy would stick his head through the railings and stuff the cake into his mouth with his claw. That way, none of the others could get at it. They couldn't get their heads through.'

'Was he always so cruel?'

Henry stared at the plane trees. Their pied bark reminded him of disease. The trees were much taller but nothing else had changed. Ragged children still haunted the square, holding tethered horses and hoping to receive a reward that was most often a kick.

'You could never tell with John. He would disguise kindness with the trappings of cruelty so that no one should find him out. I think he felt it was a weakness. I believe that's why he joined the Army.'

'To be among the poor? They say the common people are all for Queen Caroline. I hope the coronation won't turn into a commotion. Your father says the common people are all malcontent and that the Whigs use them.'

'It's not only the common people. Parliamentary careers are built upon manipulating that unfortunate female. What a time! We are crowning a king we must pretend we want for the sake of the Constitution, who has invited his mistress to the Abbey, refuses his wife, and at one time supported Fox and his Whigs against his own father. On the other hand, we are afraid that his wife who is something I cannot name, will turn up supported by the king's former party to the delight of the common herd who see her as a woman wronged and the king as an inhuman monster. It is a Roman circus.'

'Which the poor love. But there must be poor to observe the wealthy. How else would they have ambition?'

'You know, Jane, that really is an intelligent remark.'

'Thank you, Henry. I'm glad I'm capable of one now and then.' She was inwardly furious. It was through his own and her father that Henry got what work he had, yet he never acknowledged it and treated her with condescension, and feigned surprise.

'Conversely,' she continued with deliberation, 'it is the presence of those poor that makes the rich defend themselves behind a barrier of laws, and makes the trading classes aspire to the same defence. In the end the poor will too.' She knew she had said too much. Henry's petulant expression turned to quick anger at the immodesty of her persisting. He did not reply, but walked to the sideboard, lifting the covers again. His back was turned to her.

'If father does not come down soon, I shall start without him. Mutton chops and cold chicken. Lord, I'm hungry!'

'We still await William and Maria.' She reminded him only to annoy. These frictions between them seemed to produce the only subjects on which they could converse. Henry did not turn round, but his vehemence was unmistakable.

'Must you!'

'I'm sure I said nothing.'

'You irritate me deliberately and you know it well.'

'But we are awaiting William and Maria.'

'Is that another example of your wilful misunderstanding?' He turned to face her. 'I don't deny your intelligence, but you must not use it to goad me. You prick at me on all occasions. You do it before my family and my friends. Why? I'm saddled with an abundance of enemies who mortify my flesh. Woman is a soft thing, a thing of gentleness and joy, comfort and calm. A home should be a bed of sweet hay, not of nettles. Why are you so discontented?'

'Henry, don't shout. Not here.'

'I demand to know why.'

'I'm not discontented.' A literal lie.

'Then, for the love of God, do not prod at me!' As quickly as he had flared up, his attitude changed to remorse. His hands, which he had clenched dramatically in the air, relaxed and he straightened them by his sides with the uncomfortable appearance of a guardsman at ease. 'Forgive me. I'm on edge.'

'There is nothing to forgive.'

'But I want forgiveness!'

It was the voice of a child crying out. Jane took his hand, because she knew she should do it. She was equally aware that she had no desire to. It was a shock to find that these small things were becoming duties. She wondered, as she had for the last year, if the change was in her or in him or in them both : Henry found her contact the relief he desired. He continued, trying to be light.

'I didn't know that Caroline intended it to be a full family affair. With William, sparks are bound to fly. Father says he is a natural disaster. I think he wishes he was a natural son.'

'William has wit.'

'He laughs at the institutions that ensure the survival of mankind. That's his wit.'

'Henry, he has a sense of humour and tolerance.'

Henry snorted but still clasped her hand hard, as though in seeking comfort he meant to punish her.

'That tolerance allows him to be exceedingly late. Their political views would have ended them on the gallows not so long ago! He describes the law as pedantry.'

Jane laughed as she had taught herself to. The sound was indulgent and soothing. Henry released her hand and pointed out of the window.

'There they are.'

A carriage had entered the square and racketed round it in a cloud of brown dust. It stopped with some tugging and shouting from the coachman. The horses were lathered and wet. The dust stuck to them. The coachman jumped down, opened the door and let down the folding steps.

'She is trying to be elegant,' said Jane, 'and she is handsome.' William handed Maria down and took her arm.

'Ready for breakfast?' William enquired in his most solemn and conspiratorial tone. He was smiling. Maria returned the smile, with a nod at the house.

'I think *we* are to be eaten! The hungry lions are at the window.'

'I know. But of course we haven't seen them, and we're not late.'

They walked up the steps together with the stately calm of ascending to the altar in a church. William tugged the gleaming brass bell-pull.

'Should I wipe it, now I've used it?'

'William, be quiet!'

Crabtree the footman opened the door and showed them in, taking hats and coats.

'Sir, ma'am, if you will come this way please, Mr and Mrs Henry Kelleway are waiting in the dining-room.'

The watchers were now standing before the dead fireplace, which had been filled with roses. Maria noticed that they had shed petals onto the carpet like live coals and that Jane was standing on these, quite oblivious. She could not repress the thought that she would have avoided them. Henry came forward, investing himself with dutiful enthusiasm.

'William, Maria. Delighted to see you both so well. Father will be down soon, I hope.'

'Then we're not late,' Maria replied as they exchanged dutiful pecks.

'It is difficult to be late for father!' replied Jane with great charm. Maria thought that she at least had some spirit.

'There was so much traffic,' explained William, 'we began to wonder if we should ever make it at all. All the streets are lined with people. It's impossible to proceed near the Coronation route. There is tremendous excitement about the Queen.'

'The Queen?' Henry looked sharply at his brother. 'I hope you are not going to shout for the Queen.'

'Nor you for the King. I will make a pact on that.' Henry managed a smile.

'I can find myself less than enthusiastic about His Majesty. However, I believe we are to see a grand parade. And if we do not see the King, I believe we shall hardly be able to avoid his clothes.'

'They say,' William remarked innocently, 'that he has reserved a seat in the Abbey for Lady Conyngham, and needs a box for the others outside.'

'William!' Jane affected to be outraged to encourage him.

'It is all very much the talk today, sister Jane. They are shouting the odds at street corners on the Queen demanding to be crowned. Quite disgraceful. They are giving three to one she will. If I had any money, I'd have stopped the coachman and wagered it.'

'You are sure she won't come?'

'I'm certain she will, if she's half the woman she's supposed to be.'

'Do you approve of her, then?' Jane's eyes were amused and challenging. She knew that Henry was struggling with his rage and it acted only to incite her. William had this effect. Although she recognized it, she had no desire to resist.

'Have I ever said so?' William was much shorter than his brother, but his face was naturally droll and he was nimble with his limbs, full of expression and gesture. He held up his hands in mock horror. 'No, not I. I am much too cautious to say anything about what I really feel, in front of a barrister.' They all smiled except Henry. To him William made a brief bow. 'Come, Henry, a spectacle is what the people like. Do you verily believe that all those persons of idle disposition who haunt the law courts are students of the law?'

Before Henry could reply, which he was about to do with some vehemence, the door was smartly opened by the liveried footman to admit Thomas and Caroline. The intention was that she should be on his arm, but the effect was much the opposite. Thomas lumbered forward, bothered by the elaborate constrictions of his dress. His shrewd eyes took in at a glance the attitudes of his sons.

'Good morning to you all. I have detained you, I know, and I apologize. Good morning, William, I see you made it, good morning, ma'am.' He could not bring himself to call Maria by her name. 'I trust you had a pleasant journey. Good,' he continued without waiting for a reply. 'Damn me, but the weather is hot. George will lose a pound or two before he gets to the Chair. Still, it's got a stone lining and should cool him, eh? Be seated please, I've no idea where the servants are, it's anarchy in the house. They're all going except cook and pay more attention to themselves than to me. Still, they should see their King. Crabtree!'

The footman, who had stood at the door throughout, made as though to enter the room.

'To the kitchen. Tell Burges we are waiting and ask him what he's about. Devil take it, we've waited long enough. And while you are about it, make sure the carriages are ready. We want no delay.'

They seated themselves, Thomas attempting to aid Caroline who could have managed much better alone. Burges, the butler, arrived almost immediately, and in time to seat his master in his chair.

'Well, Burges?' Thomas demanded gruffly.

'I must apologize, sir, for the delay, but all is not as it should be with delivery persons, because of the Coronation.'

'Then ring the bell.'

At this signal, the housemaid and the footman appeared with hot dishes of fish and ham and buttered toast in bain maries. Caroline refused everything except the buttered toast. The men set to with a good appetite, following the example of Thomas, who ate with speed and purpose.

'There is tea and cocoa,' he said, 'but if the gentlemen prefer, we shall have wine. I shall have wine in any case. Ladies, this will be our luncheon too so we must make the best of it. Caroline, you cannot exist on toast. Burges, where is that fish?'

'No, Father,' Caroline protested, 'I have no appetite. I think the day is too warm. I could not manage it.'

The footman stood beside her with the silver dish and the smell of it made her stomach turn. She felt hot and flushed and prayed she would not be sick.

'Then drink some wine to fortify yourself. I don't agree with this fashion of the ladies who sip their weak scandal-water and declare upon its aroma and flavours and medicinal values. Their souchongs and hysons and boheas are all the same to me – a poor kind of brackish water that effects only a loosening of the tongue. A witches' brew compounded for the assassination of character!'

They all laughed except Caroline, who contrived a smile. She sniffed the bouquet of roses that had been set before her and with their sweetness managed to obliterate the rank stench of boiled cod.

'I shall breakfast on the sweet scent of these beautiful flowers.'

Thomas snorted and picked up a cold chop which he quickly cleaned from the bone. The wine circulated.

'The trouble with Coronations,' Thomas continued, with the knack he had acquired at Temple dinners of talking and eating simultaneously, 'is that they are such solemn occasions of re-joicing for all but the common people. You can't take a cold fowl and wine to your box, for some dee'd fellow would kick it over and souse the ladies below.' He roared with laughter at the thought. These young, he thought, looking round the table, are waxy imitations of the right old stock. The men are afraid to drink well lest they should be thought ill-mannered. Were he their age and offered his father's best wines, he would arrive at the Coronation slopping like a wine-skin. 'Gentlemen, fill your glasses please. Ape your sovereign. Today we are crowning a hogshead.'

Henry was shocked. 'He is still our King. God Save the King.'

'You are a prig, Henry.'

'If that's the name of loyalty, then, sir, I am a prig.'

'Don't be so stiff and stuff, sir. We all applaud the monarchy, but this Prince Charming has turned back into a toad. Or to give him the structure he deserves, into a whale. I'm no Whig, but I quote a Templar, Charles Lamb:

> Is he Regent of the sea?
> By his bulk and by his size,
> By his oily qualities
> This (or else my eyesight fails)
> This should be the Prince of Whales.

Very good. They say he is now twenty-two stones.'

William, his eyes twinkling, said :

'Sir, that is almost a libel.'

'Then it has ceased to be by the coming into being of the fact, or the fat as the case may be. No sir, if it's a libel, we have repeated it often at dinners and twice at Grand Nights!'

Maria was watching Caroline. The men continued to talk and laugh and on the surface all was merry between them. But Caroline had grown very white. She gripped her bouquet like a talisman. The clatter of dishes masked her discreet whisper.

'Caroline, are you well?'

'Yes, perfectly.' Caroline had started, her eyes full of alarm.

'You are quite pale.'

'It's nothing. It's so warm. Please don't concern yourself.' Her tone was peremptory.

'But perhaps you should not go?'

'Of course I shall. Please say no more or everyone will notice, which I should find embarrassing.'

Maria returned to listening to the men. With the wine they had become expansive, and Thomas ebullient. They would be difficult to get from the table.

Caroline was anxiously aware that Maria's eyes moved to her again and again, thoughtful and alert.

Since first light at four o'clock, a crowd had been forming outside Queen Caroline's house in South Audley Street. Inside the house, lights had burned all night, and servants had been seen coming and going through chinks in the curtains. At first, the crowd had consisted of the ragged homeless creatures of the night, wretched and stinking, who sat on the kerb watched over by several 'Charleys' – the aged nightwatchmen of the city. The crowd had been increased about four by costers, mechanics, and Smithfield meat porters, all fanatically loyal to the Queen and full of contempt for the King. Then came hawkers and traders and every sort of passing street-seller who might do some passing trade while enjoying the free spectacle. There were penny-pie sellers, vendors of pickled whelks, sheep's trotters, fried fish, pea soup, spice-cakes, muffins, milk, tea, coffee and curds – all on their way to the Coronation route for a brisk day's trade. These were joined by hucksters, travellers, pick-pockets and show-men, similarly bound, some carrying monkeys or accompanied by dwarfs whom they placed on their shoulders for a better view. A ragged quack with his fingers sticking from the end of woollen mittens set up his folding table and tried to sell pre-ventatives against the cold, composed of gin and liquorice.

Gentlemen of the Town, bloods who loved the Queen's cause or were staunch Whigs or merely enjoyed the scandal which was their stock-in-trade, were informed by their footmen who had been sent on the errand, that the Queen's coach was being harnessed-up, and left their gaming clubs or their mistresses if they had not yet got to bed; for who would get up at such an hour unless he was still going from the previous day?

Facing the Queen's house across the cobbled street was a high brick wall on top of which agile or drunk spectators had clam-bered, kicking and beating back those who attempted to follow and overturn them all. It was not early for them to be drunk, for some were always drunk and waved their penny bottles of gin and sang. This waving, tottering row of black crows observed the progress of the preparations within the Queen's courtyard and cawed out the news to those below.

'Six nags are out!'

'The coach is out and harnessed!'

Two men fell from the wall, one backwards, no one knew where, the other forwards, where he cracked his skull on the stones. He was propped up against the wall, unnoticed, while others fought to take his place. No one looked to see whether he was alive or dead.

Just before five, as London sparrows started their long day's fight for dropped oats, Lady Anne Hamilton arrived to attend the Queen, and a cheer went up, for the Queen obviously in-tended to go.

'The Queen for ever, hurrah, hurrah, hurrah!'

The unoriginal shout was repeated time and again. Coster-mongers in their broad-ribbed corduroy waistcoats and dandy scarfs, waved their caps. Gentlemen brandished their gleaming hats. The Charleys wished that a military guard had been pro-vided, armed as they were with lanterns and wooden rattles.

*

During the previous day and through the night, all streets leading to Westminster had been blocked by massive timber barriers. Few people had been able to sleep through the sound of hammering, shouting and clatter of dray horses. A long barrier had been constructed from Charing Cross to Parliament Street to separate ticket holders for the ceremony from the crush of the crowds. Specially trained men accompanied by professional bruisers had been given special instruction in the correct forms of tickets, so that those with forgeries could be forcibly removed. Parliament Street itself had been divided down the middle, with one half reserved for coaches alone, to speed the progress of traffic. All along the Thames, close by Westminster, the landing-places, wharfs, stairs and roads had been sealed off with militia to guard them. Only Whitehall stair had been left open, and here a gun-brig had been moored on Wednesday to the derision of the bargees and watermen who stripped naked and swam about it, performing acrobatics and plunges from its anchor chain. Down river, the Thames was log-jammed with craft. Steam yachts and paddlers from the south coast towns were scraping hull to hull with Thames barges and sailing craft. A thousand small boats sculled or wallowed from ship to shore and boat to boat. The Thames watermen, in their flared short-coats and brass badges, were having the harvest of their lives. They charged outrageous fares to passengers desperate to disembark and countless bags carelessly fell over the side to the wailing of their owners, always near the shore, and always where they could be retrieved from the mud at low tide.

For every form of that vast mass of parasitical life that constituted the poor of London, the day was looked forward to like a second coming. The dredger-men would fish out what the watermen nudged in too deep. The toshers expected rich pickings from the sewers that they sieved and searched, knowing just how to find the coins that always stood upright in the brick joints, or the bones, metal, spoons, forks and occasional jewellery they could expect after such an occasion. The mud-larks, mainly filthy, dripping children and pathetically bent old hags, would descend on the mud to rake and dig with their hands for coals or bones, bits of rope and timber, nails and iron, which they collected in old kettles or their own hats. The coal could be sold at one penny for fourteen pounds, and the rest in rag-and-bone shops. Crossing-sweepers expected to be tipped well, with so many horses about. Only the pure-finders would do badly, for it was dog's excrement they sought for the tanneries, and dogs would be run off the street today.

King George the Fourth had taken the precaution of removing himself from his home in Carlton House the previous evening, and had spent the night in seclusion in the home of the Speaker of the House of Commons in Palace Yard. He abhorred the unruly crowd that so frequently abused him, called for the Queen, or even threw things at his carriage. He abhorred exhausting drives, and the day would be long enough. The Yard was secure from the approach of the crowd, which, thick as corn, choked every road around Westminster Hall and Abbey. He had brought with him his own sofa bed on which he had slept well, aided by a belly full of good wine and brandy. He slept while the peers arrived to strut and fuss in Hall and Abbey, and excited women worried about their feathers and sleeves and gloves and gowns.

At precisely seven o'clock, the lord great chamberlain and the lord chamberlain of the household brought him his shirt, white silk stockings and slashed velvet trunk-hose with matching gem-encrusted doublet. Their efforts to dress him were hampered by their own state robes, so that they rustled and puffed and fumbled. Finally, amidst his complaints and oaths, they encased him in his peacock plumage from head to foot. The robes were of great weight, his train of crimson velvet spattered with gold stars was of extravagant length. Eight pages would be required to carry it. The border of the garment was in solid gold thread. His black hat, as though to compensate in scale for the bulk of the royal physique, was adorned with a ridiculous plume of ostrich feathers that looked like a small explosion. From the midst of this rose the plume of a black heron, like a giant arrow that had impaled the cloud. George was soon sweating profusely and mopping his brow continually.

'Damn me!' he shouted, 'I shall be melted away by the time they crown me! Eh?'

'It is magnificent, sire,' said the chamberlain diplomatically.

'What is the weather like?'

'Mild, sire.'

'The devil, it would be!' He examined himself in a long glass. 'Even Brummell would have to concede that he had never concocted a thing like this. I could almost wish I had asked him, that he could see it.' He mused along this line of thought for a moment. 'Have all my friends good seats?'

'Yes, sire.'

'It will get back to him anyway. He will scour the journals for an account of it. Now, breakfast.'

Below stairs in Regent Square, desperate but muted pande-monium had reigned from the start, which occasionally broke out in a brief flurry of hard words and female tears. Not only, as Burges, the butler, had said, were deliveries hopeless, so that Bessie Tate, the housemaid, had had to be sent out for the milk and fish, but the staff themselves were caught between their duties to the master and his guests and their evident desire to get down somehow to Westminster in time for the procession. Mrs Burges was cooking in her best dress, with an apron tied round her waist, trying to avoid the fat and gravy.

Out the back in the cobbled mews, Will Morton the coachman had started earlier than anyone. In fact he had barely slept. He had attended to the family barouche the night before, polishing the whole bodywork with its twenty-four coats of copal varnish, with a fine leather. He had jacked up the carriage under the axle-trees and washed each wheel with a water-brush and mop, finishing it off with a sponge. Each wheel was then polished like the bodywork. The leather and some sweet oil were then applied to any persistent stains and polished until he could see the stubble of his chin in it. Next the iron-work and joints were oiled, the axletree and wheels greased and all bolts tested for tightness. Finally the ornamental brass-work was lightly rubbed with rot-tenstone and sweet oil, carefully removed. He had no sooner finished this than he started grooming the horses with the help of the stable-boy who had thrown open the doors of the boxes and fed them. They methodically 'strapped' them down with a damp wisp of sweet hay. Any stains on their coats were carefully sponged out and then finished off with a clean linen cloth. Each horse was next turned about to have his head, ears and throat brushed, his ears pulled to please him and his mane and forelock combed. Finally, they were turned about again so that their tails could be treated in the same way, with a discreet trim from the scissors where Morton thought fit. The tails were finished off with a brush on which a little oil had been dropped so that they achieved a fine gloss. The barouche was seldom used, for such occasions seemed to arise less frequently as Thomas grew older. Only three of the six horses were in first class condition, but when Will had finished with them, no one but an expert could tell.

It was with an agony of despair that he saw the condition of the hired barouche from the livery stables as it clattered into the mews. It was covered with red dust and flecks of mud, and the copal varnish was crazed. The horses looked like winded old hacks. The three men with it grinned at him, as he stood there, brush in hand, shaking his head. One was the driver, another his outrider and the third the outrider Will needed for the barouche. Will looked at his prized silver watch.

'It's five!' He sounded tired and angry. 'How the deuce do you expect me to get that thing into condition. The master paid for six decent horses, not six broken jades. Look at them! Not one set of teeth between them, tails like a length of ship's rope. Jehu, what do I do?'

'Now then, Will Morton, don't be offensive to these choice damsels of the livery stables!' The speaker was the other driver, a large man with ginger sidewhiskers and a badly smashed nose from a fall. He spoke as though he were holding it. Jamming his horsewhip by his seat, he jumped down. 'Your master is lucky to get horseflesh at all today. He don't pay much – no offence – and the demand is something cruel. If we had oxen, or trained dogs we could've hired them today. By God, even a blind bullock!' He grinned cheerfully, perfectly aware he had the upper hand. 'You wants 'em or you don't. For the time being, I take it you is suffering from some surprise that we is here bright and early and that you wants 'em, for you'll have to pay for their coming!' The other coachmen were now grinning as well. The big man slapped Will Morton jovially on the back. 'Don't take it hard, Will. You only got 'em at all 'cos we all want to go down to the Abbey to see the Queen. Patriotic, that's what we are. We ain't going with no party what is dropping off short or wishes to view the route from afar, lar-de-dar!'

'What about the coachwork!' Will ran his hand over the cracked varnish as though he were a doctor investigating a contagious disease.

'British and best! Well, I reckon you were the boy for that. Now look at the polish you have on that beautiful means of conveyance over there. That is the work of a dedicated artist in polishing, which I have never claimed to be, and my lads will back me there. And have you a suit of livery for my man Harold here, who is to be your outrider, or you and he will look like Captain Smith an' little Pocahontas, and that wouldn't look well.' The broad over-bearing grin appeared again. Together with the smashed nose he looked wicked but not malicious. Will knew the man well.

'All right, Dick, chops for breakfast, fish and wine . . . If Burges says so and approves the coach!'

'Now that I call business! Hop down, lads.' The other two men jumped down. 'And perhaps a little tip for our services from your master, above and beyond our wages. Like you can tell Burges how he was given such a fly-specked object and worked with a merry quip and cheerful will to smart her up? Burges has the ear of your master. Scratch my back, Will, it itches. Who knows but when your master may next need a horse?'

'Who knows but he may go elsewhere.'

'Ah, Will! Unkind. Uncharitable. We are an old and trusted firm. There are some very unscrupulous people in the livery game!' He let out a roar of laughter, and strode over to the bucket and brushes that Will had been using. 'Tell Mrs Burges, our compliments and we are hard-working, hungry men!'

They set to busily, for all their bluff and banter, and with Will and the stable-boy following up behind them, the carriage was smartened considerably. Even the cracks could be lost with a skilled rub of oil. Morton wondered if he should ever get a chance to shave and change.

Bessie Tate blushed as red as rouge as she rustled back in her best striped cotton dress. She clasped the basket and milk can that she was carrying and marched straight ahead, avoiding the

perspiring men as much as possible. She felt delightfully confused and her heart was bumpy, as Mrs Burges would have put
it. Dick Bayliss, the driver, called out to her as she feared he
would and prayed he would.

'Carry your basket?'

Bessie shook her curls and kept walking, kicking up her hems
at the ankle.

'Pretty little thing, ain't she,' said Bayliss, loud enough for her
to hear, which was very gratifying and frightening too. 'All
dressed up in her crisp and rustling best. Good as roast pork!'

'Let her be!' said Will, annoyed.

'Oh ho! Spoke for, is she? Never a ring to show for it, though.'

Bessie scurried inside. She would remember every word of the
exchange and think about it tonight, in bed. Two men! Just
think of it, and Will had spoken up sharply.

'Is she from the country?' Bayliss asked. 'In my experience,
housemaids usually are. Come up to town to better themselves
as they sees it. Some of 'em will try anyways to do it,' he added
darkly, with a wicked eye on Will, 'and some of them goes down
and down. That's often the way with housemaids.'

Will was white and angry now, but as a liveried man it was
beneath him to show it to a journeyman driver.

'She's from Ipswich,' he replied, 'and a proper nice girl that
knows her place, and I don't know what you're driving at.
Works hard and talks little, she does. Not something you can
boast, Dick Bayliss.'

Aware that he might have over-stepped the mark, and seeing
his breakfast forfeit, Dick was conciliatory.

'No, I mean I saw her coming here, hurrying along. Thought
to myself, there's a pretty little thing, all pink and plump.'

'He whistled at her,' volunteered Harold, the outrider, a man
with bad skin and a spotty face.

Will scowled and slapped the side of the coachwork with the
leather, working over and over it until he achieved a dull gleam.
Dick Bayliss kept his head down and did the same. Things could
get back through a servant to a master that could do a chap in
his position no good.

*　　*　　*

It was six, and the sun was bright in the dusty leaves of the trees when Burges discreetly leaned to his master and confided that the carriages were ready. Crabtree had stationed himself behind Caroline's chair. In this automatic piece of training she felt trapped as woman of the house. Could he not have stood behind Jane? She knew this was unreasonable, but was annoyed nevertheless. Crabtree had always stood behind Caroline, and she supposed that he always would.

Burges, receiving no response to his confidence to Thomas, repeated his announcement with increased volume. Thomas, whose nose was in his glass, continued to ignore it, but Henry was getting impatient, and showed his scant respect for properties.

'We shall be late if we don't go. Come on, Father, the carriages are ready!' His irritation showed on his face.

'What's that?'

'Come on, Father, the carriages are ready. Burges has told you three times.'

'I can't see that's any of your business, sir, in my house. In any case,' said sly Thomas, 'it has only been twice. You should not exaggerate. It is a practice of solicitors but unbecoming in a barrister. Scant respect for facts, that's what!'

With a wicked grin the old man hauled himself to his feet, aided by Burges, who was visibly suppressing a smile. Henry felt his fury for his father returning, but Jane's hand rested on his arm, squeezing it in warning. He said nothing. Crabtree helped Caroline from her place, and she had to pull herself up almost as much as Thomas. Suddenly she felt quite unstable and her knees were weak. Maria and William were, thankfully, chattering about how much they had enjoyed breakfast, and about the cost of the King's clothes and generally throwing a mantle of normal noise over the table. Jane and Henry were glaring rigidly ahead, like sporting trophies.

'My shoe, I think,' Caroline murmured unnecessarily to Crabtree.

'Ma'am?'

'It's nothing, Crabtree.' She wished he was not a footman and she could have taken his arm for support. She moved slowly from the room, as the others rose and followed.

From the Tower came a dull boom, more a trembling of the heavy air, as they fired a gun for the hour. They would stop only when the King entered the Abbey. As though excited by the shock wave, the church bells which kept up their incessant yelping and clanging seemed suddenly more vigorous and louder.

'Dee the things,' Thomas protested as they made their way to the front door collecting their belongings, 'I suppose they will be louder at Westminster. Scare the horses and permanently deafen the people. Don't you want to see to your hair? We've lost Jane and Maria again. Women must do these things every half hour. I must admit you have never been like that.'

No, thought Caroline, nor have I ever had the opportunity. Condemned to sober management from my birth that killed my mother. I have never learned the arts of cosmetics. I never change the fashion of my hair, as girls and women do, after each ball at Carlton House. I have not been to Bath or Brighton. I do not collect the fashion plates from the magazines of modes. I have missed my girlhood, but I am not sure that I regret it. But womanhood I will not miss.

'Come along, Caroline,' Thomas was complaining in his accusatory tone, 'don't stand there clutching the table, take an old man's arm. The women seem to be ready. Mind you, there will be very grand company in the box. They will be tiresome, and the men drunk. It is that sort of circumstance that makes me think, devil take the King. Don't tell William I ever said such a thing.' He turned to face her at the door. 'Caroline, I know you must have your own life, but you will look after me, won't you? I can't talk to my other children, and as for their wives! And my other son is away in the Army! I know you think me a possessive old man, but I am lonely. Henry is a good man, but impatient and with no humility. Living in Kensington! He should set his hat at Gower Street, that's what a barrister should do, with an eye on Russell Square. I think he will come out well in the end, but I am an old man.'

'Father, you are not. You are able and your practice is sound.'

'I get tired.'

'We all get tired, Father.' Caroline wished for this prolonged agony to be over, the King to be crowned – as if it really mattered to her – and to get back to Charles Ware.

'Dee those children,' Thomas exclaimed as though suddenly embarrassed by his importuning. 'Come along there!' he suddenly bellowed like a master of fox-hounds, simultaneously waving an arm in the air as if indicating the direction of pursuit. 'To the carriages! Burges, where are you, man? When we have departed, if we do, you may tell the servants that they may have the rest of the day to themselves with my compliments. They have my permission to cheer the King and wish him a long reign, provided they are all home in time for dinner and no one gets drunk.'

'You know,' Thomas confided in Caroline, 'it's all bluff. Would you cheer the King?'

'I don't suppose I shall cheer anyone.'

'Come now, coronations are for cheerful vulgarity, and we have the most vulgar king. Ain't that so, Henry?' he said, as Henry joined them on the front steps. They could see the coaches being driven slowly along the square from the mews to avoid kicking up the dust.

'The Queen is more so.'

'I wager you ten guineas she don't make it.'

'I don't wager, sir,' said Henry stiffly.

'Done,' said William, quickly interrupting. He had joined them quietly, and stood at the rear. Thomas looked at William with a sort of annoyed surprise. The runt had just bitten the old dog's tail.

'Very well, sir, done. This will be no day for Whigs.' The unkind snap in no way abashed William, who responded with a smile, his best weapon and so obviously cheerful.

'Then perhaps you'll make it twenty, sir?'

'Dee me! I ain't a gambler.' Thomas seemed to writhe within his waistcoat and shirt. 'But done, sir.'

William flashed a sweetly mischievous smile at Maria. Caroline noted it and envied the intimacy and integrity these two so obviously enjoyed.

The journey in to Westminster was frightening. On a normal day, a barouche would have been treated with curiosity and a certain instinctive deference by crowds in the street. Today, instead of providing comfortable isolation from the meanness and stink of the streets and people, the carriages seemed to attract and provoke them. The isolation of the barouche felt to William like that of a Revolutionary tumbril. The crowds seemed to stare with a hungry and hostile look.

They had split into two parties of three; Thomas, Henry and Jane in the family carriage and William, Maria and Caroline in the other. The enormous crowds had been there for some hours now. The smell of drink, sweat and horses was sour and awful. The ladies carried posies that they could sniff.

William found he could not avoid the watching eyes. He found himself drawn to them. Haggard men with hollow sockets, boys that looked as though they had been exhumed, women who roared curses, and whose pocked skin and greasy hair put off even lecherous sailors. His eyes caught them all as they passed. There was no admiration. He felt that they were being noted for a future occasion. They cared not a curse whether he lived or died. It was a horrible undercurrent of the times. All morning they had stood there, drinking cheap gin, even when they could not afford bread. They watched the spanking carriages with liveried flunkeys and some with liveried black lackeys, clattering by in their arrogant uncaring world. They were curiously incurious. They might as well have been riding out of existence past the unseeing eyes of lost souls. The last time he had seen such a crowd was before the riots at Spa Fields, where they had betrayed the same incurious disdain for their irrelevant masters. They seemed to be listening to other voices now. William felt highly alarmed, but took care not to show it. Caroline seemed wholly preoccupied, but Maria, as always, spoke what he was hiding.

'This is an awful journey. What a poor and awful crowd. They stare at us without interest, as though we were cattle passing. What are they waiting for? The Queen? Or do they resent us? If they resent us, why do they not boo and hiss? Will there be trouble, do you think?'

'No, I think not,' replied William. 'The working people and servants are generally for the Queen. She is their cause. That in itself is safety, for their revolution is founded on a monarch. It will be different, you will see, when we pass through a better quarter. These poor wretches are from the slums and markets. Many sleep on the streets.'

'They are so wretched,' Caroline said, speaking for the first time. She had been concentrating on ignoring the awful smells which gave her waves of nausea, 'I had no idea there could be so many of them.'

'They keep to themselves normally,' replied William wryly, 'don't we do the same?' Caroline glanced at him curiously. His face betrayed the bitterness he so carefully tried to keep from his words.

'Are you feeling better now?' Maria asked Caroline. She had tactfully allowed all this time to elapse. The motion of the coach had become juddering rather than rolling as they rattled over cobbles.

'I am quite well.' Caroline's reply was too emphatic and she coloured slightly.

Henry, unaware of the latent menace of the crowd, saw them merely as hell might be; a bestiary of vulgarity. He was not unaccustomed to the raw material of men, as no barrister could be, but he disliked them even more when in the mass. He haughtily avoided looking at them, but discussed cases with Thomas opposite. He had little to say, for his work was scant, and Thomas might at any time start to lecture him about improving his ways. Jane sniffed at her posy frequently.

'We should have come from Kensington as I suggested,' she said. 'We should not have had to pass through these places. All the rookeries of London have spilled onto the streets to stare!'

'Why not?' barked Thomas. 'It's free, and it's their King as well as ours.' Damned feeble woman, he thought. Can't stand the smell of a crowd or a lathered horse. Henry's no better either, with his nose in the air like a parrot. Damn it, the yellow rind of butter-thick filth that rims the edge at Bath comes from the most aristocratic bodies. It is no less filthy for that. He determined to have a long talk with old Sam Leigh, Jane's father, to see if they could knock some sense into these two's heads. There were tales about Henry and some woman. Jane would be too stupid to know. But he intended to find out. He looked at Jane dispassionately. Perhaps in Henry's place he would have done the same in his youth, or by God even now, but he would have been *discreet* about it. Not threats of duels and such scandal. He tried an experimental wave to the crowd who responded with some boos and uncertain cheers. Whereupon he immediately took off his hat and waved it at them. Henry, he noticed, was trying to pretend he did not exist. These lily-white half-hearted young bucks. At least Prinny had the hide of a rhino!

He could not avoid the mounting impatience he felt when bottled up with Henry. He expected the subject of money to come up. Not only that, but he would be advised how much better it would be to plough it into the family than invest it in common business. Henry's idea of the family was himself. Thomas was determined that it should be invested for the good of all the children. Henry's blind selfishness was very distressing. Thomas watched him covertly, wondering where he got such vanity. The appetite grows by eating. Thomas would do no feeding.

In Fleet Street, a man had been knocked down by a coach, which was his own fault as he was hopelessly drunk. Some ribs had been broken, and he sat by the kerb howling miserably, not for his ribs but because he had broken his bottle. Stones and empty bottles had quickly followed the carriage and the militia had crunched through the broken glass, cursing and menacing the crowd. A Punch and Judy Show meanwhile played to no one. Punch hit Judy over the head with a wooden 'clock, clock, clock,' then screamed and rubbed his stuffed pink hands. Punch was dressed as a king, with G IV R on his chest, and Judy wore a crown. Animal 'families' were displayed off the Strand, to show that man could achieve the prophecies of the Bible. Cats, mice, geese, rats, pigs and a moulting bear, all variously maimed or secretly restrained, lay sweating and gnawing at their cages of split chestnut, ignoring each other. Dwarfs found themselves trampled upon. A monkey wearing a tarnished crown drew fortunes from a spinning wheel, or turned a card for a half-penny. The dog 'who could understand the language of humans' yelped and nodded its head at the small movements of its master's feet. Jugglers and acrobats crashed into the crowd and were cursed for taking up room. A woman who had just spilled her entire stock of pea soup over her feet sat down and screamed. People waded through it, paying no attention. The noise was unbelievable. Even the church bells were here unheard.

Outside the Abbey and Hall, a new and gorgeous world had been created. No expense had been spared and everything was in immaculate order. The smell was different too. Perfumes and pomades covered the odours of bodies. Horse-droppings were swept up by men with brushes almost before the animals had finished. The vast stands built of baulks of timber were draped with crimson and blue swags of cloth, hung with golden tassels. They were fully roofed with boarding, a haven of shade during the day, and had all been carefully tested by filling them the day before with soldiers who solemnly stood up and sat down to orders. Some of them were four tiers high, but these were cheaper and further from the Abbey. These were not tested.

The front level of each stand had been raised so that it would be higher than the bear-skins of the Guards, and the seating was raked to afford a perfect view. They were almost full when the Kelleways arrived. Each stand had been painted a brilliant colour and from the bank of people within sprouted parasols as bright as a herbaceous border.

'They cannot need them,' said Maria, 'they are all in the shade. I have not brought one.'

'It is the fashion,' replied Caroline. 'I fancy that as the day wears on, the strain of holding them may overcome taste.'

'I am no good at keeping abreast of fashion.' Maria made it a simple statement without any overtones of apology, regret or self-pity. 'It is such a prodigal use of material. What can the workers in France be paid for all those cheap trimmings? Our own are ill paid.'

'A painter is expected to have a certain style!' William exclaimed extravagantly. 'Otherwise we are not socially acceptable and would be locked out of the City at night like Elizabethan players. Style is everything in the little game here today. A painter in smeared rags, smelling of turpentine and oil, proclaims his own failure. In velvet and silk, talking rubbish, he must be a success. The same is true of writers!'

'What a jaded view you have.'

'Oh, no!' William was saying. 'We enjoy it, provided it only happens as frequently as coronations. If the King may make a solemn ass of himself, then why not all of us!'

'He only says these things to be outrageous,' Maria explained to Caroline, as a matter of form. They knew each other well enough.

It cost twenty guineas for a seat in the best boxes: 'The Royal George', 'The Eclipse', 'The Orb and Sceptre' or 'The Monarch', as much as the peers paid to enter the Hall. The two coaches stopped at an alighting platform at the rear, then they walked round to the entrance at the side. Here they presented their tickets to a man in livery, who at first sight appeared to have his face pressed against a sheet of glass. The King had employed professional pugilists to supervise all entrances to the Abbey, Hall and boxes. His clothes were tight about his barrel chest and soaked under the armpits. The party looked at each other with amusement as he waved them through with his best attempt at a bow. The man's hands were a mass of gristly scars.

'You see,' William whispered wickedly to Caroline, 'it is all appropriate to a fair. I have little doubt he's the King's Champion!'

They were warmly greeted by Samuel Leigh, whom they adjoined. Thomas and Sam were too busy laughing at each other's clothes to pay attention to the ladies and Henry had to bustle about briefly. Thomas winked at Sam, and sat down without ceremony beside him. This created considerable confusion as it was proper that the older men should intermix and now they were in the way. A lady behind remarked loudly that she hoped they would not be too long standing up for she could see nothing. Henry bowed to her, lifting his hat and apologizing. They struggled past as best they could, Caroline sitting at the end with William on her left, then Jane, Henry and Maria. Thomas seemed indifferent to the trouble he had caused and was deep in conversation with Sam.

'You know old Fairfax, the solicitor with the squint?' said Sam, 'He's back there. I just bet him five guineas the Queen won't come.'

'Dee me, Sam, but the world has gone gambling mad! I just bet the painting prodigy twenty that she don't. Seems thee or me will lose it, Sam. And I never offered him the bet, he took it, you might say.'

'Yes?' Sam sounded disbelieving.

'You know how it is.' He paused to ensure no one was listening to them, but the din around them was such that people were bellowing in each other's ears. 'I was trying to get a rise out of Henry. He needs coaxin' on. He's a prig, Sam, and I say it myself about my son. Needs more red tincture in the blood, and more pages of the Law Reports. Dee me but that face fixer there snapped me up on it and before I saw the peg I was snared.' Sam only laughed. 'He has too much Whig cheek. Told me the other day he was the first of our family in sable. Couldn't understand a word of it. His paint brushes, Sam. Laughed his head off.'

'Whig or no, he has some spirit, Tom.'

'His wit I will agree, but not his face painting and his politics. Asked me if I wanted my portrait, at a reduced rate for family! You know, even his wife thinks she is a man!'

'You're ribbing me, Tom. Plump young thing, well made. Pretty, I'd say.'

'Beauty's in the soul, Dee you Sam Leigh! Don't grin at me. Says she has no intention of making her career, as she calls it, subject to her domestic affairs. I won't tell you about her domestic affairs. Would have dealt with that when we were young.'

'When you were young, you never considered the beauty of the soul, Tom. Seems to me you were after something of a more tangible nature!'

'Dee your cheek!' But Tom was smiling.

'Brought my flask. Long and boring day here. Worse than a Sessions Court.'

The galleried stands looked down onto the most spectacular piece of construction for the Coronation. A complete winding roadway had been built, in two levels, out of timber, connecting the Hall of Westminster with Abbey, passing right round Parliament Square. The higher portion of this 'platform' was four feet from the ground, so that the main body of the procession should be clearly seen. This roadway was covered along its length with a sixteen foot wide blue cloth, with a margin of a yard on each side beyond that. Beyond that again were the railings, completely swathed in purple cloth. The King was to be seen against a fine ground. Below the main roadway, and raised only two feet, was a second way for the pages, footmen, yeomen, guards and constables, so that they could move without interrupting the view of the procession. Beside the raised roadway, men were stationed at close intervals, with hammers, pincers, saws, nails and cordage lest some undignified disaster should befall. Dressed in livery for the occasion they looked ill at ease, trying to bear their tools at 'present'. They were the subject of lively banter from spectators on foot. In addition, awnings had been set up, all drawn back, but with men in livery at short intervals, ready to release the red cords they held, should the weather suddenly change. There had never been such a royal route.

The view from where they sat in 'The Monarch' looked full on to the Abbey front, and back in the distance to where the roadway left the Hall. As they had arrived at the box at just after eight, they had had a long wait. At ten, the gun was fired that signified that the ceremony had begun within the Hall, where George was being invested with the Regalia. The crowd was immense and restive. Soldiers lined the route, at ease but already tiring. The crowd diverted itself by cheering when one fainted, and demanding more.

'The Monarch' was tiring too. Parasols had been lowered and the fresh herbaceous border of crisp clothes was crumpled and wilting.

'Sam,' Thomas murmured, seeing Jane had hardly spoken to Henry, 'we must have a talk sometime about Henry. I have heard worrying and scandalous rumours.'

'I know what you mean. But the world's full of them.' He glanced quickly at Jane. It was an appraising look, as though he wished to remind himself of someone whom he had partly forgotten. 'Anything in it?'

'I fear so. Damned disgraceful thing for me to have to say . . .'

'Damn it, Tom, don't look so long faced. It's not the first time in the history of the world. Henry may be a haughty young prig, but he has temper and ambition. Needs reins and a good hand on 'em. Man of spirit there. Lacks experience, of course, but that is only time. I blame our side of the bargain. He needs a woman of spirit, not one that lets him run. I'm old enough to be dispassionate about life, Tom. I wouldn't ha' married her, damned if I would! She must learn to fight, or she'll lose him.'

'Sam, you're too kind to me. No, don't protest. I have rare moments of enlightenment into my own selfishness. Dee, but you get selfish as the years pass! I never cured him of it, young. No mother, you see, and I never took hold of him. I'll do my bit though. He can make his union work and the devil take philandering!' Thomas was red with anger. Sam gave a warning nod towards Jane, who had turned at their whispering and was looking at Thomas. They fell silent, pulling at their trousers and shifting their feet like scholars.

So the two men were in selfish agreement that the affairs of their offspring should not be allowed to interfere with their long friendship; but in very different ways. Whereas Sam was prepared to abandon Jane as of no consequence unless she showed more strength and passion, Thomas was determined that the union of the two children should never be sundered. It seemed to him the only possible way. Each man stared at the blue cloth road, considering how he would act on his conclusion.

Their further contemplation was disrupted by an ever-increasing din that rose above the general murmur and buzz of the spectators. From the direction of Dean's Yard, approaching the Abbey came the sound of yelling and cheering, thousands of voices carrying across Parliament Square. A momentary hush fell on the vast crowd as all listened, trying to catch a few words, followed by a roar of speculation as everyone turned to their neighbour with the same question.

'Good God!' said Sam, who seldom blasphemed. 'Can that be the Queen?' The King would not approach from Dean's Yard. 'It is!' he exclaimed, as he and the rest of 'The Monarch' got to their feet. 'I never thought I would have anything to be grateful to her for,' he shouted in Thomas's ear, 'but now I have five guineas!'

William was shouting and waving at Thomas with a mischievous grin. Thomas affected not to notice.

'Be a friend, Sam, and don't look. Can't bear to see the young hound so triumphant.' Sam nodded, but could not suppress his smile.

A barouche with the royal arms on its panels and drawn by six bays of matched magnificence made its way slowly towards the platform along the west front of the Abbey. In it sat the Queen with two other women, while behind it followed a phaeton with two men. The crowd surged forward in a frenzy, bowling over the constables and nearly breaking through the rows of soldiers. Cavalry horses bucked and kicked, and women screamed in alarm. The soldiers were uncertain whether to present arms, and their officers ran up and down some giving the order, some telling the men to remain at ease, which they could not do for the pushing and shoving behind them. 'Caroline for ever!' 'God bless the Queen!' The unoriginal shouts became a tremendous chant as the enormous popularity of the Queen amongst the ordinary citizens became a united voice of sympathy. But as she passed the first of the boxes, the hissing and booing began. Cries of alarm and protest were heard from well-dressed ladies. 'The Orb and Sceptre' let loose an ululation more suited to gibbons than humans, followed by a prolonged hissing. 'The Monarch' seemed to be evenly divided in their sympathies, as it contained mainly professional men. A storm of cheering, booing, and rude advice broke from it that divided families for months from that day. William and Maria clapped and cheered, Maria actually jumping up and down in a most unladylike fashion. Thomas scowled at her like Wotan. William cheerfully waved his hat and even had the nerve to wave it at Thomas. Thomas finally lost his temper, cupped his hands to his mouth and roared at the Queen. 'Go home, madam, go home! Go to Brunswick!' then felt thoroughly ashamed, although his contribution was a mere straw in the hurricane of noise. Queen Caroline's progress was frequently stopped by the pressure of the crowd, but some officers stepped forward, ordered their men to present, and the staccato violence of their motions brought some calm to the scene. Some officers saluted and presented their swords. Some stood stonily to attention. The constables and liveried men made a spectacle of themselves, some of the new recruits running after her carriage, cheering. As she approached the Abbey there was a great commotion around the doors, with people darting inside, when suddenly the door was summarily shut.

This caused the crowds to gasp, and there was pungent quiet.

Caroline had dismounted from her carriage and approached the door on the arm of Lord Hood, who had followed in the phaeton. They seemed to move so exceptionally slowly. Was this rather heavy, dark featured woman what all the fuss was about? In leaving her carriage it seemed that she had left behind her royalty. There was an inevitability about the events that happened. The door-keepers in scarlet satin drew across the entrance. They were mainly elderly men of some standing, supported by the King's favourite pugilists. Their bearing showed they intended to do their jobs, the former with firm dignity and the latter with their mutton-fists if needful.

'I present you your Queen,' declared Lord Hood loudly, upon being asked for their tickets. 'Surely it is not necessary for her to have a ticket!' The door-keeper was politely adamant although Hood was aware that some of the other keepers were smirking rudely.

'Our orders are to admit no person without a Peer's ticket.'

'This is your Queen; she is entitled to admission without such a form.'

Caroline, who had been standing slightly behind Hood now stepped forward and spoke to the man herself. Although she smiled, it was a grimace of practice. She was white and nervous, her cosmetics showing bright on cheeks, neck and lips.

'Yes, I am your Queen, will you admit me?' The door-keeper had stiffened to attention. He replied woodenly, avoiding her eyes.

'My orders are specific, Your Majesty, and I feel myself bound to obey them.'

Caroline laughed. The sound was high and artificial. Her heavy, fleshy features crumpled and she turned slightly away. Hood persisted.

'I have a ticket.'

'Then, my Lord, we will let you pass upon producing it.'

Hood held his ticket forward, and the keeper took it.

'This will let one person pass and no more.'

Hood turned aside to Caroline. 'Will Your Majesty go in alone?'

Caroline turned to him, agitated. 'Yes, I suppose I must.'

'Come, then.'

She looked at him, her eyes seeking advice. Then she shook her head. Hood tried the door-keeper again.

'Am I to understand that you refuse Her Majesty admission?'

The keeper was not to be bullied. All day he had turned away ticketless peers, who had threatened him with everything from horse-whipping to the Tower.

'We only act in conformity with our orders.'

Caroline made a hysterical noise, half-way between a sob and a derisive laugh.

'Then you refuse the Queen admission,' Hood again persisted. A senior keeper at this point stepped forward, sensitive to the fact that this repetitive questioning might lead to trouble.

'My lord, no arrangements have been made for the Queen.'

'None?'

'I regret not. We had no orders to make such preparation.'

Hood turned to Caroline. 'Will Your Majesty enter the Abbey without your ladies?' Caroline shook her head. She seemed suddenly weary and dispirited. Hood saw that she had no will to go further. 'I think Your Majesty had better retire to your carriage. There seems little else to do in view of the lack of accommodation.' Caroline nodded. There were some hoots and laughter from by-standers at the doors.

'Go away at any rate!' shouted a voice. There was another gust of laughter at this witticism. Hood advanced towards the porch, his face red with anger. He addressed the by-standers, his voice quivering.

'We expected to have met at least with the conduct of gentlemen! Such conduct is neither manly nor mannerly!'

His angry rebuke brought no cat-calls or response. Rage had produced in him a dignity that poor Caroline could never assume. Hood turned his back on them and offered Caroline his arm. Together they walked back to the carriage, followed by Lady Hood and Lady Hamilton. The constables who had stood uneasily about the platform during this proceeding formed up at a command, and preceded them, making some show of a guard. The crowd nearby clapped or hissed, according to their inclinations. It was noticeable that many who had cheered her coming now booed her going. Thomas yelled to Sam.

46

'Dee me, but it is disgraceful! She brought it on herself. That woman cannot well stay as Queen!'

'What loyal and gentle subjects she has, Tom. She should not have been treated that way!'

'She should not have tried to play on public sympathy.'

The eleven o'clock gun caught the eye before the sound reached them. A quick gout of smoke burst out. The thump of following sound buffeted the timbers of the stand so that it shook. The procession was on its way. George seemed to attract less noise than Caroline. The soldiers presented arms. Everyone craned forward until their necks and shoulders ached. The immensity of the procession gradually became apparent as it unwound across the blue cloth, like a piece of theatre across a vast stage. But here all the gems were real, all the cloths silk and satin, damask and velvet. The reservations of the crowd towards the King and the expense were suspended by the magnificence of the show. They were less inclined to cheer the King, than to applaud the production, pointing, remarking, amazed and bedazzled. It was difficult to comprehend that it should all be for one man. If George noticed the lack of warmth, he gave no sign.

The procession was preceded by the King's Herb-woman and her six maids, simply dressed in straight white dresses decorated with a hem of embroidered flowers and a long garland. Each pair of maids carried a basket of flowers between them, which they strewed as they walked. The groundlings whistled and applauded them and shouted lewd remarks. The bejewelled snake uncoiled lazily. Towards the rear, the great canopy of cloth of gold swayed to the stately pace of the sixteen barons of the Cinque Ports who bore it and blazed back at the sun as though truly in contention. When the procession passed 'The Monarch' it had the same stunning effect. After initial cheers and applause, an awed hush fell as the surfeit of richness passed.

'It's like one of Prinny's banquets,' William said to Caroline on his right, 'all meat and no salad between!'

So much crimson and scarlet velvet, satin and silk. So much lacing and fringeing with gold.

So many gems, Orders, crowns, coronets, decorations, diadems and yards and yards of heavy trains carried by tottering pages. The slashed silk and encrusted tabards passed by and the Regalia appeared, the symbols of temporal and spiritual power appearing puny after what had gone before. Then came George, towing his train slowly under the canopy of cloth of gold.

'God Bless the King!' shouted part of the crowd.

'God Bless the Queen!' came a second shout, following the first as an echo, sometimes faint, sometimes stronger than the first cry. There were even some boos and hisses.

'Let in the Queen, let in the Queen, let in the Queen!' chanted a section of groundlings who were herded well back from the Abbey front. George must have heard, but he neither faltered nor glanced their way. He had feared it might be worse and was pleased with his spectacular show. In the heat and crush, people resumed their seats, chattering and laughing. It was only then that William saw that Caroline had fainted unnoticed. She was very white, and scarcely breathing. He reached across Jane and indicated to Henry that they must clear a space, as she had fallen down in a heap. Fortunately, their movements caught Maria's eye, and she immediately understood what had happened. Saying nothing, she pushed her way past her surprised relatives and was already beside Caroline before they could see what the trouble was.

'Let me loosen her clothes,' Maria said to William, stooping and undoing the buttons at her neck. 'Help her into her seat.'

William tried to lift Caroline, but was so tentative that he only disturbed her so that she slumped further down. He was too decorous to grasp her under the arms for fear of grasping her breasts. Maria was impatient with him.

'Take hold of her firmly!'

She would have tried to pull Caroline up herself, but William, blushing furiously, folded his arms around her. With a struggle he lifted her inert weight into a sitting position. Although as a painter he understood the forces and dispositions of weight that comprise the human frame, he had never tried to lift an unconscious body before and was amazed at the difficulty. He realized it was something he should have learned.

Other spectators were staring and the members of the family were trying to gather round, which was impossible for the row of seats was fixed. There was a brief flurry, stemmed by Maria who was firmly in control.

'She needs air, that is all. Everyone will please remain where they are for the moment. I cannot manage if I am crowded. Please sit down and let her recover.'

Reluctantly they subsided into their seats, watching Maria bending over, talking to each other. She refused to let anyone help her. Thomas turned in a fluster to Sam.

'You see! It is disgraceful. I am powerless with that woman. She is not even like a woman. She defies me and has neither humility nor modesty. Can I not attend my own daughter? Dee me, I will!' He would have jumped to his feet but Sam restrained him. He was more amused than compassionate when he spoke.

'Come come, Tom. Maria is a very competent member of her sex. A lady should attend a lady. It is only a faint.'

'Dee me, I hope so!' Thomas was white and agitated.

Sam slapped him on the knee. 'Of course it is. This noise and this heat. It would bring down a guardsman. See, she is already responding.'

Maria was waving a tiny blue bottle under Caroline's nose. Caroline seemed to shrink from it, then started back, her eyes open and focused. Maria removed the bottle, and bent close to her.

'It's all right. You only fainted. Keep still and breathe in and out. Deep breaths. That's right. Slowly now ... you'll be all right.'

Caroline apparently understood, for she nodded. Tears suddenly welled up in her eyes and she started to sob, clasping her hands tight to her face so that the drops ran out between her fingers. Maria bent over her, screening her from the view of family and strangers. She sensed the tears were not for the shame of fainting. She gave Caroline a handkerchief, tucking it into the top of the clamped hands. Caroline rolled it over her face.

'Maria ...' Caroline stopped and let out a ridiculous wail. She began to sob again.

Maria bent beside her, so that their heads touched. 'What is it?' There was no response, but Caroline started to crumple up the handkerchief like a child. Maria persisted. 'Whisper to me, here. Quickly. I think I may know. I am a wife and mother. I would tell no one else.'

'I think I may be with child.' They sounded like dying words. 'I don't know. I don't know how to know, and I'm wretched.'

'I will call on you the day after tomorrow,' Maria whispered back. 'We can talk about everything. There is nothing to fear and it is possible to tell. Dry your eyes and don't let anyone guess. It may be nothing.'

She was very business-like and brusque. Her manner had its effect and Caroline automatically did what she was told. Maria started to straighten out Caroline's hat, which had slipped awry. Only when she was satisfied did she stand up and address Thomas, who was fidgety with anxiety and anger.

'She is better now.'

'Thank you, ma'am. Am I allowed to see my daughter then? Is it permitted?' His voice was full of indignation and he spoke loudly for others to hear. Maria was equal to him and responded just as loudly.

'A woman needs a woman.'

'We will go,' he announced to Caroline, ignoring Maria, 'as soon as you feel well enough to move. There is no point in waiting for the procession to return. We've seen it all forwards, it will be just the same backwards.'

'Please stay. I'm all right now.' She took his hand, knowing that she could win that way. 'Do not put everyone to trouble on my account. It was only the noise and crush. Please stay, I feel fectly well. If we go, you will only draw more attention to me and I could not bear that.' She felt weak and giddy, but in control of her limbs again. It was of paramount importance to try to appear normal. The earnestness in her voice and the hand in his hand convinced Thomas. 'I should like to stay,' she continued, 'and in any case you can never leave through all this crowd. There is no way to move a carriage.'

She was quite right, Thomas thought. His resolve collapsed. 'Very well. But I shall sit beside you.' He turned to William. 'Will you, sir, take my seat?'

It was a blunt command, but William nodded amiably and moved down the row. Caroline wondered what Maria knew that might make it possible to tell. If it was so, what should she do? Thomas was talking to her, complaining about Maria's manner.

She tried to listen and smooth him down. Maria had had the wits to guess.

The procession did not return to the Hall from the Abbey until twenty minutes to four. The Hall had been converted into a huge theatre, festooned with rich cloth. Tiers of wooden galleries had been constructed along the length of the Hall. A wooden floor had been laid over the stone slabs. The south end, which included the boxes for the royal family and foreign ministers, was hung with scarlet edged with gold. The throne was draped all round with crimson and gold, and the table before it was draped with purple edged with gold. From the south end to the north stretched the vast banqueting table that was the centre of the occasion. At the north end had been erected a triumphal arch, in full Gothic style, thirty feet high and thirty-five feet wide, while above this was the gallery for the band. The floor had been covered with blue cloth, and side tables in green. The effect was voluptuous and rich, rather than tasteful. The chairs were in the Gothic manner and the style pervaded all forms of decoration and hangings. From the hammer-beams of the roof, huge cut-glass lustres were suspended by gilt chains, each containing three circles of candles that danced wildly, scattering facets of light. From the galleries draped with swags of scarlet, the wives of peers could look down as the peers and bishops gorged themselves, for it was to be an all male feast.

While the spectators in the street attempted to disperse in a furious mêlée of horses and carriages, the peers in the Hall sat down to the Banquet. By twenty past five, when the King entered the Hall, carrying the sceptre and orb, their appetites had attained a rare piquancy. The first course was then presented to them, served up on twenty-four gold dishes, but before the covers of these could be removed, the great doors at the bottom end of the Hall were flung open to a fanfare of trumpets and clarionets. The Duke of Wellington, Marquis of Anglesey and Lord Howard entered on horseback, the horses' hoofs thundering on the timber floor. After this dramatic gesture they stood for a time under the Gothic arch, without much sense of purpose and ignored by the peers who were now permitted to eat. Before the second course, another blast on the trumpets was the signal to throw open the great gate. The King's Champion and two com-panions then rode in, preceded by trumpeters, Serjeants-at-arms and his Esquires clad in half armour, one bearing his lance, the other his target; the Herald carried a scroll of parchment on which was written the proclamation in Gothic script he could barely read.

The Champion wore a suit of bright armour that bent the poor horse they had hired for him from Astley's circus. The man's helpless immobility lent him an air that was splendidly solemn. He was praying he would not fall off. On his helmet he wore a vast and billowing plume constructed of layers of ostrich feathers, dyed red, blue and white. From the crown of this con-fection stuck a tuft of bristling black shaped like a shaving brush. His horse's headstall was similarly decorated, and when it blew and snorted, the feathers swirled. The effect on the ladies was dramatic. The man's set face, moustaches and pale concen-tration, lent him a look of ascetic fervour that seemed to them to be the embodiment of knightly virtue. It was hard not to com-pare his manly bearing with the gluttonous host round the board. They sighed, they languished, their bosoms rose and fell in all the approved ways. Impressionable young ladies were moved to tears by the romance of him. They forgot their internal emptiness, forgot the torturing odours of goose, lobster, capon, beef, butter sauce and savoury cake. They sat upright, every one a damsel. A hush even fell over the diners who had thus been frustrated from their second course. The King sat back with a smile of satisfaction.

A curious tension suggested that they believed that even now, in this day and age, someone might truly return the gesture of defiance. The trumpets screamed thrice and the Herald unrolled his parchment and began to proclaim the challenge in a shout that hid his nervousness:

'If any person, of what degree soever, high or low, shall deny or gainsay our Sovereign Lord George the Fourth of the United Kingdom of Great Britain and Ireland, Defender of the Faith, son and next heir to our Sovereign Lord King George the Third, the last King, deceased, to be right heir to the Imperial Crown of this United Kingdom, or that he ought not to enjoy the same, here is his Champion . . .' There was a flutter from the ladies and sibilant whispers. The Herald drew breath and carefully enunciated the next line. He had practised it for days. '... who saith that he lieth, and is a false traitor; being ready in person to combat with him, and in this quarrel will adventure his life against him on what day soever shall be appointed.'

The Champion then cast down the steel gauntlet which fell with a thud on the boards. A dramatic pause followed, the Champion sitting quite still, but no one picked it up. The gesture was repeated twice and when the Champion received the King's toast, the spectators burst into applause that rolled round the rafters like thunder amongst high mountains. While Londoners enjoyed the fireworks, beer, gin, meat-pies and eels of the street-stalls, the peers engorged themselves like gannets.

From Regent's Square that evening could clearly be heard the crackle and thump of the fireworks. Down by the river, St Paul's glowed rosily in pink and orange light. Acrid smoke poured into houses, offices and taverns and made river navigation impossible for an hour. But the Kelleway family, like many others, were too exhausted to care. The King was already asleep.

Dinner had been disorganized but welcome and Caroline had retired to her bedroom, pale and unsteady. Maria and William had left with tactful haste. They noted that no one tried to detain them. Bessie Tate and Will Morton were inebriated, and Bessie was in disgrace. She had been sat near the kitchen range, vulnerable on a wooden chair so that Mrs Burges could scold her each time she passed. Bessie had been crying, and she also felt ill. Bayliss had been giving her gin.

'You are the stupidest creature,' Mrs Burges hissed, 'you got lost on purpose. Livery men are up to no good. Never trust them. The good Lord knows what might have happened to you! Will Morton is a good man – except today when he has made a fool of himself – and you are lucky he saw you home. Ipswich is it? Don't they teach you nothing about men in Ipswich. I daresay they're the same there as elsewheres and fills girls up with gin to take advantage of them just the same as here. You do understand what I mean?'

Mrs Burges stood over Bessie. Her cap was pulled on aggressively tight and straight, and her apron brushed the girl's knees. If Bessie could have smelled it, she would have realized that Mrs Burges had been drinking herself. Bessie nodded and tears welled up in her eyes again. She remembered that they had been dancing to a man with a fiddle and she had been enjoying herself. Mrs Burges snorted, and rustled back to the range where she rattled her pots noisily.

In the butler's pantry, Will Morton sat with the three men from the livery stables. A pot of beer stood in front of him, but he was hardly drinking it. Bayliss kept up a stream of jocularity, but it sounded a hollow performance, and Will did not bother to smile. It was not long before Bayliss got to his feet.

'Got to get back with my young ladies!' he announced, 'and get my conveyance through the streets without a smash. It's a good night for coach-wrights!' Bayliss grinned. His ginger side-whiskers waggled. 'Thank Burges for 'is fodder. Us nags is on our way. Come on, lads.'

They all got to their feet and Morton opened the door for them. They left with the minimum exchange of courtesies. Bayliss turned to the coachmen in the mews.

'Now that was what I call sour o' Morton. Don't like no stallion round that little filly. She was only enjoying herself, but you'd think he owned her. Don't like to see her tethered, not a spirited little thing like that!'

He laughed and winked at the men, who dutifully laughed back. 'Where do we drink then, Dick?'

'After we get them horses home. Then we'll go and see what's happening in the town. I shall be back here, mark my words I shall, just to annoy Will Morton. You see, a coachman when he gets all dressed up by a family, he undergoes a change and starts thinking that things belong to him what don't. Now that Miss Ipswich is paid for to be a housemaid and ain't no business of Will Morton.' With this philosophic observation, he climbed up on the barouche, calling 'Yo Yo Yo' to the horses.

Thomas and Henry were having a nightcap together. Jane had discreetly retired, feeling that conversation between father and son might, obscurely, be of benefit to Henry. Thomas was slumped comfortably in a leather chair but Henry would not settle. He strolled or stood, holding a glass of brandy. Thomas felt irrationally annoyed that good brandy should be so badly used.

'Dee'd tiring day for the ladies,' Thomas said, considering Henry from behind his brandy glass. Henry would, he thought, have made a good junior officer – he was too handsome for the Law and his movements too brisk and impatient. Lawyers should be ugly brutes, in direct proportion to their standing. Benchers should preferably be distorted in order to lend themselves to the cartoonist's pen. An Attorney-General ought to be deformed. Bland charm such as Henry possessed was anathema to the Bench and encouraged no trust from the better sort of client. Henry was without wit or bludgeon. His cool superior air invited no sympathy. Indeed it was clear that a man of his adopted appearance ought to know what he was about. He would be a damned fool if he did not.

'Caroline worries me,' Thomas continued, seeing that Henry had noticed he was being studied. 'Hope she's all right. I shall call in the doctor tomorrow.'

'I should think it was only a faint. It was very noisy and warm.'

They mused over this stale exchange for some moments. Thomas played with the brandy in his glass, sniffing it, rolling it about and studying the reflected world of the glass. He decided that he must get it over with or the opportunity might slip. He lowered the glass from his face.

'Henry, I am worried about you. I may as well out with it. There are things, sir, that we should discuss. You must know what I mean. I would prefer we got it over with rapidly. Hate these things.'

Henry, who had been rocking from heel to toe, came down flat-footed with military crispness. He turned his head towards Thomas with the same precision. His face was expressionless.

'I'm sure I don't. I have never been good at guessing.'

Thomas tried to remain calm, but failed. He spoke angrily. 'Don't pretend to me, sir, that you do not know. It won't do, dee me! It won't!'

But Henry was indisposed to reveal he knew anything that should ruffle his calm. He continued to look blank in an offensive manner. He even gave half a shrug. It was too much for Thomas.

'I had thought that we could discuss this without being blunt, but if you won't then I shan't choose my words, no, nor worry much about them afterwards. I am talking about your behaviour, sir. I shall continue to call you sir out of courtesy. Your behaviour has gone outside a private affair, sir, and has become public knowledge. A man in our profession should value discretion as a snail values his shell, sir, for without it he's done!'

Henry was pale and angry. 'Are you referring to rumours about my private life?'

'No, sir, I wish I were. I am referring to facts. And the facts are, as far as I can see it, that you should look to your marriage if you value it. That is perfectly plain. You may say it ain't my position to criticize, but damn me, sir, I *will* comment. And my comment is that you are making a mess of your business and a monkey of our families and I don't like it, sir! No, by God, nor will I have our names passed around dinner tables like dessert. Your name is my name and you have involved me without my permission. You make no bones about how you disapprove of the way I handle my own money, when you are always in need and I'm your appointed banker. It won't cure your ills, sir, if I give you what you ask, for I know how you'll spend it. Let us clear this matter up, sir, for I've no wish to talk about it. I would sooner we could talk about the day's events, the monarchy, that would be proper. A Coronation is still a rare event. Instead of which we have this. Won't do.'

Henry drank the last of his brandy and put it down carefully on the marble mantel. His actions were those of a courteous guest about to take his leave. Thomas watched him, shaking slightly from the fury of his speech. He wondered if Henry would yawn politely into his hand, for he had that air.

'I do not propose to enter into any defence of my position, Father, as I would find that insulting. I hope that as the family is united in involvement, it will be equally united in disbelief.'

'You deny it?' Thomas roared, much louder than he had intended.

'I don't precisely know of what I am accused . . .'

Thomas broke in, mulberry-red. 'Well, dear sir, dee me, let me enlighten you!'

Henry at last lost his temper and shouted: 'I have been indiscreet, sir, is that what you wish to hear, but damn it, sir, it is all over now. Is that enough? Or do you wish me to daub myself with pitch, roll in fire-ashes and present myself at high table!'

'It is enough, of course, if you mean to stick to it.'

Henry snorted with fury and passed quickly from the room. Thomas noted that he marched with military precision. Even in his anger he slammed no door, missed no step. Thomas stared for a long time at the fire, as though he wished to consign Henry to it. Eventually he levered himself up enough on his elbows to grasp the brandy. He settled down again with a full glass. It had been an unsatisfactory day. He wondered about the future, not only of his children, but of the monarchy, peace and the dangerous voice of the people. He wished he believed Henry had the strength to stick to his voiced intentions. He eventually fell asleep.

2

Henry Kelleway had arrived late at chambers. Even then he was early for his sole appointment that day, so it mattered not at all. He stared out of his window at the fine view over King's Bench Walk. The grass was lush and unscorched. There had been plenty of rain throughout the summer. The trees towards Paper Buildings struck poses, perhaps aping barristers. It was sunny and fine and he regretted his single commitment despite his pressing debts. He was aware this was feckless of him, but his mind was too full of his personal affairs and he felt that those of others were an intrusion. He would have preferred to stroll in Temple Gardens, like the black-gowned figures he could see below, watching the small craft landing at the Stairs and listening to the sucking and slapping of the Thames. It would have given an airing to the dusty rags of his mind.

His affairs were in a mess and he could not think indoors. He found this curious, as this was the room in which he pondered the troubles of others. The rows of leather-bound reports that seemed solid and comforting at other times, seemed now to be oppressively uniform. They were repositories of dead knowledge. They could give no advice on the exigencies of immediate action. Even a priest goes to another priest, he thought. What should I do? Shall one adulterer go to another? He smiled sourly to himself. Could any of them expect sympathy, let alone helpful advice?

The sun was yellow and more suited to October than July. It shone through the twelve panes of his window and made a distorted chequer-board on the floorboards. His room was modestly furnished; Mr Agnew and Mr Wells described it as pauperized, like its inhabitant. They lounged in sweet and supple leather, watching the gentle fading of fine silk carpets, while life was good to them. Occasionally, or so it seemed to Henry, they reached out an indolent hand to pluck some rich plum of a case. Mr Agnew and Mr Wells had been in the chambers for many years. They vied with each other with the subtle and expensive colours of Feraghan, Kerman or Kurdistan. They compared rugs from Adana, Nish and Trebizond. Henry Kellaway's boards were beeswaxed.

If Mr Agnew and Mr Wells were successful, it did not impress Mr Turvey or Mr Thackeray who regarded them as mere cocka-toos of the Bar. They disguised their success, as they thought proper so that they could scarcely be distinguished from legal parchment. Mr Turvey's face was white and big-pored, Mr Thackeray's an unhealthy yellow. Their heads seemed to be powdered with legal dust. A good brief should, they believed, be treated like good port and laid down to mature for a while. Mr Thackeray was Head of Chambers and Mr Wells was next in seniority. Henry Kellaway was the new man, and only man's mortality would do anything about that. Of the remaining bar-risters – Mr Cord, Mr Hay, Mr Croup and Mr Perrin – the last was Henry's chief problem. Perrin was a well-established young man, watchful of Henry's progress and quick to scent a poacher. His rooms were adjoining Henry's and his watchful eyes and long ears seemed everywhere. Henry believed he listened at the door or paid a clerk to do so. Perrin had ambitions and connec-tions. He was Thackeray's nephew. He maintained a rigid pro-priety about his private life and never failed to refer to Henry any rumour he had heard concerning Henry's affairs. Their relationship was full of poison. Henry had scant belief that any man could be so proper without developing wings.

Henry's door opened and Corbett, the senior clerk, came in. 'Can't you knock, Corbett?' snapped Henry with sudden an-noyance. He turned from the window showing his anger on his face. It was intolerable of the man to be so rude.

'Beg your pardon, sir, but I knew you had no one with you.'

This insolent answer was given quite courteously. The man's face was blank. Henry wisely kept his peace. Corbett and he were too deep in many things for him to protest with success.

'You have a visitor, Mr Kelleway,' Corbett continued, 'whom I have accommodated in the waiting-room.' Henry nodded, but

Corbett had not finished. 'It is a lady, Mr Kelleway, of some considerable charm.'

'I know that, of course, Corbett.' Henry was sharp and peevish.

'Ah, but you don't know about the charm, Mr Kelleway!'

Henry nodded abstractedly, unwilling to concede that his attention had been caught. Corbett was a large man with a well-fed face. His trunk was big and broad, his hands and feet large. Because of his build, he was often underestimated and this suited him, for Corbett was clever. His prominent forehead was daubed with flattened curls of hair like a Greek frieze. His eyes were of that inexpressive black and glittering kind that make one imagine inner malice. Corbett was far too clever, however, to be cast in any character. He acted urbanely through a series of roles, a different thing to every man, and often in different circumstances, leaving the real Corbett hard to find. Mr Thackeray, Mr Turvey and Mr Wells were impressed by his efficiency, cleverness and integrity. Mr Agnew relied on his judgement of rugs. Mr Hay consulted him at times on the more intricate cases of fraud. Mr Kelleway bribed him for briefs, or as Mr Corbett once tactfully put it, he had received his percentage in advance. Like many young barristers entering a fully subscribed profession, Henry was reduced either to this resort or poverty. It was done discreetly.

Much as he resented Corbett, Henry recognized the value of the man until that golden day when briefs came of their own accord, and could even be turned aside. His conscience might have been easier had he realized that Hay, Croup and Perrin appreciated Corbett's services in an identical way. But Corbett let no one know. Equally, Corbett was embroiled by this practice, for should the successful Mr Thackeray, Mr Wells or Mr Turvey find out, he would not last a second. That they must know was evident, but they could not be known to know.

Henry sat down at his desk, collecting some papers into an ordered pile. He pulled over Barnewall and Alderson's reports, splendid in blue leather with red and gilt labels. Corbett permitted himself the shadow of a derisive smile.

'The lady will want a good chair, Mr Kelleway. She is quite a beauty.'

'So you keep saying, Corbett.' He gestured vaguely at the man with a quill. 'See to it. I must be ready.' Corbett regarded the furniture as though baffled. 'That one there!' Henry was losing his temper again. 'It's the best I have. I'm not Mr Wells!'

Corbett said nothing, but pulled forward a sagging chair of brown hide. It was scuffed and cracked in places.

'Do you wish me to show them in now, or shall I ask them to wait a minute?' he asked, referring to Henry's customary business disguise.

Henry glared at the man, but his face was bland. The curls, Henry realized, must be stuck flat with oil.

'Show them in immediately.'

'Of course.'

The irksome nature of the situation was that Henry had paid ten pounds to Corbett, who in turn had paid five to the solicitor, to obtain the lady's presence. Now he must remain blandly aloof while the solicitor grinned and knew. He found his rental by borrowing from his father as his fees were absorbed by Corbett. 'If you want to build up a reputation, Mr Kelleway,' Corbett had said, 'there is no use being parsimonious, because that way lies ruin. The pickings in the end are rich. It is difficult, I know, for young men to forbear, but forbear they must to succeed. You say my price is high? There is the clerk's room to pay, and the solicitor to pay and he must pay his clerks. I cannot be responsible if you cannot yet command a good fat brief. We are only covering expenses. But you are becoming known, sir, I assure you. I put in a word for you where I can. It is beneath me usually to mention that, but as you have raised the subject, I do. There is expense involved there, sir, which I have never presumed to pass on. The world is a hard place for young barristers making their way, but it is only a matter of time until they do. As an investment, I think, it beats joint stocks!'

The lady was admitted by Corbett, who stood aside trying to look both gracious and unctious. His eyes missed nothing, as she rustled past him. Henry had to agree she was spectacular. Her day dress in light blue silk was trimmed with heavier blue material. She wore a heavy silk shawl and carried a white feather muff. Henry, getting to his feet, staggered against his desk and felt unnecessarily foolish because of it. He reached out to take her hand, aware that his chair was less than suitable. She looked at him with slight amusement that embarrassed him further, because she seemed very composed and in no way cowed by her surroundings. Her eyes were a dark brown, he noted, and her rounded neckline revealed a full figure. He stared at her, for just a fraction too long. The smile of amusement was beginning to spread.

'Please sit down.' Henry escorted her to the chair, hardly noticing Coke, the solicitor, who was a small man dressed mainly in black, with a narrow but long bald head. Mr Coke had an unnerving gaze, which was either directed at his clients or at the ceiling. For the moment he regarded the ceiling, as if expecting some astral phenomenon.

'Mrs Waters and Mr Coke,' Corbett announced belatedly. He withdrew like a thief. Henry suspected he would remain beyond the door.

Mrs Waters sat down, carefully arranging her silks about her. She smiled at Henry, winningly. He thought the smile seemed practised, but it extended to her eyes.

'So this is what you endure, Mr Kelleway. I was always told that a certain austerity prevailed in the Temple.'

'I apologize, Mrs Waters, but the chair . . .'

'Do not apologize, Mr Kelleway. I doubt if any of your clients have remarked upon it. It is, after all, the man they want, and not his furnishings.'

She smiled again, and Henry, not sure what to say, grimaced back and pushed the second and worse chair towards Coke, who hardly expected even that civility. Mr Coke sat near Mrs Waters, but at sufficient distance to regard her when he desired. He obviously did desire to, for he fixed her with a stare that might have been unnerving. From his inner pocket he produced a bundle of documents tied with pink ribbon which he laid on Henry's desk, without altering his gaze. This completed, he lay further back in the scuffed hide and seemed to disappear. Mr Coke of Wyndham and Thornhill had so long practised the act of self-effacement that he had become a human chameleon.

Henry found himself watching Mrs Waters rather stupidly. He did not regard himself as particularly impressionable, but his clients were generally a miserable bunch compared with this woman. Women of his acquaintance were generally modest and unassuming, Mrs Waters assumed. Henry liked women that blossomed in the shade of men, as cyclamens beneath an elm, blossoming in their protection. Not satisfied with Jane Leigh, he had had no hesitation in turning his attentions elsewhere. But true to his cautious nature, his women were required to conform to the same pattern. Discreet adultery seemed to him a charming thing that hurt no one provided no one was informed. Indeed, in the secret contemplation of his life, he felt it redounded to him, firstly as a man and secondly by virtue of his discretion, as a human being. These stolen pleasures were contained within a careful understanding and conducted with delicate ecstasies after afternoon tea. Mrs Waters was quite outside his experience, for she was assessing him. Her amused brown eyes embarrassed him. He tucked himself further under his desk as though it offered some refuge, crossing his legs like a shy boy. Mrs Waters continued to smile, and he imagined that her humour increased. He was aware that the silence had become intense and that Mr Coke, who soaked up nuance like a sand-box, was staring at the ceiling. He must divert attention from this overt frontal attack, but his mind was inadequate to the situation.

'Good morning, Mrs Waters, Mr Coke.' He made some play of placing the papers in front of him in an ordered pile.

Mrs Waters rustled gently in the chair, as though she found it uncomfortable, which it was until she found the comfortable worn depression where the webbing had collapsed. Henry found it was difficult to avoid her presence in a properly subduing legal manner and to address himself to Mr Coke. He was particularly aware of her gaze, and could feel at this distance a slight warmth from her as though he sat in proximity to a low fire, or as he thought prosaically, near a horse. His legal frame must sustain his life at ten degrees below that of a woman graced with beauty and nourished on compliments. Her perfume overwhelmed the smell of leather bindings.

'This is in the nature of an extraordinary hearing, Mrs Waters,' he said with cool abstraction, his eyes on the desk, 'please make yourself comfortable. What we shall do is simple. I would like you to go through the whole situation in your own words, then I will ask you a few questions. No more than that. Just use your own words.' He was faltering and repetitive. Mrs Waters was calm.

'I have no others.'

Henry, in view of the circumstances of the case, had expected a respectful pause and was annoyed. He looked up at her. She still smiled composedly, lying back in the chair with the ribbons of her hat tossed back with an air of social ease. He saw she must be over thirty, perhaps even thirty-five. Her ringlets were black as split coal, her eyes dark brown. Combined with a fair skin these features gave her a quality of intense concentration. He would have found her face imperious except for her amused mouth which had left laugh-wrinkles at the corner of her lips. Her nose was rather more prominent than Henry would have preferred in a woman, although he admired a nose in a man, but he had to admit it suited her striking style.

'I trust you are comfortable?' he inquired in a flat tone that indicated, he hoped, that it was a matter of mere courtesy and that he intended to get down to business.

'Quite comfortable, Mr Kelleway, if I consider that I had understood that all gentlemen of the Law enjoyed surroundings that would have been bad lodgings for the ancient Spartans. I find that I am only slightly disappointed. It is not really even monkish!'

'Mrs Waters, I take it that you are comfortable enough for us to commence?' He was irritated and yet anxious at the same time. His voice, he feared, betrayed it.

'Please, Mr Kelleway, I am entirely comfortable and I do believe that some bareness induces the right concentration of the mind. Forgive me for my idle curiosity and we shall begin.'

'There is nothing to forgive, madam,' Henry found himself responding, 'it is not intentional as is popularly supposed nor due to exceptional parsimony. Our habit may be a trifle simple but we bring it to essentials.' He shuffled the papers again, selecting one for scrutiny and sat poised to start. Mrs Waters still showed no such readiness.

'Come now, Mr Kelleway, I cannot be convinced that the Law has simple habits. It is a sort of regimen that conceals its strength. The Law is an old fox. Indulgence dulls the brain, does it not, or shall I say that austerity sharpens the appetite. The appetite for truth and exactitude.'

Henry was confused. Mr Coke regarded the ceiling with a smile of supercilious amusement and obviously intended to offer no help to bring the conversation under control. She was mocking him, but gently and with pleasing flattery.

'That may be, Mrs Waters, I agree. However, if we may now proceed, we have come to exercise our wits somewhat on your behalf have we not, if rather indirectly. Mr Coke here has supplied me with the essential documents of the brief which I have received from Mr Montague who is the real plaintiff in this matter.'

Mr Coke made a noise of assent that sounded as though he was gargling. He leaned slightly forward, moving with slow care, uncertain of his chair, took a pair of brass-framed pince-nez from one waistcoat pocket, perched them on his nose the better to regard the ceiling and began to recite in a nasal London voice.

'Mrs Waters finds herself, yes, very much finds herself in an unfortunate position. You will of course appreciate, Mr Kelleway, that what has happened strikes at the very heart, indeed the hearth of her home.' Mr Coke was pleased with this and shot a glance at Henry. With the spectacles on his nose and his head inclined backwards he looked like a frog staring out of a pond. 'Yes, it attacks her reputation in society and against it she can have no redress. The burden that she must bear through the case brought by my client Mr Montague, will, if her husband succeeds, wound her most horribly from motives designed I fear for that purpose. Motives designed to wound and wound coldly. Yet motives that also carry with them pecuniary advantage, for if Mr Waters evades the suit brought by my client, then he will not have to pay, by my reading of the situation, and both my client and Mrs Waters will lose. I submit that the burden she would bear is out of all proportion to mere clothes. What are clothes? A trifle. Her very home and heart and reputation will be destroyed.'

He stopped his monologue abruptly and continued to stare at the ceiling, wiggling his fingers. Henry spoke quickly lest he should restart.

'Thank you, Mr Coke. I am very sensible to the situation. Now, Mrs Waters, you understand that nothing that you say can possibly be introduced in evidence, but that we may be able to identify others who can help. Will you tell me in your ... about these clothes?'

'May I ask you something first, Mr Kelleway?' She smiled at him with a boldness that was his despair. It was impertinent, he decided, but charming. 'Do you know anything about clothes?'

'I am a married man!' As he spoke, he realized what a fatuous reply it was. He wondered why he had needed to reply in that fashion. Was he in need of some sort of defence? It was certainly the reply of a boy confronted by a woman. Was Coke smiling at the ceiling? He picked up a quill and riffled it through his fingers with a noise as dry as documents. Mrs Waters had leaned slightly forward as though in pursuit of his weakness. The rustling of her dress confused him further. It was certainly sexual and he was surprised by the thought.

'Then perhaps you do, Mr Kelleway, but please forgive me for saying perhaps. For if one considers it, my husband is also married! He knows less than nothing so it is no guarantee. I think you'll agree that marriage does not necessarily confer an understanding of couture. I believe my husband would have me make do for life on my bridal gown! It depends entirely upon the sensitivity and understanding of the man.'

'Quite. But please tell me about the clothes.' Henry felt unreasonably satisfied with this firm interjection.

'Ah yes, the clothes.'

She sighed, she plucked at her dress, she hesitated, she seemed to lose her worldly air, her head hung slightly. But all the time she watched Henry and judged him as susceptible as he was vain. However, he was handsome and that in itself presented a curiosity. It was evident that he should be doing well in the world and equally evident that he was not. Her remarks upon legal austerity were founded on the knowledge that eminence brings solidity, a certain mellow fullness to a man's room, and also better chairs. Eminent men, however, cost eminently large sums of money and Mr Coke had pointed out this obvious aspect of Mr Kelleway's advantages. In such a condition he had said, a man is vulnerable. Where dust and crust are concerned there is a difference between the dust of ages and that of effect, as also with the crust of security which should be like pastry on a pie and not mere hollow armour. Yet Mrs Helena Waters judged him capable of some firmness. She allowed herself a long examination of his features – forehead, eyes, mouth and hands too. She was rewarded by Henry impatiently riffling his quill.

'Forgive me if I do not have your legal directness. I am expected, indeed my husband's position commands, that I keep up a certain style, a certain *bon ton* as befits his position, for the *beau monde* as they say. I would sooner be attacked by cannibals, Mr Kelleway, than be found out of fashion. You must understand?'

Henry felt obliged to nod with vigorous understanding.

'One need not be a fashion plate – frankly, many of them are outrageous and immoderate. I will not walk abroad as a Chinese pagoda! But even in moderation one must try to support one's husband. I am reflected in him as he in me. How else can I represent myself as his wife? Or could! His treatment of me has been so despicable!'

'Quite, quite,' said Coke to the cornice. 'Indeed, yes quite. No less than any wife should strive for, Mr Kelleway, I think you will agree. A wife is but a mirror-glass to her husband's virtues. For as Shakespeare says, a light wife doth make a heavy husband.'

'Yes, Mr Coke,' Henry said with some asperity, 'but Mrs Waters' husband has deposed, counter to the claim by your client Mr Montague, that he cannot be responsible for Mrs Waters' debts, that he made Mrs Waters a substantial allowance for clothes. I do not mean to wound you, Mrs Waters, but this is what he has said. He will not answer for the sum owing.' Mrs Coke made an indeterminate noise which suited his frog-like crouch. Henry addressed Mrs Waters. 'Forgive me, but we must get down to the detail in this thing. I have to ask you these questions, for should he succeed in proving his defence, namely that he cannot be responsible for your debts, then Mr Montague will not be paid and equally, Mrs Waters, you will be attainted as having committed a wilful act. Did he make you such an allowance?'

'Mr Kelleway, what is a substantial allowance for clothes? How does one measure it? Is it the same for a Parliamentary candidate's spouse and for a coachman's wife? Look at me. Am I extravagantly dressed? Do you know the price of silk, Mr Kelleway? Thirty pounds!' Her voice was elegantly scornful. 'That is what I am allowed. Is that a substantial allowance? Would you shame your own wife with that?'

Henry, who had privately been thinking of ten pounds, which was what he allowed Jane, moved on too rapidly.

'Thirty pounds is still a sum of money. It will be said in court. You spent that with Mr Montague and fifty-two pounds twelve shillings besides, according to your husband.'

'Mr Kelleway, do I look the sort of woman who can dress for thirty pounds a year?' She extended her arms to him in a fetching gesture of supplication, then clasped her hands together beneath her chin. Henry found it charming.

'Quite, quite,' said Mr Coke, who had swivelled his eyes off the ceiling to gaze at her breasts with undisguised admiration. He then regarded what he could see of her ankles and gave a little shudder of pleasure.

'What is thirty pounds a year with prices as they are today?' Mrs Waters asked. 'I am sure you are a generous man, Mr Kelleway. You must know that it is no more than the price of trimmings and lace. It is what I spend in Harding and Howell on materials before I can even approach Mr Montague for dress-making.'

'But your husband alleges that he did not know of this extra account, and that will be his defence. He further says that you concealed these clothes from him, which is why he refuses to pay the bills. I am sorry if I appear indelicate but he further contends that the items of clothing are not necessaries. It is the very substance of his defence.'

Mrs Waters laughed. She managed it prettily with a hint of nervous gaiety, a rustling in her chair that showed distress.

'Mr Kelleway, are you really a married man?' Henry looked at her sharply, aware that he was not conducting things with the command he should. 'I don't mean to be presumptuous, but what man knows what his wife has in her wardrobe? Indeed, what man should be allowed to know, so that he can never be surprised? Can any man tell how many day dresses and in what materials? Bonnets and evening dresses? Hems of silk or gauze? Whether of cambric, muslin or satin? What scarves, muffs, or stockings? Confess, Mr Kelleway, that no man can.'

Henry knew for a certainty that Jane had only two evening dresses and two walking dresses and that these had been paid for by Thomas. It was a reminder of his financial affairs that he did not appreciate, and he suspected Mrs Waters was well aware of it. Her eyes showed only innocent enquiry.

'My affairs are hardly relevant.' His tone was polite but dismissive.

Mrs Waters put out a gloved hand and rested it lightly on Henry's for a moment. Mr Coke could not have been more entertained if it had been a snake from a basket.

'I did not mean to intrude.'

'I'm sure Mr Kelleway is not offended,' said Coke, sly as the serpent. 'Women are a pretty mystery, are they not, Mr Kelleway? A kind of gauze of clothes.'

'Mrs Waters, we must continue,' pursued Henry, ignoring Coke.

'It has all been said. My husband, in short, is a mean man, and known for it. Our marriage, Mr Kelleway, our marriage . . .' She sighed. 'An application will of course be made to the ecclesiastical court. It is the weakness of our sex. In refusing to pay my bills with Mr Montague, who is a good man, he aspires both to avoid his financial duty as a gentleman and vindictively to destroy my good name. My own money, and I have some, is his by legal right and yet I cannot spend it. It is monstrously unkind. A woman has no standing, no defence. It is inhuman!'

Mrs Waters was reduced to tears, or so it seemed, for she sank her face into a lilac handkerchief and patted at her eyes and cheeks. Corbett, who had found great confusion in the papers of the briefs he carried, which detained him in the corridor, grinned cynically and moved quietly back to the clerk's room.

'Jenkins,' he announced to a junior clerk who was up to his cuffs in inkspots, 'I think tea will shortly be required in Mr Kelleway's room.'

'A crying case, Mr Corbett?'

'One of the better class of Thespians, but entirely convincing to some of our clever men of the law. I don't believe she's a-losing liquid because of it!'

While Henry exhibited his superficial resemblance to Wellington in profile against the yellow sun and made manly noises intended to quell emotion, Thomas was about other business. He walked slowly from the Temple, past the ancient church embedded in chambers and shops that leaned upon it and climbed over it for support, through paved courts and under arches and colonnades. He followed a familiar route to Water Lane and although his morning's work cluttered his desk, it in no way occupied his mind. He had achieved that state of grace which is won by years of devotion to worry, where parchment and pink ribbons could be forgotten without new ones ceasing to arrive. He was able to identify, among the pleading, rebutting, purporting, verily believing, denying, swearing, submitting, staying, claiming, and very occasional judgements, those cumbrous sprints of the law before they happened. The law is a hippopotamus which must always blow much water about and snort and make a commotion before it moves, giving good notice of its intentions. To every move, Thomas knew, there was a delay, but to every delay there was seldom a move. Although the system was, he warranted, on the side of the tortoise rather than the hare, he would not have changed it for he made a good living and it was his life.

He walked slowly, his top hat tilted forward and with a judicial lean so that he looked like a mobile bowsprit. It was a sign of deep thought. Beside him walked Sam Leigh with a more rolling motion. He carried his weight before and behind him and was well wrapped because it was cold. Sam carried a silver topped cane with which he poked at the mud in cracks between flagstones. They made their way towards the Black Lion which had a respectable cellar, kept a fire lit on such days and had private booths. Carts racketed past them on the cobbled streets, running to and from White Friars dock. Although they had stepped no further from their legal sanctuary than the length of an Assize procession, the streets were full of commerce. Hoarse voices shouted and cursed. Shops overspilled on to the paved way, blocking it with barrels and boxes, handcarts of fish, trays of bread and pies. Law stationers pursued their scratching, rustling business behind dusty windows. Caged birds hung from upper windows, animated by thin shafts of sunlight, but whether or not they were singing, no one could hear.

'You see, Sam,' Thomas shouted, threading through a timber scaffold propped on the street and tied with strips of rag, 'I find business a devil. If I could put as much attention to it as I do to other people's, I might make it a success.' They paused to dodge a man and a barrel that seemed to be pursuing each other. 'It is time for shipping, everyone says that. I am persuaded of it. Trade is the key to everything. In British ships mark you, and none of this rubbish about free trade! Manufactures are too risky. You must know the men you are involved with for most of them seem to be fit for a free passage. How can you know how things are being done? The mechanics and labouring class are restless these days. Breaking machines, rioting, turning on their masters. Dee me, where will it lead? Revolution they say, but I don't see it. Wellington would never allow it.'

'Wellington never allows anything,' Sam declared with approval.

'Stability,' Thomas continued, 'but I am getting on in years and must look to the family. Of course, as you know I have made my little investments, taken a risk here and there, but on the whole I put in silver and came out with gold. I have no feel for these country canters, with a house, a horse, some trees of such and such a height that have been thrust in the ground these last few hundred years. I am a business man. You know me, Sam, it is money in the end. I will not be caught counting haycocks and slaughtering my stock so the fashionable intelligence can regale themselves by digesting my menu, once at my table and second behind my back. No. But this shipping promises a good return. We carry the world's trade, by and large.'

'Apart from the Americans.'

'Apart from the Americans. But in shipping, at least, they can prove quite reliable. Most of their captains are English or some Scotch and a deal of their crews. No, a good-found ship, copper-bottomed, can pay for herself in two years. I know of nothing better.'

They turned into the court of the Black Lion, passing under the stone arch that bore the scars of carts and coaches. The yard was filthy with horse droppings, mud, hay and feed. An ostler with an armful of yellow straw was spreading layers of it over the worst mess. Thomas and Sam clumped round the boarded walk and soon had themselves established in a comfortable booth with wood as brown as stout. A bottle of wine was set down for them, with two glasses. The room rumbled with talk, but in a subdued way as of comradeship that yet demanded sobriety. The pot-boy brought clay pipes, a candle and a taper. He was rewarded.

'So what is the proposition?' Sam asked after a decent interval spent sucking at the pipe stem, and glaring into the bowl until it glowed properly.

'I take a half-share in a vessel newly built and fitting out at Wells Yard in Limehouse Reach.'

'A half-share is a large risk. Can you not take less? What if she is lost?'

'Then, Sam, I shall be fully insured. I shall see to it with my full legal attention!'

'Who has the other half?'

'A retired shipmaster, of whom I have had a good recommendation. He will select the captain and officers. It is necessary to have a man experienced in that side of things.'

'And what will she run?'

'General cargo. You see, Sam, the clever thing is that she will not only be my ship but will run my cargo too. It is a double investment, both out and back.'

Sam grunted a judicial grunt in which disbelief was mixed equally with misgiving. 'There seem to me to be two injurious possessions a man may have that bring out litigation like worms after rain. One is ships and the other is a wife. Baron and feme, and barratry. There are chambers founded on nothing else!'

Thomas laughed. 'Some might say they were equal risks. I am getting old, Sam. An old man's thoughts turn before him to the grave, or more particularly, to those that will not share it with him. There are only two things the law recognizes – money and death. It's all one or t'other. Dee me, anything short of death always has a worth! The scales of justice are nothing but a banker's balance! When a horse dies, they boil him down for glue, use him hoof and gut. He is more use than we are. When we die they boil our kin according to the recipe of the Will. We talk of Death the Reaper. It appears to me he is Death the Raper. His scroll don't carry names of his intended, Sam, it carries a list of Bills, of Deeds, of debts and mortgages for immediate discharge at St Peter's gate, which is no more than a Court of Chancery!'

'This is a gloomy mood, Tom!'

'I feel my years catching up upon me. Don't I look it now? I feel them. Eyes, legs, memory. Veins don't lie in my flesh any more, but crawl about blue on the surface, like worms.'

'Tom, Tom, I am as old as you! There's years in us yet. Black moods come from unquiet minds. It hurts me to see you brought so low. What is it? Henry? The family?'

'It is all of it. Henry is an arrogant and wilful pup. He pesters me for money as though it were his birthright, and advises me to invest in land. I see no future in him. It grieves me, Sam, that I have married him to your child.'

'We have been through all that. I won't hear any more about it!'

'Then John is away. I have had a letter from him that gives me no reason to enjoy my victuals. There is trouble in Assam, much skirmishing and he says there must be a war with the Burmese, for they are attacking the Company and no British vessels may land at Rangoon for pirates and cannonades from the shore. This is a state that cannot go on. I wish he were home, but he writes as though he enjoys the life. It cuts me to the heart, Sam, I tell you, that he ever joined the army. I blame it on myself, for I could have stopped it if I had only kept my temper. Devil of a thing, temper. Whenever I get a letter, which is not as often as I should like, everyone says good, he is well. But how do I know that? It takes six months to get here.'

Sam puffed at the long stem of his pipe. Thomas was only fifty-four, and yet he looked twenty years older. There was tiredness about his eyes today and though his body was well-covered, the skin of his face was slack so that he appeared puffy around the eyes and his jowls were marked. Sam made an effort to cheer his spirits.

'We must get off this subject, Tom, for children must sort out their own lives.'

'They are so waxen!'

'You cannot do it for them. How were you at their age? Have another glass and let us talk about shipping. As you say, that is a future. Dwelling on the past prolongs old wrongs. Tell me about this vessel and how much you are committed?'

Henry had finally perched his pince-nez on his nose and the black silk cord trailed down one cheek like a dark scar. He lay back in the leather chair, thumbs stuck in his waistcoat pockets and tried to master his feelings of irritation and confusion. It was a pose to gain time. It aped Mr Coke. He scratched his forehead and spoke sharply to Coke.

'Mr Coke, this further affidavit from the defendant is quite another matter altogether! You should have brought my attention to it earlier. It is really impossible to deal with it at such short notice as I would have thought you should know. It is very dangerous to your client and Mrs Waters and must be answered on all points and the necessary witnesses found on our side. I shall have to consider it. We really cannot go further, it is a waste of time!'

He shut a volume on his desk emphatically, and looked over the rim of his glasses. Coke, unabashed, lowered his eyes from the cornice and looked over the rims of his. He stared at a point coinciding with the second row of Law Reports behind Henry's head.

'The affidavit has only just been sworn. Indeed, for my client, and Mrs Waters, I would say it has been sworn most tardily. I would say, in Mrs Waters' own words, that it has been sworn with ill intent. Mrs Waters denies there is one grain of substance in it.'

'But what Mrs Waters says is not evidence! We require further witnesses.'

Mrs Waters no longer looked as fresh as when she had arrived. Where before there had been something of dalliance, she now languished in apparent helplessness. Her expression indicated hurt at Henry's attitude, yet she managed a charming disposition of her limbs in the intractable chair. Henry tapped the documents with his fingers.

'Mrs Waters, your husband further states that this sum includes the purchase of other goods consisting of necklaces, a diamond ring, bracelets and other ornamental jewellery, without his knowledge. He further states that he never saw these small articles before, about the house or on your person, that these articles were expressly delivered at your instructions at times when he would not be at home. He states that the times of these deliveries were set out by you to the shop-men delivering. These are not obvious things like dresses, but are small and could be unknown to him. Why did you not present this to me earlier, Mr Coke?'

Coke's eyes slid to the ceiling. A small smile crossed his face and he took time to re-adjust his legs. 'You have had the papers, Mr Kelleway, that is a copy I have presented. Perhaps there has been some mistake by my clerk. But no, I perceive you have them. Perhaps you have been so engaged that you have been unable to peruse them?' There was insolence in his tone and Henry controlled his rage. He had no defence, for the papers were there and he had not attended to them. Coke continued.

'My client is as concerned as you are, and the lady is deeply distressed. However, although this is a most vindictive and unpleasant circumstance introduced with some skill, Mr Montague has assured me that his shop-men will testify otherwise; namely that deliveries were made during the normal working hours of the day. You will confirm this with Mr Montague when next we meet. Mrs Waters, I can see, is most distressed, and I am sure you share her concern. For her, it is nothing less than a disaster. But it must be evident that if Mrs Waters had concealment in mind she would not have had such trifles delivered.'

Henry blushed, and for a moment his manner slipped as though he were an actor who had forgotten his lines. Mrs Waters immediately intervened.

'It is really quite simple, Mr Kelleway. I have worn these jewels in plain view in my husband's company. They cannot have gone unnoticed. Enquiry has only to be made. I also wore the dresses. It is impossible for him to make anything of this, Mr

Kelleway. Can you not see it? He hates and misuses me and will use every device to secure my ruin. You have the means to cure my ills, Mr Kelleway. You are a physician for my pain.'

Mrs Waters was fetchingly distraught. Henry took off his pince-nez and removed his thumbs from his waistcoat pockets.

'Dear lady, I am sensible to the great distress all this must cause you, and other witnesses will be found if you give us the occasions and places. However, it is evident that your remedy will end in the ecclesiastical court.'

'I have advised her of that,' said Mr Coke. Mrs Waters nodded.

'Then we must answer for every item that is set down in this list, with time and place worn, painful as it may be to justify yourself so.'

'What pain is left, Mr Kelleway, when the heart is destroyed?' Mrs Waters clutched her bosom with both hands and gazed into Henry's eyes. It was risky drama but Henry did not look away. Mrs Waters was satisfied. Coke had advised her well.

In the clerk's room, Corbett was reading through a letter that Jenkins had finished writing, pausing to shake off grains of sand. Jenkins, who was copying a thirty-page affidavit, was too busy to observe whether Corbett found it correct. From years of experience he was able to talk as he wrote, his small pointed head following his hand across the vellum while the quill tickled his nose. Jenkins seemed to be all wisps. His thin hair stood up in tufts, his clothes were worn out round the extremities and threads hung from collar, cuffs, and trousers. His eyesight was by now so bad that his spectacles had lenses that made his eyes look like glass paper-weights.

'That is some lady with Mr Kelleway. Some lady in silks and stuff!'

'She is indeed, and more dangerous than he knows. A bird in borrowed feathers if you take my drift. You are a clerk who knows his station, are you not, Jenkins?'

'If you think so, Mr Corbett.'

'Then say nothing.' Jenkins made several looping lines of script that looked as though it had been flattened by a considerable wind.

'But don't he know?' he asked.

'Why should he? We get about, Jenkins, and it is our business. We know that Mr Kelleway is in a short way for briefs and in our way we assist. Now we know that she comes with Mr Coke and that properly anything for Mr Thackeray's chambers should go to Mr Perrin, who has a quick, not to say an ill-natured eye in these matters. But how is a young man to start, Jenkins, but that he parts with a little of the necessary root of all good and evil alike. Besides, Corbett has a nose for these things. There will be a reward in heaven for me from Mr Perrin, you shall see. Have you considered that the prosecutor of Mr Vesey Waters, special Pleader at the Bar, must want to jump in the fiery furnace like three heathens?'

'They was Christians, Mr Corbett.'

'They was Jews, Mr Jenkins,' said Corbett, 'and to be strictly accurate, they did not jump, they were pushed. But I don't see as Mr Kelleway will have such a chance of survival with Mr Vesey Waters, who is not a man renowned for his generosity of disposition. It don't matter who is right or wrong. Win or lose, it is a good case to make powerful enemies. Not a thing I should like Mr Perrin to become involved in. You see, Jenkins, discretion in these matters is our job, and Mr Coke is very discreet.'

'I hope no one finds out, Mr Corbett.' Jenkins had stopped writing and looked up with some alarm, his enormous eyes apparently encapsulated in the glass of his lenses.

'Find out, Mr Jenkins? I never heard anything on it to find. Mr Coke has given it to Mr Kelleway. What can there be to discover there, that is not as open as Temple Bar?'

Mr Masterson, the ship-owner, lived above his premises in Upper Thames Street adjoining Doctor's Commons. He could very well have afforded to live elsewhere, but stayed by choice. The noise in the daytime was almost unendurable. It rattled sashes, shook the buildings and threatened to star the glass in the windows. Only the width of the street separated his premises from the wharfs fronting the Thames. Shipping being his business, he would get up each morning and count the burgees without the aid of a glass to see what new trade had slipped up the slithery river by the morning tide and now lay in berth.

From Mr Hoad's Iron Wharf, Mr Randall's Lime Wharf, Puddle Dock, Sand Wharf, Copper Wharf and the Carron Warehouse crammed with castings, the signs and sounds of London's prosperity erupted into the streets. The mud, according to where it accumulated, was white, yellow or green. Squat dockers whose limbs appeared to have been twisted from ships' cordage, hoisted burdens of superhuman weight, with the skill of generations. Scavengers lounged against walls, waiting for a broken barrel, a split chest or a collapsed cart. Sharp men, with a good turn of speed, waited for wallets. The gin houses stayed open for such long hours that a man who dozed occasionally might believe they never closed. All considerations of personal safety were secondary to the passage of commerce and the pursuit of Mammon. Carters thrashed their big Shire horses to a frenzy to set them lumbering into motion with too-heavy loads, and when moving, nothing could stop them. Men had to look to their safety. Carters reminded them with a sting of their long whips. Dockers replied with curses and impressive researches into genealogy.

If the perils of terra firma were not sufficient, gantries projected from upper floors. Hooks and nets dropped from these regions of the air without warning. Barrels swung crazily, threatening to stave in windows, walls or human ribs. Small groups of men, many of them in rags and shoeless, stood about at the wharf gates seeking casual work. Large, impassive men barred their way and contemplated the percentage they would receive from the embezzling tally-clerks.

Thomas Kelleway moved from doorway to doorway. He felt very aware that the power and majesty of the Law was a feeble thing here. He felt like an eggshell, and pondered how these hard and sturdy men could be reduced to incoherent wretches by a flock of wigs and gowns. He entered Masterson's house by a side stair and went directly to the first floor, where a clerk received him and took him into a back room. Here the noise receded. Masterson sat at a big desk of gleaming mahogany in a room that was similarly panelled. It immediately reminded Thomas, as it was supposed to, of a captain's cabin. All the furnishings of the room had the same naval flavour. A brass ship's clock recorded the time, a globe stood by the desk, a telescope against the wall. Prints of fine ships, hell-bent about their trade, were interspersed with prints of vessels hell-bent on mutual destruction. A large oil-painting behind Masterson's head portrayed a spectacular scene of naval destruction, regarded by seamen clinging to spars in the foreground. Masterson got to his feet with a ready smile.

'Mr Kelleway. Delighted! Sit down. Let me take your hat and coat. Have this chair, it's very comfortable. You had no trouble finding your way? Devilish busy out there as I expect you noticed.'

'Trade appears well enough.' Thomas too could indulge in understatement.

Masterson had a balding head but bushy whiskers and a fine beard, greying round the edges as though frizzed with caked salt. He had a habit of looking intensely into the eyes of whoever he spoke to, as though by doing so he could read a barometer of the general change of weather and pressure. His eyes, however, were singularly inexpressive when he smiled or became animated. He seemed to have a second, worried mind working within, whose calculating and different thoughts these eyes reflected. He wore a short coat, that by its cut and style also reflected a life at sea. One hand had lost two fingers, Thomas realized, as Masterson proffered his left hand to shake. They both sat down. The desk between them was impressively stacked with bills of lading, logs, intractable curly charts and heavy ledgers, each inscribed in gold with the name of a vessel. A variety of wooden tallies were in use as paper-weights.

'A drink, Mr Kelleway?' Masterson indicated a tantalus that stood beside him behind the desk. Thomas thanked him and after a decent debate was handed an amazingly large glass of fine old port, which he was obliged to hold throughout, seeing no obvious place to put it down. 'To business, then. Have you given the matter your thought?'

'Yes, Mr Masterson, I have. It is a difficult business. I know so little about shipping except its risks, which we see too often in Court.'

Mr Masterson gestured with his good left hand. 'One never hears the good news. Why, if the papers were to list daily each ship that has safely returned and give a lading list to go with it,

79

then there would be no room for any other news, and a damned good thing too, I say, by God!' Masterson could have been a jolly sea-dog, but for those eyes, that were boring into Thomas in an uncomfortable way.

'It is a great deal of money,' Thomas said, 'and it is risked all at once. It is not a situation where one can put some in, follow the market and see how it runs. I am investing for my family, you see. I am at the age where one ceases to bother about one-self.'

'Come now, Mr Kelleway. I have masters your age!'

Thomas was not to be distracted. 'The estimated cost of this vessel, when fully fitted out, will be, let me see, I think we said seven thousand pounds?'

'A little bit more, perhaps, Mr Kelleway. It is about average for a general seeking ship. Let us say seven thousand five hundred pounds. Don't spoil the ship, as they say, Mr Kelleway!' Masterson gave a hearty roar of laughter, but his eyes were those of a look-out.

'Her tonnage is two hundred and fifty-five. Now what does that mean in money, in return, and of course in insurance. I am a novice, Mr Masterson, and must rely upon you to seek cargo. I would have no more idea with what to load her than I would have to sail her.'

'Mr Kelleway, have no fears, it is all very simple. I have car-goes waiting to be shipped from Bristol to Boston to Buenos Aires. The agents see to it, and the cargo is loaded under coven-ant. Take wool. Wool from Sierra Leone. There is a remote but profitable market. We value that at sale here at twelve pounds a load, which means, with our tonnage, that she ships cargo of value of three thousand pounds. What do we pay for wool in Sierra Leone, you ask? Wool in Sierra Leone is two pounds a load. Profit, two thousand five hundred pounds, less cost of crew and victuals. Cannot be less than two thousand pounds. Insur-ance covers her from the moment of sailing until the moment of return, both cargo and damage to vessel. As partners in it, Mr Kelleway, we would stand to gain one thousand pounds in one voyage. A vessel of that class, a right good boat, well-made and well-found, cannot have a life of less than twenty-five years in prime trade, and ten or twenty more in coastal. If we make only two voyages a year to the Americas and ship at home between, say, Liverpool and Dover, we cannot clear less than two thousand a year! She will be paid for in three years. What else in the world can you say that for except a coal-mine? You are not thinking of taking up with the mining shares are you, Mr Kelleway?'

Thomas shook his head, avoiding the transfixing stare of the other man.

'Besides,' Masterson continued, 'you are an eminent lawyer, Mr Kelleway, an expert in matters of insurance, a man with an eye for a document, who shall see that there are no loopholes, no omissions, no circumstances not covered. It is just your sort of experience that a man like me needs. I was at sea thirty years. Master of many a fine vessel. Know a ship from keel to royal. But cargoes are complex today and I need the legal mind. Everything else I can manage, but these insurances and covenants, it is all legal stuff, and such stuff is like a burst cotton bale to me. It has a life of its own, and will not be satisfied until it has covered the quay with confusion.'

Thomas was not yet convinced. The man's record was good. He was no Navy man, but had run armed merchantmen through the French war, exchanged shot and made port. He was not clear, however, why Mr Masterson should have fallen on hard times so that he needed a partner in his concern. The man owned only two other boats, these now ageing and of medium tonnage. Masterson, as though divining his thoughts, proffered the port decanter.

'Come now, Mr Kelleway, I never knew a legal gentleman who could not handle the ruby. Port, they say, makes you lean starboard!'

Thomas accepted another mighty glass. Mr Masterson continued to spill out details of trade, trade routes, anchorages, ports, dues, excise and all the other well-organized laws of the sea. He then proposed they should take a waterman to Wells Yard to view the vessel and Thomas, well fortified, agreed. If he had had doubts in Masterson's office, they were difficult to maintain when confronted with the vessel. It would have been an insult to have had doubts in front of her, for Thomas felt she must have ears and a heart and a brain.

Shored up on logs, she seemed a thing of the highest beauty that ought not to be standing in green Thames mud. She was a lady who had accidentally stepped up to her ankles in a mire. Men swarmed over her, confident in what they did and where they trod, using keen tools that cut with a sweet rasp on sweet wood. The ship gleamed with new black and white paint. Gold scroll work decorated her bows. Yellow pine shone with varnish. Mahogany doors were rich with brass fittings that showed no trace of sea-etched verdigris. Cream rope, black shackles and chains, lay on the deck. Thomas trod it with Masterson while men with pots of boiling pitch knelt in leather-patched breeches, hammering tow between the planks with caulking chisels. The smells were powerful and exciting. Cakes of copal were being reduced in boilers. The aromatic fumes were enough to knock a man senseless and fill his lungs with the taste for a week. Sawn wood smelled sour and sweet. The men in saw pits rasped away the long day, reducing formidable logs into tractable planks that could be cut, shaped and bent. The masts lay ready for hoisting and seemed improbably huge. Anchors and chains, bollards, windlasses, blocks and cables lay stacked in a compound. A four-pounder cannon gazed obdurately out to the Thames as though seeking provocation.

'What shall we call her?' asked Masterson. '*Intrepid*? No, too common. *Wealth of Nations*? *Croesus*? We shall have to decide for the figurehead. It is half-carved you see, for they can get as far as the shoulder without too much difficulty.'

'*London Town*,' said Thomas, '*White Tower*, *Lamb and Flag* – no, we may not, I think, call her that. What a fine thing a ship is. What a knitting together of work, a collection of parts and pieces. It is the most complex thing I have ever seen!' Thomas could not contain his excitement. Tramping the deck was god-like, he reflected, a judge could keep his bench. What must it be like when she was in motion?

Masterson was smiling with his mouth. 'A name must be something the crew like too. Vigorous or courageous, or bearing the owner's name.'

'We cannot call it *Kelleway*!'

'The *Thomas K.*,' declared Masterson. 'A fine ring to that, a fine sound. Why not the *Thomas K.*?'

Thomas felt a completely childish thrill of pleasure. He was sure he must be quite pink. In that moment Masterson gained a partner, as he had known he would.

Perrin's explosion when he saw Coke and Mrs Waters leave could be heard throughout every room in chambers.

'Hark!' said Mr Corbett sarcastically, putting a large hand to his ear like an opera shepherdess, 'the legal gentlemen are illustrating a point of law by reasoned argument and keen debate founded upon the ancient precepts of jurisprudence and laws of precedent!'

'Mr Coke's clients are my clients, Mr Kelleway,' Perrin stormed, the papers in his hand quivering as though his hands had been struck by legal frost, a paralysing disease that afflicts counsel and can only be cured by gold. 'Wyndham and Thornhill send all their briefs to me. This is intolerable, Mr Kelleway, you have been tooting!' (For this was how he pronounced 'touting'.) 'It will be known, believe me. Tooting it is and blatant tooting, too!'

Small specks of spittle followed this declaration and fell gently to the floor. Mr Perrin did not display sufficient courage to leave the sanctuary of his doorway, but hovered as though ready to run for shelter. His ears were as long in fact, as in metaphor, and he had rather the appearance of a Byzantine Christ without any of the saintliness. His eyes were not rolled piously to heaven but were hot and blazing. Henry remained infuriatingly calm.

'Mind what you say, Mr Perrin, and kindly lower your voice.' He prayed no one else would be attracted by the disturbance. 'Mr Coke brought me the case. No doubt he thought he did best by his client and it seems to me unseemly you should interfere. I have never heard the parallel of it. Nor will I indulge in exchanges in corridors.'

'I daresay Coke did, I daresay! But am I to assume that she was brought for you and your undoubted fame? The name of Kelleway has spread wide, Mr Kelleway. Allow me to congratulate you. Fame and fortune, fame and fortune!'

'What do you imply, Mr Perrin?' Henry was white with rage.

'Tooting, Mr Kelleway! In a word, tooting.'

Corbett winked at Jenkins. 'Note the legal niceties, Mr Jenkins, the rounded phrase, the considered manner given weighty thought in consideration of the facts in the case!'

'They'll be in here, Mr Corbett!'

'Undoubtedly they will, and I shall graciously receive them.'

As though his words had been heard, the big door to the clerk's room was abruptly shoved back and Henry strode in.

'Oh, good afternoon, Mr Kelleway, is there anything that you want?'

Henry realized it was a desperate game but as he well knew that Perrin was as deeply dyed as himself, he saw no reason to concede the point. It was in his nature to face it out.

'Please be kind enough to enter, Mr Perrin,' he said, 'so that we can discuss with Mr Corbett the circumstances of this case.'

'What case would that be, Mr Kelleway?' asked Corbett innocently, but was ignored.

Perrin reluctantly left his doorway and entered the room. Jenkins laid down his quill, but did not know where to look, his interest was so intense.

'Mr Corbett,' Henry demanded, 'will you please be so good as to inform my colleague Mr Perrin of the circumstances of the case upon which I have just been instructed by Mr Coke.'

'Well, sirs,' Corbett replied, 'can there be some doubt?'

'There is, Corbett. Mr Perrin believes that Mr Coke should for some reason have gone to him.'

'Oh dear me, no, Mr Perrin, I am afraid,' said Corbett, his face as grave as a dead bishop, 'there must be some unfortunate mistake. Mrs Waters and Mr Coke were to have come to you on Wednesday last, Mr Perrin, but you will recollect that Mr Coke was at that time instructing you on another brief. You will recollect the circumstances, Mr Perrin, for it was a handsome brief, the fee for which I must forbear to repeat.'

Mr Perrin's anger seemed to give place to some unease. He replied testily. 'What has that to do with it?'

'Not being able to bring his client that day for that reason, another appointment was made by Mr Coke at his client's urgent request. There is really nothing more to it than that, gentlemen. Mr Kelleway was known to be free.'

Henry was humiliated by the bland lies that tripped from

Corbett's tongue and his own acquiescence to this tale. Perrin, caught in the same sticky web, could do nothing but agree that he now did recollect the occasion. There had, indeed, been a confusion, and he was sure there was no hint of ill will. Henry was sickened by his own wretched complicity in this petty, unethical, unforgivably humiliating deceit. He was sick to the heart by the mesh of Corbett's lies. One good case, he vowed, would see him out of it.

'You see,' Corbett expounded, when the two counsel had gone, 'the gentlemen, when they are down, have a fine sense of balance as is proper in the law, but the young can come close to being indiscreet. In maturity and age they can afford to look back and smile and pay us no more than our due, but look how their fees have risen! All should be equitable, Mr Jenkins, that is part and parcel of the law and I see to it, with a special eye to you and me. It is difficult to secure your client in the market today. These lawyers are a rascally rapacious bunch.' He winked broadly at Jenkins, who, having no sense of humour, thought it all very instructive.

3

Caroline shared the house in Southgate Lane, Highgate, with Aunt Helen. This was seldom onerous despite Aunt Helen's fifty years and widowhood, as she had been left a reasonable sum by her husband who had lately been a silver merchant and smith in a modest but satisfactory way. The Kelleway family had thought little of his occupation when he was alive, but had to concede that he had made prudent provisions for Aunt Helen on his death. Although this income did not admit to extravagances, when combined with Caroline's endowment from Thomas, it represented comfort.

Aunt Helen was at present in Bath, and indeed had removed herself there shortly before the Coronation, disdaining the function and its centrepiece. 'I see no reason to interrupt my sojourn,' she had written, as though it had not been deliberately planned, 'I will be back three days after the casus belli (it is certainly no casus bellus!) for we have our own charades here. I have seldom seen the pump-room and bath more deserted. They say no one of quality is in town, which is an insult we all take lightly. This may be true, but equally those individuals of low demesne who prey upon a lady's time with their foppish and forward chatter, displaying their disordered physiques, are also absent and are no doubt moving in your milieu. At least the water is purer!'

Aunt Helen had taken her personal maid as companion and with the friends of her youth was enjoying herself hugely. That rapacious town, while not bending noticeably to the financial stringencies of the weeks before and after the Coronation, conceded the merest tilt towards its few remaining patrons out of boredom rather than anxiety.

The house in Southgate Lane was comfortable although the rooms were of modest size compared with a residence in Town.

An ample basement ensured that cooking and caring were to a standard beyond mere nourishment; Aunt Helen saw to that too. Although only Mrs Loudon, the housekeeper, and her husband, the butler, lived in, there were staff to be had from the village who were neither so rural as to be rustic nor so urban as to ask high wages. With the promptitude of rural people, they were seldom late. It was true that Highgate lacked cobbled roads, gas lighting and good shops but these were small inconveniences for straddling the divide between London and the home counties to the north. It was well served too by the stages that ran from the Blue Posts in Holborn, and the Magpie and Stump, Newgate.

Maria was apprehensive about her visit although she had arranged it with such apparent assurance at the time. In order that it should have the appearance of a social occasion she cradled a bouquet of flowers that was sadly damaged as the carriage bucked and heaved, thrashing them against the coachwork. A scattering of petals had fallen to the floor. The slow motion of the horse and the wild yawing of the body of the carriage indicated they were on the steep rutted part of Green Street. Despite the mid-summer season, sunshine and showers coupled with a strong wind gave the day a fervour of spring. The trees curtsied and embraced, tearing fragments from their leaves in their ardour.

William had wanted to come on the visit as well, despite the delicacy of the occasion. It was only with the greatest difficulty that Maria had persuaded him that his spurious presence, as he sketched in the garden, would be as unnerving as having him curious in the house. The chariot ended the long haul up the hill with a staggery canter that was just for show. The horses puffed and snorted, drops of saliva showering the driver. Maria, who scarcely knew the house, looked up at it quickly. Although Caroline must have heard her arrival, she was not at a window. Poor girl, Maria thought, with the strength of maternity behind her, she must be in terrible terror.

The house was mellowing; the yellow brick and red rubbed arches were taking on the warm patina of age and coal smoke. Far below, across the green fields of Islington and Kentish Town, she could see the thunderous pall of dirty air that hung over London. Gathering up her skirt, she stepped carefully across water-filled ruts of sticky yellow mud and rang the bell-pull. The door and railings were well painted and shining. Mrs Williams, the housemaid who opened the door, was a respectable woman who lived nearby. She gave the impression of being almost entirely white; white cap, white hair, pellucid skin, white apron. Even her lips were the colour of muslin.

'Come in, madam, Miss Caroline is upstairs and is expecting you.' She took Maria's hat and coat and then led the way to the drawing-room. Maria got the impression that visitors were not commonplace and that the pale lady had been schooled in what to say. The drawing-room was light and had delicate mouldings. The view from the rear-window over the garden was spectacular. Built on the summit of a slope, the ground fell rapidly away in an unobstructed view to the river Thames and beyond. The eastern limits of the City were clearly visible. The furnishings of this splendid room showed that Aunt Helen had had her say in it, for there was a confusion of style that gave it none at all. A fire burned in the grate, for despite the sunshine the wind up here buffeted and rattled the sashes.

Caroline had been standing by the fire, trying to appear composed but looking strung and nervous. When Maria entered, she stepped forward and they exchanged kisses. Maria handed her the flowers, which Caroline in turn admired and gave to Mrs Williams.

'Mrs Williams, put these weary travellers in water. They're beautiful, Maria.'

Mrs Williams bobbed and left. Caroline was at a loss. She desperately wanted to know the truth, but feared it. For two days she had examined the possibilities of her situation, weeping bitterly at night and repairing herself to an appearance of normality in the morning. No servant must be permitted to guess. She had at first intended to write to Charles Ware on some pretext, declaring that their relationship was at an end, but she could think of no words that were not feeble, insulting and hollow. Then she had considered expressing her fears, but had dismissed this as blackmail, for he would insist on marriage and she was not sure that she had any desire to marry, despite her panic. It was the very urgency of these promptings that made her pause and refuse to follow them. Finally, she had composed a curt dismissive note, explaining how she felt with cold cruelty; but she realized that Ware would immediately guess her purpose and come to her. For lack of a formula, she had done nothing.

Maria sat down and wondered what she should say next without appearing too eager to help. While Mrs Williams was out of the way, she must try hard to advance upon the subject of her visit, or she might be manoeuvred into a social situation over the tea cups which would make it doubly difficult.

'How do you feel now?' Maria enquired with deliberate lack of tact.

Caroline immediately coloured. 'I feel quite well, thank you.' She made it sound no more than an adequate social response, and certainly no invitation for further discourse. Maria realized it was going to be very hard work. She thought, uncharitably, that it ill became Caroline to be the maiden now.

'You may be quite sure, Caroline, that nothing you say will ever be repeated with my lips.'

Caroline was silent for a long time. The fire crackled and made rustling noises as though the flames were tissue paper. Maria waited and hoped. Caroline suddenly burst out with passion born of desperation.

'Maria, I know how good it is of you to come, please believe me. I am sensible of your journey. Please have some tea and please don't think it ill of me if we don't talk about it, and when you are refreshed I ask you to leave. That is what I should like, and I don't know any way of putting it that is not offensive!'

Maria was not to be so easily influenced, especially as she had foreseen the reaction.

'Then you must certainly allow yourself to be examined by a doctor, for your symptoms give us all alarm. You half realize what they mean yourself.'

'I will not be degraded!'

'Then the only alternative is to wait and see, which is no sort of course to follow, and is at the least irresponsible. Forgive me, Caroline, but it is my turn to offend. Do you want to live in a state of unknowing? Surely knowledge is always better than fears and suspicions. One may act upon knowledge, but fears leave one paralysed.'

Caroline seemed to ignore this homily, but when she spoke her voice was firmer and had more confidence in it.

'I was weak when I agreed to see you. It was a moment of despair. I am thankful for your help, dear Maria, but I shall think that you exploit that weakness if you persist.'

She had mustered her defence and was prepared to attack. Maria was angry at this. Her anger was partly genuine and partly assumed in order to bring Caroline to her senses.

'Why do you persist in talking as though you are a victim?' Caroline stared at Maria in some astonishment. She might have been slapped in the face. 'You have always wanted to be free of your father, or so you said when we were confidential with each other, and you have achieved it. You are an independent woman, not without means, and this is an engaging house. You are more independent than I am. Yet you will not be truthful with yourself. There seems little point to me in gaining that independence if you lose truth at the same time!'

Caroline had changed in colour from pink to white. What she might have said in anger was quickly averted as Mrs Williams tapped and then entered with the tea, accompanied by a maid. The two women lapsed into a hostile silence while the tea was set out on a small mahogany table close to Caroline. Mrs Williams seemed to sense the atmosphere for she clumsily rattled the tray. She removed herself with alacrity, almost dragging the maid out after her. Caroline moved to the table and poured tea, offering Maria a cup in a hand that shook a good deal. She had to reach out with the other hand to steady it. She picked up her own cup and put it down again almost immediately, her hands returning to a defensive position over her stomach.

'How would I know?' she finally asked in a small, cracked voice that sounded as if the bones in her larynx were clattering. Maria put her tea down in turn, aware that all their small gestures were significant. She picked her words with care.

'May we talk freely?'

There was another long pause while they listened to the fire.

'I suppose we must. Yes.'

'I am a wife and a mother, Caroline, as well as your friend. I sympathize with you desperately, for it is as embarrassing for me as it is to you. Not because what we are discussing should ever be the source of embarrassment between two members of our sex, but because I know how your sensibilities must feel trampled by even the most delicate and loving questions. But, dear Caroline, I must ask those questions.'

Caroline sat down at last. She looked at Maria and nodded, much as a condemned man might invite the executioner's axe. Maria avoided her eyes.

'A woman has normal and regular functions, Caroline.' Maria knew that she sounded like a schoolmistress. 'You must know yourself about these.'

To her distress Caroline blushed hectic red. This time, however, she replied. 'I would wish we could talk about something else! However, if I must tell you, they are not normal.'

'For how long?'

'Two months.'

'Forgive me again, Caroline, or at least try to with your mind if not your heart, for this is the worst question that I can ask of you. You understand that I must ask it?' Maria could feel her own resolve ebbing as the situation protracted. 'Have you any reason to suppose there is a reason, if you understand me ... I can really think of no more delicate way of putting it!' she ended in a flurry.

There was yet another long ominous pause, followed this time by Caroline suddenly crying out – a long wail of pain – then tears. Maria quickly went over to her, clasped her arms about her shoulders and waited.

'I don't know,' Caroline said dismally, 'I must confess I don't know. I know nothing about these things!' Maria was not entirely surprised. She thought wildly for any line she might take in this indelicate investigation.

'When I was at school, Caroline, there were certain girls of lower order and generally of poor mentality who knew about things that seemed to me as remote and mysterious as the moon. They even had books which were quite disgusting, but which were at least explicit, which the day girls bought from men who hawked them round the gates. Did you never see such a book or hear of such things?'

Caroline looked at her blankly and shook her head. With a sinking feeling Maria realized that while she herself had been only too eager to gasp and giggle at the drawings, Caroline would have been far too correct and well-bred. She must get away from the books. She did not dare ask about the man. Had he told her nothing? It suited them well not to. But maybe his intentions were honourable and maybe Caroline was refusing to see him? There was too much to try to solve at once. She resolved she must pursue one thing at a time.

'There may be a sure way of telling, but it means that I must quickly examine you.' Caroline's eyes were wild with anxiety. 'Just up here, your top,' Maria said, gesturing and realizing at the same time how indelicate, hasty and absurd the situation had become. If Caroline would not co-operate she would probably have to pinion her arms and examine her forcibly. Caroline, as though she divined Maria's wild resolve, was backing away and regarding her as she would a mad dog. Indeed, Maria looked formidable. Her black hair had broken loose from her bonnet and her eyes had a fanatical gleam.

'We have only to retire for the briefest moment to your bedroom,' Maria suggested. 'Then I will be able to tell with no embarrassment to either of us, dear Caroline. We are never told these things as we should be, but as a mother one finds them out. It is one of those entirely natural and quite charming adjustments that happen to our sex and manifests itself in most women. Let me tell you about myself, then you'll understand.'

Caroline stuffed her hands in her ears. 'No! I don't want to know! I can't bear it.'

'In some women the breasts change,' continued Maria, aware that she was really still listening. 'It is natural that they should. You know that. Listen, and don't behave like a nun. If we can retire somewhere private and I may look quickly, then nothing more will be required. You are not ashamed to show me your breasts. You must have noticed them yourself. One will do,' Maria concluded, feeling the remark was slightly derisory.

Caroline shook her head. 'No, I'm not. Only . . .'

'Come along, then . . .'

Caroline led the way from the drawing-room to her bedroom where she locked the door like a banker, trying the handle. What followed lacked dignity, for despite her promise of cooperation, Maria still had to remove Caroline's clutching hands to achieve her purpose.

The truth was immediately to be seen. The nipple was dark and extended, the corona spread to twice its normal size. Maria immediately indicated to Caroline that she was finished. She turned her back to enable Caroline to re-arrange her dress at waist and neck, playing with a tortoise-shell box. The colour, she thought, was not very different. Caroline eventually gave a muffled cough and Maria turned round. Maria noticed that she was hectic red again and, quite naturally, very nervous. She felt angry that women should be reduced to this.

'That was not so bad, was it?' Maria said practically, but received no answer. 'Now sit down, Caroline, and let us try to talk as two women.'

If this was intended to be effective, it was not, as Caroline collapsed on the bed and looked even more like an assaulted maiden. Her hands were back round her stomach. She did not dare look up.

'You can see that your breasts have changed,' Maria said firmly, 'I am sure you must have noticed yourself.'

A small nod.

'You must have been worried? No? Well then, you must have guessed. I do not think that you need me to painfully put in words what we both know?'

A shake of the head.

'It is a sure sign, Caroline,' Maria burst out with a strength she did not feel, 'at least all doubt is removed! You know, and we can face things.' Maria's mind was in a turmoil. How should she ask who the man was? There was no way. Caroline must volunteer it, and the chances of that were small. She had heard of Charles Ware, but only as a friend who visited in a most proper way. She could not, however, think of anyone else. 'We can now be practical, decide whom we should tell and when . . .'

'I don't want to get married,' Caroline declared with more spirit than it looked as if she possessed. 'On no account shall I get married because of it. If Father tries to force me, I shall have to leave the country, I couldn't bear that!'

Maria decided against saying anything more at this stage. She would learn much through patience. 'Come, dear Caroline. What you need now is the tea. I will leave you to your toilette, then come next door and we shall share a cup together. You have been under a great strain and must fortify yourself!'

She bustled from the room, her dress rustling, trying to feel and sound as much like a governess as possible. Caroline, sighing, obeyed.

While Maria administered to Caroline and tried in her insistent way to establish the facts – Maria was very insistent about facts and William equally scathing – William was trying to do business but was having difficulty in pinning down what sort of business he was trying to do. He had a visitor.

Their house in Flood Street was small but admirably suited to their state of affairs as a family of moderate means. Their neighbours were usefully varied, some even illustrious. A number were writers or painters like themselves, attracted by the low rentals and riverside accommodation. Together, their unsociable habits and hours could go largely unremarked in Chelsea village. Tradesmen, unafflicted by the same avarice as Londoners, were even prepared to deliver, and wait some time for payment.

Their house was plain enough on the outside, but with an elegance of proportion that would soon be lost by eruptions of larger houses covered with stucco and paint. It was brick-built with round arches over the upper windows and a fine pediment over the front doorsteps. Garden front and rear provided a buffer from the busy streets. The glazing beads of the windows were as slender as straws.

At the rear of the house there jutted out a large bow-shaped bay to which studio windows had been added by enlarging the opening at the first floor so that it overlooked the garden. Although the river was not visible, on still days and at night the noise and bustle of the quays could plainly be heard; shouts and curses from the bargees, the rattle of coals, timber and cobbles, the rumble of barrels, the clatter of the horses unloading – all found their way in. Chelsea had its own life to lead that had nothing to do with London. It looked after its own fishing, bread, milk, oil, building materials, meat. The occasional steam whistle from some splendid, arrogant boat shook the windows and set all the birds flying. It was not yet a common thing, and people turned out to stare. Eel fishermen made a good living. The garden at the rear of the house, tended by Maria, grew like a rain-forest.

Their studio was a working room and made no pretensions to be anything else. Their bric-à-brac and properties were for use not show. Neither of them had time for those gentlemen painters whose studios were elaborate stage sets. The visitor that William was now entertaining was portly, and above all, shiny. His boots had been polished until they looked wet and his breeches were enlivened with glossy silk stripes. His waistcoat shimmered with shot silk, his coat was of shiny black cloth and his cravat of slippery cream silk. As though this were not sufficient, his red face appeared to be newly varnished, with the varnish still trickling down. He disposed of this with quick wipes of a handkerchief. The man's hair and side-whiskers were jet-black despite his middle years, and adhered to him slightly. To William he appeared almost entirely glossy, like a new-groomed horse. The man seemed to be disturbed by the fumes of turpentine which William no longer noticed and spent much time sniffing and looking around him as though he could trace it to one identifiable source.

'Damned strong smell, Mr Kelleway.'

'Turpentine, I'm afraid. Mixed with linseed oil as a medium.'

Sir Walter Manning was all presence, William decided, and no manners. He strayed about, picking up and putting down things as though he might from these judge something of William's worth. Sir Walter was at pains to explain that a certain deficiency in imagination in himself was heavily compensated for by abundant wealth. William pondered if he was going to ask for something improper. Or for William to illustrate a small book for him. He found the idea amusing. Sir Walter was now declaring, wiping more varnish from his collar, that he did not possess the quality of perception, *that* quality of perception that men of more delicate sensibilities and long association had been endowed with. Indeed, he declared, he was grateful for it, because his very directness and ability to see a point unobscured by romantic argument had made him rich. Imagination in business, he declared, was seldom a good thing. It led clerks to embezzlement and gentlemen to speculation. William maliciously enquired into the difference. He had begun to understand his man.

'There will be no more money made out of painting Prinny!' the man declared as though he had let slip a valuable tip. As William could not see that the remark led anywhere, he kept quiet. 'What concerns me is to find someone who is good at these Gothick things. You know the sort of whatnots. Women adore them, bless their angelic hearts, to stroll around or remark a view in the garden. Most houses have them, I notice. But it's knowing what you want that's difficult. I know what I like when I see it. But not before, you understand?'

The visitor helped himself to a musket which was leaning against the wall, propped his right foot on the head of a tiger which was still attached to its skin, and pulled the trigger, oblivious of whether or not it was loaded. The flint sparked on the steel. Sir Walter re-cocked the lock and stared at the pictures around him with an expression that was not encouraging. He seemed to be suppressing his natural distaste.

William's work not only occupied two easels, but was propped all round the wall. His canvases were of two varieties, portraits or landscapes. Amongst this could be seen the work of other hands. Maria's careful drawings and watercolours were delicate and insubstantial by comparison. In addition there was a small chair and little rostrum where a child had evidently been daubing. Sir Walter lumbered over to the portraits, still carrying the gun, and began to peer at them, puffing with the effort of bending.

'No one here I recognize,' he said churlishly. William inclined his head and smiled. He wished he could afford to boot the man in the fulness of his breeches. 'What's the matter with them? Shouldn't think that portraits would be here. People take them away when they're finished, don't they?' The man looked at William sharply. He evidently felt he was on to a strong point. 'I don't know about you artist fellows, but it seems to me I have the right to be reassured. What I am trying to say, without offence, is I suppose these are not rejected? I mean, someone is going to collect them and pay for them?'

William nodded, feeling furious but seeing no reason why he should prevent the man from stumbling further into the morass of his own crassness. Sir Walter was not satisfied with a mere nod. He had come to do business and demanded to be satisfied that his choice of artist was a sound investment.

'Then if you will forgive me, sir, why are they still here? They appear to be complete. You exhibit at the Royal Academy, I know, so I would have thought there would have been a demand for them. People are in great haste these days to litter their homes with portraits. I have seen walls covered with them. Every man, woman and child of them. Not to speak of horses and dogs. And yet you have some still here.' He cocked his head slightly to one side in a self-satisfied way, and wiped his collar thoroughly.

'These works are all one commission. When they are finished, they will all go.'

'All paid for by one man?' The shiny man was impressed. He started to count the canvases.

'Yes. As you feel you need some testimonial of my work, perhaps they might do? If you look closely at them, you will observe that they are not in contemporary dress. Indeed, you may even have glimpsed a hint of armour, the sparkle of jewels, the odd battle honour draped from a parapet in the background?'

Sir Walter tried to assess if William was deriding him, but could not for William had a perfectly straight face. Feeling he should do something, he puffed round the portraits again, noting that what William had said was true. William paced behind him, acting the charming guide.

'No doubt you will have observed the strong family likeness. See, here, here, here and here. The oval brown eye, the noble nose with the strong bone here,' his hand flashed out to point, Sir Walter did as he was bid, 'the auburn hair, how it passes down from generation to generation. You will have observed that they are many generations. If you look closely you will observe that their very clothing has a respectable lineage. Take this fellow,' William indicated a man in a Caroline wig of whom little else could be seen but the face and one shoulder, the rest being a sea of burnt umber, 'here is a glint of a corselet, and here the red of a cape. See. No, you must look closely.' Sir Walter was having the greatest difficulty in doubling himself up. He nodded breathlessly. 'Well, if we look here,' William continued, striding across the studio and indicating a similar figure, clad this time in uniform, 'we see that the cloak has survived. Not just until this day, but survived the battle of Waterloo, which if you look closely, here, at this,' he jabbed out his finger like a command and Sir Walter followed it like a pointer, 'is still going on slightly in the corner!' Sir Walter stared at the swirling area indicated and then at William again.

'But these are all new paintings, Mr Kelleway!'

'I should hope so. I have not had to take up restoration yet!'

'They go back into history . . .'

'Of course. They go back to the time of Norman William and would have gone back to Alfred if my client had had the means. You will recall that these times are slightly before the historically accurate date that oil-painting was introduced to England. I can assure you, however, that many noble Anglo-Saxons had themselves portrayed in this manner! We re-write history and re-create people. It is a marvellous age.' Sir Walter had finally understood, and looked pop-eyed. 'You see, Sir Walter, my clients are so confident in me that they entrust to me their pasts. Where they have none, then a little imagination will supply it. All of us have a past, and if through some whim of history it has been forgotten, then it can be restored!'

'You make up these ancestors!'

'Re-create, Sir Walter. We have the original to sketch from before we start. It is all the fashion. You must have seen many of them yourself. They should be hung where the light is sombre, such as a stair, and creates shadows to complement the effects within the canvas. The whole effect is then rich and romantic without being too precisely historical. They should not be hung in exact order, but in a confusion.'

Sir Walter managed to speak. 'This is an extraordinary thing!' He made it sound like a personal affront. William, thoroughly enjoying himself, talked lightly on.

'Really it is not. Why should people be denied ancestry when obviously they have it? It is a kick against the increasing sameness of our lives. Are we to be a nation of mechanics, with no notion of our higher selves? Are we to be put to work, quite unthinking, quite unappreciative? We should look back to look forward, because it is like having an immense memory. One sees the parallels. There is too little romance in the world, Sir Walter, wouldn't you agree? Everything is being straightened out and squared off. The village street is being demolished, for ever, and replaced by terraces and squares. Rustic disorder is already a thing of the past. Henry Holland straightened it, now Nash. They have the same pattern book, and now Nash has lent it to his friends. They are all using the same page. Stucco and paint! It is the fashion. What is wrong with honest brick and friend stone? It is a decline disguised as an advance. Stucco is a mediocre material and it covers mediocre work. Honest brick cannot show his face! They are already planning Belgrave Square. Always squares!' William stopped his dissertation, realizing that it had become somewhat disjointed. Instead of the cry of protest he expected, there was a nod and a grunt of agreement.

'Yes?' asked William, like a lover.

'Yes.' Sir Walter said, then as though surprised at himself for making such a judgement, continued to endorse it. 'I do agree. Indeed. That is quite so.' The stout man paused to settle himself firmly upon both feet, a movement that William perceived must immediately precede some proposition.

'I am told that in addition to these portraits and scenes that you paint, you have designed some ornamental works – curiosities suited to landscape and the garden, that sort of thing.'

'I have,' said William, surprised, 'may I ask ... ?'

'I had the pleasure to stay at the country home of Mr James Hall.'

'Ah. The summerhouse.'

'Exactly.'

William looked at the man afresh. It had seemed unlikely from the start that he was interested in paint on canvas, but he could believe that such a man liked bricks and mortar.

'Can you show me the sort of things you do, Mr Kelleway? And can we move to somewhere that is away from the smell of paint?'

'Yes. If it is not paint you want, then why should you suffer the smell of it? We can go through to the study.'

William led the way through a door to an adjacent room that

served as library and study. It was lined with shelves and littered with work, but contained one good desk and three good chairs. Although the smell of turpentine had not disappeared, it had at least diminished. Sir Walter declined to sit down and settled himself firmly on his feet. He wiped his face and neck.

'I should explain that I have just purchased a property of some three hundred acres with quite a fine house. The trouble is the grounds. They are so deuced dull. I can think of nothing else to say about them except that they are as unremarkable as Hackney Marsh. I have a good gardener in now, but I need something which can be done more immediately. I am told it will be ten years before the garden has much to show.' The man's voice was plaintive. William guessed that he must be in his middle fifties and it was clear he thought ten years might be too long. 'I mentioned it to Mr Hall, with whom you are acquainted, and he said he had just the idea. Of course he gave me your name. You see, we could build in only six months. Have something done.' He was suddenly eager. William felt ashamed of his earlier mockery. The man was embarrassed because he did not know what to ask for and knew he had few social graces to perform the asking. William had made fun of an honest man because he was awkward.

'I owe you an apology. I bored you with my paintings. I thought you might wish to be painted.'

'I know what you thought, Mr Kelleway, but you were mistaken. You made me feel uncomfortable and properly I should leave. However, I have persevered and here we are apparently talking on a more level plane. I have no desire to have myself or my ancestors represented, not even in a confusion. As you have had some fun with me, perhaps you will tell me why you do it? Do you have to paint pedigrees to make a living? I doubt it. I am told you exhibit frequently.'

'I do it because it amuses my skill and because I am paid well for it.'

'I hope you do not make a habit of laughing at your patrons.' There was genuine hurt in his voice and William felt he had been quite properly reprimanded. He would not, however, beat his own breast.

'No. But I must allow myself some amusement. Otherwise the

monstrous vanities of humankind become a powerful irritant. Then I would paint no one, and I cannot afford to be idle.'

'You may be as amused as you like, Mr Kelleway, provided it is directed into my work, and not at me. I am not a man who has been long conditioned to wealth, so that I see it as no more than part of my outward appearance, like my skin. It has come to me almost recently and through business. I think you will understand me better if I say that at the outset. I am not a polished man, but I am no fool. At first I thought we should in no way get on. Now I am glad we have made a start. Let that start be a restart.'

William smiled broadly, taken by the change of direction his mischievous conversation had provoked. 'I would be delighted. If you will assume my penitence.'

'Good. Let that all be. Let us see what work we can do.' As he had now taken the advantage, he obviously felt he could sit down.

'You see, I will sit now. I always stand when another man is taller and there is any hardness between us. Firstly I should explain why I do not want this work carried out by an architect. You have expressed the reasons yourself. I want something intriguing and amusing, in the Gothick style. Unfinished. I will not call it a ruin or any such thing, because you cannot build a ruin. That is a solecism. You see, Mr Kelleway, I have even learned the right words for things, and my accent is not rough. An architect is no use to me. He will want to complete things, to organize and plan. I have in mind to create a garden that conceals its arrangement. It must be a pleasure.'

He wiped his face again and took stock of the room in which he sat. They were surrounded by Maria's elegant drawings of moths, larvae, leaves and flowers. Manning nodded thoughtfully. 'You work here, and it is pleasant. I came originally from the West Country, and from there to Coventry. From Methodism to Methodism. Then we had the Johannas and they were worse. I was in business. Nails, to start with. I don't think you have ever been far from London, Mr Kelleway?'

'No, I have not.'

'It is a bitter world and I have retired out of it. You would not believe the type of hovels my outworkers lived in. Some had windows but none had sashes that opened. The rich ones had stone floors, the poor only clay. It is a long way from London. Nailmaking is rough and ready work. They work in the room they live in and cook over the forge. My men took round the nail-rods and returned to collect the nails, and that way I did not have to see how they lived. I need some Romance, Mr Kelleway, because I have seen precious little of it. These people amuse themselves by putting a woman in a pillory, when she is carrying a child. They have fun on the first of May when they go round the village at night. A gorse bush on a woman's step indicates she is what I will not say, and a tup's horn nailed to the door can destroy a family. This is old morality and new morality together and it is as cruel as the early Christians. I lived in a big house like a fortress and paid men to stand by my doors. During the wars with Napoleon, they made an effigy of me, stuffed it with straw and burned it in front of the house. I have been shot at four times and my horse killed from under me. I have been attacked twice and have killed a man with a club in self-defence. I never was a soldier. This was while I tried to go about my normal commerce.'

He paused and looked at William, as though to judge if he should continue. William was struck dumb. His initial reaction was to resent this intrusion into his own world and to reject its ugliness. He had conceded his own ill manners and now the man was repaying him by displaying his. Yet, on the other hand, he was fascinated, for the other man was casually referring to a reality which he could only guess at, or read about in a newspaper. Manning evidently took his silence to be assent for he continued.

'You see, Mr Kelleway, I have had to deal with the other side of the coin, the one without a fair face. Your business is fair faces. Of people and of nature. I have never been a hard or brutal man. I was never an Ottoman as they called some of them. They simply hated the Owners. It is still there, all that illness, like something in the blood and it will get worse. You may think this an intrusion, but if you are to understand what I want, I suppose this is why I want it.' He stopped abruptly and looked at William, expecting a response. 'When you talk of rustic disorder, you see in your mind an idyllic scene. You believe in the nobility of toil. Well, sir, I see a mob, and I see senile children and disease. I need your eyes, because mine are scarred.'

'I cannot change your view of the world. I think, Sir Walter, that you are asking too much of anyone.'

'Do you decline? I am sorry, I didn't mean to ask that. I drive too hard, you see. You should have time to consider.' He mopped his collar. There was silence while William stared at his shoes.

'No. I don't decline. But I cannot accept responsibility for your view of the world. I can only accept responsibility for what is my own.' Manning was in no way offended. Instead he smiled, a brief nervous gesture that he mopped up with his handkerchief.

'Then we must decide what to do. Forgive me. You must ignore me when I am impatient. You will have to see the place and will need to think much further about it, naturally.' The man hesitated, pointing his toes as though examining the gloss on his boots, which looked indeed as though they had been glazed for the table. He found some satisfaction in rotating his toes gently. He was evidently making up his mind on something.

'I have some ideas of my own – perhaps they are poor things, I don't know – but I would like you to be receptive to them. Do you mind? I feel I should ask,' he finished, making the defensive thought sound aggressive in tone of voice.

'No, of course not. I should welcome it.' William found himself being patronizing without meaning to be. It was like dealing with a shy child. The shy child immediately disappeared. Manning's voice was very firm.

'But you must not be influenced by me!'

'I assure you, I will not be.' William was equally firm, but smiled as he spoke. Any hint of patronage had passed. 'I would take into account what you say, then I should probably try to convince you that I was right. We are all very arrogant! Our clients, we assume, are almost always wrong. My eye sees white where your eye sees black, what's red, green. I shall probably be over-bearing!'

'That's fair.' Manning gave another half-smile and bobbed his head like a babe. 'You don't buy a dog etcetera. And I shall have the overweening advantage of grasping the strings of the purse!'

He looked up at William after this with such straight-faced solemnity while they both enjoyed the moment as a triumph, a flowering of Manning's spirit. William then laughed aloud. Manning's head bobbed up and down again with the same unsteady motion. He, too, was laughing but as though he had little experience in it. His chest, William thought, is constricted with solemnity, or disillusion or grief. The laugh-muscles have atrophied and have no strength. Like a babe, he at first can only smile. Now he has started to gurgle, and eventually he should be able to throw back his head and roar. He had the look of a man who used to. It was a pleasant moment and touching. William did not want to say anything to snap it, for he felt they were balancing on something thin and brittle. For a considerable time there was a silence between them. It was Manning who finally broke it, the communion of their emotions making him panic. He was suddenly on his feet, mopping his brow and avoiding William's eye.

'Have you anything I can look at? Those little pictures with folding flaps, you know, that show the present scene and the proposal. I find them fascinating. A conjuring trick of the imagination.'

William nodded, sensing that his speaking would not be welcome, and started to take down cloth-backed portfolios from a high shelf on one wall. Even when Manning left after half an hour, William had no clear idea of what the man wanted, but felt that he understood why. The man was complex, but because of his manner had too often been taken as vulgar or a fool. William, putting back the volumes, felt that Manning had a sad, orphaned mind. What loss the mind had sustained, he had as yet no idea.

It was late in the evening when Maria arrived home. The strong wind had blown itself out, leaving the mud scattered with torn fragments of leaves. The clear sky was cold and the earth had pulled to itself a low fog as though to keep it warm. In High-gate the sky had sparkled like black water alive with phosphorescence. In Flood Street by the river, lamps could scarcely be seen at ten paces. Men called out, from carriages, from barges. On the river, bells rang. The coachman cracked his whip a lot, and 'hey-ooped' and hoped to frighten off footpads. It was such a night as they dreamed of.

Maria was tired when she got home. Not so much from the journey, which had been slow, but from the efforts of the afternoon and her reflections upon them. William, who had been listening for her carriage, dashed down the stairs and arrived before the servants. Maria's clothes were mud-hemmed and her pumps bore country clay, thick and hard as plaster. She kicked them off, undoing her bonnet which she gave to Susan the maid. William helped her off with her cloak which George, the manservant, carried away to clean and brush downstairs. She had not lost her vitality, however, for she immediately took William by the hand and drew him into the drawing-room in stockinged feet, where she gave William a blow-by-blow account of her encounter and struggle with Caroline, making William blush by her frank account of her final success.

'There it was, no doubt at all. Nipples as brown as tea-leaves. It is terrible, William, that a grown woman should suffer the indignity of knowing so little.' Maria's eyes were gleaming again. She positioned herself in front of the fire like a man, warming herself practically, if inelegantly, by holding up her dress to her waist.

'Maria!' William protested, with good-humoured embarrassment.

'Why not? You men lift your coat tails quite as rudely and I am presenting to the world and the fire no more than you do!' William grinned. She was sheer delight in this mood.

'No,' she continued, 'it is degrading. Clutching her mammary glands to herself like a female baboon in the zoological gardens, while I try to pull from her that part of her anatomy she is trying to conceal. Absurd. A breast is a breast. It is nothing to be ashamed of.' Her face was pink now, either with warmth or recollection of the encounter. 'But I managed it. I told you I would, you must agree. Come now, agree, I insist on it!' She made determined little bows at him, both hands being occupied with her dress.

William was most immediately concerned lest she set herself on fire. 'Come away. Forward, this way. You will ignite!'

'Don't fuss,' Maria said severely, 'you are only embarrassed because you are a man. That is true, is it not? Tell me truly, now.'

'I am not embarrassed,' William lied stoutly, 'please just move away from the fire. We cannot afford to let your hem ignite, even to make a point.'

Maria smiled and moved forward a pace or two, letting her dress fall. 'I am too hot, anyway. You men must roast your buttocks. It cannot be good for you!'

'Maria! Please keep on the subject of Caroline. What will she do now?'

'She will not marry the man. That, at least, is certain.'

'Who is he? Devil take it, I don't even know that. And what will Father say? He certainly can't be told.'

Maria padded forward in her stockinged feet. 'Why not?' There was the gleam of battle in her eyes again. William considered that these social benevolences of Maria had a habit of leading to domestic fireworks. 'It is his affair, too,' she continued, standing very close to him, in her most determined manner. 'Or has he to be protected from everything? I assume he can be expected to have some experience of sexual matters, shall we say. You can't tell me otherwise for I have no belief in your divinity, dear William!' She waved a hand in the air in an operatic gesture. 'Thomas exploits you all and you know it, secretly, in the recesses of your hearts. He has arranged things in your minds as a sailor packs a trunk; neatly, so that everything is in the right order. He cannot be told anything unpleasant that might upset him! He might come down with a bump from his fine abstract attitude to life.'

'That's not fair, Maria! There's nothing abstract about his business brain.'

'A neat arrangement for a nice mind. Caroline has been wretchedly treated. Schooled for serfdom, then sold to make her master free. She was made to feel she did you all a compelling service. Thomas is as much to blame for her condition as anyone!'

'Who is this man, anyway?' asked William, brought back to it by this assertion. 'He must have had some part in it!' To avoid any further barbs of rebuke, he made himself sound belligerent. Maria was not deceived.

'What will you do about him? At this late date?' Her attempt to sound innocent was as ineffective as William's at belligerence. 'Or will you challenge him to a duel for this catastrophe to the family honour? It is still the fashion for those with none to pretend they have some in that way. But I shall not visit you in jail!'

'I shall speak to him!' William thought he sounded insolently tough. A man to be reckoned with.

'What will you say?' Maria asked sweetly. 'That he is a scoundrel and no gentleman? You'll look so uneasy and pompous at the same time that he will kick you out of the house. What will that achieve?'

'He must marry Caroline!'

Maria let out an exaggerated sigh. 'She doesn't want to marry him. Don't you understand? I know this may all be very offensive to the common brotherhood of male dignity, but she doesn't. It doesn't follow as the night the day that because a woman beds with a man, carries his child and is glad to have the child, that she particularly wishes to marry him. Indeed, why should she marry at all? Nature's necessities over, she has enough to live off. Men are of very limited use, on occasion, and this is one of them.'

William, who considered himself free from excesses of male bias which were the cornerstone of contemporary social mores, was stunned into silence. Maria laughed.

'Don't look so bovine, William. It is not the end of the world. Charles Ware is the man responsible. He wants the child, and Caroline won't marry him. It is simple enough. It would be a mere convention and a sham, for she doesn't love him. However, she wants that babe. She is going to need our help.'

William was still silent. Theoretically, he understood the situation perfectly, but he could not translate it into terms of human flesh and blood. As for Maria she seemed like a small engine under steam.

'You are not going to make a cause of this?' William asked, mock plaintively.

Maria laughed and kissed him with tenderness, having to stand on tiptoe to reach his mouth. 'I must help. But you haven't told me about your visitor. I must hear that too.'

'He was a strange man, but touching in a way, and I like him. I have no idea what to make of him yet. He is a mixture that seems determined to separate.'

'But have you got a commission!' Maria stamped a stockinged foot on the carpet. 'Don't always approach things from the wrong end.'

'Yes!' William was laughing at her now.

'What for?'

'Now that is where you have me.'

Maria snorted with mock fury at this and went back to the fireplace, pulled up the hem of her dress to her waist and warmed herself as before.

'I shall stand here, like this, until you tell me about it. I shall call for chocolate, and George shall see me!' William sat down on the sofa, grinning. Maria became more incensed. 'I shall take off my dress and dry it before the fire! I truly will!'

'Stop, St Joan, I will tell all.'

There was a tap at the door and Susan the maid entered. She looked aghast at Maria before the fire and fixed her eyes on the carpet. Maria dropped the folds of her dress with as much dignity as possible, aware of William's broadening grin.

'The baby is crying, madam,' said Susan. 'I have fed her and tried everything but I think she has missed not having seen you all day. Perhaps if you could spare a moment . . .'

'Of course, I will see to her.' Maria crossed over to the door, pausing to hiss at William, 'I will be back!'

'Pure melodrama,' he replied.

Maria, nursing the child, was convinced that William had been unbusinesslike. She would correct that.

> Chittagong, Arakan,
> British India.
> July 1821

Dear Father,

I write this letter in a temperature and humidity better suited to the growth of vegetation than man. This place is difficult for anyone to conceive . . .

John Kelleway stared around him for inspiration, but knew it was futile to try to convey his sensations to his father. It was midday and the heat was intense. Despite the overhanging palm-thatch eaves and slat-blinds of rattan, the sun found its way in, in painfully bright white shafts, concentrated by the inner shade as though through a lens. The girl, Padmavati, stirred in her naked brown sleep, making his canvas bed groan. He could smell the warm sweaty scent of her body. It was a scent, like musk. He would write the letter, then they would make love again on the floor in the Burmese way. The bed was too small and would collapse under the weight of two. He wondered why the British Army had not considered this when ordering them as standard issue. No soldier was expected to be celibate. Except by the great hypocritical public. How many wives at home, he wondered, really believed that their husbands would remain on duty for nine months when girls were available to live in and serve for a few shillings? Beautiful brown girls, without false modesty. Who looked upon the coupling of man and woman as a celebration of pleasure in which their art and skill was an essential contribution.

Padmavati had taught him how to make love. She spoke only a few words of English, but by word and gesture, had been quite explicit what she expected of him. At first he had been shocked at her active eroticism, embarrassed by her open-eyed interest and handling of his naked body. He had felt, ridiculously, that he should cover himself up. But her tutelage was so unembarrassed and calm that he soon abandoned himself to the same sensual exploration of her body. What an Englishwoman would have thought of it, he could not imagine, at least an Englishwoman of any normal upbringing. He wondered how he would do without his Padmavati. How could he return home and marry? What woman could he ever find in London to match this earthly garden of pleasures that was Padmavati? She had taught him that he was a sensual man. Her rules were simple. 'You like? Good.'

With an effort, he concentrated on the letter again. He must try to write to Thomas the letter he expected to receive. He must allay concern, give news, give a picture that was exotic but could not be explicit. He supposed this has been the problem of soldiers for centuries. He wondered what the other men wrote.

For all the labour and the trouble of it, they should compose a standard letter, for none of them would be writing home with the truth. He dipped his quill in the tin ink-pot and continued.

... for you must imagine a flat town built entirely of timber and bamboo, which grows here to a thickness of three or four inches. The heat is terrible, for it is very damp The River Naaf runs through this thatched labyrinth, and is always busy with boats and commerce. Every building is thatched with reeds or palm leaves and you must imagine these buildings when we have had a downpour which here descends in blocks of water for weeks in the time of the rains. When the sun emerges, the town, fields and jungle steam. It is then like an infernal kitchen. Our men suffer greatly from fever but I have been lucky so you need have no fear for me on that. I have had fever two times, but each time it has not been severe so that it seems that I must have a constitution that is not easily destroyed by it. We have lost a lot of good fellows.

He could not put in the truth. Two thirds of the men with whom he had left England were dead. They had never seen the Burmese who lurked across the Naaf. They had been expended to maintain a presence. For what? So that the Arakan should be safe from the Burmese or so that the East India Company might get its hands on the gem lands to the south and east? Padmavati wore gold about her neck, and a sapphire that had come from Burma. All the women accumulated treasure. The Burmese had gems beyond the dreams of a Conquistador. Elephants, timber, tobacco, gold.

Padmavati and he had sat on the floor naked, smoking cheroots. The smell impregnated the hut. She smoked solemnly, with concentration, looking at him and smiling. 'Was good?' Yes, was very good. She smiled and looked him all over, always curious of his white body. She looked at his private parts. 'Good.' She smiled and inhaled deeply from the black cheroot. It never made her cough. The town was quiet outside. The heat battered at the thick thatch. In thousands of huts, John thought, it will be just the same. With an effort he continued to write.

The strength and ambitions of the Burmese are at first difficult to comprehend. They are warlike and ruthless to a degree unknown in Europe since the Vandals and Huns. They have no respect for our

Empire and continue to build their own, invading our boundaries, subjugating and destroying all the people that stand in their way. These people are called the Shans and they have spread over a huge area of territory in a steady movement west and north. They behave with the utmost arrogance, pursuing this successful policy of aggrandisement and conquest. It is inevitable that one day we will be forced to throw them back from Assam which they threaten again. These Shans have pushed into China and taken from the Chinese large tracts of their Empire, exterminating all the peoples of Pegu, Arakan, Laos and upper and lower Burma, which are the northern, southern and Siamese Shan States. Now their warlords threaten the borders of our Chittagong possessions, but they do not invade except in raiding parties, who loot and murder. For the moment they are assembling to the north of us and have entered Assam close to Syhet on the north-eastern frontier of Bengal. Beyond this frontier is the possession of the Rajah of Cuchar which is under the protection of the British Government.

I cannot write to you of the atrocities committed upon the people they overrun. In everything they do they have so far been successful, being well equipped with weapons of the most modern kind. They make huge cannon of their own, bigger than any pieces that we have, and are skilled in making guns. I am sure that the image you have in England is of a race of primitive tribesmen armed with knives and spears, but this is not so. They have practised war with the Chinese for so long that their martial skills rival those of any European army. There is no native force that can defeat them, even if it has ten times the number of men. We are told that if the Burmese overrun Assam, as it appears they must, then Britain will be obliged to expel them in a full scale operation. Until then, we sit and wait.

I have managed to put in some hunting, as the jungle is well furnished with game-fowl and swamp deer. Much of the area is accessible only by boat. I have heard that tiger are hunted by boat to the north but we are not so lucky. There are many elephants, but tame! They work with great intelligence and are much valued here. To shoot them would be unthinkable unless they become man-killers, as one occasionally does, stamping on his mahout, as the elephant drivers are called. To catch them, they are driven into a stockade, for the former method of trapping them by excavating pits caused too many injuries. When they have been stockaded amongst massive timbers, they are starved until they submit, then are shackled to a tame elephant whose strength is of course then much greater. That way, they learn their work. Of other animals, I have seen so many that I cannot write of them but must wait until I can give you a description.

These waterways are the main turnpikes of this area of the continent, and while they afford us the means of sport and exercise, they are also of the greatest danger, for the Burmese have war canoes with one hundred paddles rowed by their soldiers. These boats can travel at ten miles per hour, our own gunboats being capable of only five. However, you may be assured that the only action that we have seen has been a skirmish in which we exchanged two rounds of musket ball apiece with a party which fired upon us on a routine patrol through jungle. The party might equally have been of poachers or smugglers as Burmese. They hit no one, we hit no one, so that was an end of it. Our patrols are most boring and uncomfortable. It is then that our men most often fall sick with cholera or other fevers.

John stared at the pages of writing and wondered what reassurance they would give. He was bored. Without Padmavati and the escape of this hut, life would be intolerable. How could he explain to Thomas that the jungle was no more varied than a desert, that the loss of life was disgusting to him and intolerable, that he took no joy in soldiering? It was reassurance that Thomas sought in the letters that John received. Was he well? What was his regiment doing? What were his chances of promotion? Promotion came quickly with successive deaths. It was not true that John had escaped lightly from the cholera he had dismissed as fever. To survive two attacks was a rarity. The hand of death would touch him on the shoulder when he contracted it a third time. He did not think of it as if, but when. He had seen and experienced the illness too much, knew the symptoms, the point of balance in the disease when life hung by a thread. He had twice lain in the long wooden hospital listening to the other poor wretches and waiting for the progress of the disease upon himself, knowing every step it would take.

It could be quick and kill in two hours from the first symptom, or it could be painfully slow and take two days. The mind was perfectly alert up to the end. First, diarrhoea, not painful but violent, called by the men and doctors 'rice-water'. Then vomiting, severe pain in the stomach, a thirst almost beyond craving. Cramps in the legs and in the muscles of the abdomen, recurring and recurring with great agony. The critical stage, when the body becomes cold and blue in appearance, the skin dry, flaccid and wrinkled, the eyes deep in their sockets as if wearing the hooded eyes of death, the voice a hoarse whisper, the pulse almost imperceptible. Each step inevitable until this point. Then reaction must set in or death is inevitable. There is a lull, a hovering of life.

John saw it as a kite fluttering on an up-current of breeze. It was no more than a whim of nature if the kite remained in the sky or pitched violently down. His body was weak. The river delta was a graveyard. Padmavati made it bearable, but he was not prepared to die for Padmavati. He stared at her brown body striped with thin slivers of light through the rattan blinds. The light emphasized her curves as she lay curled asleep, formed curious patterns along her back, buttocks and legs. He was wasting his time writing to Thomas. The letter could be finished tomorrow. He should think of here and now and Padmavati, for he had written enough. He called her name gently but she was asleep. He went over to the bed, and kneeling beside it began to kiss her body until she awoke.

4

Henry was leaving the Temple. There had been no necessity for him to come to Chambers at all, but he felt he must keep up the pretence, if only to make Perrin do likewise. His labours had consisted of a re-arrangement of the documents on his desk and a re-read for duty's sake of Mrs Waters' papers. Corbett had been ironic to the point of rudeness.

'Nice day, Mr Kelleway. Very hot. Good to get some air in the legal lungs. Will you be returning? In case there are any messages . . .'

Perrin, who had evidently been lurking with intent, accosted him before he could leave. 'Mr Kelleway! Can I have a moment of your time?'

'Is it important?'

'I think it is. I think you should think so, too.'

'Really.' Henry was icy. Perrin was holding open the door of his room. He entered, standing just within the door. Perrin closed the door behind them, then walked round so that he faced Henry. Perrin was white and obviously determined. He rubbed his thumbs continuously against his forefingers which made a small rasping sound that was dry and irritating.

'I think you know what we must talk about.' Henry stared at him rudely. 'I am not satisfied about this business of Mrs Waters. I may as well be plain. I believe there is more here than meets the eye.'

'You made yourself infernally plain upon the subject yesterday, Mr Perrin, and I decided that you probably acted through some misjudgement and had decided to forget the matter. Perhaps you intend to apologize for what you said. If so, please do not bother. I don't require an apology, sir.'

'Damn you, Kelleway, you get no apology from me!'

'Good day, Perrin. I am sure you will have better control of yourself tomorrow.' Henry turned round and took the door handle.

'If you persist in tooting for business, then I shall take steps!'

'Will you, sir? Good day.'

'Mr Thackeray must hear, sir! We are a profession, not traders.'

'Sir, tell your uncle what you will. Persist in this at your own peril.'

'That is a threat, sir!' Perrin yelped.

'Not from me, sir. You may be nephew to Thackeray but by God you are not wife to Caesar!' Henry had then walked out. He lingered through the courts, while his temper cooled. He was certain that Perrin intended to pursue his vendetta.

It was very hot. The lawns were hard and uncomforting. Fig-tree Court was cool with black shade. The ancient tree, hung with dark and glossy leaves, was a thing of umbellate calm. Henry walked over hot flag-stones, crunched across yellow-brown gravel, crossed Middle Temple Lane and picked his way along a flagged path in Fountain Court. Here the fountain was, as usual, surrounded by the black but unquarrelsome crows of the law, their gowns flapping like ragged wings. They seemed to have assembled to drink at the fountain's lip. It was a place to cool off on a hot day, to preen and ponder. Trees overhung the simple stone bowl with its single jet of water. It tinkled onto the untroubled surface, wandering slightly with any faint breeze and leaving floating bubbles. Conversation was conducted in low, murmurous tones, but men were mostly silent, as though it were a stoup of holy water of Law. Beyond the fountain lay the hall where Shakespeare played and Elizabeth danced and beyond that, the green lawn stretching down to the river.

Henry paused, then passed on, up the steps into New Court and through the wrought-iron gate of Devereux Court, with its gas lamp and extravagant flourishes of scroll-work. The whole area was free of carriages, of sedans, of bustle. The buildings were grouped with that meandering casualness that belies the sensitivity of their placing. Tudor brick and stone. Cloister and court. Narrow alleys, tortuous as the legal mind. Broad lawns with untrained trees. Unexpected narrowness and unexpected space. Inns heaped on churches, heaped in turn on libraries, halls and chambers, all as though they had been pushed together to make space for the lawns. Yet in fifty paces, Henry was amongst the furious bustle of the Strand. The noise of wheels on cobbles made it impossible to hear or think. Coachmen yelled, beat and fought their way round St Clements Church as if determined on self-destruction, lashing at their horses or each other with their long whips. Pedestrians cowered by the gutter, waiting for some break, so that they could dash across, braving the lethal spinning wheels and iron-clad hoofs. Henry turned westward, trying to close his ears to the din.

He had one problem central in his mind – how to disentangle himself with discretion from a stale affair. Despite his air of aloofness, he had been shaken by Thomas's outburst. He reflected again that those involved are stupidly unaware of worldly-wise eyes. He was no besotted young fool, pale of cheek and poetic of tongue, and yet it was, as Thomas had said, being passed round dinner tables like dessert. He supposed that women must boast of trophies too, for he had been discreet enough. But in that very discretion, he wondered, had he been furtive? What did Jane know? Nothing, he believed. Yet she suspected. He cared little for the woman, but even that must show itself in a lack of care for Jane, when he thought he had displayed all care. Maybe he displayed too much. Solicitude may make unquiet wives. It was the devil to puzzle it out. It would be the devil to end things quietly.

He cursed his stupidity and his appetites, so well concealed, he believed, by his manner. He cursed his marriage, cursed Jane and immediately countermanded it. It was not her fault, he supposed, if she could not give him what he wanted from a woman. He should never have married her. Yet she had seemed a passionate and loving thing. He particularly cursed Thomas and Sam for putting him in a position where he had no choice at an age when he was unable to resist. That was the nub of it. He was unable to determine just when he had begun to resent Jane, but it was within weeks of being wed. She had become an increasingly reproachful figure, in his mind. Her gentle criticisms of his manner, her encouragement even, had been like thorns in his shoes. Yet he could not deny he loved her.

He was so wrapt in his thoughts that he took no notice of the carriage that rumbled alongside him. He needed total concentration to avoid being overturned, just walking. He became aware of it only when it stopped ahead of him. The door was thrown open and narrowly missed his head. He grasped it, prepared to curse the occupant, male or female, but was completely disarmed.

'Mr Kelleway!' Mrs Waters shouted, 'I have been trying to attract your attention in a shameless way. I am quite hoarse! You ignore me. What a bear you are in your thoughts! Can I take you anywhere? It is far too hot to walk and you legal gentlemen dress up so.'

The coach shuddered, buffeted from behind by the collision of another. Mrs Waters' coachman entered into an angry exchange above their heads, which continued while they talked, like a close barrage of fire. Henry lifted his hat, which he then held aloft by the brim, as though it were a sunshade.

'Good day, Mrs Waters. I did not realize. I did not see the coach. I was miles away. It is very kind of you but it will do me good to walk.'

'Nonsense! Am I not allowed to spare my counsel from this bedlam? Aha! I understand. You must be chaperoned everywhere by Mr Coke?' She laughed. 'Your legal etiquette does you credit, Mr Kelleway, but it is holding up the traffic. Please come inside. I will confess to Coke, I promise. Join me and be comfortable. I promise not to talk about my troubles. There, does that suffice?'

Henry hesitated, his hat still held aloft, then gave in. He climbed into the carriage and sat down on the buttoned leather, facing Mrs Waters. She laughed, and swivelled her eyes to the open door. Henry had to get up again to close it. She always had this ability to distract him, he thought, and discomfort him as though he were a youth. She smiled at him and banged on the roof with the handle of her parasol, but her coachman, who had successfully wedged his opponent's front wheels round against his own axle-trees, was in no hurry to be off. A small crowd had stopped to judge the quality of the exchanges of sentiment. Mrs Waters rapped again, hard and imperiously, and was rewarded by an answering knock. She gestured to the opposite window, graciously, as though bestowing a favour, but all the time her eyes flashed back to Henry with a mischievous gleam. Looking out, he was startled to see a furious face pressed against the glass of the carriage alongside. Her gloved knuckles were beating on the window but they could hear nothing. Seeing that she had attracted their attention, she drew herself up and delivered a tirade at them, of which they could hear not a word. She was a large woman, speckled with beauty spots, like pork pricked with cloves.

'Shall I shake my parasol?' Mrs Waters asked. 'Yes really, I must, it is too good to miss.' She shook the handle of it at the furious face, her lips moving silently as if in abuse. The furious lady was attempting to pull down her window, when the two coaches abruptly parted from each other and they saw her overbalance and disappear. Mrs Waters was delighted, and Henry found himself laughing with her, although he knew he ought to disapprove.

'Do you always travel like this?' he asked.

'Was that wicked of me, Mr Kelleway? Are you shocked? You cannot say that you are, for you see, it has made you laugh. I have not seen you do that before. You see, you are not so stern as you pretend!'

Henry was not sure that she should be talking to him like this. It offended his dignity, but the trouble was that she knew it. 'I believe it was your coachman who started the mischief,' he said obliquely.

'Coachmen enjoy it. So did that vulgar woman. When I am old, I shall take coach rides merely to do the same thing. Now does that shock you?' Mrs Waters had to shout to make herself heard above the rumble of the coach which was now moving at a smarter pace. Henry was bothered by the feeling that again things were out of his control.

'You are baiting me,' he replied, 'and I am not shocked. But I do not approve either,' he added sternly, but try as he might it sounded like banter. Mrs Waters was lying back, regarding him with amusement and he found this exciting. She was beautifully dressed, he noted, and he wondered how much it had cost. Had she paid for it? Was this another of those little items about which her husband was so incensed? Able to read his thoughts, she leaned forward, to speak more easily.

'Well, Mr Kelleway, you have studied me thoroughly. Do you approve? Is it so extravagant? Am I wearing vital evidence? What are your opinions of my couture – the neck, the sleeves, be candid . . .'

'I'm sorry . . .'

'You are ungallant. Never be sorry. A lady is flattered by attention, especially when it is so demure!'

Henry was suddenly furious, yet his heart was thumping like an excited child. He had no right to be travelling with her yet had offered only the feeblest resistance. Now she intended to humiliate him.

'Madam, you are amusing yourself by teasing me. I should not properly be here at all. Stop the coach if you please. I must get down.'

Mrs Waters was immediately contrite. She laid a hand upon his arm, she bowed her head. 'Forgive me, Mr Kelleway. In these unchivalrous days I had intended to pay you a compliment.'

Henry was abashed and had turned red. He was outmanoeuvred. The hand was not withdrawn and he could not be so churlish as to move. Moreover, he knew he did not want to. He covered her hand with his own. She said nothing but looked him steadily in the eyes.

'We have found each other out, Mr Kelleway. You know of my circumstance, and I know that you do not know where you wish to go, for we have cleared the Strand.'

'I was going to Charing Cross,' said Henry quickly, but Mrs Waters only smiled and removed her hand.

Henry's mind was in a turmoil. His main reaction was to leap out of the moving coach like a frightened boy, but he knew perfectly well, at that moment, that he was only delaying something inevitable and excitingly illicit. If the boy had taken fright, then the man wanted to stay, wanted to know what Mrs Waters wanted from him and hoped that he already knew. He wondered if she was so overtly intimate with all her friends, or whether he had been singled out. There was a matter of pride in that, and flattery. Did she see him as another easy conquest, a male lured by sexuality as easily as a hound by the scent of a fox? He had no way of knowing yet.

The situation had a savage irony in it. At this moment, but for this unashamedly extended diversion, he should be with Mrs Anne Johnson, until today his mistress. He should be paying his respects in a state of contained cowardice and painfully hinting his goodbyes. These hints would be ignored, because Anne would never hear what she did not wish to hear. The hints would have become statements, the responses accusations, the sum of it, a tempest of anguish and tears and bitter words immediately retracted. Words used as blows, as slaps, in the vain hope of further stimulation for a passion that had flagged and become a burden to him. She would be waiting for him, and he felt guilt about it, but qualified with reason. She had loved him, he supposed, still believed she did, so therefore still did in her own view. But his flirtation, his bedding, had excited in her a monstrous demand. Their sexual adventures, at first erotic and secret, had lost the urgency of illicit sex, had become a cloying trap. Dalliance had turned to demands, liquor to syrup, discretion to declarations and possession to possessiveness.

Henry feared any imposition on his emotions. He even found it hard to accept that it was a necessary consequence of sexual adventure. As he was able to be dispassionate about his own appetites he expected that others should be so too. There was no cruelty in his attitude, only arrogant ignorance, the bigotry of rigidly enforced self-denial. The boy who wished to jump out of the carriage in sheer fright was a more real part of him than the man who calculated to stay.

Now, instead of facing Anne's sobbing rage, enduring her clinging arms, he sat in this coach with a woman who excited him, and who clearly intended to. Henry felt satisfied that the Gods had solved things for him. He had merely to go along with her – how could he politely do otherwise – and the severance was being made. Not perhaps in the way of a gentleman, but brutally and effectively. Simply, he need never go back. There was no honour in it, but it was a well-tried alternative and in some ways more practical. No scenes, no storms. Was it the coward's part, he wondered? He could not bear emotion. Was that a coward's part?

'That is a heavy burden of thought.' Henry realized he had been staring at the floor-carpet of the carriage. He looked up. Mrs Waters was examining his face with the same warm concern. 'You have sat there for quite five minutes, you know, with a face like a Lord Chief Justice. Very solemn, very weighty, not very flattering to a lady.'

'I'm sorry. I was thinking.'

'Is your life so regimented that you must commune like a priest before varying your course? You may get out of the carriage, you know. I can ask the coachman to halt. Indeed, you may do so yourself. I have not kidnapped you, Mr Kelleway!' She was teasing him like a child again. Henry found he did not resent it.

'Then where are you going, Mrs Waters? Or shall I not ask?'

'Whatever you prefer.'

'As we are in Oxford Street, I assume we are bound for Bayswater. Have I an invitation?'

Mrs Waters nodded. 'I should be delighted if you would join me for tea. If the Law can spare you, of course. But I believe we have now come so far that it will take you too long to return, for I shall not lend you my carriage!'

Henry smiled, and in that smile his youth shone through to Mrs Waters. She congratulated herself on the accuracy of her judgement, and really Mr Coke deserved some reward.

Mrs Waters' house in Porchester Terrace, Bayswater, stood to the north-western end of the road of yellow hoggin. Beyond it lay fields. To the rear of the garden another open field separated it from Upper Craven Place. No buildings hemmed in the house, which was no more than twenty years old. The carriage swung through open gates, scattering gravel and stopped at stone steps leading to a pillared porch. Henry opened the door and jumped out, folding down the carriage steps. He took Mrs Waters' extended hand, and helped her down. As the coachman made no move to descend, Henry folded back the steps and slammed the door. The coachman sought no further instructions but immediately drove the vehicle round the side of the house, the horses knowing their way.

The front door was opened for them before they reached it by a maid who curtsied and bobbed and seemed at a loss what further to do with them until a footman arrived hastily from a side passage. He took their top garments. Henry had just time to admire the broad, chequer-tiled hall before Mrs Waters led him into a fine room at the rear of the house, which overlooked the garden. The room was high-ceilinged, with a powder-blue paper patterned with dark blue flowers. Rounded alcoves lined with books had been formed on each side of a white marble mantel. The furnishings were decorative rather than functional and Henry had the impression that they had been Mrs Waters' choice. Glass cases full of elaborate shell arrangements stood on the mantel and on tables. Long mirrors with pediments and marquetry inlay hung on each wall. Flowers in vases stood in plenty. Mrs Waters turned to Henry.

'Well, Mr Kelleway, do you like the room?'

'Indeed I do,' Henry replied, although he felt it to be feminine, except for the shelves of books.

'I wonder if you really do? I shall ring for tea,' she said pulling a silk cord before he was obliged to protest. 'Please sit down.' But as she remained standing herself, Henry did too. The maid who had opened the door appeared almost immediately and bobbed.

'We will have tea.'

'Yes, ma'am.' She was gone as quickly as she had arrived.

'Why won't you sit down, Mr Kelleway? Now you have been captured, you may as well be reconciled to it.'

Mrs Waters was suddenly confronting Henry with her amused smile. Henry, who had been gazing out of the window at the profuse garden and wondering about the prudence of this situation, was again caught like an inattentive boy. His thoughts had strayed from her, and it seemed that she knew when they did. It also seemed that she was determined they should not. He was very aware of how close she was to him, and that this was not compatible with the size of this elegant room. He was aware of the smell of her body. She was not perfumed as some women perfume themselves, like sauce poured over a dish, but rather she smelled of herbs, like a garniture. He could smell the musky scent of her hair and the fresh, slightly grassy smell of silk cloth. He felt an exciting helplessness. He was drifting without any effort of his own into an intimacy with this woman as though they had been lovers, all embarrassment removed. They could stand close, make easy contact and she showed no hesitancy, and yet, delightfully, none of this had happened. He felt strangely passive.

'You are still concerned about the proprieties, are you not? Well, be assured, if indeed you find it reassuring, that my husband has left this house.' Henry's face evidently showed a conflict of emotions, for she laughed, not in any way unkindly. 'You must decide whether it is more or less proper, Mr Kelleway. I say it is more so. Ah, here is tea.'

The maid, this time in the care of the butler, entered with a wheeled trolley. They set out china and silver on a circular burr-elm table near the window. Henry, embarrassed by their presence, returned to his position gazing out onto the garden. There was no reason why the servants should embarrass him. He knew that. Mrs Waters stood over the servants until she was satisfied that everything was correct. She nodded and they withdrew. Then she walked over to join Henry at the window.

'The garden is very fine at this time of the year.'

There was still the same note of mischief in her voice, that was in no way malicious. Henry did not have to turn to know that she was smiling at him again. He was furious with himself for hiding away in this adolescent fashion. He resolved to drink this tea rapidly and go with as much formality as he could rescue.

'I think we should have tea, then. My profession . . .'

'Don't hide behind your profession! I said when I last saw you that the law is an old fox. It not only conceals its strength, I think. Am I right?'

'What do you want from me, Mrs Waters?' What he had intended as a stern question came out as almost a cry of anguish. She let it hang upon the air, private thoughts exposed to public view. She poured tea. When she had finished she crossed back to him and laid her hand on his arm.

'Have we caught each other out?'

Henry put his arm round behind her neck, lifting the curls of hair, and looked into her eyes. He was cautious and afraid. She was regarding him quite calmly, as though they were still separated by several places. He kissed her hard and she responded with passion that surprised him. He had expected her to turn away, play the modest part. He moved back to look at her, held her shoulders, hoping to see anger, outrage or at least surprise. It was inescapable, it seemed, that he should behave like a boy who wishes to shock himself as well as his love. But there was no anger or outrage in her eyes. He felt a fool for having made the experiment. He seemed committed to a life of these acts of folly. She took his right hand from her shoulder, and slowly, never taking her eyes from his, slipped his hand beneath the thin material of her dress onto the soft delight of her breast. He felt the tumescent nipple, stroked, caressed, looking into her eyes. She kissed him hard and quickly on the mouth, then slipped aside, so that his hand was withdrawn. When Henry reached out again, she took his hand in both hands and held it, but against her bosom.

'No, that is enough. Please. You see, we *have* found each other out. We will have other times. After all,' she said, the mischievous smile returning, but with a softness, 'this is the drawing-room.'

Henry stooped quickly and kissed the small mounds of her nipples through the silk of her dress. Buds of desire. She stroked his hair. Like a lover, like a mother. Henry pulled away. His confusion was absolute. His emotions became overburdened with conflict. Mrs Waters, Jane, Anne, lovers, mothers. A boy, a man. His attempts to define himself were wholly blurred. He had set out to see one woman and had ended with another. He had been determined to end his adventures, to give no nourishment to this clinging bindweed of need that sent out such tender tendrils as a young plant, then choked and fed upon its host. Instead he had strayed into an enchanted garden with growths more exotic than he understood. He protested that he must go, he promised to return like a boy to his first girl, he skirted the tea table, which somehow seemed ridiculous now, although Mrs Waters offered him one of the two cups poured. She was perfectly calm and seemed to understand, her eyes not upset, but watching him with a warm light. He found himself shaking her hand at the drawing-room door in an absurdly formal way.

'It is a long time since I have been touched so, Mr Kelleway.'

Henry was rushing along the Bayswater Road before he precisely knew how he got there, hurrying with the pace of a thief. It was only there that he recalled the absurdity of their formal mode of address. He was immersed in a cataclysm and had found that he could not swim.

'Sam, do you think the Queen is really ill? Is it serious?'

'I think it is the end.'

'So soon? I have never liked the woman, and been plain about it. She appeals to the wrong sort of people. But she seemed lively enough at the Coronation and that ain't three weeks away.'

'Three days of it, Thomas. They are keeping it back from the people. They posted a bulletin this morning, saying: "Her Majesty is not worse, but continues in the same state as in the morning." She has not improved and shows no sign of it. I am told she is beyond all treatment. There is no man alive who can treat an obstruction of the bowel.

'I fear there will be trouble. The mob will use her to show their dislike of George. Dee me, Sam, we seem poised always on the brink of civil unrest and anarchy. It is not just the mechanics and labouring people, but merchants, bankrupt lordlings and social parasites that George would never have tolerated. It is an order of people all trying to make themselves felt. It is new people who have the money, and they want the position to go with it. I thought we had seen the last of the Queen, but if she dies, she will be a lodestone of lamentations, all in competition for the best show of deeply affected grief! What a miserable country we are! Afflicted by French and Germans! Now we behave like them.'

'There are honest men who think she was genuinely wronged. I never heard you speak out for George like this,' said Sam dryly.

'He is a vulgar king, and extravagant, but he's the only one we have.'

They sat at dinner in Middle Temple Hall, where they had been summoned by the customary blast on the ox-horn that served as a reminder if their stomachs forgot. The four great parallel tables were slowly filling as members took their seats in wigs and gowns. The oak tables, three hundred years old, bore the scars and knife-marks where Elizabethan daggers had been stuck in the wood in days of different manners. They awaited the entry of the benchers who would occupy the table on the dais at the far end of the hall set at right angles to the others as a sign of their seniority and privilege. Being a Grand Night, the benchers would bring with them their guests and the whole company could look forward to a convivial evening.

'So you are firmly committed to this investment in a ship?' asked Sam, changing the subject.

'You have a note of censure in your voice, Sam Leigh. I know you think it risky, but everything is attended with risk.'

'You could invest for a more modest profit. There is all this building . . .'

'How I hate all this building! Sam, you're ribbing me! I have stood on the deck of my own ship, and I felt excited. I confess it. Houses are dull things. They sit there as boring as my brood. But a ship is a living thing. It can move around the world, it flexes and shudders and creaks like an animal. You must walk her with me, then you would understand.'

Sam's eyes twinkled. 'It's your age, Thomas. Looking for a young filly!'

'Dee me, Sam, if I was, she wouldn't be wood! And will you believe that I have been so consumed with overweening vanity that she is to be called the *Thomas K.*'

Thomas gave this information apologetically, trying it out. But before Sam was compelled to reply, they saw Henry enter and seat himself low down the table, and were themselves joined by the two other members of their 'mess'. These Ancients made short, polite bows, and sat themselves down. The one was a tall man, stooped, with very thin wrists and cavernous cheeks, called Carmoody. His build belied his appetite. His companion, Wells, was a picture of health, and looked much younger than his sixty-odd years. He appeared robust and vivacious in manner. Yet Mr Carmoody did all the talking and Mr Wells was exceptionally silent. As a mess, as each group of four is known, they all got on well with each other. Thomas (in confidence) was accustomed to refer to them to Sam as the stork and the robin, and it described them well enough.

'Well,' said Carmoody, 'there is an air of gloom about the City today. Have you noticed? It seems that everyone is preparing for the Queen to die. There is much popular feeling for her. I am pleased to see that the bulletins are so precise about her complaint, for the commonalty would have it that she is dying of a broken heart. The pamphleteers are making money!' Thomas snorted with disapproval.

'Today she is a victim of cruel persecution, yesterday she was a whore. It is pamphleteers that stir up the people. It is an excuse for malcontents and the mob. Any occasion is good enough for them. Pie-sellers sell more pies, haberdashers sell black cloth, pickpockets have access to better-lined coats. Mechanics will use it as an occasion for protest, and to display themselves on the streets. People don't know what they want. I view it with misgiving.'

A heavy knock rang round the hall. The head-porter had struck the mace on the floor. The seated members rose as the Middle Temple benchers entered in procession, in twos with their guests. The head-porter preceded them at a stately pace, dressed in purple, carrying the silver-tipped mace. The procession walked to the high table, whereupon the head-porter struck the table with a mallet three times. The company reseated themselves and the Treasurer said Grace before meat.

'The eyes of all things look up and put their trust in Thee, O Lord! Thou givest them their meat in due season; Thou openest Thine hand, and fillest with Thy blessing every living thing. Good Lord, bless us and these Thy good gifts which we receive of Thy bounteous liberality, through Jesus Christ our Lord. Amen.'

As it was a Grand Night and he must put on a show, he said it at a more temperate rate than usual. Lawyers, like bishops, are notoriously in need of their victuals. The panyer-men, or waiters, were immediately busy, bursting out onto the floor of the hall with tureens and plates as though they had been restrained at the sides of the Hall from feeding their adored masters. They pushed among them with plates of turtle soup, with bread, with wine. They crammed and scurried, like eager mother-birds. Thomas, as captain of their mess of four, as each group is called, chose the wine and was served first, the wine passing anti-clockwise as the port would later pass clockwise – all ceremonies properly observed. The four men of the mess raised their glasses and bowed to each other, as did every other mess, first opposite, then diagonally and last to the side in silent toast; the sign of the Red Cross of the Templars, they said, that strange secret order of Knighthood whose rituals and disciplines have become absorbed into the customs of the Inns of Court.

But few members ever stopped to consider. The Order of Knighthood, whose continental branch had been eradicated in France in 1312, had been accused of unnatural obscenities, sacrilege, homosexual liaisons, 'oscula inhonesta', spitting on the Cross and worshipping the anti-Christ, but in England had become rulers of the Law. Persecuted without enthusiasm by Edward the Second, they had finally earned respectability for their honesty as bankers and as a repository of deeds and documents at a time when trust was a thing between paupers or fools. They held the wealth of lords in their stronghold by the Thames, and later the Exchequer of the King who could not risk his baggage on the road. They had quickly become expert in the settlement of disputes of ownership, having records and documents of proof. They were able to refer to precedent. By natural and proven ability, their power had increased until they had become arbiters in most matters of dispute. Now the inheritors of the Red Cross Knights who had vowed to defend pilgrims on the route to Jerusalem and had taken the vows of perpetual chastity, obedience and self-denial, called for yet more turtle soup, more marrow pies, more beefsteak, more wine. With more wine, their voices were louder in joking and arguing. The Ancients, as was their right, were plied with yet more food and drink. The tremendous oaken roof echoed with noise down its hundred foot length.

The whole scene was medieval. The dark panelling of the walls gleamed here and there with the names of the Readers painted upon it. The serving table, or cupboard below the dais, made from the timbers of Drake's *Golden Hind*, became increasingly laden with covers and plates. And as the scene was medieval, so were young men's manners. Students at the far ends of the long tables were becoming boisterous and the head-porter and his minions were hovering grimly near them. They could be expelled without redress if their behaviour outraged a bencher, but on a Grand Night the benchers would retire with their guests to continue their entertainment in private. The Hall would be left to conviviality, and the students to clown, dance on the tables, throw bread and fight the porters until they grew bored with it and went out to annoy the streets of London with their antics, aping the Bucks and Beaux. The Ancients would yarn on until the yarns ran out, or until they had been told the third time round, then those who were able would totter homewards. Some would be left to snore in their seats. There were critics who attacked the Grand Nights, but they were still few and far between and were treated as poor deluded eccentrics. After all, this was the way it had always been. Indeed it was more decorous now than formerly, when the dice would have been out on the table.

Perrin and Henry sat in adjoining messes so that Henry faced Perrin diagonally on his left. Henry had tried to ignore him, not in an obvious or provocative manner, but by avoiding catching his eye. Perrin's long face had taken on a malevolent and stupid expression with the effects of drink. The Byzantine Christ had undergone a transformation with the sagging of his facial muscles. The eyelids and upper cheeks seemed to have sagged down, making his face slack and cynical. Time and time again, his eyes flicked over to Henry, who was aware of it without looking at the man. Perrin's voice was becoming loud, and as he talked with the members of his mess he nodded sagely, but with a heavy, uncontrolled head.

Henry, like everyone else, had talked about the Queen, and her apparently worsening illness. Although he had tried to keep up appearances, his thoughts had been on Mrs Waters. He felt like a boy smitten with calf-love, and yet at the same time he felt perfectly calculating about her. She was a desirable woman, and he desired her. He must keep control of himself, he consciously lectured. Head over heart. Or loins. But her breasts kept coming back into his mind, a soft and delicious memory, almost, of something tasted, eaten and absorbed, not just caressed. It was incongruous amongst this male chaff and chatter, a mixture of bragging, joking and legal banter. Did they never, any of them, have visions that were real of sensations like caressing a woman's breasts, or did they control these visions for appropriate places, not at dinner in Hall?

Was he in some way peculiar or unique? The tragedy of humans is their inability to communicate except by words. What a roar of joyous erotic news there might be, what a fluster of worries, screaming of pain, astonishment of truth, if suddenly their heads were all to explode and their thoughts at that instant to spring out. Then we could see in an instant the true cleverness, inventiveness, sensitivity of a man. Any man. Dry little barristers might carry fabulous fantasies beyond imagination. Voluble dashing pleaders might be exposed in trivial meanness, the limits of their invention like those of an actor who has forgotten his lines and cannot improvise within the constraints of the plot. Life, after all, is a plot largely laid down by others who would be producers, thought Henry, and improvisation is the art of survival.

Mrs Waters – I don't know her real name – he thought, is what I want. Want to have, desire. Jane is what I need, professionally, outwardly. What a bitter and detestable thought. Henry did not consider himself a moral man in sexual matters, but in matters professional he had prided himself on his integrity apart from the degrading necessity of Corbett. He could dismiss that as normal if unpleasant. He liked to consider that when he became established, he would be noted for judicial strength and exactness. Yet here he was, falling at the first hurdle of his profession. Demolished by the demands of his appetite which he hardly understood. He desired Mrs Waters and had no strength to deny it, yet he did not understand what he desired. He tried to picture Jane naked, beautiful, and realized he had never seen her so. Never naked, to be looked at and enjoyed. He had felt, touched, made love to her but never seen her. He was confused again, for he could see Mrs Waters easily. She had a reality for him that his own wife did not. A soft breast, her smile, they made a complete picture. He was sculpting a model of desire.

Henry had been abstracted and Perrin seized on it. He leaned across, his head hanging forward and spoke loudly, so that others could hear.

'How is your client, then, Kelleway?'

Henry gave him what he hoped was an even and unprovocative look. The sort of look one exchanges on purely business talk. 'I have read the documents, and I think it will be quite a case.'

'But she is a beauty,' Perrin said to the table at large, 'and a man is lucky to have such a beauty. I think you are half way there. Who could resist her!'

Henry tried to laugh this aside but achieved only a sickly grimace. Perrin continued.

'She has quite taken to you, Kelleway, admit it!'

'She is a very attractive lady.'

The members of the two messes had stopped talking amongst themselves and were listening. It was the worst possible thing, Henry realized, for Perrin now had an audience.

'She was my client you know, Kelleway. That is right. Quite a beauty.' He addressed the others in a generalized way. 'Briefs are queer animals these days. Suppose they always have been, but my experience is getting worse ... when your own brief don't have your name on it, well ... Now I have heard of briefs ending up in other hands than those intended, a sort of motion not envisaged in the natural sciences but entirely according to the laws of Human Nature! Not unknown, they say. Sometimes when a father has a favourite son. Embarrassing, what? Wouldn't want that to happen to me, brings the profession low. But some say that firms calling themselves solicitors are putting out briefs without the embellishment of the name of intended counsel. Now gossip is a messenger, and you may not believe a word he says, but he certainly *comes* from somewhere and therefore has some purpose. Now if that were true, it would be scandalous. They are no more than mendicant friars hawking papal bulls, wouldn't you say?'

Henry thought how strange it was that it should be assumed that men of the legal profession should be thought subtle, clever or even polite. The trappings of the law must have been constructed to afford protection from the exposure of their grosser nature. He tried to think of a way of turning this monologue but there was something so insistent about Perrin's drunken presence that he knew any response would only make matters worse. However, the insinuations had to be rebutted.

'What do you mean, Perrin?' Direct questioning. Always a good tack.

'Financial absolution, by means of these legal bulls. Of course, like the papal sort, you expect to get more out than you put in. That was always the idea. But a papal bull don't buy you entry to heaven!'

'I still don't understand what you mean. Can you explain exactly?'

'Well, I can't help you then, Kelleway. It really is not too difficult a problem, more for the conscience than the intellect, I say.'

'Are you still trying to persist that Mrs Waters is your client? Your insinuations, sir, are intolerable. You were committed to another client, as our clerk made clear. Sir, if you cannot order your affairs better, do not take out your venom on others!'

'Gentlemen!' interrupted one of the members of Perrin's mess, 'This is not a subject for dinner.'

'This is not a subject at all,' added the man beside Henry.

'What do you think will be Castlereagh's position if the Queen should really die?' the first man persisted. 'He is very unpopular with the common people and could be the focus of their attention. He would do well to keep out of the way . . .'

This solo attempt to save the situation hung in the air unheeded. Perrin's head dropped lower and lower as he tried to maintain his position leaning towards Henry. It looked like an attempt to charge him. He was unable to keep his eyes on Henry as he intended, as his head was nodding, presenting the curled mop of his wig. He therefore propped his chin up on his fist. It gave him the appearance of a watchful dog. He snarled across the table.

'Kelleway has tooted my client, haven't you, sir? That's what I say and I don't like it. It ain't good enough. But you have a surprise coming, Kelleway, you will see . . .'

'Gentlemen,' said Henry, recovering his calm as best he could, 'I'm sure Mr Perrin is rambling rather more than he would wish us to remember tomorrow. Don't be concerned, I'm sure we can all have brief memories.'

He tried to turn aside to his own mess but Perrin suddenly lunged across the table and grasped Henry by his lapels, an action, because it deprived him of support, which caused him to fall chest first onto the table.

'Because your pater familias is among the Ancients, Kelleway, it don't mean he is on Olympus!' Perrin spoke with some difficulty, suspended as he was. His wig had slipped sideways and his nose was over the gravy boat. 'Don't be high and mighty with me. How is the lady, Kelleway? Met you with her carriage did she? Transported you, no doubt?'

Henry pulled off the man's hands, which were hot and sticky. Perrin canted onto the table, missing the gravy but with his face in an empty plate. The head-porter had already seen the disturbance and was moving purposefully over.

'I could report you, Kelleway,' Perrin yelled, fumbling through his clothing to find a handkerchief to wipe his face. 'Maybe I shall!'

'What the devil do you mean, sir? Your behaviour is a disgrace!' Henry could never keep silent when he knew he should.

'Oh! Oh! What the devil do I mean? We are gentlemen here, Kelleway, not a gathering of common public!'

Henry shook his head at this provocative talk. 'No, sir, you are drunk. I will not respond.'

Perrin sat back heavily, having failed to find a handkerchief, and mopped his face with his gown. It shone with grease and sweat. 'Now you have cast the first stone!' he declared triumphantly, 'You will listen to me. Take no more clients of mine!'

Henry, without thinking, slapped him hard across the face. It was done swiftly and no one who was not specifically watching could have seen it, but the sound rang out hard and sharp. Heads turned everywhere. The head-porter, with the wisdom of decades, was standing over them immediately. Thomas, who had been observing the scene with alarm, excused himself from his mess and made his way discreetly down the hall, taking an indirect route by other tables.

'Well, gentlemen,' said the head-porter, 'I hope there's no trouble here, or I shall have to put you out.' The big man no doubt thought it was a dulcet tone, but it was full of menace. 'There's a table full of young sprigs all gamed up down there, and when the benchers leave they are setting up two of them for a fist fight for ten guineas. Now that is appropriate to their age and lack of manners. Why don't you gentlemen pass the port and have a wager on it, civilized like, so I don't end up with the unpleasant duty of reporting someone.'

Thomas had by this time arrived. 'What's the matter, Sims?'

The head-porter was immediately deferential, for an Ancient commanded respect. Young barristers were two-a-penny, got drunk and couldn't be trusted with his wife. 'Everything is in good order, Mr Kelleway. I was only saying to these gentlemen that as the young fry over there are intent on injuring themselves for their pleasure and a few guineas, these gentlemen who seem to have some powder burning might like to expend it on that and not on each other.'

Perrin was too drunk to have the sense to keep quiet. Perhaps the presence of Thomas was the last straw. 'I'll fight you, Kelleway!' he shouted at Henry, staggering to his feet and almost falling backwards over the bench. 'Putney Heath with pistols!'

'Take him out,' said Thomas to Sims. 'Quietly.'

'No,' said Henry quickly, 'it will only make a disturbance. I'll go.'

Thomas looked at Henry with abstract contempt. There was no trace of the father in him. 'Then go.'

Henry left with as much grace as this graceless situation allowed. He had no experience of such a thing. Did Perrin mean it? If he did, he would have to go through with it. What was the legal position? Castlereagh had fought Canning and dozens before and since, but they were politicians or military men. Men of high pride and irrational thoughts. It was absurd. What were they fighting about? Because he had struck Perrin? That had been exceptionally stupid of him. Over Mrs Waters? Because Perrin had accused him of 'tooting'? It was a mess. He was afraid of what Thomas would make of it.

In the Hall, the benchers filed out with their guests. They had been too remote to see any of it. The 'young fry' immediately set together two tables, exhorting two drunk young men to strip to their shirts, the first to fall off the tables to be the loser. The rest of their members nearby either watched them, ignored them studiously or got on with their drinking seriously. Men had to shout to make themselves heard. Grand Night was Grand Night and God help the defendants tomorrow. Perrin, with a red mark across one cheek and a little blood trickling from one nostril, was playing the injured party. Thomas stood over him, angry.

'I would go into this no more here, sir. There can be no rights or wrongs in what went on. The affair is a disgrace!'

Perrin was white and silent at last. Perhaps he had begun to realize what he had done. Thomas returned up the hall and resumed his seat with the Ancients, explaining it was nothing, just a nonsense of the fumes of Bacchus. The head-porter, seeing that the two young men were now up on the tables, supported physically by their backers, gave the two messes a severe patrician glower and tramped away. Perrin's mess passed the port. Henry's followed suit. They talked quickly about other things. Perrin sniffed at the trickle of blood, ignored. He wiped it away with his gown. He was becoming sober enough to consider the consequences this might have on his career. His hatred of Henry grew as a consequence. He needed revenge.

One of the young men on the tables, swinging blindly at the other, stepped into space and landed with a bone-shaking crash on the floor. His backers argued volubly and judiciously that as he had been making an aggressive move at the time of this mishap, he could not be deemed to have fallen off. They argued it on point of law. He had stepped off, indeed advanced and walked off. Fallen off, never! The young man was helped back again in a daze. He appeared unwilling. They lunged about at each other like dancing bears while the students thumped on the boards and yelled.

Singing was breaking out at some of the tables. Old songs. Elderly counsel got maudlin in their cups. It was Grand Night, a good old-fashioned Grand Night. They talked of their own youthful escapades, exaggerating a little here, embroidering their prowess there. Thomas could not find much to enjoy and was a poor companion for the robin and the stork. He stuck close to the port until dawn got up over London. It was a drunkard's dawn, seedy, warm and stale. The wind from the river smelled like foul breath. It would be hot again, then probably rain.

Henry walked towards 'the stones' – the boundary of the Bills of Mortality where the paving of the seventeenth-century city had ended, and within which the ghastly tally of the successive plagues of that century had been totted up by the daily thousands. Cabs could ply for hire from beyond 'the stones', but within the lucrative city limits only through-stages and mail coaches were allowed to set down or pick up passengers for their longer hauls. He boarded a decrepit chariot in the Strand, which like all such vehicles had formerly seen better days in private ownership. All night carriages were filthy. The horses were skin and bone and one coughed distressingly despite the weather. Henry told the driver to take him home to Kensington. He stared out at London through the filth-grimed windows, that had been cleaned only in one circular area at eye level, so that he had a port-hole view. The interior of the coach smelled of tobacco and urine. In his depressed state it seemed a fit end to the evening. He had been clambering downwards to degradation all day. *Facilis descensus Averni*.

Why had he hit the fool Perrin? It had given him no satisfaction. It was an act of involition, yet he prided himself on his self-control. The type of self-control, he thought grimly, that he had exercised with Mrs Waters. Mrs Waters was an obsession that was with him now; he knew he should escape but equally knew he would not. He hoped that Jane was asleep. He was not so hardened in deception that he did not feel grimed with shame. He considered that he had only to call to the driver and re-direct him, and he could be with Mrs Waters. Jane would not be surprised by his absence on a Grand Night. Strangely that infuriated him, for he wished she would. But would Mrs Waters with her smile let him in? Or would she kiss him on the forehead as though wishing him goodnight, and send him on his way? It was an exciting thought and he almost acted on the impulse, giving it up only when he had pulled down the chariot window and was about to shout to the driver. It was absurd and indiscreet. She would not be impressed by Romeo and Juliet wooing. It was a folly he must contain. She must be treated differently.

Jane was not asleep, but was affecting drowsy slumber. Henry undressed in the dressing-room, hiding his body like a bashful boy, hiding his nakedness as though he were ashamed, because she had no right to see it since the body was no longer loyal to her. As though she could see physical sign of it on his flesh. Jane wondered if he might make love to her. It was Grand Night and he would be middling drunk. It seemed to her that he only made love to her in that condition these days. Then her body was left with the smell of port, lingering from his kisses. She could not bear to be kissed on the mouth and thank God he did not try. She lay still affecting sleep, breathing slowly and deeply, wanting him and hating him. He would take her with such abstract passion that she longed to hammer on his bare back with her fists and scream 'Who do you think I am?' She hated herself for feeling so eager that she listened to every action, hearing the rustle of his clothes, knowing when he would be naked. He seemed to pause, and at that moment her heart was pounding like a virgin bride.

Instead, she heard him go to his own bedroom. She wept bitter tears into the pillow, muffling all sound of sobbing. She wondered how long she could survive. She cursed herself for her inexperience, knowing no way to attract, be a coquette and all the other things she instinctively felt repugnant in a wife. But why were they? Surely, if she wanted him, she had a right to show it, if only she knew how. Other women, with their husbands like that, must find the right word or way. All Jane Kelleway can do is pretend sleep and hope for seduction. Was that any substance for a marriage? She cried miserably, curled up like a small girl.

The crowds gathered in increasing numbers for upwards of an hour before each bulletin was to be posted up. Many of London's ragged and wretched poor never left but stayed there day and night at Mansion House, Cambridge House, Audley Street or down in Hammersmith. Pickings were good out of sentiment for the Queen. Beggars did exceptionally well, especially limbless and sightless veterans of the Napoleonic wars. As though to prove that life and human weaknesses continued, prostitutes did a steady trade. Pick-pockets and foot-pads congratulated themselves on the quality of persons taking an interest in the Queen's dying. Rich pickings, stupid ways. You don't get a wallet from a mechanic that easily! Carriages and horsemen continually came and went, taking the news all over London, and from there by stage to the country.

The first bulletin had been issued on August second and posted at Cambridge House. It was from Brandenburgh House in Hammersmith, where the Queen was ill.

Her Majesty has an obstruction of the bowels, attended with inflammation. The symptoms, though mitigated, are not removed. Signed W. G. Maton, Henry Holland, Pelham Warren.

Her illness seemed to grip London. There seemed to be a general realization that this was the last act in the drama. On Saturday, fourth of August, the nine o'clock bulletin indicated no change and others followed rapidly at twelve, one, half past two, three, four and five in the afternoon. They caused a buzz because they were now signed by four physicians. Brandenburgh House and its vicinity had been sealed off to keep the environs as quiet as possible, and well-wishers were mainly turned away, although a few were allowed to sign a visitor's book, thus recording to their satisfaction that they had done their duty. At seven, a false report of her death circulated with great speed and caused widespread alarm. Many shops closed. Theatre managers, with a more wary eye to business, sent men galloping breakneck to Hammersmith to find out the truth but kept their theatres open. The riders came back, horses lathered. Still no change. The overture could commence.

By Monday, her physicians were announcing some slight relief that continued all day. On Tuesday morning, the bulletin was bad and was greeted with affected and affecting groans and tears by the sensitive ladies of better quality who were displaying the deepest signs of distress and grief.

The Queen has passed the night without sleep. Her Majesty's symptoms are not worse than yesterday.

It was signed by five physicians. Sales of black cloth and crape were enormous and haberdashers with half-drawn blinds saw it as a mark of respect to sell as much as possible, savagely undercutting the next man. If the Queen recovered they would not take the cloth back. If she died there would not be enough cloth to go round all London. That would be a social disaster in these fashion-conscious times. Better to buy and be sure. Black lace could not be had at any price; there was even anxiety about black thread. Bonnet makers were working twenty-four hours a day in black basements full of steam and naked gas jets. The women were stripped to the waist and haggard. They suckled their children at their work. Unscrupulous printers did a brisk trade in spurious bulletins claiming the Queen was better, worse, had got up, walked about, or had died, had uttered her last words condemning the King, Lady Jersey, Lady Conyngham or anyone else they could implicate. Pamphleteers declared she was dying of a broken heart, and broke into leaden verse. Everyone in trade might profit from it somewhere. The King was annoyed beyond endurance for he would have to delay his visit to Dublin which he was looking forward to. He had bought all his new clothes.

Thomas, as a supporter of what he described as the greater bulk but lesser evil, continued to work steadfastly, but on Tuesday stayed at home, cancelling his appointments and having no appearance in court. He had sent up a message by horseman to Caroline the previous day, asking if she might not like to join him at this confused time as he feared there might be some disturbance if the Queen died. In truth he was lonely. Caroline had replied by return, in a note without emotion, thanking him for his consideration but stating that since Aunt Helen was now returned from Bath she was no longer alone and was well provided for in the way of entertainment. The chances of commotion in Highgate, she assured Thomas, were even less than in Regent Square. Why, if a dog was knocked over, they talked about it for days. This reply did nothing to comfort Thomas. He felt pettishly angry at his rejection. He confided in Sam.

'I know I am getting to that old and boring age when I want to surround myself with my children like a thin man wants a winter cloak. It is the cold season of my life. I am selfish and I admit it. But at this moment she is the only one I can talk to. No, don't accuse me, Sam, I don't have other motives. She has her house and she shall stay there. I've done with trying to bring her back. Who would have children? Henry has not been near me since that stupid business, which is I suppose the only wisdom he has shown in his twenty-nine years and I should be grateful for it. His disgrace is mine.'

He sighed and shook his head. Sam, although knowing it was all partly an act, could see that Thomas was deeply hurt. There were yet more signs of tiredness and sudden ageing in him, and this worried Sam. He was disintegrating in appearance in a matter of months, yet he was a physically robust man in many ways.

'I will have to have an interview with Henry,' Thomas continued. 'This Perrin creature intends to pursue the thing. He has sent round a man with a formal challenge.'

'Good God! In writing?'

'Yes. And he intends, he says, to publish certain facts as he calls them in the journals.'

'Then he must be reported to the Treasurer!'

'When my clever offspring hit him in public at dinner? When he has a mistress his wife knows nothing about and his wife is the daughter of my old friend, and apart from this mistress, Gee knows what else! Perrin is shouting "touting" from the roof-tops and it don't go down well, Sam. It goes on, but that's different, it still ain't acceptable to the legal ear. No, we can't do that. I'd sooner consign the brat to Perrin. Dee me, a penny to a pound the man can't shoot anyway. We want two good seconds who will make sure they extract the ball and do each other no harm.'

'I'll speak to Perrin. I'll silence him. We'll have him out of the Bar!'

'Sam, you're a good friend, but Henry really must get himself out of this. I don't want to know the details and I was sparing you too. But you may as well know.' Thomas sighed and scratched the back of his head. 'There's supposed to be another woman.'

'Another woman?'

'Yes, not the last one, another one. So I am told by some long-eared owls. I don't know who, I don't want to, and all I feel is shame. I could die with shame, Sam. I was a wild boy, but not after marriage. Never. Not once. Can you forgive us all? What a wretched bunch you have married into.'

'Tom, if you continue, I shall shoot you myself! Henry don't have to accept, nor does he have to turn up.'

'Perrin will crow he's a coward.'

'So he may. But only very quietly.'

'Yes, dee me! And Henry ought to pay some price to bring his lofty snout down a bit, and his lofty appetites, too! Might bring his mind back to his marriage. What he needs is disgrace and he seems well set on course. We shouldn't interfere.'

'But what if he fights, as you say.'

'Sweet rosemary, Sam! The boy can hardly hold a straight quill! This is a ridiculous affair!'

Although it was late and dark, horsemen and carriages were moving in all directions across the rough roads and open fields between Hammersmith and London. The roads were so clogged that single horsemen, carrying the Express news, leaped the hedges and galloped over the farms with a prayer there would be no walls or ditches. They clattered through small clumps of houses, not yet villages, where the whole population stood in doorways watching the carriage lamps and naked torches moving across the countryside like an invading army by night. Horsemen thundered past brickworks and tile-kilns, where men with arms like hams were ruddy in the light of their roaring hearths.

'How is the Queen?'

'The Queen is dead!'

'Are thee sure?'

But the questions were left unanswered in the night air. The notice had been posted in Hammersmith at half past eleven.

Her Majesty departed this life at twenty-five minutes past ten o'clock this night.

M. Baillie	*Pelham Warren*	*W. G. Maton*
H. Ainslie	*Henry Holland*	
Brandenburgh House. August 7.		

Thomas had heard the rumours and uproar the night before, but would not send Will Morton all the way to Hammersmith for a frippery Queen. Instead, Will had been sent to the Mansion House the following morning, where he had been waiting since dawn for the first bulletin. It was finally posted at nine. The crowds were immense and surged forward so that constables had to keep order, pushing them back. Will was muscular and used his hard body to bore his way through the crowds, earning his share of abuse and bruises. The bulletin tied to the railings was simple.

Lord Hood has a duty to perform, and a painful duty it is, to report the death of the Queen, at twenty-five minutes past ten o'clock p.m. John Thomas Thorp, Mayor. Mansion House. August 8.

Will was hurrying back to the Blue Posts where he had left his horse, when he received a massive blow on the back, which made him whirl round, fists clenched with quick anger and alarm. He found himself staring into the grinning, squashed face of Dick Bayliss. The man seemed to be all red. The cold morning air had made his complexion the colour of sliced ham and his ginger whiskers seemed to lick round his face like small flames.

'Well then, Will, she's gone, rest her soul! I shall be seeing you again. How's Miss Ipswich?'

Will suppressed his sudden anger. 'Is that any of your affair?'

'Ho now, it might be! Young Bessie has a taking way. Now I 'aven't heard that you has any claim on her, lest you've been mighty secret with it. So me and my damsels, the choice o' horseflesh, will be back for the funeral, I'll be bound!'

'The master don't hold with the Queen.'

'A King's man?'

'He don't hold much with the King neither. A necessary evil is what he says. So don't reckon your chances, Dick Bayliss.'

'Your master can suit himself. We have been booked solid for three days in expectation. I shall take Miss Ipswich myself, if the family ain't going.'

'You'll have to ask Mrs Burges.'

'I will. Mrs Burges don't put the wind up me! Good as roast pork that little filly. Now if you is backward in coming forward, Will Morton, I don't see as how you have any right to get upset. Be safe with me, she'll be. The streets will be full o' commotion and all sorts of unscrupulous persons will be abroad. Strong supporter of the Queen, I am! Fine woman. Knew what she wanted and got it by all accounts!'

'If you talk like that, Dick Bayliss, I'll fill your mouth in with ivory!' Will was furious, and very pale. Bayliss just laughed.

'Take a joke, Will!' But Morton turned on his heel and walked rapidly home.

In the servants' parlour emotions were high. They were all agreed that the Queen was a poor unfortunate injured woman, and that George was a beast. Burges was prevailed upon to ask Thomas on behalf of them all if they might be free to attend her funeral.

'When will that be?' Thomas asked testily. 'This is all most disruptive.'

'She is the Queen, sir.'

'You know my feelings about that. Have they set a date?'

'Not yet, sir, but I believe it is to be in one week exactly, that is the fourteenth of the month.'

'No doubt it will take all day?' Burges was silent. 'Oh, very well. I shall move to my club. Monarchy is supposed to be an ordered thing, not all these scandals and coronations and dyings. Let's hope this is the last of it for some time! It is all bad for business.'

'Thank you, sir, on behalf of the domestics.'

Thomas gave a wave of his hand and Burges withdrew, silent as a shadow. In fact, Thomas had too many other things on his mind to care.

In the parlour, Mrs Burges had an audience. She was regaling them by reading from a pamphlet which Will Morton had brought back but could not read. Her own rendition was slow but full of savour.

'She is a victim of relentless persecution, she must have been more than a woman, more than mortal not to have felt her wrongs: she was a heroine and suppressed them; all but those who have an interest to say otherwise, must believe and affirm that she literally died of grief; for the disease which brought her to the grave was occasioned by the suppression of sorrow. She was forced to yield to her enemies, a blow from which she never recovered. What gave her more anguish still was the thought that her enemies would say she had yielded for money, which she cared not for; and which at last she only accepted to enable her to pay her debts. Throughout all her illness she behaved with the utmost kindness and fortitude. Her domestics were reduced to tears by it and could not be persuaded to allow her to be measured for her coffin when she desired. Her Majesty expressed her dying wish to be buried in a night-dress of her own and not a shroud. May she leave the land of her persecutors as she wishes, with the heartfelt sorrow, admiration and deepest expressions of grief and respect of her loyal subjects and devoted people.'

'Cor,' she concluded, 'don't they write long sentences!' Anything further she might have said was obliterated by the angry jangling of the bell from the drawing-room.

'Burges,' Thomas said, seeming white and tired, 'tell Morton to get the carriage out, I am going to Kensington to visit Mr Henry Kelleway. Tell him to be quick about it.'

Thomas was in an even more foul mood when he finally arrived in Kensington. He cursed Henry's folly for wanting to live in such a remote and muddy suburb. He hated the houses, with their grey and white stucco, he hated the bad roads, full of holes. The journey might ordinarily have taken forty minutes or an hour, but it had taken two as the streets were obstructed by mourners proclaiming themselves ostentatiously in their carriages, by driving up and down at four miles an hour. They affected to be deaf to Thomas's angry bellows. Many of the streets were draped with black bunting that hung dripping in the steady drizzle. Shops had dark-blinds half-drawn over windows. Lamp-brackets had soggy lengths of black cloth wound round them like bandages. Thomas kept rapping on the roof of the carriage with the head of his cane.

'This is intolerable, Morton! Tell them to move over. Let them indulge all their showy grief off the main carriage-way.' He pulled down a window, and leaning out, roared at the slow-moving traffic parading ahead. 'Make way there! Make way! Clear out of it.'

'Have some respect for the dead, damn your nerve!' yelled an elderly and irascible pedestrian. 'What are you, sir? A Republican? If I were twenty years younger, I'd horsewhip you!' Thomas beat a hasty retreat inside his carriage, as the aged man's screeching followed them unabated.

'I don't know about a Republican,' declared a well-dressed matron who had pulled alongside in her coach, 'he behaves more like a common publican!' This sally was greeted by yells of laughter and applause. Thomas rapped on the roof again.

'Come on, Morton, surely you can go faster!' he urged.

Morton was in a predicament, for despite his master's impatience, he knew that the faster he tried to force his way, the more resistance he would encounter. He wore a black scarf tied around his livery hat. Trusting to the good-will this engendered, he managed to achieve a little more speed. Perhaps it was the dismal weather, but for whatever reason, the death of the Queen seemed to have provoked a sullen and resentful mood that had communicated itself across the city. It was as though the people would tolerate no pushing or shoving or being told what to do. They believed the Queen to have died an injured woman and obscurely, all their own injuries, real or imagined, were identified with her. Authority was a bully. The King was a bully. The beggar in the street felt he could wear his strip of black and saunter down the crown of the road, flailing at any horse that tried to pass him. It was as though London had overnight passed into the direct control of the citizens, and all the careful structure of government was revealed as a puny delegated force. Will Morton felt it, and saw it in the way people walked and talked, how they would not give way for horses, for militia or police, how they booed carriages which showed no signs of mourning and tried to seize the spokes and spit on the windows. When the funeral started tomorrow, the people would be King for a day. He could feel it.

Henry was plainly furious that Thomas had made this visit. He stormed into the drawing-room, then proceeded to march up and down, pausing only to help himself to a glass of brandy. He offered Thomas none. If Jane was in, she was being kept out of the matter. This storming up and down, accompanied by snorts, went on for perhaps five minutes, although not a word was said. Thomas stood with his back to the fire and watched Henry as though he were a caged curiosity. When it was apparent that this could go on for some time, Thomas spoke.

'Sir, I have a court appearance at half past three o'clock, which I shall only just make, the state of the roads and traffic being what they are. I'll be brief. You know why I am here so we don't have to pad around the subject as though we are stalking it.' Henry stopped prowling and put down his glass. His face was white and expressionless. 'I won't dwell on what I think of it. It's without parallel in my experience. However, I am your father, and it is our name. I want to know nothing of the details. They are your affair, sir. I have thought of every possible way out of this wretched business and I have come to the conclusion, sir, that there is no way out of it.'

Henry seemed surprised and stared at his father. Whatever he had expected, it was not this blunt advice. He was in no way aware of the pain it gave Thomas to give it. There was a long pause while Henry poured more brandy into his glass, then stared at the carpet.

'I didn't expect this advice.'

Thomas merely shrugged. 'You can grovel to Perrin and apologize, and be called a craven for your pains. Then you can quit the Bar for you will be finished.' The flash of rage in Henry's eyes showed that this was no course he would take. 'Well then, you have only one course left.'

'Can we hope to keep it secret?'

'Secret!' Thomas roared, 'it is hardly a secret now with Perrin shouting all round table. Why must you make such con-foundedly loud-mouthed enemies. Can't you encourage quiet assassins who knife you skilfully and professionally in chambers? But no! You have to be the Kit Marlowe of the legal profession. We are not military coxcombs, who delight to blast out each other's livers because their dogs fight in the park. We are not politicians, who think you can solve the Irish question by removing the opposition's brains. We are members of the Bar! However, I think we can keep your meeting secret, and suspect what they may, it need never get back to the Inn. You know the risk you run? If you kill Perrin, it will be murder, or man-slaughter at least. And for your second. What right have you, sir, to involve some other friend in your affairs who will stand equally condemned under the law?'

'I do not need to be reminded of all this, sir!'

Thomas appeared to soften, seeing Henry's agitation. 'Have you a formal letter?'

'Yes.'

'He wasted no time.'

'He threatens to advertise in the Journals!'

'That must be stopped, the dee'd fool! I will see to that.'

Henry took a folded paper from his coat pocket and handed it to Thomas, who read it through in silence.

Sir,

I demand satisfaction for the outrage you have committed, in public, upon my person : I must therefore insist upon the necessity of your immediately fixing upon the time and place of a meeting at your earliest convenience. An immediate answer is expected to the above, directed to Brookes's Club House, St James's Street.

I am, & c.

James Camelford Perrin

Thomas snorted. 'How is this creature a member of Brookes's?' He gave the note back to Henry. 'Have you replied?'

'Not yet.'

'Well, I must find a venue that will not be crawling with spectators and Bow Street runners. We will have some discreet place like Chalk Farm.'

'Isn't that the place where Mr Scott was killed by Mr Christie – the two magazine editors?'

'Yes, but it is a quiet spot. Can you shoot a pistol at all?'

'No!' said Henry, very agitated.

'No matter. We must hope to the Good Lord that Perrin is no better. You had better enrol in a shooting academy, quickly. You have told Jane nothing?'

'No.'

'Then don't. No need to alarm the girl unduly. I must go, I shall be late in court.'

'I apologize for all this trouble.' Henry said it awkwardly, not meeting Thomas's eye. As he often could, he seemed at that moment extremely vulnerable.

The anger went out of Thomas. He clapped Henry on the back. 'We'll find some way out of this.'

5

When William had planned to invite some friends round for a convivial evening, it had been before the Queen was even ill. Now it had turned into a wake-night party, as he announced with some glee. Maria said it was tactless, although she agreed that as none of them gave a farthing for her, alive or dead, it would be a charade to stop it. Their company had arrived clutching bottles of brandy, and Maria who did not much care for these juvenile drinking sprees of William, tried to play the gracious hostess, hissing at him when she could get him alone. She knew the men would quickly get drunk and insist on playing the clown to the small hours. She vowed to escape upstairs to their baby, Margaret, and get to bed reasonably early. Two of the men, Jack Miller and David Carroll, had brought their newest and silliest models. Pretty and pert, they would only egg their ageing rakes to further excesses. The other men had brought their wives, or in one case someone else's wife. Maria sat beside a Mrs Lacy, a sensible matronly lady whose husband was ruffling his hair like a character from a Punch cartoon and expounding on the growth of true romantic painting. Mrs Lacy had brought her embroidery, so Maria felt free to make a strip of lace. A surprising number of paintings had appeared, from under cloaks and coats. Indeed, it seemed that no guest had come without at least one oil and a portfolio of sketches. Effie, the model with Miller, was being persuaded without much difficulty to disrobe to virtually nothing while they declared they could draw a Cleopatra of her in five minutes flat.

To increase Maria's annoyance, Miller had brought a monkey with him which he insisted on feeding a glass of brandy, proclaiming that it would then astonish them by playing the piano. Instead of which it was now drunk and hung upside down from the light fitting, snarling balefully at everyone, and pulling the women's hair. When chased off by Maria with a broomstick, it leaped at high level round the room, occasionally missing its grip and falling to the floor with a thud. It appeared to have gone to sleep on a tallboy, and no one had any desire to disturb it. Miller, a small round man with a domed forehead and very painterly beard, affected to find all this very funny and slapped his thigh, screaming with laughter. Effie insisted on doing the dance of the seven veils, her generous breasts swaying around as though possessed of independent life. The monkey leaped down from the tallboy, bit Effie on her splendidly upholstered bottom, then ran hand over hand round the picture rail, finally jumping out of the window which Maria promptly shut. The brandy was making them garrulous. They became boring and quarrelsome about painters. Carroll's model, a tall girl of beautiful proportions, enjoyed her role as the devil's advocate. Sitting on the floor smoking a cheroot with apparent pleasure, she stirred them into muddy storms about Goya through Blake to Turner and Constable. Even to Caspar Friedrich, whose work only Miller had seen and upon whom he was naturally an authority. Poor William, always Turner's advocate and never able fully to explain why, found himself under constant attack.

A terrible noise in the garden revealed that the monkey had been treed in an old apple tree by two mash-eared, tail-waving tom cats, and an expedition had to be made by lamplight to try to rescue the unfortunate beast. It evidently no longer trusted human motives, but retreated further and further up the rotten tree until the twig on which it was swaying suddenly snapped, precipitating it to the ground. Unhurt, it ran up a rainwater pipe and sat on the guttering, spitting and swearing. The girls were laughing, their clothes wet with the steady rain that had begun to fall and a huge log was pushed on the fire so that they might all dry out. The brandy was still passing freely. Maria took herself off to see her baby. It was now four in the morning. She did not bother to return downstairs, but slept badly, woken by peals and roars of empty laughter.

They were still there for breakfast, as Maria had known they would be. Mrs Lacy, a true veteran, had simply fallen asleep on the sofa with her embroidery on her lap. Effie and Miller were uncomfortably slumped in two armchairs. At least Effie looked uncomfortable, but Miller had burrowed down into the ample folds of her flesh and appeared to be asleep like a babe. Carroll and William were propped up by the dying fire, nodding uncomfortably, heads on knees. The tall girl had curled up round a cushion and was sensually asleep. Others were arranged in chairs or on the floor, according to what little comfort they could find. The room smelled of tobacco and brandy and too many bodies. 'Oh dear,' said Maria, deliberately tactless, 'did no one go home!' She was ignored, as she expected to be. The morning was grey and miserable, a persistent fine rain sifting through the leaves, through the grass and bushes. It explained why no one had stirred. Maria wondered what had happened to the monkey on the roof. Had the poor animal got off, or was it still clinging to the guttering somewhere? She pulled a housecoat about her because it was cold and started to light fires. The servants were not about yet. Wary eyes opened and watched her. Miller, unburying his head from the comfortable pillow of one of Effie's enormous breasts, swung his legs to the floor and tottered to his feet.

'Well, what a day for a funeral! A more god-forsaken, bleak, cold, wet and cheerless prospect I can't think of, except the grave itself.'

Carroll shook William by the shoulder, and was rewarded by a glare. 'Are you ready to go, old chap? We resolved we would, y'know.'

'In this weather? Be reasonable, Carroll. It's a miserable day and I have a foul head and I shall stay at home.'

'Then you will miss it, for they won't repeat it!'

'I think we can be sure of that.'

'Then it is our duty as painters. A royal funeral, a sombre occasion. Black plumes on the horses, mist, silent crowds and swathed windows, black weeds and mourning. Dripping trees weeping in the long grass. Think of the atmosphere. We may only ever see one.'

'Don't be so damned depressing,' William groaned, 'George won't last that long, will he? We all have high hopes of his going before us!'

'You will come, won't you, William?'

'I suppose I must.'

In the end, William and Carroll steeled themselves to it, while

Maria fussed round them, told them they were fools and wrapped them well in coats and cloaks.

'You look terrible, and you smell terrible.'

'We will get a cab. At least as far as Hyde Park.'

They wore long boots and Maria gave them each another bottle of brandy, freely expressing her disapproval, but glad to get them out of the house. Then she could concentrate on the others. Jack Miller should be made to find his monkey.

They were astonished by the number of people and of carriages at all points along the funeral route. People had obviously been gathering all night despite the atrocious weather. Many had kept warm on gin. Makeshift shelters had been erected under and between carts and fires burned where wood or coal could be stolen or scavenged. Hyde Park was an even more amazing spectacle. A crowd of several thousand men and women had been standing in the torrential rain under a vast, moving canopy of umbrellas. Four times this host had traversed the muddy park as contradictory reports of the route circulated. Four times they had returned to their former position.

'You see,' said Carroll, as though it was some personal achievement, 'I told you it would be amazing. They are like thousands of black wood anemones. Do you think they care at all about the Queen?'

'They think they do.'

The authorities intended to take the funeral procession into the Bayswater Road and thus avoid Piccadilly and the City itself. The rumour had circulated early and the people were equally determined that the Queen should go through the City. In Hammersmith a vigorous conflict had already ensued between the police and the people. The crowd had stopped the procession in Church Street by tearing the street up, bringing in a dense jam of wagons and carts and removing the wheels and lynch-pins. Further on they dug trenches across the carriageway, splitting open the water pipes which squirted dismally into a vast quagmire of mud.

At half past eleven, a troop of Life Guards joined the procession, declared Church Street impassable and the procession moved off towards Hyde Park Gate to the cheers of the victorious and sodden crowd. A further fracas took place at Hyde

Park Gate where the crowd slammed the massive gates in the face of the military and would not allow the procession to pass through the park, despite an exchange of threats and charges by the military, which was answered by a hail of brick-bats by the crowd, who sensed that the situation was now within their control. Eventually the procession passed Hyde Park Corner and entered Piccadilly as the crowd wished. Here, William and David Carroll had managed to force their way among the crowd on foot, to see what was happening. Piccadilly was completely blocked by men carrying banners and with their own bands playing solemn and discordant music. They had made their chosen route impassable.

'This is fantastic!' said William, 'the funeral is a shambles. The people have decided what route she shall go!' From the crowds there came a steady chant, that rolled like a rumbling growl, 'the City, the City!'

'Look at those mechanics and Benefit Societies,' said Carroll. 'See what they intend to make of it. The authorities have entirely underestimated things!' Carroll sounded excited, and his eyes were gleaming. He was becoming infected by the general air of truculence. 'You see,' he declared, 'they are like an army that scents victory. They have the whole support of the people.'

The men carried their banners and their slogans. There were carpenters, coopers, leather-dressers, brass-founders, weavers, masons and representations from fifty or sixty other trades. They stood in solid, steady ranks, each man with a black band round his arm. 'Power of Public Opinion,' proclaimed one banner, 'Friends of Humanity,' 'United We Stand,' 'Justice will Triumph.'

'They are formidable,' said William, 'nothing like this has been seen in London before.'

'It was the same at Spa Fields. You were not there?'

'No.'

'Hunt, the orator, was there. The crowd was enormous.'

'It is like Peterloo.'

'I hope to God not! Unless the crowds give way, there is bound to be trouble. The authorities are fools. How can they prevent these people unless they resort to force!'

Unable to advance along Piccadilly, the procession tried to

double back and turn up Park Lane, but this was now as effectively barricaded as Church Street. Hundreds of carts seemed to be spirited from nowhere, set in the mud and turned on their sides. Spades, axes, picks and buckets were used to throw up fortifications. There were now several hundred Life Guards and Oxford Blues along the route, trying to clear the way. Swords and pistols had both been drawn. The situation was extremely dangerous as the mass of milling humanity seemed unable to move in any direction at all, and was being compressed by the horses. Women were screaming and striking out, but for the most part the crowd was still good-humoured. Insults and cat-calls were hurled at the militia who made a show of flashing their weapons, particularly the Life Guards, unloved by London crowds. The civilian authorities quickly discussed their plight with the military and decided they must again attempt to move down Piccadilly, where the crowd would have them go. However, at this moment, reinforcements of five hundred cavalry entered Piccadilly from the far end, blocking it even more effectively than before, and once in, unable to retreat.

Another return movement to Hyde Park was attempted. This further hesitation was too much and a great yell went up. Mud and stones flew at the militia from all sides. A troop of dragoons was sent at full canter up Park Lane to see if they could break down the barricades and provide a route, but here real fighting broke out. Many soldiers were wounded by bricks and stones, and several civilians received sword cuts. The line of carts was so well emplaced that it could not be removed and the dragoons were driven back. The procession would have to proceed through Hyde Park itself, the only route left. William and Carroll found themselves swept forward by the crowd as it surged up Park Lane parallel with the funeral route in order to gain command of Cumberland Gate before the military should get there.

'Take the gate! Take the gate!' They found themselves running with the crowd, because it was impossible to do anything else.

'Stay close!' William yelled as Carroll was becoming separated in the heaving, yelling mob. Shoulders and bodies bruised him. He was unable to see what happened to Carroll but was pressed on. There was an unwavering sense of purpose about the crowd as though it communicated with a single mind. There were no leaders, no commands. This seemed to make it even more frightening. As ants move, noiseless to us, so these soaked thousands converged on the gates at the north end of the park. The gates were rapidly seized and slammed shut with a triumphant roar that set the dragoons' horses skittering and dancing. They gripped their sabres more tightly. As the military gained Oxford Street at the head of the park, unarmed men, ordinary people, dashed from the crowd, seizing the bridles of the horses, pulling them round to turn them back. The dragoons beat them off with the flats of their sabres, or struck them with the back.

'Good God!' yelled William in the direction he had last seen Carroll, 'this is a lunatic fantasy! Why do the military insist on forcing the route!'

'Because they are bastards!' snarled a man beside him. 'The Life Guards are bastards!' The man hurled a brick he had been carrying, but William could not see what effect it had.

'The City! The City! The City!' the people chanted. A strong line of troops had been drawn across Oxford Street and were being murderously pelted with brick-bats. Thirty yards of the park wall had been torn down and was being used as ammunition. William heard an order to charge being yelled, but before he had time to move he was struck hard across the head with the flat of a sword, bowled over and trampled on by a horse. All around him men were cursing, kicking, punching and throwing things. Women screamed and fought. The dragoons laid about them with the flats of their sabres, occasionally cutting at a persistent offender. For the most part they showed great restraint, as William saw many men struck from their horses by bricks and cobbles. He crawled under a hackney coach, where there was already a crowd. A man fell with a sabre cut across the upper arm. Immediately a shout went up.

'The soldiers are cutting down the people!' This statement became a yell of blood-curdling anger. William felt his head and found he was bleeding profusely. Of Carroll there was no sign. He saw a black cloud of missiles rake the dragoons like grape-shot, knocking men straight out of their saddles where they lay unconscious on the cobbles. They held their ground, however, making no further attempt to press the people back. The bombardment of missiles grew worse, as though the crowd had had time to reinforce itself, or saw the stance of the dragoons as weakness. At that moment the order to fire was given. This produced a stunned silence followed by panic, but the first volley was in the air. William tried to wrap a handkerchief round his head to stop the bleeding, as he could hardly see.

'You all right, mate? Let me tie that on,' said a gruff voice. William half turned. A man lying beside him in mud-spattered working clothes was holding out his hands.

'Thank you.' He gave the man the handkerchief and felt the clumsy hands try to knot it as best they could.

'That better?'

'Yes, thank you. You're very kind.'

'Not at all. Them bastard Life Guards. It weren't the Oxford Blues.'

A second volley rang out. There were yells and screams. People fell. 'They're shooting!' a voice yelled.

Suddenly people scattered, and the dragoons were left with the ground to themselves. At least two bodies seemed lifeless. Others were dragging themselves along the ground. A man was screaming. At a command the dragoons cantered off in the direction of the procession, and the crowd in one motion absorbed its wounded into itself. There was blood on the streets and on the pavements.

'I should get out, mate!' said William's gruff friend, putting his own advice into operation and running off up a side-street. William crawled out from under the hackney, feeling weak and dazed. He realized that the dead weight in his coat pocket was the bottle of brandy that had somehow remained intact throughout. He opened the door of the hackney, sat on the step and drank about a quarter of the bottle. He congratulated himself on his foresight. A suffused, blinding warmth spread through him, that made his legs quite powerless and his mind quite easy.

'You can come with us,' a voice seemed to bellow in his ear. His head felt like the whispering gallery of St Paul's. Words rolled round, rattled, rotated. He tried to see who was talking to him, but found he was already being propelled, or seemed to be in a state of motion, pinioned by the arms.

'Who are you?' he managed to ask.

'Bow Street Runners. You are under arrest for making an affray.'

He was flung into a long covered wagon, constructed entirely of wood, with barred slit windows It was black as a chimney inside and smelt horribly of urine. He fell over legs, felt shoes, knees, rough, sticky hands, and shoulders. Eventually he felt the firm roughness of a wooden seat and managed to pull himself on to it. Beside him, a woman was sobbing quietly in a way that allowed of no consolation. It was like the last crossing to hell, he thought. Hands reached out in the darkness and wrenched the bottle from him with a low laugh. Some eyes were accustomed to the dark. His head felt as though it had been cleft in two like an apple. It reminded him of Maria's botanical drawings.

'For making an affray. For making an affray. An affray.' The phrase echoed in his head in a confused babble. He felt suddenly very angry. By God he would make an affray! He staggered to his feet.

'Let me out of here!' he yelled, with what he hoped was a commanding voice. 'If you don't you will regret it! Let me out this instant. I'll kill anyone who stops me! I have made no affray!'

The covered wagon jolted forward and William slammed down in a heap. His last conscious thoughts were confused – the unkind laughter of his fellow passengers, wondering what had happened to Carroll, wondering what he could do for Walter Manning that would be original, wondering about the monkey on the roof.

Thomas was unable to isolate in his mind what it was about Caroline that had altered since they last met at the Coronation. She had come to visit him, bringing him the news of William's arrest. He had at first been angry, swearing it was no more than he deserved, and that he would lift no finger to help. Caroline had not argued or protested or wheedled. She had listened to him as though he was a tired old man beyond sense or reason, and this irked him more than he would reveal. Accompanying this, there was about her an air of confidence, almost of indulgence. She seemed to have ceased to care for him, although nothing she said made this clear. It was rather a form of withdrawal. She seemed well, physically, with none of her previous faintness. He also sensed there was a new and different awareness between them, operating on a different plane that Caroline found embarrassing. He recognized that he had always accepted without question that she was his daughter, flesh of his flesh, blood of his blood, but there was about her now a glass wall. The thought seemed uncomfortable, almost incestuous. He felt there was a strong rejection of his role as father.

She was a new demanding person, less tolerant. Yet when he covertly looked at her, over and over again, she did not seem to have changed. He realized, however, that the daughter had gone, she was more a woman and a wife, and this was his incestuous embarrassment. He should have seen it years before. It was part of his overbearing selfishness. Why was she more a wife? There was no overt reason for such a change in role. He must have more detailed reports. He had no news that she had a lover. What secrets was she keeping from him? A wave of self-pity overtook him. Was she not truly responsible for looking after him? He had no woman, and though he knew the thought was wretched and inhuman, it was Caroline that had killed her mother. Such thoughts bear no conscious examination, but they lie dormant in the ground like seeds awaiting their season, which is madness. He felt that he wanted to weep. Was he not of an age when he could weep? What is appropriate in infancy is appropriate in age. He could not keep control of his family without Caroline, and now she had gone too. His court work was suffering. How could he be expected to stay on top of his cases while his family caused him such concern? He would never make the Bench. It required a dedication that all these demands on him were destroying. Now there was Caroline, who should have been the prop to his old age.

Caroline stood by the long window with its heavy satin drapes, looking out on to Regent Square. There was always some movement of horses or carriages. Children played on the roadway or in the square, but their voices did not travel. She was thinking about children and the extraordinary nature of her own fertile womb. It was like hugging a sack of ripe corn, assured of a future, of fruition. She was still afraid. Life could mean death, but that was a long way away, and Maria had said she would explain more. She had never considered that men carried seed, were no more than pods, waiting to explode into the moist fertile secret dark of her womb. It was the carrying of another life that seemed to her such an extraordinary thing.

She had become reconciled to relationships outside herself, to the importance of her life of Thomas, Henry, William, Maria, Charles Ware. Their furtherance had seemed a purpose of existence, and now they all meant nothing by comparison with what was within her. She must be cautious. It was a change so dramatic that it must show. She almost laughed. It would show before long. She watched skinny boys climbing a tree, slithering on the bark, spitting on their scraped legs and rubbing them. Her centre of existence had swung right off course. These children were important. Her brothers, her father, they could manage their own lives. Then she realized it was not so simple, and that concern should span all ages. Thomas could not simply be cut off. He was dependent. He was a boy with skinned knees, especially now. She wondered how and when she would tell him. She could not wait long. Staring at the railings reminded her again of William. She tried again to treat William's plight with proper levity. She could not, for if he were found guilty the sentence would be transportation.

'Father, you must make an appearance at the prison. I am sure that if you see the magistrate you can explain he was an innocent bystander.'

'I will not pervert the course of justice. No one there at that place, at that time, could be a wholly innocent bystander. William is a fool. Turpentine is a poison. I can only think it has got into his blood. I *cannot* interfere on his behalf, don't you see? He must live his own life and suffer the consequences. There is no good in his manner of living. These artists take it upon themselves to think it an escapade to join in insurrection. No. He is lucky his skull was not split. It might have been better for us all.'

'You do not mean that.' She turned from the window and went over to him. She did not, however, as he expected, put a hand on his shoulder. This hurt him and made him angrier yet.

'A simpleton could have seen the funeral was to be used by the mechanics, reformers, combinations and malcontents.'

'The people wanted to see the Queen.'

'The people wanted to spit on the King and the monarchy. The people want a Republic. The people want to break machines, defy order and rule the country! The people are so far-sighted that it was necessary to keep more troops garrisoned in this country during the wars with Napoleon than ever fought him, in case the people in their wisdom rose up and destroyed democracy!'

'This has nothing to do with William.'

'But it has! He and that wife of his, they are full of these hare-brained ideas. But they don't work at looms. They preach the honesty of toil. Would to God he would break his pictures, and do the world a service!'

'Father!' There was a long silence. Caroline remained immobile.

'Anyway, I shall not get him out.'

'I will not ask it of you.' Thomas looked up, surprised by the tone of Caroline's voice. 'You are quite right, it is none of your affair. We can only be children for so long, and it seems we have been playing that game for an intolerable time.'

'Caroline, you can't speak to me like that.'

She heard in his voice the petulance and helplessness of a small child. Against her better judgement she put her hand on his shoulder. He seized it with his dry old hands as though he were receiving a transfusion of life.

In Newgate, William felt so ill he wished profoundly he was dead. He was hunched on a stone slab that seemed to suck the warmth from him as though it were the grave itself. He clasped his head in his hands. The blood-soaked handkerchief had now adhered solidly to his scalp. His head pulsed with pain. The babble of the prisoners was like spikes being driven into his skull. One man, either mad or drunk or both, continually leaped to his feet screaming gibberish, until he collapsed again, moaning. The cell was dark, which was a relief, lit by only one barred window in the massive walls. His mind had ceased to function, and he was resentful and angry when a hand tapped him on the shoulder. He looked up angrily, to see the blood-caked face of Will Morton, the coachman.

'Mr Kelleway, it is you, I wasn't sure, sir! It's me, Will Morton, your father's coachman. I am sorry to see you here . . .' William moved over and motioned to Morton to sit down. The man looked terrible and his teeth were chattering uncontrollably. His livery coat had disappeared apart from the sleeves, which somehow remained from shoulder to cuff. His face was cut, dark coloured and obviously bruised. 'I got kicked by a horse, then beaten,' he said in explanation, seeing William's glance. 'It looks to me, sir, that you got the worst of something.'

William struggled out of his heavy cloak, an effort that took a long time and hurt his head.

'No, you keep it, Mr Kelleway, sir, I couldn't take that.'

'Nonsense.'

William thrust it at him and Morton quickly drew it round his shoulders. They sat in the dark, listening to the moans, growled conversation and vomiting of the prisoners. The smell was appalling and William felt his stomach heave.

'My God, what a smell!'

'They swab it out during exercise.'

'You seem to know about it.'

'I have been here before, sir. For nothing criminal, begging your pardon, but for being part of a procession. Much like today. What are you doing here, sir, if you don't mind my asking? Your father must get you out!'

'Who are you calling "sir"?' said a menacing voice from the dark. 'Who have we got in here, then? What nice little trifle?'

'A gentleman who is wounded!' said Morton with more vigour than his condition showed.

A figure loomed over them, shapeless but menacing. 'A gentleman with a purse or a watch, my friend. A stock to be buzzed? A throat to be cut?'

'Don't be a fool!' said Morton quickly. 'He was cleaned out before ever he got here. Cut down he was, by the soldiers!'

The man grunted in a surly way, but seemed satisfied, disappearing again into the dark.

'How did you know about the soldiers?' asked William.

'I guessed. This place is rotten with thieves. They put us all in together. There's everything in here, shallow coves that stand in rags and stare in bakers' windows, magsmen, disaster-men, screevers, Hindoos doing shallow and selling tracts, white men dyed black and pretending to be slaves.' William stared at him in amazement.

'But what are all these?'

'Beggars, thieves. Men who smear their legs with poison so they swell up, then expose them on the street, lucifer-droppers who blunder in front of well-breeched gents and drop their wares in the gutter and get paid ten times over, pot thieves, till thieves, burglars, pimps, bankrupts and people like you and me, Mr Kelleway. Distressed scholars, decayed gentlemen, old soldiers, forgers and coiners. Men who steal washing, lead, copper, tools, ladders. Bug-hunters and muchers who strip drunken men and leave them in the cold to die. It's not the sort of sight that a gentleman often sees.'

William was appalled. 'But are there many of these people?'

'Thousands. Thousands who never work nor never have any intention to. You never see them, sir, for they take care to keep low. They pretend to be out of work weavers from Manchester or Bolton, but they come from Whitechapel. They buy tracts saying how their jobs have been taken away by the machines, but they have never seen steam except from a kettle. They look on us servants with envy. We are balanced half-way, you see, between gentlemen, honest labouring men and themselves. They are the enemies of the working man, but cry they are the downtrodden poor. They confuse the public mind so that the general cannot tell the difference between the honest poor who are dying and the criminal beggars who live off rich steaks and porter. When the working man is out of work it is advertised by articles in *The Times* and all the other journals giving the news. Before the day has passed, these beggars are tramping the streets claiming to be the victims of this latest disaster, even if it happened a thousand miles away. The public can always be relied upon to be fooled. The real victims, Mr Kelleway, starve where they are.'

'How do you know all this, Morton?' William enquired in a low voice.

'My brother truly was a weaver, sir. In Bradford. I had a brother-in-law was a sailor. He had his right leg blown off when the *Indian Prince* exploded and sank. They take the stump, sir, still bleeding, and thrust it in a bucket of bubbling pitch to seal it. The real poor cannot afford a copy of *The Times*. There were people on the streets of London within three hours of the publication of the news, who had all lost limbs, and had red painted bandages to prove it! It took my brother-in-law five days to get cleared and shipped from Ostend, and there was no mortal charity waiting for him nor anyone wanted to know. They said *he* was the beggar, and his stump was oozing, sir. He died, God bless his soul, very painfully nor never complained. And these beggars, sir, made much out of it. My brother has not the fare to leave Bradford, so he must starve where he is, yet I have seen these beggars wandering the streets of London with placards round their necks for which they have paid twopence, advertising that they are him. He lives in a basement where the sewage oozes through the walls and has lost five children with cholera. He is an honest man who would never beg, but by God, sir, he will be breaking frames rather than starve. The Owners must give way, Mr Kelleway. Honest men are being made into villains and villains are prospering and will no doubt be representing themselves as honest labouring men. The honest men are dying where they lie. When the soldiers or the tars land at Chatham, I guarantee you see no soldier-beggars or sailor-beggars for forty miles. The sailor boys would kill them, sir. Truly, it's a fine sight to see the jack tars clear a tavern or two. But who will do the same for the weavers, the spinners, or the lace-makers? Them as has the news first always puts it to best advantage, and they're the most undeserving. The truly afflicted are always too late.'

William could find no words. He reached out in the darkness and put an arm around Morton. 'You are a good man, Will,' was all he could find to say.

Will Morton instinctively moved away, and William felt it and was hurt. He did not understand that Will was simply embarrassed. William was a master and he was a servant. He felt the distinction should be maintained.

Caroline had taken her carriage direct from Thomas's house in Regent Square to Henry's in Kensington, a long drive made worse by the condition of the road which was cratered and muddy from the funeral and rains. She assumed that Henry would be at home because of her knowledge of the state of his business affairs, but was quite prepared when she arrived to find that he was in chambers.

She was pleased, therefore, when she was told that he was at home. She was shown in to the drawing-room where she found not only Henry but Maria. She should have guessed, she realized, that Maria would have been of the same mind, and with her urgency have got here first. Henry took her arm at the door and brought her over so that she could sit beside Maria on the divan. Caroline felt no embarrassment, as she had feared she might at a re-encounter, and certainly Maria displayed nothing but warmth in her welcome.

'I'm so sorry, Maria,' said Caroline, 'this is a dreadful thing to happen. Have you seen William? Is he all right?'

Maria snorted. 'No he is not all right. And he has only himself to blame. He has a crack on the head, but it will mend soon enough. It is only his scalp.'

'He could have been killed.'

'Yes,' said Maria simply and soberly, 'he could.'

'The behaviour of the military was terrible. I hear they were brutal and completely out of control!'

'The behaviour of the civilians was hardly exemplary,' said Maria drily.

'I suppose that you are here, doing what I came to do?' Maria looked questioning. 'To ask Henry if there is anything to do to get William out.'

'Yes. And he thinks there is.' Caroline decided she must not tell them about Thomas's refusal. Maria might take action and visit him.

'Do sit down,' said Henry. He seemed pale and abstracted.

163

Caroline thought he looked unwell. He was tense and even more formal than usual. 'Jane will be joining us shortly. Can I offer you tea? Any other refreshment?'

'No, thank you,' said Caroline, 'I had tea with Father.' There was an immediate silence, and Caroline blushed as the other two stared at her.

'I suppose,' said Henry, 'that you sought his help?'

'I'm afraid I did. I hope no one is angry with me? He is a senior man and I thought he might carry weight.'

'And he refused.' It was a statement, not a question.

'He has all sorts of principles about these things. I walked right into them. Yes, he did refuse.'

Henry nodded. 'Well, I'm not surprised. I expect he'll come round, but we don't have time for people to readjust their principles. I have no doubt that I can have William released on bail. In fact we were just about to set off when you arrived.'

'But that is marvellous. How can you do that?'

'I shall apply to the magistrates. There is an Inquest being heard today on one of the poor devils who was shot and killed, a Richard Honey, at number four Edgware Road. Now I know from the legal buzz in chambers this morning that Alderman Waithman has instructed the reporters of the newspapers to report the proceedings with great accuracy, lest it should appear advisable in view of the evidence to have recourse to a Court of Justice in the event of a verdict of Wilful Murder. That being the case, they must release William pending the decision of the Inquest, as it may be the military who will be on trial for attacking and killing innocent citizens. They have no grounds for holding innocent bystanders who have been subject, it may prove, to an attack by soldiers.'

'They say they were making an affray,' said Maria.

'The Inquest is open to decide that the militia got out of control, and it is open to the jury to return specific verdicts of murder, or manslaughter. They may indeed return it against the regiment of Life Guards if no positive identification of individuals can be made. In the circumstances, I shall press the magistrate that such a verdict is not only possible, but almost inevitable. There is a nice legal point, in that it is claimed that the Riot Act was read. Well, the reading of the Riot Act in no way permits the soldiers to fire on the people, but only gives them powers to apprehend. William was not even apprehended by the soldiers, but by Bow Street men. I cannot see that he is held within the law at all. The only defence that counsel for the military can offer is Justifiable Homicide, but in view of the strict meaning of the Riot Act, and the fact that no person fired on the military or attacked them with specific weapons such as swords or knives, I don't think much credence will be given to it.'

Henry, Caroline suddenly realized, never having seen him in his legal capacity, was absolutely master of his facts. He could have had little time to consider the matter and she was impressed by his reasoning. She was still concerned about his pale, almost sickly appearance. He was never very animated, but he was at the moment distracted by something. His brain was functioning well enough, but as a reflex, separate from his emotions.

Jane entered. The two women went through the ritual of affectionate greetings with her, remarking on the terrible affair of William, the strain it must be on Maria, and the clothes they all wore. Henry, never patient, strode up and down with rude energy.

'Your Henry is clever,' Caroline effused, aware that she was being crude about it, but feeling that poor Henry deserved some praise in front of his wife.

'Yes?' Jane sounded less than convinced. It was a mean response that Maria quickly covered.

'He has shown us how he thinks he can get William out on bail. It sounds clever to me.'

'The law is designed to sound clever in order to fool us all.'

'But, Jane,' Caroline remonstrated, 'Henry has such a good idea!'

'I'm very pleased for you, Maria. I hope it is successful. I cannot imagine what it is like in Newgate.' Her oblique responses were obviously going to continue, so Maria got to her feet.

'I'm sorry if we seem to be rushing off with ill-mannered haste, but we must hurry to the magistrate. While we sit here, after all, poor William is in a filthy cell full of common criminals.'

Caroline and Maria strolled up and down on the drive, waiting for Henry who was collecting his papers for the magistrate. Jane had been left on the divan as rapidly as was civil. Neither of the other two women had in the circumstances much patience with her weary depression.

'Caroline,' said Maria with a certain timbre in her voice that must, Caroline knew, precede a certain question, 'have you told your father yet?'

'No. It did not seem very opportune.' They walked on for a full minute.

'But you do intend to, don't you? If you feel nervous, then I will come with you.'

'Maria, I am a grown woman. I can manage my own affairs. I will choose my moment.'

'You do realize he will be terribly upset, whatever the moment. He will be desolate. Forgive me for pointing out the obvious, but as his only daughter, he will see it as an assault upon himself first, and worry about you afterwards. That is the way men think in these circumstances. You must expect his vilification rather than his help.'

'I don't think I expect anything else. Please, Maria, don't tell anyone on my behalf. It is my business, and I will attend to it. You have been a great help to me, but any more help will not be help at all.' Maria was surprised. Caroline spoke with an authority she had never heard before from her. She must reject us, she thought, to come to terms with it. She feels she is going to be rejected from now on. Caroline continued. 'I don't mean to be rude. I'm sorry. I don't know how to explain this, but now that I am two, I feel I have the strength of two. I don't care what others say, Maria. If Father is desolate, I cannot help him. My position is more difficult than his and if he is so selfish that he cannot see it, then he must stand on his own feet and bear it. I feel that he is the child that I am trying to protect and I am the adult. I think it has always been so. I would ask all of you to look after him, that is where you can help.'

Maria was impressed by Caroline's strength and determination, but knew that Thomas would take it very ill. It would be better for Thomas that Caroline collapsed and went to him in tears. However, he would only repossess her and what Caroline was doing was right.

'Of course, we'll all help. But you must tell before long. It is beginning to show.'

William's release was effected as Henry had said. The magistrate granted bail with good grace. Perhaps he too was shocked by the action of the military. Not knowing about Will Morton, Henry made no application on his behalf. William was most upset, and at first said he would wait in the cell until Henry had returned to arrange his bail. But Henry was very short about that.

'Your wife is outside, William. Your gestures are superb but selfish. She is very worried about you. Get out of there and look after your duty. Morton, I will arrange your bail on the way back, you'll be out by this evening.'

'Yes, sir. But I don't mind if I stay in. I have done nothing wrong.' There was laughter and obscene comment from the cell.

'I'll have you out, Morton, whether you like it or not,' said Henry in a low voice that only Will could hear. 'You needn't tell this rabble.'

He went quickly, with William propped on one arm, the bloody handkerchief still stuck to his scalp. Outside, Maria, sitting in the carriage, quickly gathered him to her, and set to work with a flask of water for his external wounds and brandy for his internal warmth.

'How are you?' she asked solicitously.

'Awful,' said William. 'Tell me one thing that has been worrying me all this time. What happened to the monkey?'

Maria hardly appeared surprised by this. 'The poor thing died.'

'I somehow thought it might. It has been preying on my mind. How did it die?'

'Rest,' said Maria firmly. 'Never mind about that.'

'But I do. It is somehow mixed up in my mind with the soldiers. Miller and the monkey. The soldiers shooting. People and things dying. It is callousness. How did it die?'

'We don't know. We didn't find it until the late morning. It was lying in the parapet gutter, all its fur soaked. It probably died of cold.'

'Animals lose all their heat if their fur gets wet,' said William, as though very wise.

'Yes, William, I know that.' She wrapped clean linen round his head. With the motion of the carriage he fell deeply asleep.

It was five in the morning. Only the pigeons stirred, flurrying ahead of the small party as they approached on foot, then settling to graze, then flurrying ahead again. They had had to leave the carriage in Primrose Vale and were taking one of the footpaths crossing the fields, Thomas riding on a horse. Far away in the woods of Belsize Park and Highgate, crows grated away. It seemed unnaturally still, as though the world waited for them. Henry was terrified. His stomach was troubling him and he was concentrating on not being sick. He felt he wanted to urinate all the time, but knew he did not. He had gone behind a hedge earlier to produce a mere dribble. He began to understand how troops must feel before battle. He was shaking and felt very cold. His one desire was to get it over and done with. The fields were sloping grassland, interspersed by scraggy hedges of thorn and may. It was, he thought, no place to die; but then battlefields are not places of scenic beauty. They are places of advantage and disadvantage.

The two other men who trudged behind Henry were his second and a surgeon. Thomas was acting as the other second. His second, Drummond, a barrister from Middle Temple who had long been a friend of the Kelleways and almost as long an admirer of Caroline, called a halt, and passed round a great flask of brandy from which they all drank readily. Even then, Henry noticed, Thomas fastidiously wiped the lip. He was slightly puzzled, for a great calm had descended on Thomas. He had the inward-looking attitude of a mendicant friar, glued to his horse and lost in satisfying contemplation. There was no trace of the irritable intolerance Henry had expected. It seemed that once he had accepted the idea, he faced it with great calm. They moved on. Drummond carried the case of pistols. Henry tried not to look at them. They were now climbing up a steep slope to the top of a ridge, and as they reached the summit, Henry saw them. Down below, a little group of four stood like executioners, each in black and apart from the others. Each quite still. Henry's heart jolted and he stumbled over a tussock. He steadied his tread. Drummond put a hand on his shoulder. 'No hurry, Henry. You'll break into a canter!'

No hurry. There was no hurry to be maimed or die. No hurry to have a lead ball tear through his stomach or bowel, shatter bone, or mercifully blow out his brains. They were plodding downhill now and he could identify Perrin. He wondered if Perrin was as scared as he. Even a man without imagination must have a racing pulse, a fevered system. Thomas and Edward Drummond went forward and two of the dark figures with Perrin advanced. His seconds. The fourth man, after a moment's hesitation, went over to Henry's surgeon, and they apparently greeted each other. They whispered in low conversation. Henry presumed they were discussing what they should do in case of varying eventualities, what instruments they had brought, where they should attempt to operate. He felt he would soon retch, and belched air. He stared at Perrin who had not moved. In the faint light at that hour, he could not read the man's expression, but he appeared to be attempting a haughty calm. The men were only twenty-five yards apart. Drummond and Thomas appeared to have finished with the other seconds. Drummond had unlocked the pistol case and given it to one of them. The man took it to Perrin, who glanced down as though it were some trifle and picked up the nearer pistol. Drummond then returned, with Thomas, to Henry and held out the case.

'Here is your pistol, Henry. They are prepared.'

'Be of firm spirit,' said Thomas, 'he will almost certainly miss. Stand firm, and above all take time. Haste in these things is no good at all. Let him fire. Do not let him think you are flurried. Would you rather have to stand there and wait for him to fire, having discharged your own? Don't give him the satisfaction, by Gee. Remember what you have been told. Bring the pistol to eye level and at arm's length. Let him fire, then take your time.'

'I may have no time to take.'

'Nonsense. The man could not hit a house.'

'The rules,' said Drummond, 'are that you are to retire ten paces from each other, then may discharge your pistols at your discretion. There are no people about and no sign of Bow Street men. The surgeons have instruments, wads of lint and all things necessary. Come, Henry, let me shake your hand. Good luck. Thomas will take you forward.'

They shook hands and Drummond retired. Thomas clapped Henry on the back, but gently, with affection not heartiness.

'Don't worry,' he said, with such calm and a voice of such conviction that Henry looked at him sharply, trying to understand. 'Come with me now.'

They walked forward and stood so that Henry faced Perrin at close range for the first time. Perrin was white and swallowed. His Adam's apple slid up and down beneath the skin of his throat in an involuntary way. It was like a living animal darting up and down.

'You will now retire ten paces and fire at your own discretion. On the count of three, gentlemen, and not before, you may commence.'

God help me, I am here. It is happening and I do not really know what is going on. A babble of thoughts spilled through Henry's brain. He concentrated on taking the pistol-grip firmly. His finger felt slippery on the trigger. He prayed the seconds had checked the flints and pan. 'Three!' He had not even heard the first two counts. Automatically he turned and walked, counting the paces. As he did it, he thought how stupid it was that they did not simply drive in two stakes for them to shoot from. At a time like this he should not be bothered by arithmetic. Eight, nine, ten. He turned, without undignified haste. Perrin turned slightly later than him. Henry looked at Perrin with a foolish feeling of the ridiculous. He must now raise his gun and shoot at the man. The situation was absurd. A crow flew by, he could see it over Perrin's head. He had a wild notion to shoot at the crow, but Perrin had raised his gun and Henry realized he was staring straight at the barrel. At twenty paces it seemed absurd that they could miss. Perrin was slightly turned, almost sideways to him, shooting as a professional marksman stands. Henry shuffled his feet round and raised his weapon, realizing he must look a complete incompetent. He was surprised he should have such a thought. He was concentrating on the muzzle pointing at him. His whole being seemed to have shrunk as small as that muzzle and he lived in parts of seconds, waiting for the puff and report that would mean the other man had fired.

Seconds passed. Henry's arm shook. He found it difficult to keep it level and steady. It kept straying sideways as he kept his eye on Perrin's gun. Perrin was holding his fire! He was waiting for Henry. This revelation gave Henry a strange exhilaration. He would never fire first. He realized that his nerves were firm enough, and that fear and nerves are not the same. The brandy he had swigged belched up his nose, and the back of his nose and throat stung with acid. That was fear. That was an animal reaction. He felt like shouting to Perrin, asking him what he was afraid of, why he did not fire. At that moment there was a loud bang. Perrin was obscured by a lazy puff of smoke that formed a ring then started to dissolve. It took Henry conscious effort of thought to realize he had not been hit. The miraculous had happened. Perrin had lost his nerve, now must stand his ground. Henry continued to aim, seething with feelings of relief. He felt like throwing his pistol away and sobbing. Yet he kept it there for five seconds then suddenly pointed it into the air and pulled the trigger. The explosion surprised him, jarring his wrist. His ears rang, for he had held the pistol close to his head when firing. He could see Perrin was animated but could not hear what was being said. Some sort of argument was going on between Perrin and his seconds, and Thomas and Drummond had now joined in. The surgeons remained at some distance, carrion crows no longer required. He simply stood, glad to be alive. After some more arguing, all the seconds shook hands and Thomas came over to him.

'Well done, Henry. Come on, by Gee, we're going home. Where's the brandy, Edward?' Drummond produced the large flask and Henry would have consumed it, but Thomas took it from him. 'We have still to walk back to the carriage.'

'What was going on?' enquired Henry.

'Oh nothing,' Drummond replied abruptly.

'What was the argument about?' Henry demanded with quick suspicion. 'Don't think you can keep it from me.'

'Perrin was demanding another shot,' said Thomas, 'he said

you should continue until one man was hit. But we have agreed that honour is satisfied. You have fought according to the proper rules, and what he suggests would involve us all in deliberate and callous crime.'

He mounted his horse and they set off back down the path. The birds were singing now. Henry wondered if they had been awakened by the shot. He found himself hoping they had not been disturbed before their normal time. The beauty of the chorus almost overwhelmed him and he realized there were tears in his eyes. He had drunk more brandy than was wise.

Thomas, astride the horse, was the only one present who knew the pistols had been loaded with a wadding blank. So much for honour, he thought, a thing for popinjays and fools whose lives are worthless anyway. Honour is the best excuse that man the animal can invent for the instinct in some members of his species to kill. He supposed the large part of those who were not of the labouring classes would be scandalized if they knew what he had done. It only proved what fools they were. He had no regrets and would do the same again without hesitation.

'You did well,' he said gruffly to Henry, who was concentrating on walking straight over the grassland that seemed to be heaving.

'I don't know how he missed!'

'Couldn't hit a house! Told you.'

It had not looked like that to Henry.

Although William's release from Newgate had been effected promptly, Will Morton had had to wait longer. He stepped out of the studded wooden wicket in the main gates into the London dawn at the same time as Henry was slumping into the carriage at Chalk Farm Tavern. Will Morton was elated. The landlord at Chalk Farm was gravely disappointed, for no one had been carried in and there was nothing in it for him except five guineas for Nelson's eyes.

Will had no money. That had gone when he was knocked senseless. The crowd may have been busy with the soldiers, but not all of them to the exclusion of business. He had lost one shoe as well, and this was a major nuisance. It had not been stolen, he realized, or else he would have had neither. Wherever a crowd had been routed, he thought, there are always people and shoes on the ground. The walk home took him by choice along Holborn, past Middle Row, the entrances to Barnard's and Staples Inns and up Gray's Inn Lane. He enjoyed the irony of his situation, being a resilient and thoughtful man. He had so often clattered this way in full livery, remote as a god. Cattle and flocks of sheep, strangely alien in the narrow streets, were jostling and slipping in Holborn on their way to West Smithfield. Will had never seen this before and stopped, fascinated. It seemed that all London's food was on the move. Cattle on hoof, pies on trays, bread on carts, vegetables in wagons and on barrows, milk in hand-trolleys with churn-shaped tanks. The cattle bellowed, the sheep bleated. A few last words before the executioner's knife. It seemed ludicrous to Will that this rural intrusion should batter its way through these city streets with their fragile bay windows and overhanging gables, be-spattering the pavements and doors. The poor beast would end up in illegal shambles in the cellars around Smithfield, murdered with long knives.

Will took the paved roads to make it easier to walk on his unshod foot. The last bit of going was painful and bruising, for as he neared Regent Square the road was of hard gravel, broken flints and round stones like cobbles. He limped down the steps into the area with a sense of relief and triumph. Once in the servant's hall, he was treated like the returning prodigal. Crabtree and Burges tried to retain some order, for the preparation of breakfast was under way, but it was no good, they all wanted to hear his story. But despite his sense of security and comfort, Will sensed that there was a current of alarm in the attention with which he was greeted. It was as though they hoped to distract his attention with solicitude, to conceal something from him.

'Where's Bessie?' he asked. He had not seen her. There was an awkward silence. 'Where is she? Out for the milk? Too early.' This, it seemed, was the matter they were at pains to conceal. 'Tell me then!' he demanded in a voice that rose in inflexion. Burges was trying to hand him a pot of ale, an obvious diversion which he ignored. He felt a sudden alarm and looked from face to face, only to find that they avoided his eyes. Mrs Burges assumed authority.

'Sit there, Will Morton, you are in no condition to move.' To the others she said, 'Everyone get on with their work. The master still expects his breakfast. Will's back, you've seen him, and he's well. We'll have a little talk, and I want no one lingering about by the door. Are those knives ready yet? I thought not. They never are. Burges, we are behind hand!'

Mr Burges, who seemed inured to this form of address, nodded mildly. 'Yes, my dear. We should get on.' He ushered them all out of the room while panic mounted in Will's mind. Mrs Burges was too quick for him, for she spoke before he could frame a question.

'Will, we are all servants and must behave with a decent dignity and propriety. You are very lucky to be rescued the way you have, for you have brought shame on us all. Do not mistake curiosity for approval. We are all very happy to have you back, but the master has been very sullen and silent about it. No, don't interrupt! You remember the night of the Coronation! I had occasion to speak with Miss Bessie for her stupid behaviour and going out dancing to the fiddle and such things as a girl should not do with strange men. Well, she has done it again, and has put an end to herself.'

'What do you mean! Killed herself?'

'Oh don't be stupid, Will Morton! Put an end to herself in service in this house. She left this house, like some other foolish persons I could name, to go to the funeral. And like some other foolish persons, she fell in with bad company. All arranged is my opinion. She has brought us a disgrace, for she never came back till morning, and even then was not sober and smelling horrible of gin. Do I have to tell you any more?'

'Where was she?' Mrs Burges stiffened and looked hard-lipped and prim.

'We was not interested in the whole story. It is not for a respectable woman to repeat. She was with that low creature Bayliss, and I shall say no more, for I find it too difficult. I told her she was a stupid girl, but did she pay any attention? She never intended to. The long and the short of it is the master dismissed her. "Mrs Burges," he said, "I will not tolerate this sort of behaviour. The servants must realize it brings disrespect to the house. The girl must go immediately." So she has been dismissed and gone.'

'Where has she gone?'

'How should I know? Was I to go with her to see her right? She took her things in a bag and has gone. Maybe back home to Ipswich. We won't employ country girls again. They have no . . . well, I won't say it. I am telling you special, Will Morton, for I always reckoned you had a fancy for her. Well, she ain't worth it. She's not good enough for you. Pretty little thing, and bound to catch at a man's heart, because they is always such fools over looks. Takes away their breath like a kick from a horse. But you see where it gets them and you should consider yourself lucky, that's what Mr Burges says . . .'

She went on, repeating, dissertating. Men are fools. Country girls can't be trusted in big cities. Will was no longer listening. He was stunned. It was too much after coming out of Newgate. Troubles were heaping upon him. How could he trace her? Bayliss, he thought with hatred, he will know about this, one way or another. He found himself contemplating with satisfaction what he would do to the man with the crushed nose. In an abstracted way he realized that this was all wrong, this murderous violence. It was what the crowds and the soldiers had done to each other. It was sickening. Yet he would do it. Bayliss was a big man but he was not afraid. He would find some way of catching him unawares. He would not be fair with Bayliss. Honest men made into villains and villains prospering. He remembered what he had said in the cell.

The maroon coach with cream lines arrived without warning. Caroline had been sitting at her desk, watching the sun slanting in on the carpet and doing those boring but necessary chores of the household that Mrs Loudon must pass to her. She was checking the housekeeping books and making a list of orders to go to Highgate merchants and shop-keepers. The sun made patterns that distracted her, for she was too ready to be distracted. When she heard the coach stop she got up in immediate panic and went to the front window overlooking the lane. She felt a certainty that was immediately proved right. It was Charles Ware. She had read but not responded to his last two letters so had inevitably brought this upon herself. Aunt Helen must be got rid of for she would be sure to linger in the room, trying to look distant but bright as a city sparrow. She would miss no word or nuance and what she and Charles Ware had to say to each other could tolerate no overhearing. Caroline felt frightened and the confidence that had been so much a physical part of her over these last two weeks seemed to have deserted her. She must not be embarrassed. It was desperately important that she should remain cool and aloof. She felt that she was blushing and wished she could will herself to stop. She tried to make her mind blank, to forget how she had been used without understanding, and how he must have known. When she saw him momentarily as he left the carriage and walked to the door, she felt outrage. Outrage at him and at men. At her father who had used her, then bought his release from guilt. At this man who had knowingly used her body, aware of the consequences of what he was doing, impregnating her without her knowledge or consent with his seed.

She had had time to think about it. She must not be dishonest. She had experienced a desire to be touched and kissed by him. What they were doing had been of a sexual nature and she had known that, but no more. She was not disgusted now, as she had been at first. She was angry. Not with a hot rage that would burn itself out but with a cold rage that would endure in unforgiving hostility. That her liberty from Thomas should be brought to such an abrupt end at times seemed to her intolerable. Then she thought of the child, and saw it not as a burden but as another liberty. In its freedom she could express herself. She felt quite calm about it. But she must have the child. It was hers by right. It had been introduced into her by stealth. She heard the raps on the door downstairs. Three knocks, heavy, with a pause between them. Even this suddenly irritated her. It was both ponderous and pretentious, drawing unnecessary attention to the act. She heard Loudon let him in, a few words, then Loudon came up the stairs. When he entered, Caroline was back at her desk again.

'Mr Ware to see you, Miss Kelleway.'

'Who is that?' It was Aunt Helen who had appeared at the door.

'Mr Ware, ma'am.'

Caroline stood up. She felt that she would be better standing after all. 'Show him up, Loudon.' When he left she turned to Aunt Helen. 'Aunt, you must stay and meet Mr Ware.'

'I had every intention of doing so, my dear.'

'But I would like you to leave us so that we can talk. I have no time to be tactful, Aunt. Forgive me.'

'I had every intention of leaving you, although I hope I can trust you together.' Her eyes were amused, coy. She assumed they were at the start of a romance. Or did she? Aunt Helen was no fool. Did she guess anything? Caroline could not tell. 'Don't worry, Caroline, I shall be discreet in retreat but shall want a full account of it afterwards.'

Steps came up the stairs, and Ware entered the room, trying, Caroline realized, to look purposeful. He looked crestfallen when he saw Aunt Helen and was not able entirely to disguise it. His strides shortened to a more normal walk. Caroline felt that he looked absurdly theatrical in the deliberate way he behaved and decided that she would view him as in the theatre, from the safety of a box. Ware politely shook hands with Aunt Helen, wishing her good afternoon, and repeated the performance with Caroline, looking hard at her with what he evidently considered was a bold expression. She divined that it was intended to convey passion, determination and manliness. She wondered if he practised in a mirror, like girls practise smiles.

She felt quite unattracted to this man whose seed she carried. On the surface she supposed he would pass as handsome. He was big, well-built, well-dressed, with fair hair and grey eyes. He would have looked magnificent in uniform, she thought, but his cheeks were too rosy for civilian clothes. He looked too much like an elderly boy. Yet he was only nine years older than Caroline. His mouth, when she considered it, while he still muttered about the weather and the roads, was perhaps too narrow, a sign, they always said, of meanness. He was a country squire inserted into the clothes of a London buck. She looked him over dispassionately, aware that he was now embarrassed. There was about him a too-fastidious neatness. His boots were spotless, his trousers uncreased. He even sat with the care of a woman, arranging his coat and trousers to suit the cut of his cloth and not his comfort. That was unnerving in a man. He had been a bachelor too long.

'It is a fine day to be out on the road,' he was saying, apparently to both of them, puzzled by Caroline's distant air. 'It would be a good day for walking.'

He had been divested downstairs of his hat and coat, but was still carrying his silver-topped cane, an omission he seemed only now to recognize and which threw him into momentary confusion. Loudon rescued him by stepping forward and relieving him of the object, an act that Ware seemed for the sake of dignity not to notice. Caroline wished that he had. It would have been more human and could even have been endearing. Loudon slipped discreetly away. Charles Ware addressed himself to Aunt Helen. He turned to her, physically, his feet shuffling round, so that his back was to Caroline. The snub was a petty reminder.

'I trust that you are in splendid health after the waters at Bath?'

'Have you ever been to Bath, Mr Ware?'

Charles looked taken aback. 'Yes, madam, but I found it very crowded. I did not find the waters to my taste. Quite the contrary. The sea-bathing at Brighton is quite the thing, with chariots that run right into the sea.'

There was even something about his phraseology that Caroline found pedantic. She had not noticed how affected he was, how he lacked any fluent turn of phrase and answered in pleasantries even when more was asked of him. Aunt Helen laughed.

'I doubt whether the waters are supposed to be to anyone's taste, Mr Ware. I certainly have no great taste for other people's bath-water, for they say it leaves the bath straight for the pump-house tap. I would not go out of my way to put a toe in it. As for Brighton, a respectable matron like me cannot be seen there. Good heavens, Mr Ware, the ladies and gentlemen, as they call themselves, slip into the water without garments and are none too particular how they come out. I am surprised at you!' Aunt Helen was teasing him, but Charles clearly did not know it.

'I did not mean to suggest that you should indulge in that, madam!' Charles protested automatically. How artificial he sounded. Caroline moved impatiently towards her desk, for ill manners are easy, she decided. Shrewd Aunt Helen took the hint smoothly.

'Caroline, I will leave you now if I may. Forgive me for being so abrupt, but I have affairs to attend to.'

Aunt Helen smiled and left them. They were alone. Ware studied the carpet thoughtfully. I am, the action said, measuring my words, eliminating trivial matters. You are, thought Caroline, going to be pompous.

'Caroline, you must know what brings me here?' Caroline said nothing. 'I have written to you twice and received no reply. I take it that you received my letters?' Caroline nodded. 'Then why did you not reply?'

'I did not reply because there was nothing I wished to say.'

Ware did not seem hurt, but puzzled, and puzzlement did not suit his face. Instead of looking intense or curious like leaner men, he looked bovine. Nevertheless, Caroline was painfully aware of her heart thumping; she was beginning to feel ill and had to swallow. Ware stepped towards her and put a hand on her shoulder. She did not move.

'Caroline, tell me what is the matter?' His voice was coaxing and the question seemed to run round and round in her head like an echoing whisper. Could he really not guess, or was it all a bland pretence? She understood the duplicity of Thomas, but did not think she could deal with this. How could she explain and would he understand or deliberately fail to understand? She thought, quite coolly, of what Maria had said. This man and she had done in a time of passion that 'dreadful thing' the tea-table gossips so loved to whisper about. Old ladies with crabbed faces, limp skin and viperous tongues. What did he remember? Was it just one of many encounters? Perhaps it was nothing to him, although it had pleased him enough at the time. Caroline, what is the matter? I am with child, that is the matter. What is the matter? Love is the matter, care, concern and understanding, not demands and thanks for pleasures. What is the matter, Caroline?

He stooped and tried to kiss her but she moved away, hearing him tut like a schoolmaster. The sound annoyed her violently. It was petty and mean. His responses were so inadequate. They had always been gallant or polite but not direct. She wished she could turn and accuse him – the pointed finger and the tongue of scorn – but knew she never could. She was trapped by the lie of silence that women must maintain, pretending they have no memory, no past images. We will not remember the bed, the deranged clothes, closed eyes, the hands, the weight of his body, the awkward pauses while he tore at his clothes, the fear and panic, the failure to realize her pain, his noises of pleasure that sounded gross and animal. What is the matter? He had left her utterly bewildered. He had been tender, wanting to kiss her body, too personal, and she had cried, apologized, dressed and sat and drunk tea. He had been polite and gallant, called her his love, kissed her at the door when they parted and all the time he had known and she had not. It happens all the time, it is how life goes on. What is the matter, Caroline?

She felt him come closer and kiss her on the back of the neck and shoulders as she stood still as a statue. His arms were round her waist, his hands reaching upwards to her breasts, those brown-stained breasts spreading their goodness and richness, not for him but because of him. Even knowing this, feeling revulsion, she could not push him away. She could marry him, it had been done thousands of times. He had said he wanted to marry her and she wanted to be cupped in a man's hands, her whole being cupped and the being within her, to give them both safety. When he began to caress her, she immediately moved away, and with bitterness she heard the same tutting noise, petulant and selfish. She stared out of the back window over the green fields and hawthorn hedges to the black scar of London. It looked like debris from the Great Fire with only the white spires of churches and the dome of St Paul's rising from black remains. The dome was a breast. The mother nourishment of the Church.

'I wrote that I wanted to see you. You read my letters. You know you love me, Caroline, let yourself. Don't torture me with this silence.' Poor me, the voice said, pity poor me.

'I read your letters, but felt I could not reply.' Her voice was firm.

He seemed genuinely surprised. 'Why not?'

'Because of what has happened.'

'Caroline!' He used this exclamation to step forward and

attempt to take hold of her again, caress her, extinguish her thoughts, transform her into the thing he wanted. All this was clear in her mind. She wondered how she could marry him, feeling as she did, or if it was important. She supposed not. A marriage of convenience like so many others. It would give the child respectability. She turned to him with decision. Ware was red-faced and looked uncomfortable but whether from irritation or suppressed passion it was difficult to say.

'I have not replied because I am in no position to reply.' She searched for tactful words, for the harmless euphemisms, but knew there were none. 'I am with child.'

Ware stared at her, his face slowly becoming pale. His mouth hung open like an idiot. His eyes began to dart about as though seeking some escape. She found that now she had said it, she was impersonally calm and able to look him up and down and examine him as a prospective husband, an extension of herself or she of him in name at least, if she could bring herself to love.

'Are you sure?'

'Certain.'

'Then I must marry you. Of course. You have nothing to worry about, my love. What sort of man do you think I am?'

His protestations continued but the scales had dropped from Caroline's eyes. Those awful, predictable words, like doom. Are you sure? Then I'll marry you. If you're sure. Then, only then. The gentlemanly thing. We can arrange it tidily. The child will be born in wedlock. He showed neither joy nor horror, made no attempt to put an arm around her, smile or comfort, but explained, explained it would be all right. Are you sure? Then I'll marry you. There seemed to her no more chilling words to express lack of love than that bleak question and response.

'No, I will not marry you,' she said. She interrupted what he was saying, but she had not been listening to it in any case. She did not intend the statement to be as bald as it was, but she desperately needed to interrupt his flow of platitudes. His mouth shut tight and his thin lips seemed all bone, like a fish. 'You don't love me,' Caroline continued, 'let us not play games. What happened was just an incident. I thank you for your gallant offer, You have said all a gentleman need say. There is no need to continue further.' She knew how cruel she sounded, but she felt cruel, in defence of herself and her child. She would decide their future, not this man. 'I want this child and I have money and a family who will help. I want you to know that you are free to go, that I want nothing from you, and that I don't bear you ill will. I hope you understand. You only think you should marry me because you think it is what you should do. We should both regret that forever.'

Whatever Ware had been expecting, it was not this forceful and reasoned rejection. It was outside his knowledge of female behaviour. Tears and lamentations were expected. To indicate his concern at her confusing reaction, he sat down heavily on the divan, shaking his head. Caroline thought it would have been more appropriate had he asked her to sit, been solicitous, frightened of her in this novel state, as she in a way was frightened of herself. It confirmed her suspicions of his selfishness. It was a declaration that he wished to remain the child. She wished he would go.

'But Caroline, if I do not marry you, will you forgive me if I spell out what the consequences will be? What about your friends and family. You will be seen to be disgraced. I will have disgraced you!'

Her instant anger at this unthinking insult gave her a feeling of dissociation. 'There is no part of me that feels a morsel of disgrace. You have disgraced yourself if that is how you feel.'

'I did not mean to upset you ...'

'I am not upset,' she replied untruthfully, moving towards the front window. He was fool enough to believe it.

'Well, then, we ought not be talking about things like this. We ought to be planning, being logical ...'

Logic, thought Caroline, is an unhappy substitute for love. Outside, ordinary people were moving about their business, with or without love, with or without marriage. Behind her she could hear him tutting at her inattention. He was pursuing his theme of logical persuasion, almost as though he knew it was the surest guarantee of abrogating the courses he proposed. In the street a carriage passed and a bandy black dog darted out, snapping at the heels of the nearest horse. The horse, town-wise, paid no attention. The dog returned to its doorway, dejected. It lived to dart at coach-horses and it never seemed to have the sense to give up. One day, she thought, it will be kicked or crushed, but it has no notion of that. Perhaps Charles Ware lived in much the same way, with no notion of the consequences of actions until they occurred.

'I want the child. I have a right to it.' The words were flung at her, a spear in her turned back. The impact of what they meant had the desired effect. She turned to face him in sudden fear. It was a thing she had never contemplated. The child was hers, enfolded within her, she told herself in panic. He had no right any more than a thief who also takes by stealth. Yet at the same time she knew that her emotions were wrong in law. What he said was true. She must appear unruffled or he would press the point. She thought of the black dog rushing out to snap and going back again, dejected. She could not deal with it cleverly, for she did not know of any answer. She must react by instinct.

'I would rather you left,' she said in an even voice, that she managed to keep low and normal. 'I have said all I have to say and I would much rather we did not prolong the discussion and make it unnecessarily painful.'

'Caroline!' Ware got to his feet. Even in this action he straightened the tails of his coat and tugged at his waistcoat to straighten any crease. He came towards her attempting an appeal. The dog was darting out again. She neither moved nor avoided his gaze. The gaze was not impressive. Seeing her attitude, he stopped, slapping his hands hard against his thighs. He was very angry.

'Very well, but this cannot be the end of this conversation. I will give you time to think of your legal position, and the position of our son. I have, I think, made my position clear and behaved with propriety and honour as a gentleman. You have rejected me. But the child is ours, Caroline, and you may not reject me on that count. I ask you to think of that. Take advice from your family. I will make it plain I wish to marry you. You will see.'

He was angry and, she noted, there was spite in his voice. Again she was surprised, for it had not occurred to her that she might not be the prize. That this bluff, fastidious and angry man might want a child. Did men want children? Had that been his purpose? That was a fantasy. These were more questions for Maria.

'Yes, you have behaved correctly,' she replied, 'but I shall not change my mind.' She admired her own mendacity. Thomas would not think he had behaved correctly. How could these words release anyone but a child from the responsibility of their actions? She felt a fierce but exhilarating anger at his words that was more powerful than mere rage. It was combative and, she realized, ruthless. Charles Ware glowered at her, red-faced, tutting with a sharp irritating noise. It was like the alarm cry of a blackbird, click click, or two pebbles being rapped together. He would fly away.

'Then I will let myself out. I will give you time to consider that I repeat my offer of marriage.'

Caroline wondered if ever a proposal of marriage had sounded so grim. Why did he sound so much like a man thwarted from completing a contract? How dare he give her time to consider, as though she must weigh the terms in the balance. 'Thank you,' she replied politely.

He made a curt bow, shook his head in an uncomprehending way, tutted again and was gone. She heard him thumping heavily downstairs, in an exaggerated way, all part of the act. She had a momentary pang that he had not kissed her cheek or at least her hand, but it was unreasonable because he did not know that she intended this to be their final parting. Going back to the window, she stood where she was concealed by the lace curtain. Ware walked quickly to the carriage, not stopping to look back. It was strange, this union with a man that provided them with an inseparable bond although she was indifferent to him. In the street, he meant nothing to her. Aunt Helen took her by the elbow before she realized she had entered. Caroline jumped. Aunt Helen shushed her as she might a child. 'There there, my dear. There there!' Caroline realized she had been listening throughout. 'Everything will be all right. Don't be upset.'

'I'm not upset, Aunt Helen. I'm glad you know. Please don't ask me any more just now.'

'Of course not, but you should have told me, you silly girl. Aunt Helen will look after you.' She sounded quite delighted at the prospect and not at all reproving as Caroline somehow felt she should be. 'We must tell Thomas, you know, there will be arrangements to be made.'

'Arrangements? I don't understand.'

'A little holiday.'

'I am not going away from here!'

'There there, my dear,' said Aunt Helen with transparent insincerity.

6

William started the journey to Buckingham like a child on its first outing. Clearing London by the Bayswater Road, the carriage rattled through the villages of Acton and Uxbridge by the turnpike road to Aylesbury. He soon tired himself by hanging on to the seat while craning from one side of the carriage to the other, his copy of Cary's *Roads and New Itinerary* on his knees.

'*Amersham*, on r. is The Rectory, Rev J. T. Drake; about 1 m. on r. is High House, Capt Windsor.
1m. beyond Amersham on l. Shardloes, T. T. Drake Esq. Just thro' Amersham on l. The Dowry, Mrs Drake.'

The list was endless as he strained his eyes to catch glimpses of masonry, or rows of trees. He felt he ought to try to absorb the countryside. It seemed to be singularly flat and dull. Excellent for farming. The carriage rolled past unheeded farm buildings. Cary's *New Itinerary* showed no interest in mere tillers of the soil, only 'The Country Seats and their Possessors.' It was all very grand. He wondered how Manning could fit into this. How would it feel to be excluded? What did one do to be considered the possessor of a country seat? It made him realize that he was a Londoner and foreign here. He reflected that even the cows looked different. His experience of the animals was confined to the wretched beasts stalled in the cow houses of the city dairies of Saffron Hill and Liquorpond Street, shut up without light or proper ventilation, tethered at all times except when eventually led to slaughter. He had sometimes seen the more fortunate beasts from gentlemen's stables that were led daily by servants through the London streets to graze for an hour or so in Regent's or Hyde Park. They too were tethered and docile. The cows he saw kicked up their heels at the sound of the carriage and cantered alongside it on their side of the hedge, snorting and tossing their heads. He hoped he would not be expected to do anything for animals. He thought of the wretched monkey that had sat on the roof like a gargoyle.

The carriage took a small turning off the turnpike, which became almost immediately a yet smaller track. The thorn hedge and briars scraped against the coach and the wheels felt soft in the deep mud. There was no roadstone here. They were lucky the weather had been dry or the horses would have been in trouble. The day was sunny with banks of racing cloud that made dramatic effects across the fields of ripe corn. They suddenly came upon reapers. They seemed a huge gathering in the deserted plains of corn. It was alarming, like suddenly coming upon a secret army and not being sure of their intentions. There must have been only thirty, men, women and children, but they seemed a multitude.

A line of men, perhaps a dozen of them, moved in an oblique row across the field, swinging scythes with rhythmic skill. Larks made a din, disturbed from the field. With each delicate stroke the sun flashed briefly from the blades and the corn toppled over quite gently, as though it had been surprised. The fearful sharpness of these long blades with such a lethal caress made William feel chill. The men looked up at the passing carriage but did not break their rhythm. Behind them, women and children gathered the corn into sheaves, tying each one with an expert twist of stalk. They showed slightly more curiosity, but never hesitated in their job. Faces turned, but hands remained busy. They were inexorable in their purpose. A carriage had no meaning to them, not being 'Possessors of Country Seats'. Had he rode in a hay wain, they would have paused in their work.

Suddenly they were out of sight and he was deep among trees and green hazel hedges that arched over them. Green light filtered down reluctantly as though it were a struggle. It was suddenly cold and William imagined it must be like this under the sea. It seemed hostile and oppressive. He had the feeling that the vegetation was bearing down on them and he was glad when they burst out into the sunshine again. Behind its evident beauty, he felt, there was something frightening about the country. Association of ideas? The reapers, death and darkness? The sinister tones that lurk in Claude and Poussin where mankind seems poised in an idyllic moment immediately preceding destruction. It was his fanciful mind.

He suddenly saw the house. It was brick built and situated on a slope of no great elevation. Alongside the shimmer of glass indicated a conservatory or greenhouse. The carriage lurched suddenly, throwing him against the window so that he banged his forehead, and they turned sharply through a Doric arch connected on one side to a squat gatehouse. The carriage stopped. William could see the way ahead was barred by a high solid gate that would have protected a castle. The coachman was shouting to a man who appeared, giving his name. The man had obviously been caught eating his lunch, for he was still chewing as he opened the gate. William was surprised that it should be shut. They passed through onto a well-made drive and the wheels rattled smoothly, throwing off mud. They passed through flat green parkland studded with mature trees and William was able to see the house properly.

It consisted of a large central block with two wings and gave the general impression of having been designed by three different architects. The central block was very flat-faced but relieved by a central portico supported on stunted Doric columns of stone carrying an overweight pediment. The whole looked as though it had sunk bodily into the ground. It had obviously been grafted on to the façade at some later date. The wings and façade were rendered, the rendering stopping short at the gable-ends to resemble stone quoins. The gable walls and rear of the building were in the brick that was visible from the road, which revealed that this had once been a much simpler and more pleasing house. The wings, in newer brick, were another addition. They ran out at forty-five degrees from the main building, creating an awkward space in front and an ugly view from the rear. The plinth of the building was executed in mock ashlar work, stepped in two stages with a splay. Gothic details, William noted, mixed with Greek at an Italianate angle. It was an ugly house, the front unsoftened by creepers or roses. The pebbled drive stretched right up to the walls.

'Well, what do you think of it? Neither fish, flesh nor fowl, eh?' While he had been staring about him, Manning had appeared and was half-way down the steps of the portico with a footman behind him. He had deliberately spoken before William should turn and see him. They shook hands, Manning very cordial as though determined by physical exertion to raise the warmth his house lacked. 'The grounds are equally undistinguished as I'm sure you noticed. You see my problem.' He indicated, with a stiff little jerk of his arm, the grounds before them. He still seemed glowing and shiny, his clothes as tight as before, his stock wound round his neck like a bandage.

Grassland stretched away and down from them, without perspective or any feature. It was undistinguished by woodland or water. The small wood through which William had passed before the gatehouse was too far to the left. In the far distance the fields were yellow with corn and William imagined he could see the flicker of light from scythes. There was nothing. No church spire marking a distant village, no nearby houses. Well, he thought, it is as clean as a new canvas. He wondered if Manning had bought the place simply because it had no character. Was he so uncertain of what he liked that he preferred to buy anonymity?

'It is rather flat,' said William inadequately. He realized that Manning was bouncing from toe to heel and was very excited.

'Come in then. You've come a long way and must be hungry. I'm a poor host to keep you out here. You must watch out for me, or I shall bully you, remember!'

His head nodded up and down with the pleasure of remembrance. William was touched. He must be a very lonely man. He followed Manning inside while three servants appeared to take his baggage. There were only three pieces, so they processed with it with undue pomp, complete in livery and wigs. Manning obviously intended everything to be done in style. William pretended not to notice but thought that he would have to restrain Manning, or his taste would run to the vulgar. The servants wore padded calves.

After they had dined well, Manning suggested that they might take a tour of the grounds immediately around the house so that they could walk off dinner and exchange ideas. William readily agreed, for Manning's eating explained the constriction of his clothing and William was not accustomed to it. The interior of the house had been a pleasant surprise for it had been untouched by the builders of the exterior additions and they had eaten in a pleasant room with a fine mantel and good plasterwork of the 1780 period. Their progress round the house was necessarily slow, for Manning puffed a lot, and stopped frequently, as though to admire a particular aspect, but in reality to regain his breath. William could not help noticing that Manning wore boots that shone like mirror-glass and that he stepped daintily to avoid dirtying these. The grass was dry, but the earth soft in places. They retreated from the house some four hundred yards. William was wondering how to frame his questions on cost and intentions, when Manning spoke.

'I know it is early, and I said I would not influence you, but I have a vision of what I would like to look back and see here.' He paused hesitantly, as though expecting William to stop him.

'Yes?' said William encouragingly.

'I detest as I'm sure you do, Mr Kelleway, the degenerated repetition of formal gardens that is the curse of this country. They are foreign to us, a product of the austerity of imagination of the French and Dutch, who do not believe anything is good unless it can be set out with a square, compass and dividers. They must have symmetry at all costs. I will not have symmetry at any cost. I want no display of magnificent dimensions where my gardener can display his knowledge of geometry. Rousseau said that the grand air is always melancholy, that man's little-ness is but increased. Now William Kent understood that. I have an admiration for his work.' He stopped suddenly, as though he had shown altogether too much of his hand.

William was fascinated. 'Please go on,' he encouraged, 'this is all a great help.'

'Kent's tools were perspective, light and shade. Where anima-tion was wanting, he supplied it by means of buildings, temples, summerhouses, paths, water, trees, walls. But he went too far in planting dead trees and decay. I like Repton's work. I like ruins. But none of this funereal decay. No mausoleums, no mutilated inscriptions, urns, weeping willows, yews, sepulchres, cata-combs or cemeteries laid out for dogs and cats! Make me some-thing with water. Moving water. I like the sound of it and the sight of it. Here there should be some point of emphasis, some structure. Perhaps a canal leading to the house. A bridge. A boat that I can use. A garden house in which I can study or simply sit. Rustic, enchanting but no melancholy. I do not like the Grecian style. It is the style of tombs and death. Make me something romantic. The house is hard. Soften it for me. I hate the Grecian front. Remodel it. I would like a maze, with arbours. A garden as the Elizabethans had gardens, for pleasure and amusement, not for philosophical gloom.' He mopped at his face with his kerchief. His eyes were sparkling and he was obviously excited.

William was infected by his mood. 'Then we can have galleries, roofed with green vines, outdoor banqueting rooms in the same manner covered with hops, woodbine, musk rose and cucumber, walled arbours and garden houses, labyrinths and mounts that you can ascend to see the way out, surrounded by water in which you can fish, and hollow within, with curious grottoes, water . . .'

'Yes,' declared Manning, 'that is the sort of thing! And perspectives to quaint towers that you can ascend to catch other vistas, views. A camera obscura with a window slit and mirrors . . .'

'We can have a scent garden. You must shut your eyes and be guided by the fragrance. You walk on crushing camomile, guided at intervals by lavender, sweet briar, wallflowers, white violets. We will have strawberry leaves to walk upon, and matted pinks, and clove gilliflower . . .'

William stopped abruptly and both men fell silent. They were equally embarrassed by their own outbursts of enthusiasm. Manning was deeply touched and was struggling to conceal it. This communicated itself to William who paced away a short distance as though assessing the view. He was troubled at finding such deep emotion in his client, for it meant his expectations would be high. He hoped he could live up to them. He walked back to Manning casually.

'Well, I must get on with my work! There will be a lot to be done. I must first make a survey and then start to work up some rough ideas. It will be quite a task.'

'Please do not be embarrassed, Mr Kelleway,' said Manning,

ignoring William's dissembling, 'if I say to you that I think you are the person for the task.'

William wished he felt at all confident. Manning was now walking on as briskly as he could. They were heading back to the house. That is enough of emotion, his manner said.

They retired to the drawing-room with the french windows open onto the sparse gravel that served as a terrace. They could hear the restless settling of late crows, like a quarrelsome household. Far off, the scream of a fox made them both start, then nod agreement. A fox. It was still and the candles ran no wax, consuming themselves in their mysterious transformation from matter into light. Manning was still tightly dressed, a prisoner within his self-imposed strait-jacket. Or was it armour, William wondered? They talked with restraint, almost with reserve, as though they were afraid they should become too open and emotional again. They both seemed to understand with instinctive delicacy that this was a shared secret. Whereas for William it might be commonplace, for Manning it had been a frightening experience. He had revealed the soft flesh within his carapace.

Manning offered brandy freely, which William for the most part declined. He wondered how much use Manning made of it, for he had seen him drink only one glass of wine with lunch. The bottle steadily emptied, yet it had no effect on the man.

'I have a brandy in the evening,' he had said. William wondered what this warded off in the night. Did he sleep badly? A footman stood motionless at the door, perhaps ready to renew the bottle. William wondered why he did not dismiss the man, for another of Manning's habits was always to be accompanied by a servant in the house. That there was no lady Manning, William could only arrive at by deduction, for the subject of family or kin had never been mentioned. He guessed the man had been married, for the furnishings of the house had not been assembled by a man preoccupied with business. Their present arrangement he took to be Manning's work, for objects stood in unexpected places, much as though the men who had removed the furniture had been told to put it in such-and-such room and leave it.

'You see.' Manning was pointing to the last gory streaks of sun that lit up the clouds. 'Death of a day.' This melancholy thought was delivered as a commonplace. It was true there was no beauty in the sunset. It looked like grey rock banded with red sandstone, the lower strata an unpleasant red.

'What will it be like tomorrow? What version of the rhyme do you believe?'

'Fine, I should think. My gardener told me I should listen to the crows. They are much more knowledgeable about such things! Whatever their use, I don't like crows. Unpleasant birds. Anonymous and with no charm. How are your portraits, Mr Kelleway? I confess I regard them much as I regard crows? Am I a barbarian?'

'No.' William laughed. 'At the moment I am working on "Ivanhoe", and I must be honest and say that I like it.'

'Is it for the Royal Academy?'

'Yes. Although it is not finished, it has been well received so far.'

'Well, it is just the fashion. I have no sense for fashion myself. Is it exciting?'

'Both exciting and romantic. Full of colour and chivalry. No more dull portraits. But there will be many others along the same theme.'

'You make it sound like a manufactory.'

'We have to sell in the market-place, too! You should attend. There might be things there that would take your fancy.'

Manning gave this proper thought. 'I might, Mr Kelleway. If there are real delights.'

Further conversation was interrupted by the crunching of footsteps on the gravel outside. Two men dressed in livery paced slowly past the open window without a glance. Their steady tread and sense of purpose puzzled William.

'Your servants work late or walk late.'

It was not the correct observation for a polite guest. Manning appeared confused. He pointed his shiny shoes.

'They go round the grounds,' he finally said. 'I suppose I must tell you and should have told you sooner. I told you I was never an Ottoman, but I was an Owner. I have had my troubles, and made my enemies. I mentioned it to you. I am not a violent man but have been confronted with violent forces. Wheel-breakers, loom-smashers, armed men. They gain in strength. Rick-burners and frame-breakers. They would not let me bring in the machines. They burned down my mills, destroyed my nail shop and iron foundry. I cannot expect you to understand any of this, Mr Kelleway, but can only ask you to believe that I paid the best wages I could and needed the machines to survive. Cobbett's men distributed pamphlets and these people who were once trusting, honest labourers became a mob. They were chained and fettered. Many were flogged. But still the pamphlets circulated and they sowed ideas that sprang up as monsters.

'You will remember the meeting at Spa Fields, but I think you will know nothing of what happened in the north. In 1817, the whole of the country seemed as if it would go up in flames. On the ninth of June, three hundred men from Derby Peak gathered with scythes, bludgeons and guns, marching to Nottingham demanding arms and support. They were quarrymen, stockingers, iron workers – my men. They killed a farm servant who would not open the doors. At Nottingham they were scattered by Hussars. In Holmfirth, hundreds of textile workers rose the same night, incited by Radicals and traitorous sheets – the Black Dwarf, Reformist's Register, and scurrilous lampoons. They said they would fight for Liberty, that their liberty was secure, all England was in arms and that the rich would be poor and the poor rich. That was their deal. They were dispersed by a few shots. Of the Derby men, thirty-five were arraigned for high treason. Ten lawyers prosecuted, only two were there to defend thirty-five men. I have no love for rioters, but there was no justice in it. There was a spy among them, for which I suppose I should be grateful, called Oliver. Brandreth and the other leaders were hung. They were not even allowed their "last words" on the gallows.

'Then there was Peterloo, about which everyone knows, but in between there were the small battles, skirmishes, deaths, hangings and brutality. Some of their leaders were fine men. All this, Mr Kelleway, was in the normal way of business. London prospered and shut its ears to what was happening. The nearest it got to it was in the House. After Cato Street, when they executed Thistlewood, Ings and the others, we had more trouble. In Scotland the banner went up, "Scotland Free or a Desart". We expected them to invade and unite with the Yorkshire men. They marched in Barnsley, hundreds of them, but nothing happened and they dispersed. They burned my mill that night, for it was strongly barred and they could not get in to break the looms. Men were killed. We did not shoot, the building fell on them.' He stared out at the sky which was now black.

'Then I had to leave. Until then they agreed I paid fair wages, but the prices were dropping, I could pay no more!' He turned to William, his face glistening in the candlelight. He seemed to be pleading for judgement. William could think of nothing to say that would comfort the man. He could think only of his life in Chelsea at that time. Manning might as well have been speaking of Peru. 'So a sentence hangs over me. It was not my fault that the wall collapsed!' Manning suddenly got to his feet and walked rapidly up and down before the window. 'I told them to get back, I warned them. They were unable to see the danger, the weight of the machinery and the beams. I shouted to them and they fired at me with muskets! They were throwing timber and carts into the flames. It all came down.' He stopped suddenly and mopped his brow and neck. 'Have some more brandy, Mr Kelleway. I apologize for my lack of manners. But I warned you my eyes were scarred.' William declined, but Manning poured himself a large drink and sat down again. 'So now I must surround myself with servants I hope I can trust who will protect me, and salvage something of pleasure and beauty from my life if there is anything to be had. Do you see now, Mr Kelleway?'

'I see,' said William, 'but only like a child.'

He lay for a long time awake, listening to the night sounds, hearing at intervals the sound of feet upon the gravel, moving steadily, with an occasional low snatch of conversation. He wondered if it was all exaggerated. Was it still happening throughout the country? He thought about the funeral and the soldiers and the militancy of the people. There would have to be reform, a whole upheaval between servant and master. He thought of the sabres of the cavalry and of the solid row of men, scythes swinging across the field. They had not enough interest in him to pause in their work. Just a blade of corn. Were they what Manning feared? He slept badly and dreamed of violent things he could not remember when he awoke.

Fountain Court can be the solace of lost souls and lost causes. It can also be a mere distraction from the affairs of the legal treadmill. A turn or two around the fountain is said to have inspired the legal archaeology that has won many a close-run case. In the abstracted vein, Sam Leigh found himself making an unconscious detour on his way to Essex Court. Perhaps the music of the water lured him, or the dancing diamonds of the jet. He was dismayed to find Thomas standing beside the basin, staring into the pool as though he had lost his soul in it. He was oblivious of Sam's approach. Perhaps a more tactful man would pass by, Sam thought, but that man would be less of a friend and more of a coward not to approach a man with such cares.

'Thomas?' He spoke gently. 'Thomas?' Slowly as a tortoise Thomas turned to him, first head then body, with cumbrous effort. Like a tortoise his skin hung limp about his neck. 'So I find you here too,' he continued kindly. 'As we get older we spend more and more time like herons staring into the water. I wonder what fish it really is that we all look for? Lord Chancellor's sinecures? Prothonotary, Clerkship of the Hanaper? Chaffwax? Or is it the Bench? That will come.' He was talking to allow Thomas to regain his composure. He had caught him unawares with such a look of pain that it seemed the only thing to do. 'I think the Bench is only a short distance away, why don't you sit down?'

Thomas looked at him, comprehending his feeble joke, but allowing himself to be taken aside and seated. They stared over Garden Court and the gardens to the Thames, always busy with sails. Sam allowed silence to fall. Thomas should take his own time. Other counsel passed, inclined their heads. Sam greeted them for them both.

'Sam,' said Thomas finally, 'I am old and I am slipping. If I were a carriage horse and so unsteady at least I'd get mercy. My man was found against today, and he should have got off lightly. Summerson came up to me afterwards – he was prosecuting – and said as much. He would not have pushed so hard, he said, if he had not thought I would have fought back like an old dog. Sam, I could not have been more defenceless if my man had turned out to be a Catholic.' There was a long pause which Sam let run. He could hear the carriage horses clopping along Fleet Street and The Strand, the rattle of wheels and shouts of horsemen. Sparrows came down from the trees to drink at the lip of the fountain bowl. They were Temple sparrows, spoiled and unafraid. 'I cannot consider myself fit for the Bench,' Thomas stated.

Sam made for the heart of the matter. 'What is it really, Thomas? You *are* an old dog, but you don't fool me. Ain't that what a friend is for? We all miss a few, like fishermen, but we go back next time with a better lure. Tell me, Tom, and don't divert me with this stuff.'

Thomas scuffed at the gravel with his boots, then spoke to the ground he had exposed, head hung, leaning forward to avoid Sam's eyes. 'It is the family.'

'We have discussed that. There is nothing about those two we can't talk about. What is it now?'

'No, not Henry, though Gee knows he has made enough trouble. Or William who is a natural disaster. The only place for Whig painters is in the Tower! And, by Gee, he will get himself there if he continues. He was imprisoned for making an affray. You knew that?'

'Yes. Arrested, but not imprisoned, Tom.' Sam's pointed correction had the desired effect.

Thomas sighed and came to the point. 'You're right, I must discuss it. My mind is confused. Not so much confused, I suppose, as binding everything into a docket marked irrelevant. It's Caroline. Not to mince matters, Sam, she is with child.'

Sam was surprised, but tried hard not to show it. He was too good a confidant. Yet he did not know how to reply, for his thoughts were racing through all the possibilities and permutations of the situation, seeking the softest question that would encourage Thomas to elaborate without being bluntly offensive. All his questions he judged offensive, so he took the oblique approach instead.

'She did not appear to be well at the Coronation.'

'I'm not surprised! Dee me, I'm not surprised! All these harpies descend on me to tear at me at once. I am smothered by them all! My children will compress me with problems, the country is beset by lack of discipline, Radicals are everywhere. The country will be a Republic in twenty years, Sam, and I can only trust that God in his mercy will do me the honour of taking me before then! What has come over us? We beat the damned French, yet they still conspire against us everywhere, and because of them we lost the American Colonies. A pirate Republic run by rogues and radicals – for who can tell the difference? Catholics will have their emancipation, and Ireland will become a part of Spain, you'll see!'

At his raised voice, heads turned on adjoining benches, and aware of it he fell abruptly silent. The outburst, though brief, had done him good. Sam probed gently.

'And is Caroline well? I trust so. She is a fine girl.'

'As well as can be expected. You know, I have discovered what it is like to feel murderous. It is a form of absolute grief when all things that we cling to seem not to matter. She is my daughter, Sam! I loved her more than I can explain.'

'You do me an injustice. I have a daughter.'

'She was more than a daughter!'

'No, Tom, she was and is your daughter. No more no less.'

'When Margaret died, she looked after all of us.'

'Thomas, she was a babe. When she grew up she cared for you. You are not seeing things with clear eyes.' It was the first time that Sam had heard Thomas mention his wife's name for years. He recognized the turn of Thomas's thoughts and immediately saw the danger. It was like another death to the man, or the re-living of an old death. He must disentangle the two women in his mind. 'When she was a babe, you did the caring. Of course you care for her now!'

'Now I don't care to know her.'

'You don't believe what you are saying. Walk with me in the gardens. Move your limbs. It is good physic for the heart.'

'You won't move my heart, Sam. This has been a secret thing kept from me, a disgrace in the family. I do not even know the man, and she will not say. She says she will keep it from me for fear of what I'd do. My daughter tells me that! What would you do? An illegitimate child! She says she will not marry him. Will not. *She* has decided!'

'Will he marry her?'

'He has asked her but she has refused! Sam, I cannot tolerate it. It is a canker.'

'But you do not kill the rose!' Sam was fierce with him. 'Of course it seems a tragedy, but you must not be so hasty. These are early days, she needs time and support.'

'She will get none from me!'

Sam said nothing, letting the brutal pronouncement stand. He hoped that Thomas would see the ogre within himself that had spoken such pitiless words.

'She may do what she wishes. It is her own life and the child's, as she tells me. She has no need for me. And I offered her my open house! What more could I do? I was prepared to help in every way, although I tell you, Sam, there were tears in my eyes.'

'Who were the tears for?'

Thomas looked at Sam uncomprehendingly, then slowly he reddened and the look turned to anger. Sam met his look evenly. Their friendship surely could stand this, or else in that moment he was prepared to sever it. Thomas seemed to understand the utterness of his danger; seemed to consider the implicit choice in the other man's attitude. Perhaps he saw distinctly for a moment and recognized the pettiness of his words before they were covered over as a sea-rock is covered over by angry waves. He looked at the ground again, his face losing its violent colour.

'I'll walk,' he said, as though it were a concession.

'A good bottle and a pipe,' said Sam in a kindly voice, 'is a kind heart's ease to a buffeted man.' The strength of their friendship re-affirmed, they would consolidate it. Sam felt in need of solace himself. He was too old to put ancient familiarity to the test in such a way. New friendships would be beyond them both.

'Do we have to be buffeted so cruelly at this age?' Thomas asked. 'We are old vessels, our timbers are unsound, our sails frail, our caulking gone.'

'The sea don't change,' replied Sam. 'Old ships have more barnacles. We feel it more.'

'I can't comprehend it, Sam. We were always so close and she has nearly destroyed me. I will stand your disapproval, for I can't bring myself to forgive her. She may do what she may. I must make my position clear.' Sam said nothing as Thomas got to his feet and they walked across the court. The bridge had been re-established between them. Sam felt that he did not mean it. In time he would see and understand. Selfish Tom that he loved.

'Have you seen Dick Bayliss?' It was the same question over and over in all his known haunts, in tap-rooms, in stables. The list of inns was endless. Cross Keys, Goose and Gridiron, Belle Sauvage. Dozens of inns, busy with coaches at all times of day and night. Swan with Two Necks, Saracen's Head. Tired men. Five in the morning for the Bristol coaches, half past for Banbury, Carmarthen and Gloucester at six, leaving at intervals all day until seven in the evening. Post coaches later. Tired passengers, exhausted horses wet with sweat, arriving at all hours in between. A whole country perpetually on the move, with coaches to within miles of the smallest villages. A whole country dependent on the horse. Six hundred short stage routes within London alone. Omnibuses and private carriages. England had become mobile in a way the world had never known. With it too came the long hours, red-eyed men, pale boys, expendable horses and noise, perpetual, hellish noise. Cobbled streets had their hard granite scored by the sheer volume of rattling wheels. One hundred and fifty-eight return journeys daily to Paddington, one hundred and four to Camberwell, seventy-two to Blackwall Docks. 'Have you seen Dick Bayliss?' So many places to ask. Men too tired to comprehend. Women and boys too busy to listen. Tired inns, almost worn away by activity, the very timbers of post, floor and doors thin from human contact. Tables scrubbed until the knots stood out. The continual feeding and drinking of humans and horses. Their bedding, their waking and their waiting. Yet, somehow, it all ran to time, accidents excepted.

'Have you seen Dick Bayliss?' The coach-horses stood patiently in harness in the yard of the Arctic Bar, waiting to leave. Will Morton had to shout to make himself heard over the racket made by the men heaving up trunks and boxes onto the coach. Passengers stood about, shouting at them anxiously, fussing over their possessions or their farewells. The kitchen windows were open and the sound of pots and plates being crashed down in haste made the horses prick their ears and move. The man he shouted to patted the nearest horse. He wore a pocketed leather apron and was himself making a din. He went methodically around each horse, dogged by Will, tapped at each fetlock and picked up each hoof in turn, cradling it in his leathern lap. He then checked it for damage or stones, hammering home a protruding nail, inserting a new one, taking a file from the apron pocket to rasp at hoof, or another file to cut at iron.

'Why?' said the man without pausing and apparently without interest. He did not bother to look at Will. 'What is it to you? Do I know you?'

'I'm a coachman.'

'Oh.' The man was unimpressed. So were thousands of other men.

'Regent Square, for Mr Kelleway. The master hires Dick Bayliss for making-up.'

'Oh.' The farrier moved round the lead horses and Will followed him round, rubbing their noses.

'I can't find him.'

'Oh.'

Clap, clap, clap. The shoeing-hammer made a flat noise on the iron of a shoe. The man dived under the traces and was between the horses, oblivious of their hoofs, pushing the animals firmly apart to get at their feet. The horses neither shied nor kicked, but looked back at him with the docility of complete trust. Will saw he was a real horse man, without malice or sentiment. A man that the animals knew was without cruelty, and equally, Will saw, a man who would not ascribe human motives to his animals. Such men were unstable with beasts. Will ducked under the traces and pushed between the horses to join him. The farrier looked up with sudden and natural anger. It was a trespass on his job and craft. Within the traces, he was within his workshop walls. The shoeing-hammer came up in his hand.

'What's your game?'

'You know Dick Bayliss.'

'Have I said so?'

'No, but you haven't said you've never heard of him.'

'Mister, I don't like a man between my horses when I'm working. This is my patch.'

'I would feel the same. But I have to find Dick Bayliss.'

The man bent down and picked up a hoof, let it go again. Will leant against the adjoining horse in his own accustomed way. Perhaps it was this casual act that made the man soften, for it was the act of a man who works with horses, not the act of a liveried fool who wrenches at their mouths and flays them with a whip.

'All right, I know Dick Bayliss. What do you want him for?'

'For making-up from the stables. We only have one carriage.'

'Bayliss a friend of yours?' The man watched Will closely. It was an awkward question, for Will had to judge what the farrier would think of Bayliss. Would he like the rough and ready man, or detest him as much as Will?

'In no way. We pass the time of day, o' course, but he don't keep a clean carriage nor curries his horses.' He tried to keep any trace of anger from his voice. The farrier seemed satisfied.

'He's got a runaway tongue. And I seen him kick his horses. No good.' He ducked under the horse's belly and was out the other side. Will followed him.

'Where is he, then?'

'Down the road.' The man indicated the direction with a nod of his head. 'He's changed stables. That's why you can't find him. Shouldn't want him if I was you. Don't keep his carriage no better and his nags is skin and bone. You get no service from hacks like that. Got no sense of beauty in him. Just look at these.' He patted the sides of one of the big bays. There was no self-indulgent pride in his voice, it was a statement of fact. 'Now I have things to see to. They're on the road in a minute.'

Will wished him good day and was given a brief nod in reply. The passengers were clambering into and onto the coach. As he walked down the yard, he had to stand back to the wall to allow an incoming coach to thunder past in the confined space. The horses were hot and streaked with dust, the coach spattered and stained. Its name, in cream on black panels, was *The Telegraph*. Underneath, in smaller letters, London–Colchester–Ipswich. He was immediately buoyant with hope. Perhaps she had gone away. Gone home. He walked quickly up the street looking for the livery stables. The sign advertising them was no more than two hundred yards down the street. The stables were approached by a long passage that opened out into a courtyard. Will walked halfway down the passage, feeling like a thief. From where he stood he could see that the courtyard was entirely contained within buildings.

The stables occupied two adjacent sides of the court, and behind them rose a high brick wall, cutting them off from the yards of the buildings beyond. There was only one way in and out. He must find somewhere to wait where he could keep an eye on it. He retreated quickly up the passage, heart thumping, and walked up and down the street trying to appear casual. He was grateful for windows and shops in which he could stare as he thought, keeping an eye on the entrance to the passage, or watching it in the reflection of window-glass. If he kept this up for long he was bound to be conspicuous. Although the street was busy enough, the shop-keepers would get uneasy if he kept staring in. He told himself he must loiter, look at the time like a man with an appointment. Then, if he was being observed, he could appear to get impatient, tap his feet, take up his station well down the street, out of the sight of immediate shops, then return in, say, an hour. There was nowhere he could sit. No coffee-shop, inn or gin-house. There was not even anywhere to lean, on railings, wall or porch. He could not sit down, for he was too well dressed for a vagrant.

It was nearly five. Bayliss must be back within an hour, unless he was engaged for the day and the evening. What was the position, he asked himself, idly looking at pairs of braces, or gallows, that were becoming quite the fashion? Mrs Burges had said she might go back home to Ipswich, and here he was close by the Ipswich stage. If she had gone back, how did he stand to her and how did he stand to Bayliss? He had never made things plain to Béssie and Bessie had been shy in return. This was no time to start doubting his rights! The low creature Bayliss, as Mrs Burges called him, must have his due. But what was his due? In the searching and looking for the man, his revenge had become cold soup. His rage was yesterday's rage, re-warmed.

Good enough but not the same as fresh rage, ready for blood. He carried no weapon. Suppose Bayliss was armed? He might well be. Coachmen carried pistols. Would he go up to him and knock him down? What then? Kick him, break his ribs, crack his skull. If he could only be sure what Bayliss had done! He felt in the pocket of his coat for his clasp knife, aware of the unreality of the situation. He was no stranger, as no man could be, to the frequent rioting and fighting of London streets, whether by apprentice boys or vicious young Bucks. But this premeditated attack, coupled with his nagging doubts, made him feel sick and full of fear. Perhaps when he saw Bayliss his hate would revive. That was what he told himself. He found that he was holding the knife very tight in his pocket and consciously let it go.

He walked farther down the street, for the haberdasher with the gallows was peering curiously at him from the interior of his shop. The crossing-sweepers, wretchedly dressed boys stationed at each corner with their bare feet caked in mud, eyed him watchfully. Their minds were as keen as a banker's scales. They knew they could expect only a small tip, if any at all, for their perfunctory brushing aside of droppings. They were waiting for him to cross. Will, with the instinct of his kind who is neither a master nor of the poor or labouring class, felt in their glances an innate hostility. He was unacceptable to them, neither of them, nor sufficiently removed from them, in his good clothes paid for by his master, with his trained carriage and polite mannerisms. He had the trappings of a master without the necessary money. He had the servant's despising for beggars and the poor.

The street here was filthy – worse than the city streets but not worse than those around Smithfield. The deep layers of horse droppings and other filth formed a hard crust that was never removed, but in the summertime was reduced to dust that blew into houses and food, covered hair and clothes and choked the breath. When it rained the powder was washed away but when it dried out, the smell was appalling. They said the stinking layer deadened the sound of the carriages. It was just one thing to put up with. In poorer quarters, human effluent was disposed of in the same way. Even here, there were no covered sewers, no proper water and cesspits overflowed in open runnels down narrow streets. Earth privies were seldom emptied. Londoners did not like hot summer days, for they brought unknown death. This area felt uneasy, sandwiched between the rookeries and the better streets of Bloomsbury. Tradesmen would always be quick with suspicion. Will thought of the farrier and the readily raised hammer. A commonplace. A man who expected trouble as a daily event and was capable of dealing with it quickly. He felt even more afraid but steeled himself with thoughts of Bessie Tate. The morals of men like Bayliss were like those of savages. He realized that in this sort of area, Bayliss would have the advantage. Tradesmen would not help. If Bayliss set the whole stables on him he could expect no mercy. He must wait and get him alone. Here there was a deep divide and he must be very careful. Two beggar men of the type he most despised were eyeing him thoughtfully. As he stared in a baker's window with complete disinterest, he was approached by a child.

'You shopping, mister? Look at them cakes!' He looked at her, trying to master his alarm. She seemed to be about twelve or thirteen. Her clothes were old yet laundered. She had been smearing her cheeks with some red colour, probably a metal oxide, like a little Punchinello. Her hair was shiny with grease. She probably dressed it with mutton fat. On her feet she wore the remains of satin slippers several sizes too large, without soles. One was at right angles to her exposed foot. 'You shopping, mister?' she demanded more loudly, taking his look over her as an advance.

'What do you want? I'm not shopping. Go away.'

'You're looking at them cakes!' the child declared unabashed. 'What do you want?' She winked at him and gave him her idea of a coquettish smile. It was a pathetic grimace. Will was not shocked but very embarrassed. Again, as a servant he was part of a deeply respectable group who rarely encountered such approaches. More rarely than those either above or below him in rank or income. 'I'm over twelve,' the child reassured him, 'it's all right, mister, it's legal. Ain't got the clap y'know. Don't I look a nice young virgin just what as a gent might like? I got a brother an' sister to support, mister, and I ain't dear. Nice chance for a young virgin. Just round the corner. Mam's out an' we'd have a room.' She said this in a wheedling tone and Will felt so awkward and unable to deal with the situation that he felt in his pocket and gave her two pennies.

'Go away. Leave me alone.'

'What's the matter, mister? Frightened?'

With a derisive laugh, the child ran off, her slippers sliding about her skinny legs like leather washers. Will saw the beggars converging on him and quickly moved on, crossing the street. The worldly-wise lad of nine who swept before him with a birch-twig broom got a penny to his surprise as Will escaped. From the other side of the street the opening to the passage was obscured from time to time by the passage of carriages and carts. He saw the first carriage turn into the passage but the driver was a small man, not at all like Bayliss. Perhaps he would only follow Bayliss today and find out where he lived. He would return better armed, literally. He wondered where he could obtain a pistol without it being known. He told himself he would use it only in self-defence.

He was staring in the windows of a butcher at the gory remains of cattle – it seemed this shop only sold innards and offal – when in the swirling panes of glass he caught sight of Bayliss. In livery on a carriage, he was hauling round the lead horses, using his whip as though he must compress them into the passage by violence. The horses baulked and bucked as a result. Bayliss cracked out at them with his whip. He seemed even more violent than the Bayliss Will remembered. But then he realized that Bayliss had always treated him as his master's servant and that he inherited the respect due his master, by proxy. Will's heart was thumping away uncomfortably. He would wait where he was until the man left.

He looked desperately for any shop where he could buy some trifle and yet keep an eye on the passage. He had no idea how to buy tripe, but thought he must have a plate to put it on. He saw a tobacconist's shop further down the road, and although he did not smoke, made for it with relief. The man behind the counter already had a customer and this gave Will more time. He examined pipes set out on a rack, as though contemplating buying a briar, clay or meerschaum. The customer, who was enveloped in blue smoke with a rank smell, was obviously a dedicated smoker and took his time pinching at the tobaccos laid out in wooden bowls on the counter, lettered on their sides with gilt, discussing the bird's eye, plug, honey-dew, and cake. When the man left with a length of black pig-tail, the tobacconist coughed pointedly to attract Will who was still beside the pipe-rack. Not knowing what to do, he purchased half a dozen cheap clays, taking as long as he could, and left. The tobacconist had obviously expected more of him.

The respite was sufficient. From the passageway, Bayliss suddenly emerged and walked off, turning to his right. Will thrust the pipes into a pocket, hovering in the doorway until Bayliss was well ahead, then set out in pursuit. He still had no clear idea of his intentions. The furtive act of following the other man seemed to sap his rage. He felt that he was engaging in a criminal act.

Bayliss turned off the main road and down a side street. It was narrower and dirtier again. He was heading towards the rookeries beyond. Will Morton became more uneasy and more aware of the narrow boundaries that a man dressed respectably as he might tread. The houses overhung the street and were black with soot. Masonry and brick were decayed, doors repaired with crudely nailed boards. The people in the streets were increasingly tattered in their appearance. Within three hundred yards he was in the world of the poor. Bayliss walked boldly, without fear. Only a fool would accost such a man. Will Morton, lurking and lingering, could not adopt such poise and swagger. He was aware of eyes on him, everywhere. From upper windows where haggard females leaned out, from the dark of doorways that served as shops, pawnbrokers, gin palaces and brothels, all under one roof and sometimes in one room. They were in the slum area of St Giles. He was spat at from above. Rotten planks had been laid on the stinking ooze of the streets, and they squelched up and down in the liquid filth as he trod on them. No sunlight could find its way down to dry out this muck and no carriages used these foul alleys except to bring out the dead on the carts of poverty. The smell of excrement and rubbish was nauseating and he held his nose. He was jostled by shapeless figures, and once felt swift hands run over his body for a purse they could not find. It was like being scampered over by a rat, and he recoiled.

Bayliss moved on and Will forced himself to follow. Other figures, carrying trays of trinkets, called to him, jeeringly. They did not even try to sell here. He was jostled again and again. Obscenities were snarled at him, but he did not pause, sensing that was the purpose and that it meant real danger. How easy it would be to be dragged into one of those dark doorways. He had heard about such things. Men disappeared and were never seen again. Bodies chopped up and dropped in cesspits. Or, some said, they boiled men's bones for soup. It was a far cry from Regent Square, yet only half a mile. Bayliss suddenly disappeared.

He had turned sharply to the left and seemed to have walked through a black brick wall. It was a trick of the light, for when Will got closer he saw there was a narrow archway and a passage no wider than to allow one man. He moved down it cautiously, and was surprised to find that it opened out into a cobbled yard which he recognized as George Yard off Long Acre. They had passed through the worst areas, and although still a slum, the yard had been well constructed. Bayliss was only sixty yards ahead of him and entering a stair that ran up in the angle between two buildings, serving them both. He had traced him to earth. He watched. He could see each floor as he passed it, and whether he turned to left or right on the landing. Bayliss disappeared on the third floor, turning left. Morton climbed the stairs, opening his clasp knife with shaky hands and holding it in his coat pocket. The third floor door was unremarkable. Old paint was reasonably clean. Almost without thinking about it, he hammered on the iron knocker. He must not think about it. He would falter. Bayliss opened the door. Whatever Will Morton had been expecting and suppressing, it did not happen. His grip on his knife was aching. Bayliss seemed stunned for a moment, then his big face split into a grin. He seemed genuinely delighted and he made no offensive move. Morton was nonplussed.

'Will Morton!' Bayliss roared. 'Bess, it's Will Morton, the livery man from Regent Square!' Before he could move, Bayliss had reached out and slapped him on the back. 'Get no work from there, eh? Short shrift and a tight girth for this old barb. But I'm a stayer, Morton. Bess!'

She appeared at the door before Will had time to reply, and

the sight of her was effective as a kick on the head from a horse. He stared, stupidly bemused, while she smiled at him, cautiously and with affection for an acquaintance. Yet there was a wary look in her eyes. Will was a grim and white-faced figure, and she hoped there would be no trouble, that his visit was no prelude to persecution. Will saw that her curls had lost their spring. Her hair was becoming lank, lack of washing he immediately thought, no Mrs Burges. In that thought he realized again that she was really a child. But her eyes sparkled and her face was happy, if apprehensive. Some of the kitchen pallor had gone from her cheeks and her natural healthy colour was returning. She could not obtain that in this sombre court. Bayliss must have been taking her out. He forgot that he had half expected that she had returned home to Ipswich. He forgot his rage and released his grip on the knife in his pocket. He had expected to find a hollow-eyed, bruised hag, victim of debauchery and ill-treatment. Instead, she was modestly well-dressed and seemed sure of herself and Bayliss. She looked at Will kindly, but with reserve. He thought it the remote look, civil, but without passion, that betokened an absence of years rather than of days. He no longer knew her.

There was no wedding ring on her finger. Her eyes intercepted his quick glance and she hid her left hand behind her skirt. Bayliss said nothing, for once, watching this interplay of assessment. He saw Will Morton seem to shrink and grow bent before his eyes. He knew what it meant, for he had seen it in many men. Muscles that were keyed up had relaxed. Tension puts bulk on a man, conveys an animal warning. Will was completely confused. By all his standards she was an immoral woman, fallen and living in sin. His morality, that of the servant's parlour, allowed for no half-way house between heaven and hell. She was abhorrent to him as a fallen woman, yet he could not hate her as he should. The line between cohabitation and prostitution was mere words without a marriage. Yet had his master taken a mistress he would have accepted that without condoning it. With his own, among servants where standards were absolute, there were only two standards, wed or unwed. He knew she was a whore, yet was jealous. He was mute, confused, and hardly aware that Bayliss was ushering him in. This was all wrong. Bayliss the

Brute was patently happy and as Bessie took his arm, Will turned to run. Bayliss took his arm firmly.

'Come in, Will, be a friend. We don't have many visitors, Bess and me. How did you find us, eh? We thought we left a cold trail.' He had ushered Will into a gloomy room that was nevertheless clean. Whatever could be polished, had been. What could be scrubbed was clean. A low fire burned on the range. Will averted his eyes from the bed in the corner. He was sick with jealousy for the Bessie Tate that had been. This strange likeness must be a double, as this Bayliss must be another Bayliss who had his arm around this strange Bessie. He seemed a tender man, his gestures and looks were loving. The ginger-haired oaf stood before his domestic hearth as though he would ape a gentleman, yet he was putting on no play-act. 'Some spy-wife ostler that ain't no Billie to Dick Bayliss? Well it don't matter who speaked on me, for I have an honest job with rough jades. And what do they say about this showful pullet?' he demanded giving Bessie a squeeze to show he did not mean it.

She coloured. 'Oh Dick!' They were the first words she had spoken.

'That was what I call uncharitable, Will Morton. Your master is the real gent, sending my Bess to pad the hoof in a wicked place like London. Light a glim, Bess, and give Will a shove in the mouth – only gin, for I ain't a rich man yet! Sit down. You ain't hardly your talkative self.' Bessie lit a candle and stood it on a table. Bayliss turned a wooden chair around and sat astride it. Will, still uncertain, sat down on another. He felt he had entirely lost control of the situation, and yet he ought to be in command. His strength was to have been Bessie's undeclared affection for him, his rage at her seduction. He was disarmed. 'We're goin' to make it legal when I has enough saved, and I shall buy a hackney or two of my own. You shall see me polish them then! Oil the leather too, be my own master!'

Bayliss talked on, elaborating his plans. Bessie Tate put the bottle down before them and returned to the range to stir at a pot. She smiled occasionally, and looked towards the ginger-whiskered man with the crushed nose and big, scarred hands. Will hardly listened. He excused himself as soon as he could, Bayliss demanding a promise that he would come to see them again. 'Isn't that so, Bess? Ain't that what we want?' he asked at the door.

Bessie looked at Will with a remote smile, concerned with her cooking. 'Yes. Goodbye, Will.'

It was colder than scorn. When he got to the foot of the stairs he realized that his pocket was full of broken clay. He had sat on the pipes without noticing. He flung them down in the court, turning his pocket inside out as though to clear out every fragment of the memories of his Bessie Tate.

Williamsburg,
James City County,
Virginia.
October 1821.

Dear Father,

I realize that this letter must come as a great surprise to you, since at my last I was still in India and the Army. Also as the new location from which it comes is, as I know, a country about which you have opinions and indeed reservations.

Shortly after my last letter I was taken ill with fever again, and as you can judge, recovered. In consequence of the fever, however, I was much weakened and my physique distressed so that I have been invalided out, it being obvious, I am afraid, that I should not recover unless I left the Indian climate for good. My regiment gave me the fare of the passage which I took this far and a pension which is so derisory that it may accumulate in their books until a date that it becomes worth collecting. I have, however, been provident in saving in India and have some funds with which I hope to start up business here. This seems to be a prosperous place through farming for which there is an abundance of slave labour.

The need to comfort and console others. John stared bitterly at the sunlight moving on his desk, making patterns of ovals that disappeared and recurred as the light filtered through the leaves of the tree outside. It reminded him of other patterns of sunlight. Of a brown body striped like a tiger. His letter was a lie. It was Padmavati who had contracted cholera. He had come to the hut one day, through the empty streets of noon, but there were people outside, sitting in the shade under the eaves. Old women sat waiting, knees drawn up to their chins. They

211

reminded him of vultures. They watched him with impersonal, inquisitive black eyes. He knew immediately something was wrong and ran up the wooden step. A young Arakanese whom he had never seen stepped from the shadow into his path, his hands up, his arms stretched wide. 'What's going on?' John demanded but the man looked at him blankly. 'No speak,' was all he could say. He tried to stay in front of John, waving his arms and walking backwards into the hut. He talked urgently in his own tongue. John was aware of other people in the darkness of the hut. They sat on the floor, burning incense. The air was sickly sweet with the smell. Padmavati was lying on his wood and canvas bed.

At first he thought it was an old crone. The beauty of her smooth body and face had already collapsed. Her dark eyes were sunken and dim, her cheeks hollow and the lips that smiled were drawn back to reveal her teeth as though in a snarl. Her firm breasts seemed like wax that had melted, slid, and set in wrinkles. Her bones made lumps in her loose skin where she had been smooth and round. The young Arakanese was still trying to keep him away. He had hid his eyes and yelled. He could not remember much about his first reactions, except for the sound of his own shouts that rang in his ears. Horror and rage that expressed itself in a savage noise like an animal howling. He had forced the young Arakanese aside and bent over the withered head. He had called her name, too loudly, for she must have still been able to hear. In a croak she said his name, and something in Arakanese he could not understand. She could hardly move her lips, which seemed dry and glued to her teeth. He looked around desperately for water, making wild gestures of drinking from a cup to the faces all around him. A woman draped in a sari came forward with a brass cup which he tried to put to her lips, but the water ran down the sides of her mouth and cheeks onto the pillow of his bed. He knew she was dying. She had passed the crisis, there had been no reaction, and she was sliding away.

He expressed his grief in pointless violence. He shouted obscenities at the attendant women and ordered them out of the doorway. They stared at him understanding only that he had gone mad with grief. He kicked out the little brass bowls of incense so that they rolled down the step and lay smoking in the street. He pushed at the women, who fled from him. The young Arakanese struggled with him, talking, explaining something that John could not understand. He seized the end of the bed, indicating clearly that he wanted to stay. John had drawn his pistol and put it to the man's head, showering him with screaming curses. Had the young man resisted, John would have blown out his brains. He realized two days later that the young man was Padmavati's brother. That he had destroyed and disrupted the family's quiet preparations for death according to their religion. In his selfish grief he had demolished a sacred ritual, left her unshriven.

He had sat by her bed in the furnace-heat of noon, waiting. Without the burning ud-buti sticks the other smells of the room crowded in on him against the concentration of his mind that Padmavati must live, even though he knew she could not. Brass and clay bowls had been used for the degrading course of the illness. Violent smells. Flies buzzed around the pots, blackening the lips where they found something to feed on. He wanted to kill the flies, but could not leave her side. Padmavati, he kept saying, Padmavati, because he knew no other words and cursed his stupidity in not learning the rudiments of their tongue. He hated the flies and wished them dead, saying to himself, oh God, if there is any strength in the power of prayer, kill them now! But they crawled and multiplied in number everywhere, trying to land on her eyes. He beat at them, always missing, as they circled and returned. It was a sort of madness. He sat for perhaps an hour, fighting with the flies before he realized she was no longer breathing. The eyelids did not respond. She was dead.

John watched the dappled light playing across the desk and over the paper on which he was writing. The quality of the light represented a temperate and kindly climate. In Arakan, light fell in bars or blazing pools, lay still on the ground like a substance. Here there were shades within sunlight, and it moved and mingled with these shades, insubstantial, kind. He wiped at the sparkling in his eyes with his thumb and forefinger and they were wet.

His 'savings' were Padmavati's gold and sapphire necklace

which he had taken from her body – not for theft but because she had no other possessions he could take and he felt desperately in need of something. It did not belong to the shrunken corpse on the bed, but to the brown and smiling Padmavati that was his. He would never tell anyone what he had done, but her family would know and would think him a thief who robbed the dead. It was their gold, their treasure. He wondered if it had ever been reported to the authorities. It was very possible. He had taken the first ship available from Chittagong to Madras and from there had sailed round east Africa to Capetown. Here he had changed ship for the Guinea Coast and Atlantic crossing. He had tendered his resignation in writing before sailing so that it would be opened when he was already well away to sea. The long voyage had been good for him physically but the distance did not diminish his sense of guilt and loss. He could see that his behaviour had been close to madness and that his two illnesses had so weakened him as to demand from Padmavati not just sensual pleasure, but security that she could not have given had she lived. He had wanted to hang on her as a drowning man will clutch his rescuer, so that both die.

He contemplated the hatred of his behaviour that he carried within him these few months. He knew now the degree of his instability. He had wanted from a simple native girl a whole range of emotions of his own creation, had sought to see in her the fulfilment of his own deficiencies. He could entrust no woman with that. With an effort he continued with his letter, knowing that he was seeking to justify himself and so fulfil the needs of Thomas. He was not so hard that he could deny them.

The climate here is excellently suited to my continuing recovery and I think I am now fitter than I have ever been. You must realize I could not come straight home to England in my former state, nor could I contemplate returning without trying to make something of myself again. Here, I can hope to do it in a land where we speak the same tongue. It is nearer than Australia and in many ways like England. I hope to start up in business but have not yet determined where or in what manner. I hope then to be able to return home in order to visit you and all the family. I know nothing I can say will allay the surprise you will feel at this turn of events, but believe me, sir, it is for the best. I will remain in close communication – closer now than formerly – and for the moment I lack nothing and have adequate capital so you must not worry on that score.

He read through what he had written and was dismayed at the thin apology of his words. There was no robust consolation to be plucked from them by even the most eager father. He contemplated tearing them up and starting again, but soon considered it useless. If his father must not have the truth, then he must put up with poor lies. It was all he felt he could manage. He opened the drawer of the desk and took out Padmavati's necklace, laying it deliberately on the sheet of paper that was to travel to England. It was a poor act of defiance, substituting the letter for the reality of revelation. Perhaps he was trying out the feeling or believed that some imprint of the jewel would communicate itself by the paper. It was like a gesture of superstition. The necklace would be his wealth. What he had genuinely taken as a keepsake in his madness he would now sell as a thief, quite sanely. For he was no thief, he told himself, in Padmavati's eyes. She would not have minded. The necklace would buy a plantation or a farm or a business of substance. The sapphire sparkled in the dancing ovals of sunlight. John watched the effect. In it he found a hypnotic peace.

7

Autumn sat on London as though the devil sat on the chimney-pots. People were trapped inside, or moved like newly blind, feeling their way along walls. The choking, sulphurous fog brought death to the elderly and unwary. It was the hunting season for robbers and cut-throats. The carriage trade gave up. On the river, the greasy water rubbed at the yellow muck, failing to grip or move it. It seemed determined to cling where it was, parting for boats or the occasional carriage, only to close immediately and firmly as sand. In St Paul's, the preacher could not see the front pews. The destitute slept in peace. Leaves turned gold on city trees, then quickly black and fell unnoticed. Everyone who could afford a coal fire built it up to keep out the damp cold. Tile kilns, brickworks, foundries, tanneries and breweries added to the filth. Aristocrats affected to be bored in their country seats, and broke their limbs in pursuit of foxes.

In Wells's shipyard, the overseer waited for some stir in the weather. The *Thomas K.* was ready to launch. A light wind strayed down the valley of the Thames in the third week and London awoke like Rip van Winkle, slowly and rather dazed, looking about to see what had happened in the interval. Masterson immediately sent a horseman to Thomas in chambers, apologizing for the short notice, but saying the launch must be made in case the weather closed in again. Thomas returned a note that he agreed.

On baulks of timber immersed in the green Thames mud, the *Thomas K.* looked as fine as any new ship should. She was bedecked with bunting that hung completely still as though cut from plank. Half the width of the river could now be seen, flowing noiselessly past as though it were indeed oil. The sounds of work had ceased except for the men fitting the launch. The inclined plane could be seen disappearing into the murky water where it presumably continued but was abruptly cut from sight. Men with buckets of tallow and grease daubed the side of the bilgeway and sliding-plank. Only the dog-shores prevented her from a premature slide into her element. Thomas had surveyed all this with the nervousness of a landman.

'Is she safe? Will she keel? What is to prevent her?' Wells tramped round the ship with Thomas and Masterson, checking, reassuring, laughing off Thomas's fears. His men had been supplied with barrels of ale for the occasion and allowed to bring their wives, provided no woman touched the ship. They stood a short distance off, very merry, the sound of their laughter strangely deadened by the lingering fog. Thomas wished it had been sunny, but above all just wished to see her safely afloat. A small platform had been erected that smelled strongly of new-sawn pine. The timber was rough and unplaned. A strip of cloth had been draped over the rails as a concession to the sense of occasion the owners would expect. It had been inexpertly tucked into swags which were fixed with bright copper nails.

They waited for the tide and they waited for Sam, Henry and Jane, William and Maria. Caroline had not been asked. Thomas tramped the heavy timbers of the deck feeling intensely depressed. His children seemed determined to rob him of his honour and his pleasure at an age when these were carefully constructed things, built up over years and not likely to be built up again. The ship, he thought, seemed to symbolize it all. So much work, so much saving on his part had been put into this investment for the family. So much labour by others using skills it took a lifetime to perfect. Now his children had pulled it all down. His life was as hollow as the ship's hold. The ship was young, however, eager to fill that hold, had long work ahead of it. With what pleasure he could have waited for Caroline before all this, or written to John. He could not even long for Sam to arrive, for he was afraid of Sam's censure. They would make a fine launching party. He wished he could be one of the shipwrights for they at least would get a real pleasure out of it.

He listened to his feet clumping upon the deck. It was funereal. That shadow must be closing upon him as relentlessly as the incoming tide. He wondered again if all families were like this, and wished, as he had begun to recently, that he had more

217

friends and acquaintances. He could not compare, except with Sam, and there was nothing there he was proud of on his part. He blamed it on the loss of their mother and the wilful and irresponsible insistence of Caroline that she should leave his house. She had said she could not be a fleshed ghost of the dead. The very thought of the words hurt. Yet here he was, who had determined never to think of her, brooding about her on this occasion when he should be full of pride. He hoped William and Maria would come respectably dressed. It would be too much if they came in some outlandish weeds. He would not put it past William to come dressed as an admiral. He would have gone on brooding if he had not been interrupted by Masterson, very spruce in his tail-coat and black beaver. Thomas could not understand what Masterson was saying.

'I've got a trumpeter,' he said.

Thomas stared at him in confusion. The remark seemed to be relevant to nothing and he wondered if he had heard the man right. 'A what?' Perhaps it was some new nautical term.

'A fellow that blows a trumpet, to give a fanfare over the launch.'

Thomas stared at Masterson incredulously. He was so far from such frivolity that it seemed utterly absurd. 'What on earth for?' His tone was rude .

Masterson looked put out but managed to cover it with a smile so that he grimaced. 'We should have some music. Something to raise a cheer as she goes down the plane.'

'But those fine fellows will give us a cheer,' said Thomas, indicating the workmen who were in the state to cheer anything, even a shipwreck.

'I thought we should have some music. We'll dispense with it if you don't want it.'

'No, no. If you've hired the man, let him do his piece. Let him stay well away from the platform. I can't stand loud noise.'

'We'll pipe her in,' said Wells who had overheard this exchange, 'we always do that with bo'sun's whistles.' Wells said nothing about the trumpeter. He could not imagine what the mixture would sound like.

'Isn't a trumpeter unusual?' Thomas persisted crabbily. The idea seemed to him so peculiar. He had never envisaged a ship being launched to the sound of a trumpet. There was something so thin and brassy about the instrument, something so superficial, that it struck him as ridiculous. Perhaps it was because Masterson had interrupted his brooding thoughts, which were sombre with emotional echoes built up of complex sounds like a great organ within a cathedral. This ridiculous trumpet was an interloper and he was prepared to be difficult about it if only because it dispelled the organ music from his brain. 'And if we are having whistles I can see no point in it. I think the trumpeter should be dispensed with. A fanfare would be a ridiculous pomp, and one trumpet a mere pizzle!'

Masterson, although obviously upset, thought it prudent to shrug and agree. He went off to cancel the trumpeter. 'Don't forget, I'll pay him just the same,' called Thomas. He wondered if he was behaving irrationally, for it was all such a silly thing. Wells seemed pleased, however, and was nodding his approval with a smile. 'Whistles for a ship,' he said, 'trumpets for human frailty, bugles for war and drums for death.'

Thomas was greatly struck by the yard-owner's remark. There was something philosophic in the manner of shipbuilders, that had not changed with these unruly times. They seemed to season like their wood, very slowly. Wells was humming to himself and running his hand over the thick varnish of a mahogany rail that seemed to Thomas to be as glazed as a boar's head. The man seemed to find pleasure in the feel of it. He caught Thomas's eye.

'Tide is nearly up now. I hope your party shows soon. The Thames is a faithful slut; she keeps good time! This lady must be blessed. You can feel she's ready for it.'

The fog blew off the river in wisps, full of the reek of coal. Thomas picked up an end of rope, beautifully lashed, which still left a thick round brush of hemp. He smelled it, perhaps unconsciously copying Wells's pleasure in the senses of the ship. It smelled new and good, something like hay and something like pitch. The varnish smelled new and good, the empty holds smelled of pitch and wood. Here he had built a new and beautiful world. His spirits lifted.

The launching party arrived in time, the three carriages pulling up in the yard almost in convoy. It had been a long journey although only four miles after crossing London Bridge. They had had to follow the winding of the Thames along the terrible riverside road through Shadwell and Rotherhithe to Trinity Street, sometimes cobbled, sometimes mud but always congested with commerce. Heavy carts blocked the road completely, ships loaded and unloaded with wooden derricks swinging low overhead while foremen or ships' mates roared at the traffic and their own men. Cases, boxes and barrels were continually in the way, and scant attention was paid to moving them. Parbuckled barrels were wrenched from their holds by dockers who kicked them down the road to their destination at their own pace. Commerce was master here and carriages a mere annoyance. Everything seemed to have to cross the road to warehouses. Bales of jute, hemp and cotton, grain, wool, timber, tea, machinery, beer, rum and wine. The warehouses shot open doors at three, four or five storeys above the street and from each one swung a gantry and tackle like gallows.

It was a part of London that none of the visitors had ever seen before. Henry and Jane viewed it with annoyance and distaste. The coolness between them had become coldness now. In the last few weeks it seemed to her that he had become increasingly well-mannered towards her but without any familiarity. She thought she might as well be accompanied by a butler. He showed her no signs of affection, but was solicitous to a nicety. Of love-making there was none. She did not know how to invite affection, as she thought of it, and this added embarrassment gave her a feeling of deep injury. It was natural to her to conceal this completely and return his impersonal civilities with polite expressions of pleasure. She felt she understood the agony of a mute who longs to speak. It showed in her eyes when Henry caught her sometimes looking at him unawares, but it prompted in him a quick revulsion. To be together in a carriage for this length of time was a long suffering, like being in bed, listening to him undressing each night, and wondering if he would come in. At first she had wondered with longing. She knew when he had undressed. There would be a pause while he picked up the lamp and in that pause she held her breath and lay quite still, wanting to miss no small hesitation or nuance. There was not the slightest move to her door. He went straight from the dressing-room to his own room, the light fading from under the door. She would almost stifle before she realized that she had not let out her breath lest in even that small noise she missed some fragment of important intelligence. Listening like someone afraid and hunted, she thought.

Now they jolted along making pleasantries about the intolerable condition of the roads, as polite to each other as at a public engagement. At first she had wondered with longing, but now she wondered with fear, for if in some way she had been found wanting, she must be found wanting in this as well. Why should she not be afraid of this stranger? She would not be shamed that way. Yes, the roads really were intolerable. Yes, the fog seemed to be lifting. Yes, it really was a long way to the shipyard. A conversation by omission is worse than silence.

Sam Leigh was enthralled by what he saw, and lacking a companion, chatted cheerfully to himself, pointing out the sights. He had not forgotten his hip flask. The wispy mist was breaking up and had suffused slightly with yellow sunlight. There was an occasional glimpse of the flat back pancake of the Isle of Dogs on the northern bank and of ships, barges and luggers on the river. Sam would not allow thoughts of Jane to intrude upon his pleasure at the outing. It took a conscious effort to push it to the incoherent recesses of his mind, but it was like Sam to succeed in this endeavour.

'Fine ships, fine ships!' he exclaimed, 'twelve, thirteen, fourteen. Twenty-two barges. Come on, sun, break through. Should be a joyous occasion. Haven't been down the river since I was a boy. What a place. What work, squalor. By God, what a marvellous sight!' Sam rose to his feet, swaying with the motion and thumped on the roof of the coach, shouting to the driver to stop. He wanted to watch the marvel of one of the rope-walks that abounded by the river. The two coachmen pulled up, covertly feeling for their pistols, for they had come armed to this uneasy district.

The rope-makers walked backwards down the full quarter-mile of the ground, six from each end. Each spinner carried round his waist a huge skirt of heckled hemp that he fed out at an even rate, varying his pace to get the thickness constant.

They retreated from the big wheel that drove revolving hooks to which each man had fixed his yarn, feeding out the oily tow between finger and thumb, the hand protected by a woollen rag. Hooks set out at intervals along the length of the rope-ground took the weight of the spun yarn. The men were absorbed to the exclusion of everything. It was heavy, demanding work. Later, the strands they had formed, each a quarter-mile long, would be fed into the multiple steel mouth of the forming wheel that would twist and countertwist the strands while the strain pulled the heavy machinery up the long iron rail on the ground. Twist and countertwist until the carded hemp had become hawsers as thick as a forearm.

Sam thought, and not for the first time, that Thomas would have been better advised to put his money into things like this. There would always be need of rope. There would always be ships but cargoes were a chancy trade and too subject to fashion and the whims of war. Even sail might be at risk if steam power ever proved to be what was claimed of it. But steam ships would still need rope like men needed shoes. As he thought this, he saw that the rope-makers walked bare-foot over the ground. He was not immune to such rebukes to his own conscience and called to the driver to drive on. The rope-makers must cover mile upon mile in a day in their endless tread, always backward, soaked from head to foot in oil. He wondered if they walked home backwards, if indeed they were as unable to walk forwards as the average man can walk back. He had no right to feel sorry for himself or complain about anything. He took a reassuring swig from his flask knowing full well that he did it to state his confidence in his own privileged position and knowing full well he was not deceiving himself. He imagined, correctly, that Henry and Jane would not even notice the rope-makers. Their eyes were filters through which only clarified, clean sights passed. He sighed for his own old, worldly generation that had so much more sense and took another swig from his flask.

William and Maria drank in the sights and sounds, describing them to each other as though everything must be repeated in order adequately to snare it. They larded everything with adjectives too rich for the mean reality, but it was only enthusiasm. They were too ready through predisposition to see noble toil. They meant no harm in it, for it was a painter's wonderland of colours and picturesque scenes, but increasingly William became uneasy and stopped effusing.

'What is it?' Maria asked, immediately sensitive to his change of mood.

'We should be made to get out and walk,' said William. 'We are living in castles and are quite out of touch. Turner would catch all this, I never could. I paint romance and he paints reality. Which is the better?'

'People demand romance. Life is too full of reality.' Maria did not sound convinced.

'You know perfectly well that that is the sort of reasoning I revolt at! Why should I care what people demand?' Maria smiled at him, she had no need to put it into words. 'Yes, I'm compromised. We all are by the creature needs of our miserable frames.'

They passed the rope-walk. They stared out of the windows at the twelve men, six from each end, approaching each other in the middle. The men did not look up. Their eyes were on the yarn, their dirt-caked feet moved steadily, automatically. Their action had the same inexorable quality as that of the reapers in the field, and the image flashed into William's mind. It contained menace for those free to move, and stubborn persistence. It was the persistence of the crowds that turned the funeral of the Queen. It would have its way. One day.

Mr Wells stood on the pine platform beside Thomas, and Masterson stood on Thomas's left. Behind were Mrs Wells, Miss Wells, a girl of twenty, Sam, Jane, Henry, Maria and William. Behind and slightly apart stood the master ship's carpenter and his wife, embarrassed by their position on the platform, and embarrassed by being dressed in their best clothes, which were not good enough, beside all these City swells. Thomas was ridiculously nervous. An address to the Bench was never like this. About forty workmen and their wives were chattering below while a dozen determined and hefty-looking men stood ready by the dog shores and keel shores, ready to strike them out with sledges. They spat on their hands, eyed the shores and joked with each other. Thomas envied their familiarity. He was still convinced the ship might fall over and was concerned for the safety of the men.

Aboard, a crew of half a dozen men hung over the stern waiting for the launch. They would attend to her capture and enslavement lest she try to slip free down the river. Thomas wished Caroline was with him. He could not escape that thought, and support. Not the present Caroline but the Caroline that was, the unbanished image. A man had finished tying a green bush of some species to the bow, where it hung over the figurehead of an undistinguished plump young woman whose clothing had slipped from one violent pink shoulder and who was making a peering gesture, with her right hand shielding her eyes. Thomas wondered what the significance of this was. She looked as though she was trying to see through the shrubbery. He made a brief speech when Wells called for silence, thanking the men for their fine work, trusting she would be a happy and profitable ship.

'The good Lord bless the *Thomas K.* and all her crew.'

'Lord bless the *Thomas K.* and all her crew!' chorused the workmen with impious jollity. Wells nodded. The bosun's whistles blew a squealing chorus that might have been anything or nothing and the men with heavy hammers set to as though it were a logging race. Wedges flew, shores dropped out and the ship quivered, paused as though to have a last look at its birthplace, then sighed down the tallow greased plane into the peasoup water of the Thames. The workmen let out a cheer, while Sam, Wells, William, Maria and Thomas gave a hurrah! The restraining cables pulled up taut and she was afloat. She seemed to Thomas to find the water to her liking, sitting high as a duck on a nest. They returned to Wells' office with a great feeling of anticlimax, to take refreshments before their return to London. Thomas felt there should have been so much more in it for him. It was, after all, a kind of birth, yet he did not have the child. Life seemed this way to him at every turn.

He was congratulated by everyone in turn, including Masterson, which slightly unnerved him. After all, the man was half-owner. There was a hearty naval air about the man when he talked to others, but he adopted an almost obsequious tone for

Thomas. Perhaps he was unaccustomed to doing business or embarrassed that he could not put up all the money himself. Thomas hoped he would grow out of it, for he was to run the trading side. Henry was polite to Thomas, almost cordial. Their shared experience had drawn them much closer together. Whatever Thomas thought of Henry's behaviour towards Perrin, he had to concede that the boy had behaved with courage. Damn it all! He was proud of the boy. No damned fool like Perrin was going to pull down the Kelleway name with tricks and nonsense! He only wished that Jane could look more lively. The girl seemed wholly abstracted and he supposed he would have to rescue her as Sam was gaily in conversation with the Wells's pretty daughter. He excused himself from Henry.

'Come along, Jane, I hope to make my fortune on that ship. Henry tells me he has got a good case. I'm delighted to hear it. It is not perhaps a spectacular case for the law books but will make good stuff for the journals. It is the stuff of reputations when some silly woman fights the thing out in public. It is a sort of game of revelations. He will have half a dozen such cases in a year, you wait and see. You must become his expert on couture. I confess my total ignorance on the matter. Give me a fraudulent company or for that matter a good contested swindle!' He realized that Jane was staring at him with incomprehension. His stomach seemed to shrink within him at the concealment which itself exposed an unhappy situation. Young Henry should have been delighted. But what other motives were there that he could guess at and pray to God were nothing but the stupid terrors of an old fool?'

'I'm sorry,' Jane said politely, 'Henry didn't tell me he had a good case. I am very glad to hear it.'

'Probably didn't want to bore you with it – barristers are terrible bores to their wives.' Jane appeared genuinely uninterested, but he wondered how much of it was an act. 'I just bore anyone who will listen.' He passed quickly on to other things, trying to persuade himself the damage would only be slight. He was angry with Henry that he should have put him in a position to compromise himself.

Oh God, thought Jane, make some refuge for women. They are so easily exposed to such damage from which they emerge wanting, whatever the case, and they have no redress. They are either stupid or are being kept in ignorance for some secret motive known in the coterie of men. Yet my victory is my lack of interest – in Thomas and through him in Henry. I have embarrassed Thomas and Thomas has found this concealment out, whatever new secret it contains, and he will pursue it. Now I have a stranger in the house. Let Thomas pursue, I will sit and watch the chase, for I am sure that I am not involved. The stranger will find no refuge with me.

William and Maria were talking in great good humour with Mrs Wells, a very spirited matron dressed rather too loudly to be quite fashionable, but, Maria thought, a delight amongst these ghosts. Outside the workmen were drunk and dancing to a squeeze-box and mouth-organ. She would have liked to be part of it, a thought that shocked and delighted her. Her father would never have hesitated.

Mrs Wells had somehow managed to get the footman attached to her as though by an invisible but irresistible cord. Thus she was able to summon up a silver tray of glasses of Madeira with a forward motion of her hand. The footman responded magically. He took pleasure in Mrs Wells, for Mrs Wells was drinking and he approved of it. He approved of Sam for the same reason. He thought the others a dull and preoccupied lot. The Madeira was of course intended for the gentlemen, being a great fashion at that time, but Mrs Wells thought it a fine cordial, warming to the constitution.

'This is no episcopal "tent", my dears,' she remarked, taking another glass and pushing the tray towards William and Maria, 'but has a goodly taste of the grape!' She had, she explained, developed a taste for it on that island when she and her husband had been there on shipping business. 'Did you enjoy the launching?'

'You must have seen many of them,' said William. 'It is a fine sight, filled with magic. Trees are so much of the ground, the earth. They are sawn and shaped and take on a shape that seems as natural to another element as they first seemed in their own. I cannot imagine the timbers of a ship being transformed back into trees. They lose their identity completely. I find that fascinating.'

Mrs Wells was lost by this, but beamed sweetly. 'But you are a painter, Mr Kelleway. You see things differently from ordinary people. I am an ordinary person. I enjoy the Madeira. You know,' she continued on an entirely different thread, 'this office is no place to entertain. It is too hard and work-ridden. The carpet is only here for the day, and so are the curtains. That screen over there conceals a mess of papers. What a terrible wife!' She laughed in a jolly way, motioned and secured another glass of Madeira. 'Such a pleasant cordial,' she murmured.

Perhaps attracted by the laughter at some inner level, Henry drifted over to join them. The Madeira immediately appeared. The footman observed with disgust that Henry toyed with the glass throughout. William introduced him in more detail than had been possible before the ceremony. Mrs Wells obviously had less interest in barristers than painters. Maria smiled to herself at the airy way in which she dealt with him.

'How is it, being a lawyer, Mr Kelleway?'

'I am a barrister, madam.'

'Are they not lawyers? Forgive me, Mr Kelleway, I really am confused in such matters. Do you wear a wig and gown?'

'Yes,' said Henry stiffly.

'That must be fun!' exclaimed Mrs Wells. 'Do have another Madeira. You must take several, you understand, to appreciate its full flavour. Did you enjoy the launch? Oh dear, so much like asking if you enjoyed lunch! No, I suppose not really. When all is said and done, there is not very much to it. In a way it is sad, like a deserted ballroom, for the yard is empty as soon as the ship touches water. It is a party which is over as it begins. All we can do is sit and look at her floating out there.' She sounded quite morose and Maria realized the Madeira was taking effect. 'Perhaps we should all sit down,' continued Mrs Wells, 'if anyone has remembered chairs.' She motioned with her hand and the silver tray was presented in front of her. 'Thank you, but what we really need is chairs. We have had a long and tiring day. I daresay my husband has some somewhere.'

'Yes, madam.' The footman departed to some ante-room and reappeared with a wild-eyed companion, none too steady on his feet. They carried hard wooden chairs such as clerks use, and placed them down. Mrs Wells subsided gratefully.

'How is your case going? We have all heard it may make you some name,' Maria asked Henry while these proceedings continued.

'I think it will go well enough. As for making my name, I suppose anything between husband and wife is good enough for scandal. I believe this lady has consumed enough Madeira,' he added, dropping his voice. 'I doubt if she will be able to get up again.'

'Sit down, my dear!' roared Mrs Wells.

'Thank you, in a moment,' smiled Maria.

Mrs Wells, thus frustrated, shouted William into an adjoining chair and treated him to her views on painting. Maria wished she could have listened, but Henry was determined to keep her. He came quickly to the point.

'Maria, how is Caroline? I cannot ask Father, and I so rarely see you.'

'We do not live so far away. But we live in different worlds and must reconcile ourselves to it, isn't that true, Henry?' He wished she would not be so keenly to the point.

'I suppose it is. I cannot commend Caroline but I cannot condemn her like Father. She lost her youth to us. Is it so terrible to snatch at motherhood? It happens all the time. One child in six, I believe, is born out of wedlock and in the so-called aristocracy the proportion is even higher.'

'You are justifying it. I don't feel it needs justification, and I shall look after her. You are making a case for her in your heart, Henry. I don't feel she has committed the slightest crime. If you wanted a child, would you not simply have one?'

Henry was so astounded by this statement that he was unable to do more than twirl his half-full glass. Maria unnerved him completely. He supposed he admired her as much as he feared her. She had no place in his concept of what a woman should be, yet she was in many ways his conscience. She touched him lightly on the arm, as though she understood and wanted to comfort.

'It is a hard thing, Henry. You administer the law and it has no room for hearts. They hung a boy of nine two days ago because he poked a stick with a rag through the bars of a colour-merchant's shop and stole a swab of pigment. No one but the

law could make a case for that. You have no right to a conscience. You must forfeit it with your profession.'

'I will not permit you to be so hard on me!' Henry was flustered and angry. 'She is my sister!' He said this louder than he
intended, and coloured, looking round to see if anyone had
heard. 'Thomas is too hard,' he said, almost whispering, 'and I
want to know how she is. You have chosen to turn my anxiety
into a personal attack. How could you do that?'

'She is well, Henry, and I will always be delighted to keep you
informed.' She spoke with such warmth that Henry's anger
evaporated. He bowed to her stiffly.

'I am really very much beholden to you, Maria.'

'And I believe I am to you.'

He moved away to stare out of the window at the ship. What
had she been driving at? Maria would never preach the abso-
luteness of right and wrong unless she had some motive. He
feared she must know, or guess about Mrs Waters. Mrs Wells
roared with laughter, making all heads turn. Her legs were stuck
out straight in front, showing her ankles. Her strong yellow dress
was becoming crumpled. It did not suit her rosy complexion
and shone round her chin like a huge buttercup. Henry was
thankful for her vulgarity, for he was in no mood to participate
in any civil conversation. But before he had time to wonder
where he could discreetly hide, there was a knock on the door,
and the unsteady footman escorted in a young man. He had
been riding, and was wearing Hessian boots and riding-coat. He
carried his top hat under his arm, and was dusty and perspiring.
They all stared at him, and the young man was naturally embarrassed. He did not carry with him any hint of alarm, but
rather looked as if he expected a welcome. Wells stepped over
to him, shooting a glance at his wife, who sat up straighter.

'Yes, sir. Have you business?'

'I have a message for Mr Thomas Kelleway and have been
told to ride here immediately by Mr Justice Fellowes.' He felt
in his coat and proffered an envelope sealed with red wax to the
room at large. Thomas took it. 'I believe it is pleasant news.'

'Thank you, sir,' said Thomas with a grim scowl that stiffened
the young man up. He opened the envelope and read the paper
within. He stood for a long time contemplating, his head nod-

ding gently up and down. 'Sam, the Parliament has made me a Bencher.' His head nodded up and down again. Sam rushed over to congratulate him. Thomas grasped his arm, whispering, 'Take me out of here, Sam, for I feel I shall make a fool of myself. This is all too heady a cup.'

Sam led Thomas outside to an office, the others congratulating him or warmly clapping him on the back on his way. Only Mrs Wells was unaffected, for she was snoring, bolt upright, attended by the footman lest she fell.

Henry was working by the light of four candles. Other parts of London might blaze with the naked flames of gas, but not the Temple. An occasional Court or Alley was illuminated by one of the intruders that cast its comparatively brilliant glare on homing counsel, but in chambers, wax or oil was the rule. The gas-light of London might be the wonder of Europe, but members of the bar are not easily impressed by the facility of science. They reserve their admiration for the invention of some new contortion of defence that will occupy my lords the King's Justices for a year or two. They have heard that machines called 'portable steam engines' are in use in Yorkshire for pulling coal from mines, and that they are not uncommon. They have even heard that plans are afoot to link town to town and carry members of the human race, but regard this as an improbable event and an enormous risk. However, risk ever benefits lawyers, so they are philosophical men.

The weather was cold, and he kept a meagre fire burning. Coal was expensive and Henry was beginning to feel the strain. To be more precise about it, he had long felt the strain, but Jane had begun to notice the scarcity of money for the ordinary wants of the house. Henry lived in fear of paying the servants' wages. The housekeeper alone, without allowance for tea, sugar and beer, cost forty pounds a year. They lived as though his income were three thousand a year, when it was less than a thousand. He could ill afford the money he spent on Mrs Waters. Beside the documents of her case that surrounded him on the desk were sheets of paper covered with figures. They proved over and over again the insolvency of his practice of the law.

He relied on Jane's money to survive. It was a pretty picture. He found that he resented Jane increasingly, when she queried his business affairs. She always used the same pretext that he must have outstanding accounts that he had omitted to collect.

'You are too careless of your fees,' she said in one of their encounters, 'it may be a charming quality in a man of the law, but it is beginning to embarrass us at home. I'm sure that Thackeray or Turvey don't extend such privileges for long. Can you not speak to Corbett? The man is not doing his job.'

'Corbett does his job well enough.'

'Then why does he not attend to you?'

'Jane, there is not so much outstanding as you presume. I cannot command expensive briefs. You know that very well.'

Jane was silent for a long time. When she spoke, he was alarmed to see her close to tears. He would be unable to comfort her, even to put an arm around her. 'I have no head for business,' she finally said, quickly leaving the room. He had not followed her and she had not expected him to. They lived on exchanges of insincere civility, heavy with suppressed anger. It was never Jane's inclination to stand and fight. Her head for business that she was so ready to dismiss was all that ensured their survival. In the morning she did her own round of the kitchens after breakfast, not relying on the housekeeper alone. She checked that work had been done without waste and handed out articles required from the store cupboard. She talked with Cook, comparing the costs of food, always managing to make it appear like zeal and not anxiety. It was a depressing struggle.

Jane insisted on making her visits and morning calls, but received no thanks for trying through conversation to build up Henry's limp reputation. He had never cared for social gatherings and was dismissive. They gave few dinners these days because of expense. Jane pleaded as good reason that Henry had an abundance of work and was frequently very late. This latter at least was true. Yet they still had to maintain the linen, plate, silver, china, glass, servants and cellars that were a necessary part of the fiction of Henry's success. Jane had borrowed money secretly from Sam, who had asked no questions, knowing the answers too well. With his aid she managed to keep up her own appearance and pay the tradesmen. The similarity of her own situation with that of Henry's case was too bitter to dwell on.

Jane had tried to resign herself to childlessness. They always slept apart now and she could see no possible end to it. She had ceased weeping and had thought out the realities quite coldly. She would be glad of children, without love, she had decided. It had at first seemed a desperate thought as it struggled to emerge from the laced-up recesses of her unconscious. It had grown into something that could not be suppressed. She envied Caroline. She, Jane, had all the trappings and none of the results in human terms of happiness and a home. Henry feigned that he was unaware of these deficiencies. His women were his total distraction. She knew enough about the male animal to know that her longings would remain unfulfilled while his guilt or his passion made her repugnant. Yet many children were fathered without love, as the tales told by her calling friends recounted, skirting round the subject and talking in low voices, but making it perfectly clear. It was said that drink could achieve the necessary situation and she decided she would not shrink from it. Henry might alter if she were with child, but she put no faith in it. It was not even important. It was the child she wanted and surely he could not remain indifferent? Anything would be better than civility.

Henry could not settle to his work. It was clear and cold outside, and none too warm in his chambers. He stared out at the street lamps and the night sky. The stars seemed big and low. On Monday there had been another bad fog with accidents and fatalities at the Elephant and Castle. The thieves had had a holiday. He wondered if it might turn to fog again tonight for there was a look of frost about it. He pulled his curtains again and slumped in one of the depressed chairs. He had earlier demanded the newspapers from Corbett, who had observed that as all the other gentlemen had finished with them, there was no reason not to give them to Mr Kelleway. In his restless mood he was able to appreciate the sublimely incongruous disposition of the news. In newspapers, the world thrives on great or trivial incidents. The bulk of man's affairs is of no interest.

The *Courier* and *The Times* were concerned about the situation in Turkey. In Constantinople the Janissaries were being executed each evening to the sound of cannon. Lord Strangford and Count von Lutzow, the Austrian Ambassador, were incessant in their efforts to preserve peace between Turkey and Russia. At home, Carville colliery near Newcastle had exploded, and fifty-two men and boys of the fifty-five working there had been instantly killed, the force of the explosion being such that the body of one boy was blown high out of one shaft and fell again to the bottom. They were using naked candles while they worked at an intruding seam of rock. 'A remarkable incident in Ayr' was reported. While a gentleman in Wellington Square 'was busied with his toilet, a pane of glass in the window near which he stood was instantly shivered into pieces, and a fine brown pheasant darting across the room struck violently against the opposite wall and fell stunned to the floor. It is supposed that a hawk had been in pursuit.' It occupied as much space as the colliery disaster. Henry turned to the Law Reports with some anger. He hoped the gentleman enjoyed his pheasant.

John Jacobs was indicted for assaulting Ellen Alderson and stealing from her person a bonnet, one shilling in money and a handkerchief. Found guilty. Sentence – death. The Jury recommended clemency for the prisoner. The Common Serjeant said that he would put forward the Jury's recommendations of mercy but that this sort of incident had become too common an occurrence. The prisoner should not put much trust upon it but prepare himself for the awful fate to which his conduct had subjected him.

Henry Harris (14 years), Richard Prendergrass (12 years), and Michael Anderson (only 10 years old), were indicted for stealing from the person of the child P. Wright in the parish of St Giles a coral necklace. Found guilty. The two younger to be flogged, the older put into a place of refuge for the destitute. A workhouse.

Henry laid the papers down. The columns were full of similar things. Two-thirds of the cases were children, desperate but experienced rejects from society. He looked over Mrs Waters' papers. The sums of money, the extravagance of dress, the accusations. If the case should go against her, it would mean social disgrace for a while. Mrs Waters, allowed thirty pounds, had spent a hundred pounds on clothes and as much again on jewellery. John Jacobs would hang for a bonnet, a shilling and a handkerchief. Perhaps it was his depressed state and the contemplation of his own financial affairs that pricked him to a lively sense of outrage and pity for these unfortunates. It was also honest recognition of his own fall from grace.

He was hopelessly embroiled with Mrs Waters, wanted her desperately with the passion of immoderate youth. His marriage to Jane had been gently arranged, had been put in his path since birth.

He thought that he had devised the means of defence for Mrs Waters. The nub of the issue would be the evidence that showed that Vesey Waters was exceptionally mean and severe in his domestic and business dealings, and above all that there had been no concealment. Mr Montague had been a pleasant surprise. By appearance a John Bull, he had shown himself to be shrewd and tactful. He valued the trade of women, he said, as Henry might well understand, and generally found them better customers than men. He had every reason to suppose that Vesey Waters was perfectly aware of his wife's purchases, and had no reason to suppose there had been any concealment. The goods had been delivered openly. It was true that the times of delivery had been pre-arranged for specific times, but these were all within his normal trading hours. There was no doubt about the loyalty of Mrs Waters' servants, because, for Mr Montague, he had their affidavits. They stated that her clothes were always in plain view if her husband had an eye to look, but that as he treated her dress with indifference, never showing the slightest interest in it, they doubted whether he cared. If he cared, then he did not comment. It could also be shown that on the dates of deliveries, Mrs Waters could have had no certain knowledge of her husband's movements and that he could on any of the days returned home at any time. His absence at work merely coincided with the working day of Mr Montague's delivery men. As a pleader at the bar, the length or brevity of any day's proceedings were quite uncertain.

The jury would have to decide upon the question of necessities, and here he would have to make his case. It must be proved that she had been no more than reasonable in dressing up to the position required of her by her husband's station. It was embarrassing that Vesey Waters was a member of the Bar. He had groaned with disbelief when Corbett had with so much relish pointed it out.

'It is not a case,' Corbett had continued, 'that I can see any way of your winning, Mr Kelleway, to the entire satisfaction of your career. They say that Mr Waters is a man who bears a grudge with as much good grace as a bad tooth. It is always a bad case when a man of the Law is brought in as the defendant.' Corbett had shaken his head with heavy gloom. He was enjoying himself enormously.

'Then why the devil does he not pay up?' Henry had demanded angrily. 'That would be an end of it. It is sheer vexation.'

'Ah, Mr Kelleway, we should not speak of a member of the Bar in that way.' Henry went pink with anger, and stared at the man. 'Mr Waters will see it as a matter of impugned honour. He wants to be judged and cleared.'

'I realize that, of course. Kindly do not discuss Mr Waters.' Henry was short and rude. 'Damn it, Corbett, that is gossip!'

Corbett drew himself up with an attempt at hauteur. 'It is bold of you to speak like that, Mr Kelleway. Perhaps you have received further briefs?'

Henry glared, but was wise enough to hold his tongue. Corbett left with elephantine dignity, leaving no doubt that he was contemplating a suitable revenge. Henry heard him complaining to Perrin in the corridor. He had been wise to keep quiet.

The knock on the door surprised Henry, and he immediately closed the *Observer*, folded up the papers and thrust them away in a drawer. It could not be Corbett, for the man had gone home and in any case would merely have tapped and entered, knowing well that Henry had no client in consultation. The concealment of the newspapers made him feel slightly ashamed. It was a sign of his professional uncertainty, his determination to present a good face. Thackeray would have continued reading, even in the presence of a client, just for long enough to establish that the client was really an intrusion whom he would deal with as a favour. There was a second knock, like the first, tentative yet rapid. Whoever it was was concerned to come quietly.

'Who is it?' Henry called, but either the person did not hear him or did not like to reply. Henry felt a slight pang of fear. Mrs Waters would not be so indiscreet as to come to his chambers alone in the evening. He prayed not. Then it might be a thief or robber who had slipped in past the porters. He got up from his desk and opened the door abruptly, keeping himself to one side but with a foot strategically placed to stop it opening more than a few inches.

The man outside was a complete stranger. He wore clothes of inferior cloth, not tailored. He had the appearance but not the manner of an artisan. Around his neck he wore a spotted kerchief. His boots were heavy and coarse-grained. Just behind him in the corridor stood a porter with a very watchful eye. Like all his sort, he was intensely suspicious of the artisans and the poor, always keeping one eye on the rookery of St Giles just across the road. He would not leave until he was satisfied with the man's intentions. Henry was heartened by his presence. The porters were burly, tough men.

'What do you want?' asked Henry. His tone was not polite.

'Are you Mr Kelleway?' The man's voice was firm enough. His accent was strange, part London, part northern. It was difficult to know which was uppermost.

'Yes.'

'May I see you, Mr Kelleway, on a matter of business?'

'I am busy. I am a barrister. There must be a mistake. Do you need a solicitor?'

'I know you are a barrister, sir, and I have no need of a solicitor. If I may explain why I have come to you,' the man looked at the porter and back to Henry again, 'I lent a silk handkerchief to your brother, and we became acquainted in Park Lane. We shared rooms for a while as well.'

Henry took a moment or two to make the connection in his mind, then he stood aside, opening the door. 'Very well. Come in.' He nodded to the porter who lifted his beaver in response and moved down the corridor as though he fitted it. Henry closed the door and returned behind his desk where he remained standing. 'Now then, what is it you want? You understand I can take no instructions from anyone direct but only through a solicitor? What is this about my brother? I am grateful for the help you gave. Of course I will compensate you for the handkerchief, and shall be delighted to add to it for your pains.' Henry's delight would have curdled milk.

The man was quick to respond. 'No, sir, I don't want no ex gratias.' The phrase surprised Henry. He must have showed it. 'You are wondering, of course, what I am, and I will try to explain. You do not know me, sir, but I saw you when Mr Kelleway your brother was released after the funeral of the late Queen. It seemed to me, if you will forgive me saying so, that you had matters sewn up and arranged proper quick. I took the liberty of finding out your address in order that I might pay you this visit.'

'I still don't understand. Would you be good enough to come to the point?'

'I will come to it directly, sir. But it is a difficult matter in some respects. If you hold the Combination Acts to be dear to your own thinking, the prosecution and jailing of newsvendors and the brutal exploitation of children, then I had best stop now and you may show me the door. I will go away, sir, and you will never see hair nor hide of me again, of that you can be sure. But if you are a brave man, as I believe you to be, then I would beg you to give me a fair hearing.'

Henry was nonplussed. The instincts of a London gentleman of his upbringing and class were unreasoning and immediate and were to tell the man to get out. He knew, historically, of the condition of the Spitalfield weavers and of the actions of the Luddites, Jacobins and Paineites. These had for him associations of conspiracy, secrecy and violent revolution. They represented the anti-Christ to the establishment. But London was to a great extent ignorant of the Combinations, the more moderate groups of artisans and craftsmen, banned by law but allowed through prudent necessity. There were those that smelled of Radicalism. There were those who campaigned for the abolition of the Corn Laws or the Malt Tax, for a ten hour working day instead of the twelve or fourteen often worked. These moves were the subject of campaigns in Parliament and out, and respected men championed them. Henry and his contemporaries talked about them but knew little. Of the condition of the labouring poor, the vendors of news-sheets and of child labourers, he knew virtually nothing. Occasional cases of gross abuse of labour appeared in the Courts, or the arrest and sentence of a newsvendor. Sentence was given and the ill removed. It seemed to Henry that life went on much as normal and without any great need for change. Indeed, opposition to the established order appeared clearly to him as treason.

Yet the man before him was reasonable and his speech, though coarse, was coherent. He evidently meant what he said and would depart at a word. He did not look the sort of man who said things he did not mean. Henry looked at him again. He was well-shaven and his face ruddy – a man who did a good deal of travelling on horseback. He evidently did not work in factory, mill or mine. The man's blue eyes held an expression which belied the humility of his approach. If anything, he looked like a country squire who had fallen on hard times. Curiosity is the devil. Henry had to know more.

'I have no truck with Radicals!' The man smiled, but said nothing. 'Perhaps you had better give me your name, sir, for then I can hear your business and perhaps know what it is you want.'

'My name, sir, is William Watson. I represent men, women and children who find themselves in trouble with their masters or who are prosecuted under our existing laws. I represent to a degree Mr Hazlitt, Mr Hone, Mr Cruickshank and Mr Carlile. The Combinations deserve to be heard in their own defence as any man deserves to be heard before the law. In brief, Mr Kelleway, we have extensive funds, and if we are to proceed in a lawful way, we must have the law behind us when the law attacks us. We must find counsel for the defence. Without counsel, we get no hearing and summary justice which is no justice at all. We have other counsel who will undertake our defence, but we need a man in London. This is the reason for my approach. I know no counsel, and although the thread that has led me here may seem very slender to you, sir, it is the only guide I have.'

Henry did not know what to say. The proposition seemed

unreal. 'Forgive me, Mr Watson, but have you any idea of the cost of employing counsel?'

'Forgive me, sir, but you can have no idea of the extent of our funds. Our revenue through dues is fifty pounds a week. The carpenters alone have a reserve of two thousand pounds.' Henry looked at the badly-dressed man, wondering if this was some joke, or if he was being mocked. The man had the nerve to smile at him as though in sympathy at his bewilderment.

'You cannot have such money!'

'Our dues are a penny a week for each member. You may work out that we have over twelve thousand subscribing members.'

Henry, without thinking about it, sat down. Only when he was seated did he realize he had succumbed to his surprise in such a conventional fashion as to spoil his image of poise. He attempted to recover by lying back somewhat in his collapsed chair and displaying his Wellington profile. Mr Watson politely demolished the situation by asking if he might sit too. Henry nodded.

'Men have made their reputations with us,' Watson said, 'though I don't say you have any need of such nonsense. I don't mean in any way to be impolite, Mr Kelleway, but we have become accustomed to be forthright with words. Nothing would be asked of you outside your normal profession. You would not be asked nor would be welcome to attend any meeting of the Combinations, unless,' he added with a smile, 'you were prepared to take the oaths. It would not be permitted.'

'What about this sort of thing?' said Henry, opening the drawer of his desk and pulling out the newspapers. 'The *Observer*. Old Bailey, Saturday.' He read from the paper. ' "The Constitutional Association. The King against Charles Sanderson, at the prosecution of the Constitutional Association." It is Mr Adolphus speaking. "It has been discovered that the prisoner was a tool in the hands of a set of base wretches, who have declared that nothing shall ever stop them from vending the poison which, for such a continued period, they have disseminated all over the country. The parties, into whose hands the boy unfortunately fell, have declared that they will never desist from publishing these infamous libels; and the object of the institution is not to punish persons who act ignorantly, but those who, in defiance of all law and its consequences, persevere in their illegal practices. It has been satisfactorily proved that the prisoner, prior to his entering the shop where he sold the libel in question (Carlile's shop in Fleet-street), was a virtuous and honest boy, in the employ of a respectable man, and that he was seduced to sell the offensive works, not knowing that he was violating the laws of his country. The boy was in want of a situation, when he was induced to enter into the employment of the creatures that he has described, and was now sorry that he had been guilty of the offence imputed to him." That is your Carlile. Is that the sort of defence you expect me to take up?'

'Carlile is in Dorchester gaol. He produces the *Republican* from there. Many of his bookmen are there with him. I read the newspapers, Mr Kelleway. What is the infamous libel? It does not seem to me that the words of Mr Adolphus are entirely without defamation. If you read *The Times*, you will find another perspective put upon it.'

Henry coloured. 'Adolphus defended Thistlewood and the Cato Street conspirators. I would have thought you might have had some respect for him for doing that job.'

'Adolphus is only concerned to further his career. We are no conspirators, but good artisans!' Watson spoke with some temper. He reached out and seized *The Times* from Henry's desk, and opened it. 'Here you will find the same report of the trial, but if you care to refer to the leading page you will find that their comment more accurately reflects the situation. Listen! "The Mock-Constitutional Association has sunk a step lower than even the efforts of its honorary Secretary and the employment of boy-spies could reduce it – it has been praised by Mr Adolphus. We certainly shall now scarcely think it worthy of further notice : we have too much generosity to trample on the fallen. For the particulars of this last and fatal assault upon this unfortunate body, we refer to the Old Bailey report." The question is, Mr Kelleway, do you agree with *The Times*, or accept the report without comment like the *Observer*?'

'Let me see!'

Watson handed over the paper, indicating the column. Henry read it through again and was silent.

'You see,' said Watson, calm again, 'the Constitutional Association is dedicated to the suppression of anything liberal or critical of the Government or condition of the people. The boy was put there by them. In everything we do, false and vicious rumours are circulated.' Henry wanted to protest but allowed Watson to continue. 'We say, for instance, that Spinners live in abject slavery. This is said to be libel. But I shall tell you, Mr Kelleway, how they live, because in London you may not know. They work fourteen hours a day, they are locked in, men, women and children in a temperature of over eighty degrees. They work three hundred and thirteen days of the year. There is no water provided for them to drink except at teatime which is half an hour. Even the rain-water is kept locked up. There is no ventilation, there is the smell of gas and the air is white as fog with cotton fuzz which they must breathe. Many die before they achieve the venerable age of sixteen, Mr Kelleway. They have a system of fines which confirms a state of slavery that does not exist in our houses of correction. If a Spinner is found washing himself, a fine of one shilling, opening a window, one shilling, spinning too long with his gas-light in the morning, two shillings, for remember they work both day and night with the wonderful introduction of gas lighting. Any Spinner heard whistling, a fine of one shilling, any Spinner leaving his oil-can out of place, six pence, any Spinner being five minutes late, two shillings, any Spinner being sick and not able to find a replacement, a fine of six pence for steam, per day.

'As Cobbett has said,' Watson went on relentlessly, 'by heaping people together there is produced proof of the most corrupting immoralities. I do not wish to shock you, Mr Kelleway, but if I must, I must. In Tyldesley in Lancashire two Spinners, found together in the necessary, are fined one shilling. We are cramming humans together like animals in a pen and creating consequences where the most loathsome vices break out like the disease hatched in that heat. Yet if we are to print what we know and see, we will be imprisoned and fined. But they will not stop us. The Combinations are our strength. In the mills, when men ask for more money, they bring in women to do the work. Now with steam power, they bring in children to do the work of women. And we are proud of it! We are the greatest exporting and manufacturing nation in the world. Our Minister for Foreign Affairs bombasts other nations, urging them to follow England in her humanity and abolish the black slave trade. Good God, Mr Kelleway, there are men in the north who would change their lives this instant for the freedom of a black slave!'

Watson was suddenly silent, embarrassed by his own passion. Henry too was silent as though trying to find some words of refutation. He knew instinctively that the man opposite spoke from personal knowledge. He knew too that he was right in what he had just been saying. He did not know if he would agree with the man on many of his other views, but he knew that he, Henry Kelleway, like all his kind, lived on the misery of millions. It was all a far cry from Mrs Waters' dresses and jewels. Was this to be his penance? His life was foolish enough to deserve it.

'We want no Adolphus, Mr Kelleway. We need honesty and integrity. There will be plenty of enemies who will try to destroy you inside and outside the Law Courts. I have no idea if you are our man, I'll be honest with you. Only you can decide.'

'Who are you, Mr Watson?'

'I was once a publisher myself.'

'And now?'

'I do what you see me doing. Try to get men to help us. However, I have said all I came to say, and more, no doubt! Please think on it. I can return.'

'No,' said Henry quickly, and before he had time to think about it and rationalize his motives, 'I won't think. There is no need to think. I will be glad to act as defence counsel if you need me.'

'I will approach you through a solicitor of course!' Watson was beaming.

Later that evening, he blew Helena Waters' hair from his face, gently, first to one side, then the other. She lay half across his chest, her hair hanging down on him like a fine curtain, her breasts soft on his chest. Lamps were lit in the room so that the servants should really believe that Mr Kelleway, the counsel, had come to confer with his client. Henry looked at her. Jane would never have lain in the light, naked, never lain upon him in this way. She would have trembled behind her sheet, begged for the lamps to be extinguished, blushed and protested. Poor Jane. He felt momentarily sorry for her, for she missed so much. He was unable to see in Jane any quality in her modesty, overwhelmed as he was by Helena Waters' sensuality. He reached down her back, stroking her body from buttocks to shoulder. She nestled her head down beside his, and he was aware how heavy she really was on his chest. The only problem of pleasure is satiation, he thought. We notice weight, we feel hot, our skins stick together. Nature is a moralist and imposes these discomforts, at first gently, then insistently, as if to remind us that this is only an interlude and there are other things to do.

'You know,' he said softly to her, 'because of you, this afternoon I committed myself to something I shall almost certainly regret.'

'Because of me? What was it? And why because of me?' She propped herself up again so that she could see him. Henry thought, she is heavy, and she is much plumper than Jane, too. I can hold the flesh upon her back, soft as it is. Skinny Jane is all ribs, almost a child's body. He wished his mind would not play these tricks upon him. 'I thought you had finished the papers for my dreary business?'

'Yes, I have.' He ruminatively ran his hand beneath her arm, cupped her breast. She gave no sign of noticing. Jane would have hid her face lest her expression showed distaste or pleasure. Lest her expression gave her away at all. 'No, it is nothing to do with your case, which can now take its course.'

She laughed. 'Has it not just taken its course! You may take that course again!' Henry was embarrassed now. He was tired and he still felt that he should get home that night. As though reading his mind, she said, 'You must stay the night, provided you leave early before the servants are about. My husband never comes here now. He stays in his chambers or at his club. Come, Mr Kelleway, I shall think you a lawyer of very poor stamina who cannot satisfy his client entirely!'

She was laughing at him, but Henry was discomfited by her

mention of her status as his client. His position, he thought ironically, was invidious enough.

'I have taken on another case, or it may well be cases. I think I only did it from a sense of guilt.'

'Guilt?' There was asperity in her question.

'Of a kind. It is very complicated.' He felt her move slightly from him. He was on dangerous ground. Henry was not sure if it was intentional or a reflex. It was only the third time they had lain like this but already he was becoming aware of her subtle uses and her demanding nature. 'I have been asked to be defending counsel, as far as I can see, for unspecified cases on behalf of London's newsvendors and Combinations. They want representation, and I have been approached to provide it. I said yes.'

'What an extraordinary thing!' This time there was no doubt. She moved from him and sat upright on the bed. Henry stared at her body in the lamplight. She made no attempt to conceal her nakedness. He could not see her face too clearly because of the shadows cast by the flame. 'Is that sensible?'

'I will do no more for them than I would do in any defence. All will be done properly through solicitors. It will merely be another brief.'

'But these people are involved in sedition and blasphemy. They are mechanics and artisans and publishers. You should not become involved with them. I can find you cases with people of some standing in society. You had no need to look for them in the gutter!'

'There are many respectable men among them and many respectable counsel will defend them. Why should they be treated differently from any other party?' Henry was annoyed by her reaction and her possessive response.

'No matter what you say, you will make enemies. You cannot expect to draw clients from good society if your business is with these types of people. Why did you not consult me? Does making love to me give you this guilt?'

'No!' protested Henry untruthfully.

'What is it, then?'

She stood up and put on a robe. The gesture was as definitive as though she had encased herself in armour. Henry sat up and swung his legs over the bed. He reached for his clothes.

244

'I think that I feel I am too privileged. Perhaps I am too indo-lent and do not care enough about issues outside my own life. There is terrible injustice and poverty in the country. I was moved by what I was told, that's all I can say. I felt I wanted to help. These people are fighting for their very lives, for their health, for their release from slavery. At least it seemed like that to me.'

'And cases like my own seem trivial?'

'I have not said that. You are putting words into my mouth. You have been disgracefully treated. You know I think that.'

'Do I?'

Henry stopped dressing, stood up and seized her by the shoul-ders. She tried to pull away from him, but Henry pulled the robe open, stripping her of her armour, and pushed her onto the bed. After a while she stopped struggling. They both know that he did it so that he did not have to answer and because it seemed the only solution in the short term. They both understood, it seemed, that the long term should be deferred. Henry felt wretched that he had come so suddenly to that state again with another woman. Mrs Waters' misery was no less deep than his own. It was all going to end so quickly.

8

Court of King's Bench, Westminster. Michaelmas Term.
Nisi Prius.
R. Montague Esq. v. V. Waters Esq.

Mr Justice Cranley looked like a silk cocoon which had been
laid in the dark recesses of the huge oak chair on the dais. His
full-bottomed wig and parchment face were the only parts that
could be clearly seen in the dim light, and his white goose quill
fluttered as he made a note. He wore the judicial black silk robe
trimmed with ermine, silk girdle, scarf and scarlet casting hood
appropriate to the proceedings. He was a slight man and seemed
lost in garments. The barristers wore their black gowns of stuff,
with white lawn bands tied round the collar and their short wigs
of thirty curls with a bald patch on top. Defence counsel Mr
Ward had ostentatiously placed his purple bag on his desk to
attract Mr Justice Cranley's eye. Henry could not do likewise for
such treasures of status could only be given by King's Counsel as
marks of approval.

The court room itself was off old Westminster Hall, the scale
and majesty of which left all concerned except the lawyers
suitably cowed before they even sat down. There was a considerable crowd of spectators. Henry had been right in expecting some notoriety to attach to the proceedings. So had Corbett. He wondered who they all were and prayed that Mrs
Waters was not among them, although he could not very well
see. Defence counsel Mr Ward was scribbling vigorously as a
largish man gave evidence from the box. Henry was pleased.
The witness was nervous, which gave him a simple honesty,
but he was also articulate and fluent which gave Mr Justice
Cranley no opportunity to interrupt, as he enjoyed doing, 'to
have it again, in English'.

'Now, Mr Freeson, you delivered dresses to the house of the defendant on several occasions. Can you remember how many occasions?'

'Four, sir.'

'You are quite sure?'

'I am quite sure, sir. It is all recorded in my day-books, along with the address and goods.'

'Was there any time given when the goods were to be delivered?'

'Yes. There was a time. It is noted in my books.'

'Is this unusual?'

'No. Ladies are accustomed to hold engagements at certain hours on any day, and it is quite usual for them to wish to see the dress when it arrives to ensure it is as they would wish. If it is not, then I take it back with a note.'

Henry had been very nervous at first. He was sure that no prisoner could have felt worse. But as soon as the proceedings had begun, he had started to relax. He wondered if Mr Ward had had the same nervous attack, but doubted it. Mr Ward was very experienced, especially chosen by Vesey Waters. Mr Ward showed no emotion of any sort until he had a witness on the run, then would display his acting talent with a wide range of expressions of doubt, disbelief, ridicule and contempt.

'Were your deliveries to the house of the defendant made at the same time?'

'No, sir. I have other deliveries to make. It is not possible.'

'But they were all made within your normal delivery hours?'

'Yes, sir.' There was a slight stir among the jury, and Henry felt that it had been well taken. Waters had insisted on a jury trial. He would make much of the question of extravagance. Henry sat down to allow Ward to proceed. Ward stood for some time in silence to invest his words with as much weight as possible.

'Mr Freeson, were these dresses you delivered expensive?'

'As to the price, sir, I have no idea, but they were very good, sir.'

'Over what period did you deliver these four dresses?' Freeson had to think hard. Ward delivered the answer. 'No matter, Mr Freeson, I have a record here that they were delivered over a period of only four months. That would mean one dress a month. Is that right?'

'I did deliver them over that sort of period, sir. It will be in my day-book ...'

'Oh, it is, Mr Freeson. Would you say that you are accustomed to deliver clothes so frequently to other customers?'

'I couldn't exactly say I am accustomed, sir.'

'Then give it to us in English!' interrupted Mr Justice Cranley with a certain sound of triumph in his voice, which was much more penetrating than his frame would suggest.

'Can you be more explicit, Mr Freeson?' Ward pursued.

'Well, sir, I meant that some customers have deliveries even more regularly than that. We are a respected concern ...'

'There is no room for advertisement in this Court!' interrupted Cranley. Freeson was being thrown off stride. Henry wondered if Cranley was sympathetic to Waters. Were they friends? They were both from Lincoln's Inn.

'Let me frame the question again, Mr Freeson.' Ward was now being extremely helpful. 'There are, of course, extremes. Would you say it was more common or less common to deliver dresses at a rate of one per month?'

'Less common.'

'A good deal less common?'

'I suppose so, sir.'

'You shall answer yes or no, sir!'

'Then yes, sir.' Freeson blushed and looked angry.

'Indeed, few women order dresses at such an interval?'

'Yes, that is so, but sir ...'

'No buts, Mr Freeson. Your answer is yes.' Freeson shrugged. 'Is it yes, sir? You must answer to the Court!' Ward turned on his sudden severity quite savagely. 'The Court cannot interpret the movement of your shoulders!'

'My Lord!' Henry was on his feet. 'The witness is being harassed!'

'No, Mr Kelleway, I do not believe he is. I cannot interpret the movement of limbs into English. The witness will refrain from these movements and give a good answer.' Henry sat down. Freeson had gone from pink to pale. Ward addressed him again. 'Your answer please, Mr Freeson.'

'Yes.'

'You mean that few women, in your experience, order dresses at the rate of one a month?'

'Yes.' Freeson was tight-lipped.

'Thank you.' Ward sat down.

Henry rose again immediately. 'I would like to examine on one point made by Mr Ward. How many times did you deliver to the house of the defendant?'

'Four, sir.'

'In one year?'

'Yes, sir.'

'Would you say that that is more common or less common compared with other customers as the number of dresses purchased in a year?'

'More common.'

'Would you say it is the generality?'

'Yes I would, sir, in my experience.'

'Object! My Lord, the witness is being led!' Ward was up.

'You will refrain, Mr Kelleway. The jury will pay no attention to opinion on what is or is not generality. The Court is not interested in opinion or experience. Mr Kelleway, you will not put words in the mouth of the witness.'

The silk cocoon rustled angrily. Henry was perfectly happy to provide him with a deferential bow. When Henry sat down, Mr Coke was caught with an expression of surprise on his frog-like face. He was praying that Mr Walters would not hold it against him as well. Henry was not losing like he should. Mr Montague patted Henry discreetly on the back.

'Good man, Freeson,' he whispered in Henry's ear, 'and you did it well.'

Henry found that he was enjoying himself. Coke found that he was not, and yet he should be. Vesey Waters was hunched beside Mr Ward like a black vulture, and Coke felt sure that his eyes were upon him.

The evidence of the butler followed smoothly. The man appeared detached and could not be ruffled in his corroborative evidence on delivery. Unfortunately he had a very male ignorance about clothes and all attempts to obtain proof that the garments had been worn at all were fruitless. However, he would give no ground to Mr Ward, who naturally took this as proof they had not. The butler reiterated that he was quite unable to say, one way or the other, one piece of female attire looking very much the same to him as another. As to colour, Mrs Waters had several garments of similar colours that were currently fashionable, and he would not be able to tell them apart. Mr Ward sat down frustrated.

Mrs Gibson the cook provided the surprise that Henry did not want. He had only ever encountered the butler and a maid on his own visits, and then only once. He had no knowledge that such a dragon was concealed in the basement, and the thought that she could have seen him made him feel very cold indeed. Mrs Waters had mentioned her in passing, but had given no indication that there was any bad blood. Mrs Gibson was definitely for the defendant. She bristled with hostility towards any question that put her master in a less than favourable light. Mr Ward was carefully cool, knowing well the dangers of letting her useful prejudice become unhelpful ire.

'Mrs Gibson, you have been cook to the defendant for how many years?'

'Twenty-two, sir.'

'A long time. Has the defendant in this time ever contested a bill?'

Henry protested. 'My lord, this is not relevant to the case. Are we to examine the household accounts or are we to continue with the case?'

Cranley conceded the point. 'Mr Ward,' he said, 'you must confine yourself to the goods in question.'

'I wished to prove, my lord, that my client is in all respects a gentleman who has honoured his tradesmen. It is relevant to the case to show that an exception has been made in this account from the plaintiff, and that the exception is a single event and for a specific purpose. I wished to show it was in no way the custom of the defendant to deny payment.'

'My lord!' protested Henry again, 'Mr Ward continues to make his case!'

'Sit down, Mr Kelleway! Gentlemen, you will both observe the rules.'

'Very well, my lord,' Ward continued smoothly. 'Mrs Gibson, did you see these dresses delivered?'

'I did. They were delivered by the delivery man to the tradesmen's entrance which is beside the kitchen.'

'And the goods that came with the dresses, the jewellery?'

'I did not see the jewellery, but the delivery man said that he had and he handed in a receipt. The receipt also listed the jewellery. It was signed by Mrs Waters. The man would not leave until he had the signed receipt as proof of delivery.'

'Did you say anything to the man?'

'To Mr Freeson? Is that the man?'

'It is.'

'Thank you. Please continue.'

'I said to him, I hope Mr Waters knows about these, I really do, for it seems a lot of money to me. That's what I said.'

'Did Mr Freeson reply?'

'He did.'

'What did he say?'

'He told me to mind my own business, sir! I said I was sure that my master's business was mine if there was money being spent what he didn't know about!'

'I must protest most strongly, my lord, about the continued insinuations being made!' said Henry. 'This is most irregular.'

'Quite so, Mr Kelleway. Mrs Gibson, you must refrain from repeating chatter. Mr Ward, you must not encourage it. The jury will ignore the witness's remark.'

'Really, my lord,' Ward protested, 'the witness is only repeating what she said in answer to my question. It is either a matter of fact or it is not, that she said it.'

'She has expressed a supposition which she cannot support. It cannot be admitted.'

'Very well, my lord. But, with your permission, I propose to ask Mrs Gibson certain questions close to this subject because I believe it to be important as a point of law to show that some objection was made by a servant to the shop man. It is, I think you will agree, an important issue at law if it can be shown that a doubt had been raised in the mind of the shop man as to whether the goods were properly ordered within the defendant's knowledge. You will, my lord, be aware of such an issue as precedent. The onus would then transfer to the shop man to report the situation to his employer.'

'I agree that as a point of law it is perfectly proper, Mr Ward, but you must not stray.'

'Thank you, my lord. Mrs Gibson, I want you to answer me carefully. It is true that you said to the shop man, "I hope Mr Waters knows about it." Is that correct?'

'Yes.'

'Thank you. And on what occasion was that?'

'When he brought the second dress, which was in green silks, striped, with gauze, and a necklace with green stones and a gold ring with a green stone. I think they was jade. I don't know much about stones, not having any myself, and not holding with ornament.'

'Did you remark on anything when the shop man returned on the two following occasions?'

'I didn't like to, sir. He was sharp with me.'

'Thank you, Mrs Gibson.'

Henry was quickly to his feet. Mrs Gibson glared at him. She was short, grey-haired and obviously fiery. A woman of stern principles. That at least was how she would see herself. She and Mr Vesey Waters must share a common contempt for the world.

'Mrs Gibson, who actually received these packages? You would be busy in the kitchen, would you not?'

'Yes, I was busy in the kitchen. The housemaid took them in and gave them to the lady's maid who took them to Mrs Waters.'

'Then you really never had an opportunity to see them?'

'I did!' Mrs Gibson was outraged. 'I saw them large as life. The window looks over the area, I see everything that comes and goes.'

'But it was really none of your business.'

'Well I never! They was coming into the house. The master paid for them!'

'No, he hasn't, Mrs Gibson, which is why we are here.' Mrs Gibson was controlling herself with difficulty. Her head started to wobble about independently of her short body. She was very offended. 'However, you certainly saw the packages?'

'Yes, sir, I certainly did, each time they was delivered.'

'And you actually saw and read the receipts?' There was a

silence. Mrs Gibson's head wobbled even more.

'I saw the receipts.'

'And you read the receipts? You left the kitchen, came to the door, and when the house maid came back with the signed receipts, you read them before giving them to the shop man.'

'I never said that, I never did!'

'I suggest you never read any receipts, but heard about the items later. You have no first-hand knowledge of any receipt at all. Is that not true, Mrs Gibson?' She would not answer. Her face was flushed and a stubborn look formed about her mouth and lips. 'Is that not true, Mrs Gibson?'

'You must answer,' said Cranley, 'and answer the truth, in English.'

'I saw the receipts. Clear as I am here.'

'But you never read them, Mrs Gibson, I know you did not.'

'I never read them. But I saw them and I was told what was on them.'

'Quite. And how could you possibly know that the second delivery of packages contained a striped green silk dress?'

'Because it did!' Ward protested to Cranley.

Cranley addressed himself, unfairly Henry thought, to him. 'Mr Kelleway, can you advise us of the purpose of this close questioning?'

'I can, my lord. As the packages were wrapped in thick paper, and bound with ribbon as is the custom with Mr Montague's shop, and as they were taken upstairs intact to be examined by Mrs Waters as her maid will testify, there is no way that Mrs Gibson can say that she knew what was in any of the packages as first-hand knowledge as she claims.'

Cranley was bound to concede. 'Go on, Mr Kelleway.'

'Mrs Gibson, you were told what the packages contained, were you not? You believe you know the contents of the second delivery. You do not, I put it to you, have any idea what the other packages contained. The reason is that the lady's maid herself does not know, because Mrs Waters opened them in private. Is this not so? What knowledge you profess is only servant's gossip. Thank you, Mrs Gibson, you may step down.'

Henry sat down abruptly. Mrs Gibson looked as though she might never be moved. An official touched her arm and she angrily brushed him off, darting glances defiantly round the Court as though looking for anyone with whom to conclude her unfinished business. Mr Justice Cranley spoke to her with the courtesy of a slave-master.

'Stand down, woman, or you will be put down!' Mrs Gibson left.

Mr Montague looked impressive. The jury would like him, Henry felt sure. That had to be weighed against the too obvious fact that they would believe Vesey Waters. If he could dent that belief, then the collapse would be utter, for a man of the law must be above all petty considerations, domestic or otherwise, when he gets himself in front of a jury. Henry guessed that he could rely upon Mr Ward to make much of Vesey Waters' position. He also guessed that Ward would dispose of Mr Montague quickly. He must not hang around in the eye of the jury too long. Ward was indeed to the point.

'Mr Montague, is this the first action that you have ever brought in respect of the debts of a wife?'

'No, it is not.'

Henry judged he would not object. It would be tactically wrong. He sensed that Ward would welcome it, for there was something about the way Ward was standing with his back half turned to him.

'Then it is your experience that ladies do sometimes ignore the limits of their allowance and purchase things other than necessaries?'

'It is my experience that they sometimes do.'

'And do you think, Mr Montague, that a tradesman has a responsibility in this matter?' It was a question that Henry had rehearsed with Montague and he was delighted to hear it asked.

'I most certainly do.'

Ward immediately took the opening provided. 'Have you exercised that responsibility in this case?'

'I have.'

'You feel you made adequate enquiry, had adequate assurance that these purchases, to this considerable sum, were made with the knowledge of the defendant?'

'I felt that no enquiry was called for.'

'Why? Is that exercising responsibility as you say you have?'

'Because Mrs Waters has for years been a regular customer.'

'Did she always spend so much?'

'No.'

'Was this the first time she had spent so much?'

'Yes.'

'Then how could you feel that no enquiry was called for? Did your shop man not report his conversation with the cook?'

'He did not, and I would never let the gossip of servants influence my decision regarding the honour of my customers.'

'But still you felt that no enquiry was called for although the sum the defendant's wife was spending was greater than you had ever known her to spend?'

'Mrs Waters does not spend a great deal on clothes. Her husband has been adopted as a prospective parliamentary candidate. I assumed that these arrangements were in connection with his station.'

'You assumed, but made no enquiry to the defendant?'

'No.'

'Thank you, Mr Montague.'

Ward sat down, well satisfied. It was a solid point at Law. Henry saw it had to be answered, and was brief.

'Can you tell the Court, Mr Montague, when you decided to approach the defendant in order to secure payment?'

'When the defendant's account exceeded fifty pounds.'

'Is this your normal practice?'

'With every customer.'

'Thank you.' He felt he had contained the point. Whether it was accepted as reasonable the jury must decide. In the end it would be decided upon that principle.

Mr Vesey Waters had some difficulty deciding how he was to play his role, and this lent to his appearance an uncertainty of style wholly foreign to his normal court appearance. As an experienced pleader, he felt completely at home, and was prepared to treat the Court with lofty disdain. As a shrewd defendant, he must be sympathetic, honest, and neither lofty nor lowly. As a wronged husband, he must be hurt and bewildered. The combination was less than perfect. It came together as slightly scornful petulance. Juries would not like it, no matter how much they respected the man's position. Waters refused to look at Henry at first, as though he was beneath contempt, and addressed his answers to Mr Justice Cranley.

'Mr Waters,' Henry began, 'you have stated that you made your wife a perfectly adequate allowance for clothes. Will you please repeat for the Court the amount of this allowance?'

'Thirty pounds.' Mr Vesey Waters did not like discussing money. The words were forced from him.

'I'm sorry, Mr Waters, I did not hear.'

'Mr Waters said thirty pounds, Mr Kelleway,' Cranley supplied in a bellow.

'Thank you, my lord. Mr Waters, can you tell us how many dresses your wife possesses?'

'No.'

'Well, can you tell us if she possesses a great many?'

'No, sir, I cannot. The Law does not understand the words "a great many". It is a subjective term.'

Henry saw that Cranley would not intervene, he was enjoying it and liked to see young counsel put in their place.

'Perhaps in these circumstances you will permit the Court to be the judge of the Law, Mr Waters. I can appreciate it is an unfortunate situation that you find yourself in.'

'My lord, this is too much!' Ward was angry.

'Yes, Mr Kelleway, that is too much.' Yet Cranley did not sound severe.

'I apologize, my lord, if I gave offence. I intended to convey condolence.'

'I object to this line of questioning, my lord,' Ward said very forcefully, 'it is insinuation and has no bearing on the evidence.'

'With your permission, Mr Ward,' Henry continued quickly, 'I will ask Mr Waters a question.' Ward sat down, still angry. 'Does your wife possess more than ten dresses?'

'I believe she does.'

'But less than twenty?'

'In that order.'

'You are by no means sure?'

'No.'

'Do you take a great interest in clothes, Mr Waters?'

'No.'

'Would it be true to say that you are little concerned with clothes, and do not much notice them?'

'It would be true to say that I am little concerned with clothes. I do, however, notice if too many appear.'

'You have stated that these clothes were purchased without your knowledge?'

'That is so.'

'The thirty pounds a year that you allow your wife, does this include for the purchase of jewellery?'

'Yes.'

'Shoes?'

'Yes.'

'Scarves, shawls, stockings?'

'Yes!' Waters looked full at him now. Balefully. 'It is a clothing allowance, sir. I believe these are all items of clothing?'

'And you never saw any of this clothing?'

'I did not.'

'As far as you are aware?'

'I have said I did not, sir. You repeat yourself.'

'I would be obliged, sir, if you would answer simply yes or no.' Henry regarded Waters with a calm he did not feel. He was playing a dangerously provocative game. Mr Coke, behind Henry, felt he might swoon away at any moment. He sunk low in the hope of dissociating himself. 'I must ask you to think very carefully about your answer,' Henry continued. His tone was ominous and something in it conveyed to Vesey Waters that it might not be mere bluff. The same impression came through strongly to Ward. He leapt to his feet.

'My lord, I must protest about this bullying of the defendant. This is quite out of order. Mr Kelleway pursues with veiled threats. Quite out of order!'

Cranley, who had leaned forward with some interest, concurred, but without much edge to his rebuke. 'Mr Kelleway, what is the point you are driving at? Will you please get to it, if there be one. If there is not, then I shall view it most seriously.'

'My lord, the point is very real. I can prove that Mr Walters was seen in company with his wife when she wore these clothes and indeed these jewels that the defendant claims never to have seen.'

Cranley stared at Henry hard. Henry stared back, aware that Cranley had very mixed feelings indeed. That a pleader should be caught like this was quite outside one part of his code, but nevertheless the desire to protect a brother of the Bar was strong. It was prejudicial to the good name of the Law itself to have this sort of scene.

'I see. This is very serious, Mr Kelleway. I hope your proof is good?'

'It is, my lord.'

Ward was of course standing, flapping the sleeves of his gown. 'I must most strenuously object, my lord. I have no knowledge of this matter. We are not prepared for it.'

'Do you wish to adjourn, Mr Ward?'

'I wish to consult my client, my lord.'

'Very well.'

Ward bent down and he and Vesey Waters remained in stooped conversation for a few seconds. Waters was shaking his head. It was not clear what he meant until Ward turned to Cranley again.

'My client will not adjourn. He says he sees no reason to do so.'

Henry knew that he had his man. If Waters was adverse to an adjournment, then it must be because he was afraid of the introduction of more evidence, and would prefer to try to fight it out as it was. Cranley told him he might continue.

'Mr Waters, can you remember that you had an engagement to dine on the evening of the fifteenth of June this year with James Turner Esquire?'

'I remember the occasion, I do not remember the date.'

'It is sufficient that you remember the occasion. Can you remember what your wife was wearing?'

'No.'

There was by now some noise and gossip around the Court among the spectators. Waters looked at Henry with such venom that Henry knew he was lying. Whether he had ever thought about it before or not, he would never know, but there could be little doubt that Waters saw everything and remembered. He knew he was teetering on the brink and could not go back. He must know where the information came from, for he certainly had not given a diary of his appointments to Ward.

'On that occasion, I put it to you, your wife wore a green striped silk dress with pale green gauze.'

'I do not remember what my wife wore. I have a bad memory for such things.'

'I hope you can substantiate this, if you are going to pursue it, Mr Kelleway.' Cranley sounded severe now. Perhaps he reasoned that the sooner this were over the better. The more extended it became, the more public notice it would attract in the news-papers. If it went to a second day, gossip would fill the Court with the public and reporters. He considered that, in the circum-stances, Waters was probably right not to adjourn.

'I can substantiate this by eye-witness, my lord. The dress I have described is one of those purchased from Mr Montague, as I shall recall Mr Montague to attest, and is one of the dresses the defendant claims never to have seen. The defendant's memory is clearly at fault. I shall call the lady's maid, who will declare that the defendant's wife has only one striped green silk dress, that it is the one purchased from Mr Montague, and that on that evening her mistress wore that dress.'

'My lord, I protest that the Court should be used in this way. Mr Kelleway is quite out of order. Is he to be allowed to intro-duce his own evidence? His behaviour is monstrous, my lord!'

'Your behaviour does you no credit, Mr Kelleway. You will kindly wait until I ask you how you intend to proceed. If you in-terfere in this way again, I shall be most severe. It is my last warning.' Henry nodded obeisance. It cost him little, for he knew he had made all his points. 'Mr Ward, I think that your client must nevertheless answer on these points.'

'I can answer them, my lord,' Waters said, his voice loud and angry. 'I have no recollection what my wife wore, and I am sure that I was never made aware in any way whatsoever that my wife was wearing new clothes.'

'Now, Mr Kelleway,' said Cranley, 'but proceed with care.'

'You have no recollection, Mr Waters, of what your wife wore?'

'No!'

'But it is possible that she could have worn some of these clothes?'

'It is always possible. I would not have noticed. They certainly were not brought to my attention.'

'Do you recollect that on the evening of the twenty-second of June you attended a ball at the house of William Colquhoun Esq?'

'I recall the occasion.'

'Do you recall what your wife wore?'

'No, I do not.'

'Could it have been yellow satin?'

'It could have been almost anything. I have said I do not recollect.'

'My lord,' Ward protested amid a growing buzz of talk around the Court, 'must my client be subjected to this close questioning? I object most strongly to it.'

'I am unable to uphold you yet, Mr Ward. Mr Kelleway is precise about his dates and places. Perhaps he will quickly come to the point of it!'

Henry was thinking fast. He could not sustain his examination without objection much longer. Then he would be compelled to put up a new witness, the lady's maid. Ward would then be compelled to ask for an adjournment. He must know that if the witness was introduced on the following day, then Waters would have to fall back on the simple defence that he did not know his wife's wardrobe and was not informed that the dresses were new. Waters and Ward both had enough sense to know it sounded weak, for at least it would prove there was no concealment, prima facie. Whether they could then carry this into a point of law that verbal revelation was required as well, he did not know, but it would be a contentious business and he doubted they would risk it. However, if he could drive them to adjourn on the issue of necessaries, he felt he had already raised enough doubt about there having been concealment without being obliged to present a witness. He did not relish the thought of Cranley summing up. He was sure he would be partial to Waters and raise such reasonable doubts that would adjourn the whole proceedings to the realms of equity where it could be chewed over by toothless old dogs of the Law who would find some way of modifying the verdict. He responded to Cranley.

'My lord, I will not pursue the point. Mr Waters, have you, during the time that is covered by the purchase of these dresses and ornaments, been accustomed to entertain or be entertained frequently?'

'I am sorry, sir, but I do not understand the word "frequently". I do not believe it is recognized in Law.'

Henry gave Waters a stiff bow. 'Then I will re-phrase it, Mr Waters. We are dealing with a period of just over four months, commencing in May of this year and ending in mid-September. In this period, how often would you say that you were about on a social occasion, accompanied by your wife?'

'I really cannot recollect exactly.'

'I have asked for an approximation.'

'I do not think I should give inaccurate answers. I would have to refer to my diary.'

'Come now, Mr Waters, for the information of the Court, was it twenty times, thirty times or forty times? Which is the nearest as an estimate? I will not hold you to an error of more than ten.' There was some hubbub from the spectators. Cranley demanded silence. Waters was silent too. 'You surely can answer, Mr Waters. You have been, I believe, a very busy man.'

Waters was so angry and his face so rage-red that he could hardly bring himself to speak with an civility at all. 'Perhaps thirty times.'

'Thank you, Mr Waters. That would be the number of times that you were accompanied by your wife?'

'Yes!' It was a strangled snarl.

'And you did not at any time during this period believe that a new dress was necessary for your wife, nor consider whether or not she was adequately dressed as befitted her station?'

'My lord, my client cannot answer such a question! It is put so that if he answers yes or no, it is equally repugnant. Mr Kelleway is using trickery! My client is not conversant with his social life in this way.'

'Your client cannot answer yes, Mr Ward!' Henry said with asperity.

'This is too much, my lord. If we are to be pressed on such matters of detail, then I would beg leave for an adjournment. My client must consult upon these trivial things that the plaintiff has seen fit to raise.'

Cranley looked shrewdly at Ward. He knew then, as Henry knew, that it was all over. All the better, Cranley was thinking. Settle it out of Court. A thoroughly nasty little case, neatly prosecuted. If young Kelleway had intended to bring it to this, then he showed better sense than he had ever heard of him. He thought it must be young Kelleway, because he could not see that Ward had engineered it.

'The case is adjourned. Another time will be set.'

'Thank you, my lord.'

The Court rose as Cranley went out. Ward ground his teeth and waited for the room to clear before writing a note for his junior to take to Kelleway. Mrs Waters, who had sat anonymously at the back throughout, slipped away. She felt no elation for she had won nothing that mattered to her. An adverse decision might have brought Henry to her again, but now he would shy away. She could not promise herself that she would not pursue him.

Mr Coke, receiving the congratulations of Mr Montague, was unable to make up his mind whether it had been a great victory or a terrible mistake.

Aunt Helen was in an extraordinary state of excitement. It had started with the first false labour pains and had endured now for two days and nights. She seemed to thrive on it and rather than wilting, was gaining strength all the time. Caroline had been put to bed in the back bedroom, normally vacant, that looked out over London and was the opposite side of the house from the rattle of carriages along the Lane. She had sent a messenger to both the doctor and Maria, telling them that she would summon them when her labour really started. She had almost become a girl again, both in spirit and looks. It was the best reassurance Caroline could have wished for, because she was afraid. Yet, like Aunt Helen, she was also very excited. When she looked at herself in the hand-glass, she saw that she was quite pink and flushed. It rather surprised her, for she had supposed she would look wan and ill.

Maria received her second summons at twelve on a Friday.

Dear Maria, can you come at once. I would value your help. I could never abide hired help for such an occasion. They would be more concerned to know where the father was, bully the cook and count our silver, by which I am told they estimate the value of their services. I must not prattle. Please come. Aunt Helen

Maria arrived within three hours. Another carriage was drawn up by the side of the house. She imagined it would be the doctor's. William had wanted to come too, but Maria had insisted that it was no place for a man, as he well knew, and that someone should look after their own child, Margaret, the domestic affairs, the cook's daughter's painting lessons, the unhappy vegetarian cats and his own work for the next Royal Academy, for which she had great hopes. William had not been entirely gracious about it, but had had to concede. Maria, too, was immensely excited.

'Aunt Helen, this is wonderful!' She found herself effusing as she rushed into the hall.

'Yes, isn't it! Slow down, Maria. Everything is well under control. The doctor is with her now but he says she is not due just yet. Shall we have a little cordial? I really am quite fatigued, and I know you must be.' She kissed Maria, who then realized that Aunt Helen smelled quite powerfully of brandy.

'Aunt Helen! You have been at the brandy bottle!' Maria was smiling at her chidingly. She and Aunt Helen had much in common. Together, they were positively conspiratorial.

'And why not, my dear? It is a stimulant. Good Lord, if they can give it to you when you faint, why can't you have it before you do!'

'Can I see Caroline?'

'In a moment, when Doctor has finished. The most agreeable part about other people's babies is that you can actually enjoy having them. I can't say that having one's own is without discomfort. I do hope it will be a boy!' Maria was ushered into the drawing-room by Aunt Helen who poured her a large brandy in a crystal tumbler more suited for sherbet or lemonade. 'The doctor's name is Foster, just like the Doctor Foster who went to Gloucester in the nursery rhymes, but he doesn't like you mentioning it!' From which Maria gathered that Aunt Helen already had. She was not surprised.

'Sit down, Aunt Helen. You must have been on your feet for days.'

'Yes, I suppose I have. Oh dear, I have forgotten about a nursemaid. I had intended to advertise for one immediately – she must have impeccable references. Oh, I do hope Mrs Loudon is keeping things going in the kitchen. When it comes to it, there are so many things one never has. The first one is always the worst.'

Maria could not help but smile. Considering the circumstances, Aunt Helen had no tact. Aunt Helen saw her smile, and put out an arm on her hand.

'My dear, I have no tact at all, have I! What a thing to say! Still one never knows, the right man may come along. Have you ever seen this creature Ware?' Maria shook her head. 'Well, he has been round to the house again, you know, but I saw him off. Caroline was upstairs and did not know. Just as well. It would have upset her. Oh, come on, come on!' This last was obviously aimed at the doctor, or alternatively Maria thought it might be encouragement for Caroline.

'Come now, Aunt, you cannot sustain this all day and night. You lie down here and let me look after Caroline for a while. We are good friends and I can manage perfectly by myself.'

'I suppose you have experience in these matters ...'

'Aunt Helen!'

'Well, of course, dear, I know about your charming child. I am most unreasonably in a whirl. Oh here comes the doctor!'

'Sit down!' Maria was firm.

There was a knock on the door. Mrs Williams the housemaid, who looked tired – no doubt through dealing with Aunt Helen – opened the door to admit Dr Foster, a slight middle-aged man with luxurious side-whiskers and a strong voice. He bowed with a little inclination of his head upon finding Maria in the room as well.

'How is she?' asked Aunt Helen.

'Good afternoon, doctor,' said Maria advancing to him. 'I am Mrs Kelleway. I have arrived to help.'

'Good,' boomed the doctor, and sounded as though he meant it. He cast an eye at Aunt Helen. 'That will be perfect. Are you acquainted with childbirth?'

'I have one child myself. I think so.'

'Then I must see Mrs Loudon to make sure we have everything ready when we need it.'

'Is she well?' asked Aunt Helen.

'She is perfectly well, madam. In fact she is in the very pink of health. There are no signs of any complications, and it is just a matter of waiting. I estimate it will be no more than a few hours. It would be most useful, Mrs Kelleway, if you could sit with her quietly. I am sure it would be much appreciated.' He implied strongly that Caroline had not had much quiet previously. Maria smiled. Caroline must have spent much of her time reassuring Aunt Helen.

'Then I shall go up to her.' Maria was quickly out of the room and up the stairs. She opened the door quietly. Caroline lay on her back, eyes shut. 'Caroline?' The eyes opened, and Maria was delighted to see her smile. 'Is everything well?'

'I am very pleased to see you, Maria! Yes, the doctor says everything is well, but it does hurt so!'

'Are the contractions frequent?'

'No, not yet. I feel so fat and heavy, but I am very happy. I think I am also afraid, but I suppose that is natural.'

'Yes, of course! You look extremely well. I will sit with you, if I can find anywhere.' She moved linen, towels, basins and jugs, pulled up a chair to the bedside. 'I only just managed to stop William. He would have been here with me! Aunt Helen is downstairs on the sofa. I think she could well do with some sleep!'

Caroline made a face. 'She has been marvellous, but she can be very tiring.'

'I won't tire you. Just relax. What shall we talk about?'

'Give me your hand, Maria. Talk about anything. Tell me about William's painting, or about this venture in the country. Tell me about anything.'

At three in the morning the house was a blaze of lamp-light. It was a cold clear night, and fires were stoked up in every room. Mrs Loudon staggered up and down the stairs with kettles and bowls of water. Aunt Helen, who had fallen asleep in the early evening, made a rally unassisted by brandy and fussed at the doctor, who eventually asked her to leave Caroline's room. At three-thirty she gave birth to a boy. At five, Aunt Helen and Maria were allowed to tiptoe quietly in and gaze at the swaddled form. Caroline was pale and asleep for some time. She too was well. As they crept from the room, leaving the doctor and Mrs Loudon in charge, Mr Loudon the butler appeared, coming up the stairs.

'There is a gentleman at the door. His carriage has just arrived, madam. A Mr Thomas Kelleway. I have shown him into the drawing-room.'

'Oh,' said Aunt Helen. It was all she could manage.

'Thank you, Loudon,' said Maria, and went down the stairs ahead. She found that she was nervous. Who had told him? It must surely be a good sign. Thomas was pacing about in front of the fire, leaning forward as though out for a walk with Sam. There was no trace of reserve in his manner. He might almost have been the husband.

'How is she?' he asked with such touching eagerness that Maria had to forgive him for his past behaviour. 'Is the child born?'

'She is in perfect health, and the child too.'

'When was it born?'

'Only just over an hour ago.'

'Boy or girl?'

'A boy.'

Thomas stopped pacing and searched for a handkerchief. He blew his nose. 'And Caroline really is well? There were no problems?'

'None at all,' said Maria.

'I did not expect you to come,' said Aunt Helen. 'We did not know that you would want to be informed.'

Aunt Helen was not one to soften as quickly as Maria. She, after all, had lived with and supported Caroline through this long time. Thomas had no answer, but merely stood nodding his head as though acknowledging that he deserved the rebuke.

'I suppose she would not see me?'

Aunt Helen was about to make a tart reply but Maria forestalled her.

'I am sure she will be very comforted. She is asleep now, but I will ask the doctor to tell us when she is awake and you can go in.'

Thomas was suffering torments of emotion. He suddenly sat down. Maria realized then that he was not a young man, and that he must be both tired and burdened with heavy remorse. She poured him a large brandy, as Aunt Helen had done for her, in a tumbler. He took it and drank.

'Thank you, Maria. This is all a great excitement. Could I impose upon you, Helen, to remain here?'

'Yes, Thomas, you may.'

'How did you hear about it?' Maria asked.

'William told me. He thought I should know.' William, thought Maria. Clever, interfering William, who had judged things just right this time. Thomas was fumbling in his coat pocket. 'I could not bring anything with me for Caroline, for them both. I left at once. You must have a terrible number of things to buy, bills to pay. I would like to get this over with, Helen, but please don't tell Caroline. For the boy, and Caroline, and for the things they will immediately need.' He put a purse on the table, tentatively as though it might be construed as an insult. 'I couldn't think of anything else, immediately, to help.' He coughed nervously. 'It is a poor thing for a father to seem to be buying his forgiveness. But it is practical and you will need it.'

Maria felt sorry for him. She said what he wanted to hear. What was also the truth. 'What will immediately help, beyond anything, is that you are here. As for the money, we will need that too. For your new grandson.'

Aunt Helen gave a little cough that indicated that she at least was not giving this whole-hearted approval. Thomas looked at her.

'I know, Helen, I know. I have had a four-hour drive through the night to think about it. I don't expect to be forgiven, but I can be giving.'

Part Two 1827

9

The three-master *David* lay for half a day off Tilbury waiting for the tide. Fog hung low on the greasy water as though it exhaled vapours. Small ships moving down the main channels drifted by without hulls, only their spars and sails showing. It gave the impression, through half-closed eyes, that the *David* itself was moving. The outflowing Thames bubbled against her cable and sides.

John, who was thus squinting at the passing sails and listening to the water, was on the deck early. Charlie and Nell, the two children, still slept in the small cabin they all shared. He was loath to wake them for they had not slept well during the crossing. Their faces which had been so full of health were pinched and their eyes pouched with purple folds, looking as though they had been beaten. The Atlantic had done the beating. It had not been kind. At times the small cabin had been an evil-smelling hell. The children had wept that they wanted to die. Unable to eat, retching, unable to sleep. It was a hard thing to put them through for such an uncertain reception.

The fog was thick as cannon-smoke and the morning sun made it golden, occasionally breaking through with painful brilliance. John was reminded of the Mississippi. He could hear and occasionally see other ships and their crews. There were shouts, laughter, whistles and the squeaking of pulleys accompanied by the deep chanting of men. They could have been slaves at work. The monotonous pulling rhythms seemed to have no language in the muffling fog, only a driven purpose. He realized that he was viewing it all as a foreign port, just as he might view Bombay, Dakar or Boston. The Mate, passing, wished him good morning and told him they would be up-river by noon. The man's west of England burr emphasized his divorce from his own land for he scarcely understood what he said. The ship was English, carrying cotton, and John and the two children were the only passengers. The Captain had felt obliged to have him to dinner in his cabin each evening although John had felt the man would have preferred otherwise. However, he insisted that a paying passenger should not eat with the officers or crew.

John was elegantly dressed for going ashore in pearl-grey coat and trousers, cream silk waistcoat and brown boots. Too dandy, he imagined, for London, but fashionable in the Eastern States. He smiled as he thought of his broad-brimmed grey hat. He must buy a beaver immediately or he would attract a crowd. Around him and aloft, the crew went about their business in blue or white trousers, frayed in rags to the knee, their shirts bleached by salt and wind, their rancid hair tied in pig-tails with tallow or butter. Their feet were always bare. The men looked at him with envy and some with too much appraisal. He must be careful ashore. Here, as in Boston, there was no place for landsmen among sea-wolves. The men lifted their heads from time to time like dogs scenting. They could smell London in the fog and were thinking of wives, whores, ale-houses or old scores. Some would be without money, all lost in gambling during the passage. His present safety was solely due to the savage laws of the sea. It was a thing he understood well from the Army.

John left the rail of the ship and climbed backwards down the mahogany ladder to the cabin. It smelled sour below decks. Charlie and Nell slept together in a bunk with the ends of a sheet jammed in their mouths for comfort, their small bodies curved into corresponding commas. In Nell he saw her mother. She would be beautiful. Her dark, tired eyes and limp open mouth reminded him, as they had done throughout the voyage, of the incredible day when he had come home in the cool of a scented evening and found the two children clinging to each other, silent with shock and battered. Louise, their mother, had wrecked the house. Outwardly there had been no sign of what there was inside. The horse was ambling: he had been singing to himself. There were no old crones, no immediate signs of warning like Padmavati. The house seemed to drowse in peace. Louise had tried to set fire to it with an oil lamp but mercifully the black maid had seen her, rolled up the carpet that was ablaze and thrown it out of the window. Louise had scratched and bitten the poor woman quite severely, fighting to be allowed to destroy.

But what? Her children? John did not know. She had fled where no one had been able to find her. Perhaps she was dead.

They had searched for her of course. Hostile parties of men had tramped over the plantations with dogs. They were efficient and full of hate. Maybe they thought John had killed her or at very least they were sure he had driven her to suicide. He had had to face Louise's father, a weak little bully with a goatee beard whom John used to find a figure of endless fun. He had come backed with an armed escort because he had not the courage to come alone. They told John he must get out, baying at him from a distance but gradually approaching nearer. If he did not get out, his plantation would burn. They could not guarantee the safety of his life or his house or even his bastard children. It was the first time any one of them had spoken directly to him for four years. He could smell the whisky on their breaths.

They were, they declared, Christian men, who could no longer tolerate his pagan behaviour in their land. The minister smelled of whisky too, and carried a bible in his right hand as though it were necessary to perform the exorcism. He said that John was Satan in their midst, from a safe distance behind other men, that he had seduced and taken a woman to live with him unashamedly and unwed. The plantation owners with their quadroon mistresses hissed their approval. The minister said that John had isolated the poor creature from her loving father for lust, siring bastards in defiance of the laws of God and man, cutting himself off from the human race and rejecting with contempt and arrogance their advice, prayers and concern. The minister was tall and thin with spectacles and ill-suited to echo the wrath of God. Next time they came, said one of the bolder men, it would be with torches and guns. They would hunt him from the country like a coyote.

'If thine eye offend thee,' said the minister, 'pluck it out and cast it from thee.'

No one paid any attention to the two children. The black maid, who loved them, hid in the doorway, her eyes round with fear. The next day, she too was gone. John would have liked to reward her but did not get the chance. He picked up Charlie and Nell, still hugging each other, as delicately as though they were fledglings fallen from the nest, gently examined their bruises and cuts. Physically they had not been badly hurt. He had wept when he had carried them to his bed and seen them lying shaking and white.

Louise at first had laughed with him. In the excitement of their early passion it was easy to point at and deride the hypocrisy around them. John was dashing, foreign and experienced and she had never met a man like him. He had travelled the world, made money, had views so outlandish and had seduced her with such gentle consuming passion that she felt neither furtive nor guilty. When they set up house together they merely did openly what others did covertly and John made it all seem as romantic as elopement. The small-minded bigots who ostracized them seemed as unimportant as weevils. Yet the weevils worked away and slowly destroyed them. They entered her mind. The birth of the children had brought joy quickly, sundering stresses. It seemed that Louise could face the isolation and contempt alone, but could not bear to see it pour like foul vomit on her bastard children. They had both laughed when they called her slut. But Louise could not laugh when they whispered 'bastards, bastard boy, bastard girl!'

Words said in shops made her turn in quick anger. Sometimes innocent, often not. Words like bath, barrels, basket, brushes. Said in her direction with an innocent look by women who then ignored her. Their trade was not welcome so they had to buy far afield. They began to quarrel with each other. Louise demanded more and more passion from him until it became a burden, and then she would accuse and accuse that she had been led and educated to this and now what, now she was the king's whore? Her derangement expressed itself first in tempests of awful tears. The house was full of the sound of sobbing by night as though it were haunted by a distraught ghost.

'Whited sepulchres,' the minister had declaimed, 'which appear beautiful outward, but are within full of dead men's bones.'

Ye have ploughed wickedness, ye have reaped iniquity; ye have eaten the fruit of lies: because thou didst trust in thy way . . .

To gather the children up and put them gently to their beds with comforting, with soothing, that was useless as chaff to a starving man. He had tried to bleed for them, unconscious of the imagery, but had only degraded himself with drink. Their wounds were within their minds. Looking at them even now he wondered to what extent they had truly recovered. Charlie was a bright, quick boy who rejected affection, Nell a pretty child who craved it. Only this change and time would heal them.

They had never found Louise. His cotton had been burned down. Torches moving in the sly of night. He had sat on the porch on a chair in the full light of an oil lamp, glass in hand, singing. If they wanted to shoot him, he was there. He wondered if the minister had sanctified the holy flame that would cleanse this iniquity from the face of the land. The raging line of flame was impressive. He had released his slaves, telling them they were not to fight the fire, but were now free. The slaves were bewildered as any captive beings who are suddenly thrust back into a world they have forgotten. Then, after the first hesitations, they disappeared silently. He had no feelings for them one way or the other. They must fend for themselves, like him.

This, he thought, is how Nero must have felt. He only regretted that he had not had the foresight to fire the fields himself and deprive them of that pleasure. They had chosen the night with care, for the wind swept the flame across his land like the advance of a wall of blazing lava, but it never veered towards the house. By dawn it was done. He had strolled through the thick powdery ash for a mile. It was still hot in places and could be stirred to a glow with his boots. It was a landscape of Hell that appealed to him. Nothing on the ground had survived except the stumps of gate-posts. No living thing ran before him in the deep ash, yet overhead a lark sang, birds passed over on their own business. It was a vision that he wanted to capture in his brain and be able to recall because it was so bizarre. After an hour he had returned to the house, roused the sleeping children and carried them to the carriage he had made ready as the flames were dying. There were few possessions he cared to take. He preferred to leave the furniture to trouble the consciences of the farmers. They would have to take it or leave it to rot, but either way it was not theirs. They had driven away on a brilliant, sunny morning. He knew they would be watched.

At midday the *David* creaked her way up-river to London Dock, putting John, the children and his possessions ashore by boat at Wapping New Stairs, where a carriage could be hired from there to London and a carter found for the boxes. The day was dry and humid. High cloud prevented strong sun from breaking through. John thought how dark his children looked compared with the pallid skin of the dirty urchins that scrounged around them for anything easy to steal. The same in all ports, he reflected, the same poverty in the midst of a traffic in riches. He wondered where he should lodge as he intended staying in a city inn until he found his feet. He knew not to ask the carriage driver, who would be on commission. He felt nervous because of his proximity to Thomas and wondered if the old man had somehow sensed his return. Thomas still had the power to produce this response of quite childish fear, when blazing cotton fields had seemed to him a mere entertainment arranged by the devil to display for his pleasure the workings of human folly. He realized that he had managed to remain dissociated from the events around him and indeed from other people to an extraordinary degree, but he could not escape from the reality of his family.

Caroline had the french windows flung open that commanded the magnificent view over London. The dome of St Paul's, like a grey up-turned tea-cup, dominated the blackened plain of city roofs that was pricked everywhere by thorny spires. The garden was sweet with the scent of roses and honeysuckle. In the room, roses overwhelmed the vases in which they had been arranged. Aunt Helen and she sat sewing beside the open doors, enjoying the evening air. A flurry of swifts screamed and chased repeatedly around the garden and over the house. So beautiful in flight, so ugly in voice. They exchanged only a few words, content with their work, which was more a pleasure than a necessity.

Aunt Helen had shrunk more into herself and seemed much older except for her same lively eyes and tongue. Her erect body had crumpled from being housebound. She sewed without the aid of spectacles which was really remarkable as she was engaged in delicate work. Cows were making a noise in the fields below, returned from the evening milking and indulging themselves. Because of the warmth, other windows were open and the curtains moved slightly in the modest breeze they enjoyed on the hill. They could hear the sound of stage coaches quite clearly as they pulled up Highgate hill, but only looked up and then went on sewing. They knew each coach by its time. To-night they were all slow in pulling up the gradient. The horses would be in a sweat. Men did not shout and crack whips, but were subdued, sympathizing with the horses and thinking of the next change' and ale, cool from barrels in deep brick cellars.

The last six years had been kindly ones for Caroline. The child, now called Edward Thomas Kelleway, had been a foun-tain of emotional delights in which she had openly indulged her-self in a way that only Henry and William could criticize. Maria encouraged her, for she was not spoiling the boy but enjoying the babe, the infant, the child as an extension into a second life granted her when all expectations for the first were over. Thomas had become over-indulgent as though he now felt the boy to be his own, having made his peace. He behaved, Maria thought, as though he had sired it, and with her quick compre-hension understood that this was both his adjustment to Caro-line and the child's illegitimacy. She did not approve but under-stood. Caroline firmly kept Thomas at a distance from the boy. His possessive faults would be with him until he died. He could not be content unless all his family belonged directly to him, without generation but simply as his children.

'It must be very hot in town,' said Aunt Helen, 'I suppose it will rain soon. This cloud will lead to thunder.' She required no response. Their domestic ways were companionable and relaxed. The ring on the door bell which they could hear clearly down-stairs took them by surprise.

'Who on earth can that be? It is an unsociably late hour for visitors. You are not expecting anyone, Caroline?'

'No. No one at all. Perhaps we should clear away our sewing.' She felt suddenly and irrationally nervous.

'I don't see why people should have to keep such late hours. I have no intention of seeing anyone tonight!' Aunt Helen paused, and an alarmed expression crossed her face instead. 'Oh, I do hope nothing is wrong!'

'It is probably a mistake. Someone has been given the wrong

number.' Caroline tried to sound calm but was alarmed. They never had late callers. Had something happened to Thomas? It was the most obvious conclusion, but she knew very well that something else worried her more.

Mrs Williams had evidently answered the door, because after a pause during which the two women listened like surgeons for a heartbeat, there was an outburst in which her raised voice predominated. The male voice of Loudon intervened and there was an interchange of male rumbling. 'It's a man!' said Aunt Helen, only to fill the silence of their listening. Steps proceeded quickly up the stairs, almost in a scramble.

Aunt Helen looked pop-eyed. 'Good gracious!' she shrilled, and commenced stuffing the sewing down behind cushions, darting about the room. Caroline did nothing, but stood quite still. She was very white and had Aunt Helen been less concerned about the social graces she would have been alert enough to know why. Loudon opened the door in a curiously obstructive way, as though trying to block the doorway with his body. He was out of breath and he addressed Caroline.

'Madam, Mr Charles Ware is here and desires to see you. I said that you had given instructions that you were not to be disturbed, but the gentleman stepped past me!'

'I did,' said Ware, shoving past Loudon again. Loudon stared helplessly at Caroline, unsure what to do.

'Is it your usual practice, sir, to push aside servants?' Caroline was shaking, more with fear than rage. She had not seen Ware for four years when he had last made an attempt to visit her. He had been turned away at the door then, and she had only seen him through the lace curtains, filled with panic. After this long time she had believed that that had been the end of it. As a person, he had no reality to her any more. He represented an abstract threat, yet he had come alive again.

Ware had put on weight. His face was becoming pudgy and rolls of flesh formed two rings above his collar. His red face had an even more hectic colour and the skin over his cheek-bones was tinted with an ugly lattice of purple veins. His clothes were still far too tight and grotesquely youthful for his burgeoning middle age. His side-whiskers had become increasingly ginger and Caroline thought that he looked like a hot and pompous mayor, complete with bustling manner. She could not recognize anything in him, now that she was confronted with him again, that she could remember in the man she had known so long ago. She had distanced herself from him so much that six years seemed six centuries. She remembered him as an abstract being, a portrait done in oils of someone long since dead. It was unreal that this man was father to her child, for that man was dead. She nodded to Loudon who stood guard at the door lest he should be required to escort Ware out. Although Loudon was ageing and corpulent himself he looked considerably annoyed and flustered by Ware's ungentlemanly entrance. The hot weather made for short tempers. Loudon withdrew with reluctance. Caroline knew he would hang about on the landing outside in case he was required. She had the support of her servants.

'You are looking well, Caroline. Very handsome indeed.' The same pedantic speech.

'I would much prefer that you addressed me more formally, Mr Ware. You have no invitation to visit, let alone at this hour. Indeed, you know well you are not welcome. It is almost ten. I would be obliged if you would go.'

As though to banish evil spirits with the power of light, Aunt Helen was moving round the room lighting oil lamps with a taper. The evening fled from the room. Their peaceful communion with its delights was ended and Caroline resented it. Aunt Helen was right in what she was doing for it indicated plainly that whatever he had come about was not to be treated in the soft light of a social call but as business. Ware was annoyed by Aunt Helen and tutted each time she moved to and fro between himself and Caroline without so much as a glance. Caroline could smell the strong fumes of brandy from Ware. He had been taking courage, and had indulged in it.

'Good evening, then, Miss Kelleway,' said Ware, with insulting emphasis on the 'Miss'.

Caroline coloured. Aunt Helen abruptly rounded on him, making him jump. She waved the taper in his face, in danger of igniting his side-whiskers.

'You are a coward and a bully, sir, and no sort of a man. How dare you come here at this hour and behave like this. You have been drinking, for I can smell it. I have a good mind to light your breath with this taper for you would almost certainly explode! That is no way to visit ladies. You must leave immediately.'

Caroline subdued Aunt Helen gently by taking the arm that brandished the taper. She puffed it out. 'What is it you want?' she asked. 'You well know that I do not wish to see you, and you have forced your way into our house past the servants. There can be no explanation for this behaviour. I wish you to leave, Mr Ware, is that clear? We have nothing to say to each other. If you have come in some way to embarrass or insult me, be assured you will not succeed. Good night, sir!'

'But we have, I believe, something substantial in common. You cannot unsire our child.'

'How dare you!' Aunt Helen was pink with fury but Caroline continued to hold her arm.

'You have taken him from me,' Ware continued. He stood quite still, holding himself as though he were on parade. His voice, as always, had a peculiarly dull quality which made it easy to ignore the significance of his words. 'You have locked him away from me, his rightful father. I do not know what you have poured in his ears, but a boy needs now to be in the care of a man. He must be taught other things than mere woman's ways. A boy must learn to ride and shoot. What sort of namby-pamby are you going to bring up if you are allowed to confine him to this cell of women! When you saw fit to reject me and the generosity and genuine feeling of my offer, you did not think that I would accept, did you? Since when have women controlled the house? You have had a great deal of slack rein, but devil take it, we shall put an end to that! You may reject me if you wish, but you shall not speak for the boy. I shall see to that.'

Caroline realized it was no surprise to her. It was an unconscious threat that she had lived under for years. It seemed no less monstrous when expressed. She had to concentrate hard to grasp that this wooden brandy-flushed man had come to take away her son, the flesh of her flesh, that he genuinely laid claim to the boy, that his words were no brutal joke but the statement of his intent.

'He is mine. I cannot listen to this nonsense and I must ask you to leave. You have forced yourself on us. I hope you still have some scrap of behaviour left in you that will persuade you to behave properly!' It was all nonsense. She talked only so that she could attempt to cross to the bell-pull, but Ware was too quick for her and moved with short swift steps between her and it.

'Oh, no. You have made me wait, Miss Kelleway. You have been utterly selfish and treated my boy as your own. I need a son and heir, and I have one. I have waited for the right time, been patient. But you don't seem to truly comprehend, Miss Kelleway. I have come for my boy.'

Caroline was only momentarily put off by this staggering declaration. He spoke as though he were death come for a promised soul. She screamed at the top of her voice. In the still hot air the sound seemed magnified beyond all human proportions. She screamed again and again, surprised at the violence of the sound. Loudon burst through the door, astonished and obviously frightened as Ware rushed instinctively at Caroline. Whether he intended to gag her or hit her was not certain. Loudon tried to grapple with Ware but neither man was lithe or fit. Instead of hitting each other as Caroline had assumed, they indulged in an almost comic pushing match, shoving each other in the chest, puffing, and hoping to overturn the other. In the circumstances the effect was so bizarre that Caroline felt inclined to giggle hysterically. First one shoved, then the other, like two pouter pigeons. Aunt Helen, whose aggression was well aroused, picked out an unpleasantly long needle and jabbed it without hesitation into Ware's well-filled breeches. He let out a roar, but could do nothing about the wasp behind him while confronted by Loudon. Caroline heard running footsteps on the stair, evaded the three combatants and rushed to the door. A man she had never seen before was running down the stairs with Edward Thomas grasped under one arm, still three parts asleep, limp and protesting at the interruption. His thumb was still stuck in his mouth, his eyes shut. The man shoved Caroline aside. She did not dare to attempt to trip him because of the child, but she screamed and screamed again.

Mrs Loudon darted out below, looking terrified, but had the wits to sum up the situation in a moment. She flung the bolts shut on the front door, turned the key in the lock, removed and fled up the first flight of stairs towards Caroline. The man, weighted with the child, was too slow.

'Is the back door locked?' Caroline yelled.

'Yes Ma'am,' Mrs Loudon puffed, 'there's no way out for him!'

Ware emerged from the drawing-room and charged down the stairs past them. His accomplice had dumped Edward Thomas on the stone floor where he curled up and resumed sucking his thumb. The man pulled and rattled at the door uselessly. Ware was panicking.

'For God's sake, get the thing open!'

'I can't. The bitch has locked the door!'

'What bitch?'

'Her!' The man pointed at Mrs Loudon who was craning over the banisters.

Mrs Loudon let out a loud warble of alarm and passed the key to Caroline. Ware turned about and started up the stairs towards them. Caroline and Mrs Loudon fled higher, or at least Caroline succeeded for Mrs Loudon, out of breath, soon collapsed on the stair and could only puff and wail. Mr Loudon, looking bruised but bull-like, reappeared from the drawing-room. Seeing his quarry he went into battle much as he might have served tea. He first stopped Ware with a surprisingly gentle but effective hand on the chest that was almost deferential. Ware was surprised by it just long enough to pause. Loudon hit him hard on the head with a blue and white china plate that shattered and fell down the stair well. The pieces then fragmented on the stone floor. Poor Loudon had hoped the blow would knock Ware out, but being inexperienced in such things and not wishing to find himself arraigned for murder, it merely knocked Ware to his knees on the stairway where he shook his head like a stunned prize-fighter, mouthing oaths. Loudon backed into the drawing-room in considerable alarm, searching for further weapons. His training was too good to allow him to use the well-shaped vases that comprised the good china. Instead he sought by instinct some inferior and expendable piece, but these all seemed to be small and useless.

He was saved from a further confrontation by violent hammering on the front door. First one, then two, then three pairs of fists beat upon it and men's voices called out. Caroline's piercing screams had alarmed the neighbours. To encourage them, she screamed again from the top of the stairs, amazed at the facility with which she produced such a blood-curdling noise. The knocking stopped and heavy thumps beat against the wood. They were trying their shoulders against it. Ware's accomplice, who appeared to be no ordinary rogue, but some gentleman friend, was white and scared. Edward Thomas slept on unconcerned where he had been dumped, knees drawn up in his nightshirt.

'We've got to get out, Charles!' the man shouted and dashed for the rear of the ground floor.

Caroline ran down the stairs, past Ware who watched her in bovine wonderment, as though this had been none of his doing. She flung herself on Edward Thomas and yelled for help. The crashing at the door redoubled. Ware, rising to his feet and clutching the banister, was immediately confronted by Loudon, armed with a poker and a Wedgwood bowl which to Ware's fanciful eye he brandished like a sword and targe. He ran awkwardly down the stairs, his tight clothes ridiculous. He stopped by Caroline as if to speak. She expected oaths, imprecations or threats, and looked full at him, believing that thus he could not bring himself to strike her or harm the boy. She was astonished to see that his eyes were brimming with tears.

There was a tremendous crash at the front door and a shiver of yellow wood flew off onto the floor. Paintwork crackled. Someone had brought an axe. Ware fled the way his companion had run, and she heard the crashing of a window at the rear of the house. They would break their way out. She found that she was sobbing, and had been for some time without noticing it. Her dress was soaked. Loudon, shouting to the men outside, obtained the key from Caroline and opened the door before it was finally brought down. Caroline was aware of a confusion of faces, anxious or inquisitive, touching her, asking and trying to help. She tried to quiet them, told them to their astonishment to go away. The child stirred but was still asleep. Mrs Williams appeared, roused from the village, and took control of the house and the spectators. Caroline and Edward Thomas were put to bed together and Aunt Helen was content to be ensconced in the drawing-room with a very large brandy, describing the proceedings with flutter and relish. The well-meaning and the curious were thanked and gradually but firmly dispersed. It was dawn before the lamps were finally turned down and snuffed.

Caroline, awake and hearing the voices downstairs, lay shivering uncontrollably. She felt cold and clammy despite the heat and the sheet stuck to her like a shroud. It had been a near thing. She went over the events endlessly, blaming herself for all the trivial things the mind exhumes, spectres of the unconscious. Things she should have done, things she should have said that would have sent Ware away, cowed, without provoking his insane actions.

It seemed impossible that it had really happened, and Caroline realized the danger in this. The whole episode was that of an unbalanced man, an uneasy mixture of farce and ruthlessness. What if he had been armed? She would buy a muff pistol and keep it to hand lest he should try again. She realized that she would use it without hesitation if he did. Edward Thomas, asleep, was of her body. She put her hand on his hot forehead. He moved slightly to avoid the contact. It seemed incomprehensible that the child was half Charles Ware. Mentally, she had contrived to make his being into a virgin birth. The child was an unconsummated regeneration of her own cells. She fell asleep as the birds started singing, dreaming of rain that turned to toads, toads that soured milk and were put into churns to make butter; of Charles Ware as a giant toad, bursting his waistcoat and breeches, but it was not Charles Ware because she was very clever and when he was not looking but eyeing a glass dome of wax fruit, flicking his long tongue, she pulled off one of his shoes to reveal his toad's claw. Then he confessed who he really was, became tiny, and she captured him by sweeping him up in a dustpan and throwing him out of the window onto a dusty street that was a great plain of fine sand where she knew he could not survive in the heat.

John was surprised how little London had changed in his absence. So much had happened to his life that he felt it ought to be reflected in the streets, as it seemed to him a monstrous passage of time. He found that he knew his way about the streets and alleys and even knew the names of some shops and inns.

The streets were busier than he remembered them, and he had to be very careful of the traffic. The roads were surfaced with compacted stone, where before there had been packed clay, split with ruts. Now the drivers cracked their whips like madmen, and raced even faster. Carriages were more numerous than he could have believed possible. Only the hackneys remained unchanged, drab things with chipped paintwork pulled by hollow horses.

The day was bright and hot again, Londoners complained of the heat and dust. Ladies with parasols made walking a hazard. They complained to each other about the heat. Shopkeepers complained to customers. Strangers complained to strangers. To John it was very strange, for he felt it to be a pleasant day. He was walking to the Temple from the Blue Posts inn in Holborn where he had spent the night. The children had been left behind. He wanted to break things gently and was afraid of the task.

The queer jumble of narrow streets around the Temple were wrapped in their own shadows like barristers in dark gowns. The shops here were fusty law stationers, sellers of second-hand wigs and gowns and of barristers' bags, booksellers crammed with Law Reports, pens and inks and caricatures of judges. In dim interiors John saw men on high stools, some with candles in the daytime, endlessly copying in copper-plate script the three, four or six copies of the documents of the case, whatever case it was. It seemed a severe slavery to John and he stopped to peer into a sunless interior, wondering what kept them chained to their job. The premises were terrible and ill-cared for. The shopfronts had illegible inscriptions where the paintwork had either peeled off or was covered with grime. Only the poky windows gave some hint of what went on within. John was intolerant of the Law's insistence on dust and must. This dislike of change seemed to him a convenient action for parsimony. It was not so in the Americas.

He knew he was dawdling out of fear. He would much have preferred to have announced his impending arrival by letter, but there had been no time for that. He had even considered writing a letter from the Blue Posts to Thomas, saying he had arrived, but condemned himself for cowardice and abandoned the idea. He had rehearsed the part he would act, for he must not allow himself to be gathered up as the prodigal and thus leave the way open for Thomas to take him back as a child whose actions could be reprimanded as a child's. He knew Thomas would do that. Yet he had seen so much that Thomas could never imagine, knew himself to be a man in the facile terms of the world in his own right and not by some appointment of Thomas. But he could not convince himself. He had been assailed by doubts during the Atlantic voyage. Was it a man who had behaved with lunatic grief over Padmavati? Why had he sat on the porch while the burning cotton made a fiery sunset to the end of his second stolen life? He stole like a child, but did he give anything back? It had begun to assail him. It seemed to hold the key, but he wondered if we ever stop being children while our parents are alive. And when they are dead, what are we? Men were all around him in the streets, but he could not see that they had anything that made them different from him. He thought he had identified manhood as a form of selfishness, a withdrawal from the world, a stop to thinking about others and their misfortunes and a concentration on the self. But what difference is there between that and the taking of a child? He had come full circle without understanding. He must keep Thomas at a distance for it would be too easy to succumb.

It took him some time and several enquiries to be given correct directions to Pump Court. The porter pointed out number two, where he ascended a cold flight of stone stairs, the treads of which had been worn to a bow by the dragging steps, he imagined, of weary litigants. The walls were shabby and had been painted long ago. He found Thomas's name in gilt script on a board on the first-floor landing, where it headed the list of names of men in the chambers. The silence on the landing was so absolute that he hesitated to interrupt it by knocking on the door. He was panicky, and had to make himself do it. There was a long pause and he began to think he had not been heard when the door was opened by an elderly clerk, very correctly dressed despite the hot weather.

'Yes, sir?'

'I have come to see Mr Thomas Kelleway.'

The clerk looked him over with a perfectly open stare. 'Have you an appointment, sir? I do not believe I have any appointment for Mr Kelleway this morning. He will not see chance callers.' The man had thick grey hair and wore spectacles with plain glass for effect. Despite his tight coat and collar he did not seem to be perspiring. His face was professionally wooden, in the way of butlers and footmen.

'No. But I am Mr John Kelleway, Mr Kelleway's son, just returned from America.'

The clerk remained wooden. Sons returning from foreign lands were not always welcome by their fathers. He stood aside, however, and opened the door a civil width.

'Come in, sir. I will see if Mr Kelleway is free to see you.'

He showed John into an austere little cupboard of a room furnished with only a table and two wooden chairs. John felt sweaty. He wiped his face and hands quickly with his kerchief.

Thomas burst into the room like a welcoming dog. John was astonished at how he had aged. He seemed much more stooped, so much smaller. Thomas flung his arms around John, seemed to jump up at him, pounding him on the chest and back, then he stepped back to take stock of the long view and leaped at John again. The clerk permitted himself a smile and discreetly left them alone. Thomas had not uttered a sound. He sat down on one of the chairs and stared at John, shaking his head in bewilderment and holding out his hands, palms upwards as though he cupped within them all happiness.

'It's good to see you, Father. I'm sorry this has been such a surprise!' Thomas let fall his hands as though no longer able to support the weight of joy, and shook his head in amazement, never taking his eyes from John. 'I was unable to write. I have only just arrived . . .'

John was becoming slightly anxious at his father's muteness. Thomas suddenly started to struggle from the chair as if to launch himself upon John again. John took both his hands and held him in the chair. To his alarm he saw tears in the old man's eyes. He must tread carefully.

'John,' said Thomas finally, 'this is such a surprise to me, you must allow me to lose my composure. Why are you here? Are you from Virginia? Devil take it, my legs have failed me! I think my wits have failed me.'

'Yes, I'm from Virginia.' He sat down facing Thomas in the other chair. 'I had no idea how else to communicate with you but visit you. Are you sure you are all right?' Thomas had gone white and suddenly appeared ill.

'It is only the shock, sir! It is not every day your son walks in after seven years. John, it is good to see you!'

'It is good to see you, Father. You look well.'

'Nonsense, I am my age and look it. I feel it too. You have come back in time.'

John ignored this line of talk. 'Well, are we going to sit here and stare at each other? The very least I can do, if you can abandon your work, is fortify you with strong spirits. This instant. It is the nostrum.'

'By Gee, sir, it is! If you will help me from this chair which seems to have sunk under me like some trap, we shall sink a glass or two outside these dusty walls and you shall tell me, sir, what the devil you mean by appearing from nowhere to make the stars run in an old man's eyes!'

He wiped at his face and John helped him from the chair. Together they negotiated the stairs, Thomas holding on. By the time they were walking across King's Bench Walk, he had regained his normal strength and was full of a thousand questions, bent forward as usual like a bowsprit and moving automatically towards the Black Lion. He was proud, and introduced John to other men on the way.

'This is my son, John, just come back from Virginia. Gave me the shock of m'life! Fine way for a boy to turn up!'

John shook hands with men in gowns and wigs whose names he did not catch or care to remember. Thomas was calming down. It was a small tedious thing to do if it took the excitement out of him. All the time a part of him stayed well outside the situation, wary, observing the degree of pride, love and possessiveness. He supposed that he had always had that discipline for circumspection. He was thinking of past times and past places. It might make him seem a cool fellow but he knew it was self-protection.

'Father, I'm no prodigal!' he protested when this process went on too long. 'Let us have this drink.' The edge to his voice was enough to make Thomas stop and look at him, letting the black ravens of the Law slip by.

'Can't I be proud of you?' Thomas asked rhetorically. His voice was quickly petulant and hurt. John said nothing, but smiled to cool the graze. 'You're right, I'm boring you with all these people; they mean nothing to you and to tell you the truth, most of them mean nothing to me. I'm being selfish, you know. I've been alone a long time. Makes a man want everything his way. There's time for everything. Let's have that drink.'

Beware, thought John, the old man has become more subtle with his years.

They tramped up Water Lane, dodging through the usual brawl of commerce. Thomas led the way into the Black Lion, dodging without a glance the crates and boxes and handcarts. Passing under the stone arch of the yard, he stumped ahead of John around the boarded walk to his favourite booth. The court-yard stank, in the heat, of horse-droppings which had been piled to one side by the ostler. They watched him watering the brown dust in an effort to keep it down. The man was stripped to his trousers and was brown as a chestnut horse.

'What should we drink for a homecoming? What is appropriate, eh? It *is* a homecoming?' he asked anxiously.

'Yes, it is.'

'Then the only important question is answered and do you know I forgot to ask it till now! That does not mean I shan't bombard you like a man-o'-war with others. But now we have a reason to drink the best we can lay our hands on. Pot-boy!'

Thomas insisted on ordering up the oldest bottle of brandy the Black Horse could find in its cellar. It arrived encrusted with dust and cobwebs which Thomas flapped at with childish delight, making a great play of coughing and choking.

'When this was laid down, I must have been a mere boy! The world was a different place then.' He sighed at the turn events had taken. 'Tell me, why are you home? I have not even asked that! Your last letter said everything was well. I confess, now you are here, that it made this old heart ache because I thought to myself, the boy will stay. We shall have an American branch to our family, and what shall I do then!' Thomas laughed and thumped the table. 'Shouldn't like that, sir, shouldn't indeed. Republicans!'

John had considered his answers to all key questions. 'The cotton failed. An absolute disaster.'

'Are you ruined?'

'Almost.'

'Almost is not had!' Thomas declared with pride, 'almost is a narrow squeak. Any man with anything in him has, in my experience, been almost ruined at one time or another.' He poured the brandy, his hand slightly shaky with excitement. 'The thing is to get out with enough for recovery. I have sold very fast myself in the past. Sold short, but got out with something in the palm.' He handed John a very immoderate measure and picked up his own. 'Your health, John!'

'And yours, Father!'

'Have you the price of your existence? The necessaries of life, I mean. I ain't prying, sir, but I wouldn't like to see you run short when you've newly arrived. By Gee, you must have so much to tell me, I don't know where we shall ever begin. I would have liked it as a boy you know, seeing the world, going places.' John forebore to remind Thomas how he had been opposed.

'I can survive, sir, and have a little over.' A little over of that fortune from Burma. A dead girl's dowry that was still with him, shaping his life and helping him when he deserved no help.

'Then, sir,' Thomas declared loudly, 'you have escaped well. You are clever with money. Lord knows, it don't run in the family. If it weren't for your old father, I don't know where the money would come from. Your brothers show a woeful lack of understanding for investment. Money is a tree that must be encouraged to grow, nurtured and tended. To put it in banks is to plant it in sand. Banks, sir, are a scourge. They sterilize the seed of growth? So you have a little over. Where are you lodging?'

'The Blue Posts, Holborn.'

'That is a coaching inn. We can do better for you than that.'

'I have only just arrived, sir, give me time!' John managed to laugh it off and Thomas joined in too, making nothing into a great joke. 'How are the family?' John asked, anxious to change the subject. He would tell Thomas more of his own affairs when more brandy had passed his lips. His chance enquiry seemed to wound Thomas, who poured out more brandy to fill a pause while he considered what to say.

'They are all over the place.' He pushed across the filled glass. 'Not actually, you understand, but I don't know, they seem at sixes and sevens all the time. Have you eaten yet today?'

'Yes, I have. Go on about the family.'

'Well, your brother William has made a great ass of himself. You will find out. He has become successful at his daubing and it has all gone to his head. This Royal Academy is just a parade for fashionable peacocks. He has always thought himself too clever and now that they idolize him he is unbearable. He takes pupils and teaches other daubers how to daub. He designs follies and suchlike nonsense, and I daresay soon you will see him tramping round London dressed as a troubadour, which is his more moderate form of attire!'

'You are exaggerating.'

'No, I am not. These people make a world of simpering nonsense, knights and damsels. Romance? Rubbish!'

'But he is making money from it.'

'It seems to attract moneyed fools.'

'Then perhaps he is not so stupid.'

'It doesn't suit me, there's nothing manly in it.'

'You're being too hard! How's Henry?'

'Taken leave of his senses.' John smiled and filled Thomas's glass. 'He has found his mission in life defending pamphleteers and scandalmongers. He defends the Combinations, who are groups of workers that think they can adapt the Law.'

'But is he good at it?'

'I don't see there can be good in it. He has made his name for it, if that is what it is about. Times are troubled. They want to repeal this and repeal that. All politics!'

'And Caroline?' There was a brief pause, then Thomas slapped the table as though in sudden remembrance. It was a contrived gesture that John noted.

'But you won't have heard the news! It will be a shock to you. You see, I have nothing for you but this type of thing. You must let me explain the circumstances before you pass judgement. It was certainly a grave shock to me, I can tell you, sir, but now I understand it.' He stopped, irritatingly.

'Go on, what is it?' John demanded in some alarm. John was trying to read Thomas's face but could not decide what his expression meant. It seemed composed in equal parts of pride and embarrassment. Also, Thomas was blushing, a thing that John had never seen before. He waited while Thomas took a good draught of brandy.

'You have a nephew' John stared at him blankly. He was thinking of William and Maria. He knew about young Jonathan, their third and youngest. 'Caroline has a baby.' John was not as astonished as Thomas had imagined.

'I didn't even know she had got married. When did this happen?' A natural reaction. Thomas became even more fiery of face. He turned his glass about and glared at the brandy for inspiration.

'She isn't married.'

'What?'

'She isn't married.'

'Oh.' John sounded very solemn for he had a wild desire to roar with uncharitable laughter. Not at Caroline but at the reverses that fate deals to all plans. 'Is she well? And the baby? Is it a girl or a boy?'

'They are both very well, and it is a boy. Caroline is a fine girl. You have nothing to reproach her for!' Thomas looked up at John challengingly. It was too much for John, who started to laugh. He simply could not keep it down. Thomas stared at him, pop-eyed. 'There's nothing to laugh at, sir!'

'That's nothing,' John said before he had time to think about the prudence of the matter, 'I have two!'

His laughter hurt him. There was no mirth in it, but anguish and relief. He did not know if Thomas understood that and did not care, for now it was out, he felt unburdened of more than the mere concealment. The thoughts that haunted him and seemed to crowd about him were put into momentary retreat. He had behaved like a child, he knew, and done that thing which he had vowed not to. He wondered why he could not be self-contained as he imagined Thomas must be. When it came to it, he wanted Thomas's absolution. He could not see that Thomas had just sought and received his.

John helped himself to another glass of brandy, drinking it

down defiantly. Another childish act, another small step back. It was not the way he had envisaged things – the long talk, the gentle revelation, the stern shock and the long road back to acceptance. He had blabbed it out like a schoolboy. Perhaps he meant to create a wall of rejection, he told himself, behind which he could sit and feel affronted until he wanted to come out. Thomas showed no signs of rejection. He was stupefied.

'What on earth do you mean, sir?'

'I mean what I said.'

'Is this some joke about Caroline? It has been a very serious matter to us all. The poor child needs support. I don't see any cause for laughter!' His misunderstanding hurt John more than any scorn.

'I would not joke about Caroline, sir,' he replied frostily. 'If you had listened, I have just told you that I, too, have two children. They are at the Blue Posts now.'

'Two children?' Thomas was at his most bovine. 'You never mentioned any two children. What sort of two children?'

'Mine, sir. A boy and a girl. I daresay quite like other children. I meant no joke. I have two children. You have two more grand-children. I am sorry to break this to you so abruptly, but there have been so many circumstances and other things.' It sounded lame. Thomas obviously thought so too.

'Well, good God, why have I never heard of it?' There was an awkward silence while Thomas stared at him. John said nothing but looked back at him mildly. He was thinking that Thomas's eyes looked weaker, his skin seemed to be ill-fitting. It is a pity nature cannot tailor us better for our declining years. 'I am astonished. You never said a word of it, sir, and yet you had every opportunity. You have not been the most punctual of cor-respondents, but I believe I received all your letters. Not a word of it! Now words are beyond me. Are your children very new?'

'No.'

'Then I am even more astonished. You arrive without any warning to set kegs of gunpowder under me and offer no ex-planation. Where is their mother? When were you married? Who is she? It must be some time ago, sir!'

'Their mother has left them,' replied John obliquely. He could not bring himself to add further to the confusion at that time. Time was a necessary ally. 'I am looking after them.'

'Good gracious, are you determined to pole-axe me? What else is there? I thought that it was I that had news to break to you. You are too cool by far, sir, in concealing all this from me. It hurts me more than I will say. What do you mean, she has left them? What has been going on? I thought we trusted each other and had no secrets, but if you cannot confide in me more than this, then, sir, it is a sham to call me your father!'

Thomas reinforced his outrage with more brandy. Despite his protestations, John was unable to dispel the feeling that these masked a certain satisfaction or even a secret delight. It would have been too tame, he supposed, if he had returned in due order, all things arranged. In a way these surprises were expected of him and in this respect he had played into his father's hands and strengthened the expected image of himself. That, immediately, would be no bad thing, but he must not allow the story of his circumstances to become mere table-talk for retail at Temple dinners. He would not be consumed and patronized. Thomas was continuing on the theme that no true son should keep such news from his father and that as a son is an extension, a branch of the tree, these things should in nature be fed back to the sturdy trunk of the father. John decided to make the dutiful responses. They would be less colourful and less useful to Thomas in the retelling. Instinct told him that if he allowed himself to become part of his father's narrative then he would become part of his father.

'I did not tell you all this because I did not wish to hurt you. It is one thing to tell you face to face, but consider your alarm if I had committed it to writing from that distance.'

'The deuce, it has hurt me more now!'

'But consider my point.'

'I see no point. What have you up your sleeve next, what other conjuring tricks, sir, what other sleight-of-hand? What was their mother's name?'

'Louise.'

'Of good family? Pretty?'

'Yes, both.'

Her family would certainly have said so. Cotton aristocrats

with more money than Thomas could ever amass. Her dark hair and skin, their fiction went, were inherited from her Spanish grandmother who had been the daughter of a nobleman. Like wild wheat that springs up every year whatever crop is planted, this colouring was the wild strain that persisted through their generations. He had never believed in the Spanish grandmother. When they talked of her it was with haste and embarrassment. They were too emphatic about her origins and too vague on detail. His children had the same skin, olive despite their long weeks on board ship. He supposed he would support the same fiction because it was easy. His life was a hotch-potch of fictions forced on him by expediency. There was nowhere he could commence with the truth except within himself. As long as he could retain that bulwark he would not become the sham his father saw. If the world is oiled by fictions, so be it. An individual's truths are too painful and not welcome.

'Then what happened?' demanded Thomas loudly, clearly becoming exasperated by John's silences. 'I'm sorry, this is impolite of me. I am behaving like the Inquisition and this is no time or place to talk of it. Forgive an old man. We have plenty of time.'

'There's nothing to forgive. You are entitled to the bare bones, anyway! In your position, I would be much the same. In brief, she was unstable.'

'Went mad?' Thomas blurted out.

John looked at him, wondering why he had not fully identified this crassness before. Thomas's emotions were those of a nine-year-old. His reactions and vocabulary no better. It seemed surprising, as it had always done, that a man learned in the Law should remain so undeveloped in his relations with life. His job brought him into contact with every aspect of human failing and ambition, and John felt that he should be entitled to assume that some accumulation of understanding had occurred. Yet here was confirmation that it was to the contrary. Thomas was looking at him with interest as though he expected a straightforward answer to his straightforward question. John felt furious, but remained bland. It was, after all, part of the fictional world he had re-entered.

'I wouldn't put it like that. I think she found family life a strain. You cannot compare life there with here. We found it impossible.'

Thomas appeared to be trying to grapple with this in terms he understood. 'Quarrelled you mean?'

'That sort of thing.' The next fiction. A string of them would eventually be spun to form a skein that could be transformed into a woven garment with shape and form.

'You should still have written to me, sir.' The rebuke was plaintive, not angry.

'The reason I didn't is simple enough if you consider it. As we humans are, we always hope to resolve matters for the best before thrusting the burden of them upon others. It is more pleasant to send good news and more pleasant to receive it.'

Thomas nodded, mollified. 'I suppose that is your way. You consider others too much, you know. The purpose of a family is to give support.'

But who is to give support to whom, John wondered? He was prepared for Thomas's next suggestion, but was unresolved how to answer.

'You all must come and stay with me, of course. The house is completely empty now that Caroline has left. No question of it.' He raised a silencing hand that then descended on the brandy bottle and refilled his glass. 'It will bring the place to life again. An empty house is a dead sort of place.'

'We can discuss it, but I must see to my affairs first.'

'You may see to them much better from the house. You must arrange it immediately. You cannot look after the children!'

'They must recover from the voyage.'

'They will recover much better if properly looked after. You can't find a place of your own, you have no money.'

'I have a little.'

'I suppose this is your dee'd pride? Can't you take a loving offer?' Thomas was becoming angry. John knew his attitude was unreasonable and unthankful and that the practicalities of such an arrangement must in the end outweigh his emotional resistance. With the children attended to, he would be a free agent to a greater degree.

'I accept with pleasure, Father, but don't wish to impose on you.'

'Impose? I shall impose on you, sir, to tell me what you have been doing with yourself these years. Your letters have been very clams. They must be prised apart to find the information that is hidden within. Caroline once said that the most informative thing about your letters was the address!'

John contrived to laugh. 'I have not come home to sink into your armchair. You must expect me to try to put my own feet squarely down.'

'I would be gravely disappointed if you did not. You know, sir, you don't look like wax.' Thomas struggled to his feet, clutching the table. He was so bowed that his head almost touched John's. Leaning further forward, he slapped John on the shoulder. 'Nor do you feel like wax.' John, puzzled by this incomprehensible remark, merely smiled at him. His father was evidently the worse for the brandy. 'Come on, then, let's see these children of yours and get them out of that inn. Actions achieve, words deceive!'

The two set off unsteadily on foot. The heat made them sweat and the brandy tasted cloying and dry in their mouths. John followed Thomas, absorbed in his own thoughts. To him at that moment it was all a foreign land.

His thirst could be slaked with tea with Padmavati, sitting naked in the cool shade in the hut that the great thatched eaves provided. Padmavati handing him a brass cup that was itself cold to the touch, moving gracefully in the striped shadows. Cool water from a clay jar suspended by a cord from the roof. The glow of cheroots in the secret darkness. Her feet were as hard as an animal's. She had pads of thick skin and could walk barefoot on the baking earth where he could only hop and complain while she laughed at him. Her feet hard and dry but the rest of her body indescribably soft and firm.

'Good?'

'Yes.'

'Good.'

None of it was gone, for he had it with him.

Louise had feet as white and soft as blanched roots and yet her body was more angular, her bones less compactly clothed in flesh. They drank sherbet and cordials or expensive wines that John brought from afar. In the early days, she liked to drink wine in bed then make love. Children of the grape they had called Charlie and Nell. They were delivered in the bed of their conception, and Louise had taken pleasure in it. The doctor had to be brought forty miles from a neighbouring town. She had torn the sheets to shreds to help ignite the carpet. Her idea had been to burn the whole room.

Strange people milled around them in thousands. Carriages and horses clattered everywhere. He bumped into people and things, half dazed with brandy and with London. The torrent of people never abated. He felt claustrophobic panic and wanted to run and yell and disperse the nightmare. He had consigned himself to hell. No more cool shade, no more love. Thomas, ploughing ahead of him, seemed to have claimed him and to be leading him into the furthest recesses of these regions of terror. He was shaking and ready to scream, when Thomas suddenly stopped.

'Are you all right?' he asked.

'Yes,' said John illogically, 'I think it must be the brandy.' They were at the Blue Posts inn.

'Let's go up, then,' said Thomas and was on his way ahead of John before John could collect himself. 'Which room?'

The two children were lying on the bed asleep despite the hour of the afternoon. Their bodies still craved sleep. They were both curled up, utterly relaxed, Nell with her thumb resting on her lower lip. The counterpane was of dirty pink cotton that showed up badly in the sunlight. Thomas stopped his headlong progress the moment he saw them and changed his entire manner, approaching the bed as anxiously as a bird-watcher approaching a nest. John remained in the doorway, watching Thomas's face. He was still dazed. The room was hot and Thomas's slow approach and the children's shallow breathing gave the moment a dream-like quality. There was no sound. Thomas walked as though treading through deep water.

The old man looked down on them for a long time, holding his breath, then moved carefully backwards in the same strangely slow way. They went out of the room together and John quietly shut the door. The corridor was single-sided so that they were looking down from the glazed gallery into the inn yard. Thomas looked slightly puzzled and did not immediately say anything, but stared down at the endless activity of men and horses. John knew why and wondered how Thomas would approach it.

'They are handsome children,' he said with a note of doubt in his inflection, 'quite dark-skinned. The sun I suppose. Not your colouring ...' He left the statement hovering to become a question.

'Their mother's,' said John, 'her grandmother was Spanish. She was a striking woman. Spanish dark hair and eyes.'

Thomas nodded and put his hand on John's shoulder, his face showing relief. The fiction was complete. 'Very handsome children,' he said, 'the girl will be a beauty! They must leave this place immediately. Even the bed-linen is filthy.'

'When they wake.'

'Yes. Yes, of course, let them sleep until they wake. I find it very difficult to believe. They are my grandchildren, you know.'

Ah, Padmavati, what children we should have had, John was thinking, there would have been no disguising. No fictions. No need to flee, no need to return here to this selfish man.

'Yes, they are your grandchildren. It must give you quite a shock to acquire a family as rapidly as this.'

'Indeed, John, indeed. Arrange to move them now, then you can tell me what you have been up to. There are years about which I know nothing!'

10

The first rockets fanned out like pink ostrich feathers in the sky, then were followed by a bang and cascade of crackles. The ink black water of the lake reflected a perfect image of the plumes. Two men released more rockets from a gondola moored on the far side of the lake. This time they released drifting curtains of green smoke containing slowly descending emerald lights. The crowd exclaimed, the ladies' polite exclamations sounding like the crooning of doves.

Manning's new garden sparkled with colours. Fairy-lights in coloured glass jars were suspended from trees, lined the steps and paths or glowed mysteriously from subterranean tunnels. Green lights were placed by the waterfalls or floated on the water itself on green wooden discs secured among the lily-pads. A tower, lit by flaming torches in wall-mounted braziers, dominated a ridge to the left, while the tangle of jagged rocks behind the lake rose higher and higher to form a cone like a volcano from which red and orange light flickered. From this issued a sudden rush of rockets that exploded loudly, making the spectators jump. A band played incongruous airs in the heart of a clump of young trees. The bandstand of boughs forming rough Gothick arches had been draped with garlands of honeysuckle intertwined with roses. There was, as Manning had intended, no formal order to it, and he was busy with puzzled newcomers who came to seek his advice.

'You must go where you please!' he was saying, delighted and agitated at the same time, 'you must do what you will, see what you may see, discover what sights you can. There are things hidden, there are things to smell. There are no excursions here, no tours!' His shiny face made him a chameleon as he moved amongst the lights. 'I assure the ladies there is nothing frightening, nothing funereal or sepulchral. Only a feast of the senses.'

The doors of the house were flung open and all the lamps were lit in windows. William had indeed transformed it. No trace of the neo-Grecian remained. Except that it occupied the same position and was mainly the same shape, the present building bore no resemblance to the previous austere mixture of brick and stucco. It owed much to Strawberry Hill, and something to Ashridge and perhaps even a little to Fonthill, as William would readily confess. Wyatt was the inspiration, he said, he the disciple with a vision. Maria did not like him in such moods. He had had too much success recently, in her opinion, and did not know how to digest it. His enthusiasms which before had had a delightful childlike quality, now too easily turned to childish petulance. He exhibited and postured annually at the Royal Academy where he had had the honour to be insulted by Turner, who suggested he might like to change his palette for next year and use colour instead.

In the dark of the evening, it was impossible to see just how much the façade had changed. Crenellations and brackets could just be seen, deeper black against black. In daylight the whole thing was revealed as a froth of honey-coloured stone. The stucco had been removed along with the dumpy portico, and the building refaced. Tudor windows dominated the front, with square mouldings over doors and windows, the spandrels over the arches rich with foliage tracery. The external walls of the central block were covered with panelling, with bands of quatrefoils to emphasize the horizontal and vertical lines. Abutments divided the walls at intervals, although they had no obvious purpose but to fly upwards above the line of the parapet, ending in startling pinnacles. The parapet itself was embattled along the whole length of the building and pierced with recurring devices. Walls ran from the house and into the gardens, similarly embattled, unifying the landscape with the building. William had applied himself with care and scholarship, observing correctness in most things and mixing nothing by more than a century or two. The neighbours were astonished, William was overweening and Manning was delighted. Even in the course of its construction the house had become well known and savants visited it to view, and to talk with William. The combination of his painting and building activities had made him famous, and Maria found it very trying.

The evening was calm and had not yet turned chill. A moonless night had been selected so that everything artificial in lighting could be seen to best effect.

'We cannot have rockets going bang in the face of the moon!' William had declared. 'It would be insulting and unaesthetic. If there is a hint of rain, it must be cancelled. Be arrogant about it. They will all come again.'

Manning had smiled at William. 'You are sure that you have made all this, and that this has not made you?'

Now William watched it all with a feeling of deep satisfaction that showed on his face. Maria was not in an amiable mood. She had never seen him look so smug, yet she had warned him of it many times. Their home was less a home now, and more a shrine at which she felt she too was expected to worship. He was ignoring Maria's irritation, determined not to be distracted by her from his success.

'Come, Maria, take my arm and walk round with me.' The very graciousness of his manner was infuriating.

'We have been round it all twice and I know every bit of it, anyway. Is there any need for us to have to go through it all again?'

'If it bores you, I'll go alone.'

Another eruption of rockets shot from the mouth of the 'volcano' and spattered the sky with silver and gold. From where they stood by the house they looked down on the water and could clearly hear the gasp and chatter of the crowd. They watched the reflection of the sparks blow aside and die.

'It doesn't bore me!' Maria retorted with more anger than she had intended to show, 'but you are making rather a parade of it.'

'You see, Maria,' William continued as though she had not spoken, 'there is no such thing as sophistication. It is a means by which those who wish to distance themselves from themselves, convince themselves with a smokescreen. The atavistic pleasures cannot, however, be denied. Fire and water. They love fireworks!'

'And why not? Don't be so pretentious, William.' She knew

she was rude and unkind, but she could not bear to see him so inflated.

'I think you misunderstand me, Maria.' His voice was querulous. It made her hackles rise.

'I don't think so. I asked why they should not love fireworks. I do. I also love colour and music, sunshine and so forth. I think you have it wrong. It *is* sophisticated to like what you like. I don't see that what you just said means anything.'

She was tired of living with a sage. William was wearing a hermit's cloak made up by a stage costumier in bottle-green silk. On his head he wore a floppy hat with a brim and pointed crown like a hood. It was pulled down sideways. From the point of the hat, which hung down to his shoulder, sprouted a bunch of wax and wire foliage. Manning had asked his friends to dress 'in the picturesque'. His servants were dressed as heralds.

'You are being very perverse tonight. It is my duty to move about, to be seen and talk to people. This is partly in my honour, and I shall not be unsociable. It is also the culmination of years of work, and I shall be seen if I wish. I shall go round again.'

Maria thought of the endless drawings she had prepared for him – she was much the better draftsman – and the years of her own work that had been interrupted for the sake of this enterprise. It had started off as an aside but had gradually taken possession of more and more time. They had never conceived how much detail the builder would require. When William started on his Academy canvases, he relied upon her to keep the flow of detail going.

'Then forgive me if I don't. I shall be happy to sit here and watch the fireworks.'

William strode off, glad to leave her and annoyed. This grating had become too much of late. He could not see the purpose in it.

Thomas and John arrived with Caroline. Manning had insisted the whole family should come although his house burst at the corners. John and Caroline had exchanged conversation in front of Thomas like lovers in front of a chaperon and Thomas had shown as much ill-concealed curiosity. There was a strong bond between the two and great curiosity. He was annoyed that he felt he was being excluded from some exchange that was more direct than that between a father and his children. He had not realized for many years, as none of his other children had given him any cause, that there are secrets between brother and sister that exclude a father.

They had had no previous opportunity to talk at any length. John had been taken on a rapid tour of the family where all the civilities were observed. Henry had been polite and remote. Jane and he no longer maintained any pretence but went about their separate ways. Jane looked very much older and unhappy; darkness surrounded her mouth, caved her cheeks and eyes as though the shadows of her life were already upon her. William was condescending and off-hand. He had other more important matters to attend to, he seemed to imply, than returning brothers. John vividly remembered the old William, and held his peace until he could understand this pretender. Maria had been warm and effusive as ever. He divined that some of it was aimed at William.

Caroline had welcomed him with a hint of embarrassment which he found charming and which infected him as well. It lurked about in the carriage with them, a constraint as though between two criminals on the same charge. Thomas was the police officer. He sat like one, between them, upright and talking in stilted sentences.

In the darkness inside the coach, which was only relieved by the pale light of the lamps outside, they could have talked with intimacy without their unwitting jailer. We are sinners bound together, she was thinking, but with John we can poke fun at the saints.

The road was heavily scented with honeysuckle. It had infused a strong brew in the warm evening air. Bats flapped low over the carriage, delighting to dive between the horses' ears, while Morton cracked a whip at them. It was so intensely dark that their pace was only little above walking. The carriage lamps no more than rubbed at the dark.

'Was it really quite sumptuous in Virginia?' Caroline asked. 'Or is it all stories that one hears? They are so often exaggerations. I suppose it is defence.'

'Yes, it is for a few, but only a few. But everything was imported. You can have no idea what importance a common object assumes if the replacement must come from England or France or even New York. Even in the Army you can be sure that supplies will arrive eventually.'

They had been talking in this vein for some time. As it was now so dark, Caroline felt able to adventure further. 'Your children are very handsome. Nell is quite beautiful.'

John looked quickly sideways at the silent officer of order between them. He was hoping they would give away valuable evidence. Yes, Nell is beautiful. She is the image of her mother. Instead, he replied, 'So is Edward Thomas. A fine boy and very clever. I wonder what he will turn out to be?'

Caroline smiled to herself in the dark, but did not reply. Thomas was playing the part of Wall. His silent presence was a Niagara of noise. The din of his silence drowned out speech. Thomas must have been aware of their reticence for he suddenly got to his feet and leaped out of the coach door, nearly being knocked out by an elm branch. He cursed under his breath, while John reached out a hand and squeezed Caroline's arm in conspiracy. They would lose him and talk later.

'Morton, you fool, is that the fireworks I hear!' Morton was taken aback.

'Yes, sir, I can see rockets.'

'Then you are the only one! Good God, man!' he exclaimed, having lost his temper with the branch, 'do you think we have come all this way to miss them while you sit on the roof and have a view! I want to see them. Thrash these nags up a bit. They are asleep! If you can't get more pace out of them, you shall soon have a job driving a hearse!'

'We can't see, sir. There is no moon and the road is narrow. The lamps don't light more than a few yards and there is a ditch.'

'You don't need two on the seat. Get that fellow down and let him run ahead with a link, or we shall miss them all!' He clambered back in and sat down. 'I like fireworks and haven't come all this way to miss 'em. It will be the only good thing here. The rest is William's nonsense.'

The man climbed down from the driver's seat and ignited a big torch from one of the coach lamps. It seemed very bright although it was only orange flame, and produced a rope of black smoke. The unfortunate man, clad in full livery, puffed ahead in front of the horses whose amble quickened to a fast walk. Thomas got up again to peer out of the door.

'I can see rockets!' he declared. 'I tell you, I shall go home if we have missed them! Ha! Ha!' he shouted, making swipes at a fluttering bat.

John pondered on the scene, enjoying its exotic qualities. The whole scene, through time and absence, was foreign and strange to him and he saw it with fresh eyes. They came suddenly upon the gatehouse. It was ablaze with light and the drive from there on was lit by lanterns at intervals of twenty feet.

'Come on, Morton!' Thomas bellowed, and would have left the puffing linksman at the gates if Caroline had not stopped him. The poor man scrambled on behind, still clutching his burning brand, and at far too great haste they galloped up to the door. Thomas's greeting to Manning was perfunctory. Caroline smiled at Manning, who was rather bewildered as he watched Thomas walking full tilt for the lake.

'He adores fireworks, and is afraid he may miss them. I'm sure he will return in a more sociable frame later!'

John took Caroline's arm. Manning, mopping his face between arrivals, envied Thomas. He wished he could see his own fireworks.

'Well, sister Caroline?'

'Well, brother John?' They had moved aside where they could slip quietly away.

'Do you want to watch the pyrotechnics?'

'We can see them from afar. Having lost Thomas so easily, I don't see why we should allow ourselves to be so easily caught.'

John laughed, and Caroline smiled at his laughter. She liked to hear it because it blew away sere years like leaves.

'Remember, the whole family is here. We can't hope to avoid them all.'

'Let's go through the grottoes. They are all by the lake watching.'

They went through a passage made of large slabs of rock that became a tunnel. The mortar joints had been raked out and filled with earth and ferns to give the appearance of nature. Piped water dripped into pools set in blue-lit recesses to the side, where fish swam in clear water.

'What a piece of luck for William,' said John.

'It would be more luck if he appreciated it. William has made us all sad. He sees it as being a divine gift that is his due. Kissed by the Gods. You must have noticed.'

'He made it plain enough. He never seemed interested in material things. I think it is still an act.'

'Maria is having a terrible time. William cannot see it. There is nothing wrong with him except this conceit which makes him a child.' They watched the carp moving sluggishly in the pool.

'And what about you, Caroline?'

'I am very happy. Father has been very kind in every way.'

'He owed it to you.'

'That's a very harsh way of looking at things.' It was not a rebuke, but rather a sensing out of John's reactions to see if they matched her own. John understood.

'No, it is realistic and not unkind. We are all selfish in our own ways. God knows, I have been selfish in mine. You were robbed of the most precious thing in life, your own youth. Father knows it.'

Caroline did not want to continue on this line. 'What about you, John? Where have you been so selfish?'

'What do you mean?' His tone was sharp.

'You said so just now. That you have been selfish. We know nothing about you, you know. You have told us a clever history, made us a schoolbook from which we have learned the dates and places but otherwise absolutely nothing. History is about people as well as places. Have you so much to hide?'

John thought for some time. The plopping water played a dreary and repetitive tune. 'I can't answer that until I know what other people hide.'

Caroline was not pleased by this response. 'Can you not answer that by judging for yourself? You cannot put the responsibility on others.'

'Did you?'

Caroline turned away, annoyed. 'I had no choice. I think you are confusing the issue. There are people here who will still ignore me. You will see them turn away. They are more tactful now, but it is still the same. You should tell us because I am certain there is something to tell.'

'I'm not ready yet.' The cry of a child.

Caroline walked on.

Thomas was annoyed to discover he had lost them. At first he craned about, but seeing Sam Leigh with Jane, he moved over to join them. They greeted each other warmly, to the stares of surrounding spectators. Anything they would have liked to say was interrupted by a succession of explosions and crackles as various set-pieces were lit.

'Good display!' Thomas shouted in Sam's ear. Sam nodded. They watched the remainder through to the climax, the men in the gondola vying with the demons in the volcano to ignite the sky with tracery. Maroons exploded that made the ladies squeal and shook the ground, then it was over. The darkness that fell seemed thick as a cloak and for some time the spectators stood, unable to see. The servants dressed as heralds appeared with torches and guided the way to marquees set about the gardens.

'How is it all, Sam? I have only just arrived. I nearly missed the fireworks.'

'It is all very modish, I'm sure,' said Sam, which was so uncharacteristic that Thomas stared at him rudely. 'Very well, Thomas, I tell you it ain't my sort of thing. Damn nonsense really, but I didn't want to say so because of your William.'

'Makes no difference to me, Sam. If it's nonsense, it's nonsense. William was always a young ass.'

'I didn't say it isn't all very fancy and probably clever, but it is all this Gothick stuff again, and to tell the truth, I can't understand it. It is not only a thing, it seems, it is a frame of mind. Where they get it from, I've no idea. There are three hermits living in those rocks, permanently employed. They rattle bowls at you and tell your fortune! Did they tell yours?' asked Sam, diverted.

'No, they did not, nor get a shilling either, which is what they want. They will have a lean time when we've all gone.'

'I think the perfume garden is beautiful,' said Jane, speaking for the first time. She had arrived with Henry for the sake of appearances, but moved around on her father's arm.

'What's that?' asked Thomas.

'Shall I take you?'

'If I can have a drink afterwards.'

Jane tried to laugh, but no laughter showed in her eyes. It was like pain. Thomas felt it himself and took her arm in his.

'Let me borrow this girl, Sam, but don't stray. We shall have that drink.'

'You will find me waiting in that tent,' said Sam, as he moved away.

'What is this garden, Jane?' Thomas asked pleasantly.

'It is an Elizabethan idea that William has made into a game. It is planted out with fragrant herbs, aromatics and sweet blooms. You must walk a path blindfold holding a cord, and try to guess what they are.'

'I can't tell a daisy from a rose!'

'Never mind. You are supposed to enjoy it, that's the important thing.'

They walked together over the lawns, past other entrances to the grottoes and lighting effects. In two places, small groups of musicians had taken over from the band and were playing string pieces while ladies listened, perched on rustic bowers. The gentlemen stood, trying not to look bored.

'He has certainly spent a lot of money and thought of everything.'

'Yes,' said Jane, 'and there is to be dancing later until dawn and more fireworks to herald in the day and a champagne breakfast. At midnight there will be a formal opening ceremony by Sir Walter in the grottoes. He has a surprise he is keeping till then. Everyone has been told of it!'

Thomas stopped her suddenly, as they were temporarily clear of other people. 'How are you, Jane?'

Jane turned away from him. 'Let's keep walking.'

'Jane! We are kin, and it is the breaking of all our hearts, your father's and mine that you and Henry are not mended.'

'Please?'

'Very well. Forgive me for asking. I'm no good at subtle things.'

'No.'

'That's blunt from you, Jane,' said Thomas with some admiration.

Jane stopped. 'I think the time has long since come for me to be blunt, only I am no good at it. I have tried to be blunt with Henry, sir, but only bruise myself against the wall of his deafness. If I had the weapons, I should stab him!' Thomas stared at her as though she were a new species. 'I know what you have all thought, and that has not helped me. You must not mind if I speak of Henry in the abstract, because that is all he is to me. He is a successful man with the Combinations now. Has made his name defending them, and yet he cares as little for them as he does for me. I do not have any weapons with which to hurt him but I hope for his sake that if he treats them as badly as he does me, he is properly prepared. I have had three glasses of champagne to enable me to say this to you. Are you shocked?'

Jane was white faced, her hollow eyes angry with emotion. Her face in this mood was hard and lacked beauty. For a moment Thomas was being permitted to see the bitterness that she contemplated in herself in the mirror at night, as she practised the art of ugliness, removing any traces of beauty from her face that might present to the world the wrong impression of her true state. Thomas was very distressed. He had declared that she was waxen so often that he had come to believe it. Because she controlled her emotions he had overlooked her brains.

'I said once to Henry that it was because the rich defended themselves behind the barrier of the law, that the poor would be obliged to aspire to the same defence. I am poor. Very poor in spirit. I have considered divorce.' Thomas was taken aback. It had never entered his head that they might become involved in that whole hideous formality. Jane evidently knew what he was thinking. 'I know what is involved,' she said, 'and I am not at all unaware of the processes. I am prepared to apply to the ecclesiastical court for a divorce *a mensa et toro*. I am prepared to bring a charge of criminal conversation against Henry in the civil court.'

'But this is terrible!' Thomas was agitated and his arms rose and fell at his sides in a helpless gesture. A situation of such long standing seemed set in its ways and he was alarmed to realize that Jane was not prepared to tolerate it with the tactical abstraction of Sam and himself. He had believed she would accept her lot, indeed had never considered that she had much choice. He wondered if she had been chattering to that damned woman Maria. 'You can't do it, Jane. What would your father say?' He knew it was a cowardly refuge, but he suddenly felt very old and weary at the permutations of human difficulty with which his children presented him. Could they not manage their own affairs! As though in answer, Jane was continuing. Her voice was low and flat, seemingly without emotion but her mouth worked on the words like sour gooseberries.

'Henry has shamed me, and you both knew and kept silent, thinking I didn't know. Well, I do. Do you know that Mrs Waters is here tonight? I have never met the lady. Are you going to introduce me, for I'm sure Henry won't? Are you shocked that I know? What motive, sir, did you and my father have in concealing such things? No doubt you are convinced that you were protecting me and the sanctity of marriage. Perhaps you were only protecting your friendship!'

'That is an intolerable thing to say, madam. I won't listen to it!' He felt shaky and needed to sit down. Jane saw, but had no compassion.

'We arrived here together tonight, we shook hands with Sir Walter, and I have not seen him since. Where is he now? Are you being kind to me? Keeping something from me in case it should hurt me? There is nothing left, sir, that could hurt me now, and that is a very dangerous position for Henry to be in. Before long I shall be too old to have a child, yet I am married. I won't have one with Henry. No, don't pretend to turn away. As you said, we are kin. What can you or Father do to make up for that? You have perpetuated this situation, and I won't have it.'

The tears were running down her face but there was no sobbing. She had so muffled her emotions over the years that she no longer wept. Her tear ducts still functioned involuntarily but that was all. It was more terrifying to Thomas than any womanly outbreak because it was so controlled. He tried to put an arm around her, to usher her into the lee of some trees where no people passed, but she wriggled away from him. In the trees a dove cooed, stupid noises of sympathy.

'Let me be seen to look ugly! It's the truth!'

Thomas said nothing and they stood in silence for a long time. He looked out over the gardens with their fairy lights and caves, string orchestras, tents and people. He could hear the music, faintly. Couples passed, or people in groups, talking, laughing. It is this setting that has done it, he rationalized, all this damned frippery nonsense. He wondered what to do next. His immediate response was to suggest something that would take her mind off it, but something warned him this was wholly inadequate to the situation. The trouble with women was that you couldn't treat them like men, suggest a stiff drink, get it out of the system. He was totally at sea. It was left to Jane to take the initiative.

'I've finished.'

The burbling dove sounded sleepy. He was unaccustomed to late nights. An owl screeched in a nearby wood. The leaves of the tree stirred and they listened together to the night noises that seemed to distance them from the problems of man.

'What shall we do?' Thomas asked. It was both a general and a particular question.

'Go to the scent garden.' Jane sounded matter-of-fact.

'But what do you intend ... about the things you have been saying?'

'I shall tell Henry the truth.'

'Not here?'

Thomas's selfish reaction was immediate. To his surprise Jane laughed. Thomas, stooped and anxious, took her arm in his hand. She did not resist. At that moment she welcomed human contact and the transparency of Thomas's selfishness made it impossible to sustain real venom. He weighed heavily on her arm and she wondered whether it was deliberate, or whether he really was becoming so infirm. He was perfectly capable of leaning on her for effect. She would make no comment that would allow him to indulge in self-pity.

He allowed himself to be blindfolded by a black servant dressed in a tabard and fumbled his way along the silk cord that zig-zagged through the garden. He could feel with his feet that he was walking upon different textures, and his legs brushed against leaves that seemed brush-like and spiky. Heavy perfumes assailed him, and sharp, acid scents. He could identify none of them, although Jane followed behind him, murmuring names and explaining he should notice this or that. It astonished him that she could behave with such calm again. After a few minutes under the blindfold he began to feel panic. He found that he could not suppress involuntary thoughts. He was moving in a dream, without senses, following a cord that led to nothing. He lost all sense of direction and began to feel giddy. His heart beat faster. The musky breath of blossoms made him feel sick. Age. Faculties and body fading, he thought. This is surely like death, this cord, this blackness. He tore off the blindfold before the finish and sat on a seat to the side, panting for breath. When he regained it, he felt it had been a near thing. The first real struggle. He watched Jane with resentment. She had not followed him away from the garden, but continued on her course, slowly. She seemed serene and he wondered why the devil she had chosen this occasion to upset him, when he was only being polite.

Henry walked into Mrs Waters unexpectedly. He had not even known she was there. She had been dancing on the boarded floor laid on a lawn, and stepped off, laughing, in front of him. The man she was with was about his own age. Henry immediately disliked him. Henry was with Sam and they had been talking Law, watching the rotating dancers.

'Mr Henry Kelleway!' she effused in a fashion he knew to be false. Her face was almost immediately blank of expression. Henry was no better. Instead of grappling with the formalities of introduction, he stared at her, trying to read the closed book of her face. Sam Leigh, who knew perfectly well who she was, took control of the situation.

'Excuse me?' he said, 'do introduce us.'

'I'm sorry. Mrs Waters, this is Mr Samuel Leigh, barrister.'

Sam gave a punctilious bow. The man with Mrs Waters returned it. 'Mr Searle.'

'Mr Kelleway is a brilliant barrister,' Mrs Waters continued, 'at least I had reason to believe so.'

Henry knew he should smile and move on. Sam had already started to do so. It was her use of the past tense that galled him as it was meant to. It was also an irrational feeling of excitement in his stomach.

'Mr Leigh is more eminent than I,' he replied merely in order to stay in the same place.

'I don't doubt it,' said Mrs Waters with a ravishing smile at Sam, which stopped him as effectively as a bullet. Sam himself marvelled that at his age he remained entirely naked to such glances. He felt rather proud.

'Not at all, not at all,' he protested, blushing. 'This is a very fine place, is it not, Mrs Waters?' Thus Judas, he thought.

'Very entertaining and picturesque. The hermits strike me as being dirty, however. It cannot do them any good to live underground. It was designed by Mr Kelleway's brother William, the painter,' she explained to Searle. 'He was the man in the cloak you said was such an odd fellow.' Searle looked irritated and Mrs Waters laughed gaily. It was such a sound as young girls practise for their first ball. She was mocking them. 'A talented young man. His poor wife!'

'His poor wife?' Henry was trying hard to show no sign of anything except courtesy. He must not be annoyed.

'His poor wife is sitting all alone by the house with Sir Walter for company while her husband is the centre of admiration and attraction. It is always the same, Mr Kelleway. We poor women are eclipsed. Is not Venus the moon and Jupiter the sun? It must be years since we last met, Mr Kelleway, and I hear that you labour hard for the enemies of our society and are the scourge of the Owners. That sounds a great deal for a simple barrister. Mr Searle, would you permit me to ask Mr Kelleway to dance so that he can tell me what has shot him to this eminence?'

Searle murmured assent as he had to but his face betrayed understandable annoyance. Henry saved his anger until they should be out of earshot.

'It is a waltz. Do you waltz, Mr Kelleway?'

'Of course, madam!'

'One is never sure with legal gentlemen, they can be so archaic. And they are very careful where they put their feet!' With this aside and another dazzling smile at Sam that excluded

Searle, she walked with Henry onto the boards. 'How is your pretty wife?' the men heard her ask as they started off round the floor.

'Tell me, Mr Searle,' asked Sam politely, 'what do you do?'

'Do, sir? I do nothing,' replied Searle bluntly.

'Oh,' said Sam and conversation lapsed completely.

'Why did you come?' asked Helena Waters. Henry was nonplussed. 'To dance with me,' she explained.

'I could hardly have refused,' he replied stiffly. He was concerned to hold her far from him so that he looked stiff as a heron. He could feel her trying to move closer to him and at first resisted. Short of a farcical struggle of pushing in the middle of the dance floor, he had in the end to give in. He was aware of her considerable strength of body as well as mind. The music of the indifferent band had the merit of giving them privacy.

'You shan't push me away,' she said, 'I won't be held at arm's length. You can't pretend to indifference during a waltz.' She looked at him closely, and very openly. 'You haven't changed much, Henry. A little older, which suits you. Your face has a few more wrinkles and I prefer it. Only young saplings have smooth bark.' Feeling compelled to return some sort of compliment, Henry inclined his head to her.

'You have not changed at all, madam. Your beauty is . . .' he faltered.

'Enduring?' she supplied. 'No, Henry, don't bother to pay compliments, I know my own state of preservation, and I am no younger either. There's nothing there to talk about. Your work goes well, I hear.'

Henry shrugged. 'Yes, it does.'

'It warrants more than a shrug, surely? It does in my life anyway.' Rebuked, Henry was silent. 'No enthusiasm now? Do these people deserve your attentions and your sacrifice? They owe you a lot, you know. Still, they have made you an eminent man.' She was trying to emulate the amused, open expression with which she kept the world at bay, but he could see it wither away as he looked at her and her eyes showed pain. It terrified him lest it should turn to tears. She guessed his feelings and answered for him. 'No, I don't weep, Henry. I did, but what's past

315

is past. Isn't it?' It was a direct question to which he did not respond. 'I can still feel sadness though,' she continued. 'Are you happy?'

'Yes,' he said with the abruptness that means no.

'Poor Henry. We had such a short time together. Our pursuit of happiness was a flurried chase.'

'I don't think we should speak about it here,' he whispered urgently.

To be heard but not overheard, he leaned forward, his lips brushing her hair. He could smell her perfume and for a moment turned back years, wanting without thinking to kiss her neck. He recoiled, startled. Her eyes, regarding him, had the same expression that he used to know. His heart was thumping like a schoolboy daring to touch his first girl. It irritated him that his emotions were just a youth's.

'No one can hear us,' she said reassuringly, 'I think you still love me. Can you say you don't want me?'

'You never hesitated about the point!' He thought how she had waylaid him in her carriage and carried him willingly off.

'I have no time for dalliance. You should know that. We put on all these fine gowns, and you put on these tight trousers and stiff coats but our bodies are entrapped animals beneath them, just the same. No miraculous change takes place. It's all a sham. Look how people eye each other around the floor. What do you think they are thinking? Cupidity, hate and desire.'

'And Mr Searle?' To his surprise she laughed with genuine amusement. 'Mr Searle has ambitions concerning me, but as he is a dull child his ambitions will remain unfulfilled. I would like to think you are jealous, but you don't think I would let him lie with me?'

Henry was reduced to embarrassed silence by her directness. He had forgotten the breathless delight of it. He had never talked to any other person in such an easy way. 'You haven't changed at all,' she said with warmth, his stupid, youthful heart thumping. He knew he should break off the dance immediately, but knew he would not.

'You've forgotten, though,' she rebuked him. 'We were able to say such things to each other. Why should a woman not talk of lying with a man? Does it make me unmentionable? Cannot a husband even tell his wife he desires her? You have forgotten everything. I had high hopes for you, Henry. When a man is hungry he should eat. It is a compliment to the cook!'

'Helena, be quiet!'

'No one can hear!' They moved round on the boards to a position nearer the band. 'Years have gone by now. Will you visit me again?'

He could not bring himself to say no for motives he decided were honourable, so responded with what he told himself was tact. 'I will one day.'

'But you haven't asked me my address.'

'I assumed it was the same.'

'It is, but you did not ask. Now I doubt your intention. Henry, we are both unhappy. That is a waste. My bed is yours.'

Henry kept dancing mechanically. He knew he was blushing. Mrs Waters was looking at him so directly that he was convinced that they must be standing naked as Adam and Eve on the dance floor. The music suddenly stopped. There was some polite clapping. Henry had to look at his clothing to convince himself.

'You see,' Mrs Waters continued, 'what stuff clothing is. You are making sure of your disguise!' They walked off the floor, Mrs Waters taking his arm firmly and squeezing it. 'Promise me you'll come or I'll embarrass you more!'

Henry nodded. 'Yes.'

Searle and Sam stood in Englishman's silence, which is a state of suspended animation agreed by mutual disinterest. They were relieved when the couple returned.

'Thank you, Mrs Waters,' said Henry returning her to Searle, whose arm she did not take. 'Mr Searle, if you will excuse us, we have other realms of this entertainment to visit.'

'I'm rather slow on my feet,' said Sam, 'and take time getting round it.'

'Certainly,' said Searle with too-obvious relief, 'good evening, gentlemen. No doubt we will encounter each other again, making our *petit tour*.'

'Thank you for the dance, Mr Kelleway.' Mrs Waters looked polite, urbane and amused.

As they walked between rows of lights towards the rock constructions, Sam suddenly stopped and turned to Henry. 'That woman seemed to me to have ambitions for you.'

Henry managed to laugh. 'She has ambitions for all men,' he lied without thinking.

'I wouldn't know about that. I'm only interested in you.'

'Sam!'

Sam grunted and they moved on. Why, Henry pondered, did the lie slip so easily from my tongue? It defamed her. Would it spring so easily from my mouth if I loved her? What is it I need from her? Or she from me?

'Maria!' David Carroll was genuinely delighted. 'I've been looking for you. Your genius husband is the lion who cannot be approached so I could only hang about him for a word and be sent off with a buffet from his paws. Why has he left you here? He's holding court down there. I think this will go to his head. You will have to be very severe with him about the house, or he will give up working.'

Carroll had remained a constant friend through the years. His amiable nature was impervious to William's new-found arrogance. Carroll declared it a mere pose, a *jeu d'esprit* which would pass. He had become comparatively successful in his own right with landscapes of lowering Alps.

Maria sat on a swing seat twisted with browning hop vines on which the flowers were still aromatic, and rustled as the swing moved. Although people moved about her all the time, she had a distracted manner that had discouraged polite conversation. For Carroll, she immediately stopped rocking and moved over.

'Shall I swing this thing?'

'No, David. An idle thing for the sake of idleness. However, it made me seem occupied and kept conversation away. I have been left here because I am bored, and don't want to see it all again.'

Carroll laughed. 'I can understand that, but it *is* Willie's day and he may as well have his triumph. There will be money in it in the end and more commissions too!' His enthusiasm was touching, his simplicity less so as it seemed to Maria to be too akin to William's. How they must have things revolving about their uniqueness!

'I have no place in this sort of thing,' she said, 'these grand parties are a kind of human stew. We are all pushed together like so many ingredients, mixed and simmered, and emerge as something different. Our nature has been changed. What went in, neat, precise and natural, comes out a confusion of shapes and tastes. A goulash, acquiring a little of the tang of everything. I never feel better for it.'

'But Maria, you worked so hard for Willie! It is your triumph too. He could never have done it without you.'

'Is that my reward, David?'

'Maria, you are taking it all very seriously. Is there something the matter?'

'Yes. These grand affairs give delusions of grandeur. If I won't subscribe to them, William gets upset.'

'That's just Willie's temperament. He wants to sweep everyone along with him! It's natural enough. He only gets hurt because he wants everyone to enjoy it as much as he does.'

'But that is utter selfishness! It is the same as people who insist on reading you bits from books you would rather read yourself. He has changed, David.'

Carroll looked at her worried face and after sustaining his ebullience for a few moments in appearance and pose, seemed to crumple. 'Yes, I suppose he has. We all have.'

'Yet you haven't started believing in yourself.'

'That's a very enigmatic remark, Maria.'

'No, it is not. And you fully understand me. When you and William got up to nonsense, it was nothing. High spirits. There was nothing inflated about you, rather the opposite. William has been so praised recently that he believes his worth.'

'He deserves it,' said Carroll stoutly, as a man in defence of fellow man.

'Do you really believe him to be so good?' Maria's question was very coolly put.

Carroll bridled. 'Come now, Maria, that's no question to ask a friend! What do you want me to say? That he isn't the best painter since Giotto? Of course he isn't. But why do you want me to say it? I won't be led into it, it's not fair. Willie has become a bit arrogant at times, but he will get over it. He's the fashion. That's success. Of course he isn't the greatest painter the world has seen, but I won't tell him so, and I hope you won't tell him for me. I wouldn't do it to him!' He paused. 'Anyway, how are the children?'

Carroll's blue eyes were innocent, but Maria felt deep anger. How easily the conversation could be diverted to domestic matters. Here, Carroll was plainly saying, are your affairs. Stick to them. He meant no harm, indeed she doubted if he meant anything by it. She slipped into the easy routine of narrative, but her mind was busy. Margaret is doing well with her lessons. Yes, she is seven and she is a promising painter. Yes, it is a pretty talent in a girl. Jonathan is teething, badly, and Henrietta, aged four, has a terrible temper. No, the cook's girl has given up painting lessons with Margaret because the cook insists she must go into domestic service and her place is in the kitchen, so Maria and Cook had a scene, as a result of which the cook gave in her notice. No, William was not amused by it. William was not amused by much.

'Maria!' called William, hailing them from an unnecessary distance, 'David! You must come with us. The grand surprise opening is going to take place!' He referred to a crowd of about fifty that swirled like a cloak at his heels. He was enjoying every moment of it, Maria could see, and she realized she should not, reasonably, resent it. A shrill bell started to ding excitedly from the ruined tower. 'That's the signal,' he called, 'it's midnight!'

Thomas, who had finally located Sam in the darkness and confusion, was scathing. 'Melodrama! And what a waste of money!'

William and his host were escorted by servants in tabards who carried links to lead the way. Other servants moved in the darkness, replacing wicks in the fairy-lights or adding blocks of wax.

'There will be more fireworks afterwards!' called William's voice from somewhere ahead.

'Come on, then, Sam,' said Thomas. 'I missed half the first lot, but I shan't miss this.'

Some people who had been trailing about in a young maze unable to find the way out, trampled through it like sheep, flattening the young box trees.

'There go the men who govern us!' exclaimed Sam, pointing to several eminent Members of Parliament.

Manning was standing on a jutting rock below a heap of large slabs that owed a great deal to artifice and nothing to nature. Torches had been lit and stuck in brackets all around so that he addressed the crowd like a medieval lord in hall. To suit the part, he wore a gorgeous cloak edged with ermine, a heavy braided waistcoat and braided shoes of material. The colour of the cloak was indistinguishable in the torch-light. Two servants stepped forward at his sides, produced silver trumpets with a flourish, and blew a fanfare. Thomas thought it too ridiculous. John, still standing with Caroline, was mesmerized by the torches which reminded him of other scenes. His guilt was heavy on him and he realized then that he must make some attempt to find Louise. It must be possible to trace her somehow. He was horrified by the powers of destruction that he fleetingly saw within himself. He did not listen to Manning.

'Honourable Members, ladies and gentlemen! I hope that you have been diverted by our surprises and the small curiosities that have been prepared for you.'

He fumbled about in his cloak, and finding a kerchief, mopped his forehead. The effect of regality was not enhanced. Maria, whose eyes were ever sharp and critical, noted that he stood upon a small wooden plinth concealed by his cloak to give him more height.

'Those of you who are my neighbours will, I hope, have the opportunity to enjoy it often. Those that have come further, I hope to welcome frequently.' He paused, mopping again, and addressed the ground. 'I have tried to make here a garden to remind you of former days. Mr William Kelleway has created, I believe, a triumph.' He paused for murmurings of appreciation and polite applause. 'We live in an age where the unbeautiful machines on which our prosperity is founded are blackening our land, where unbeautiful forces seek to destroy our very country and our democracy. We need to return to an older form of beauty, to ease our eyes, with perfumes that enchant the nose, with simple rustic pleasure in flowers, trees and water. In brief, I have seen enough of ugliness and ask you to enjoy simple

321

beauty. Behind this rock is a cavern that has been concealed. The water beyond passes over it so that it falls past it on the far side forming a curtain through which you will dimly see the ruins of the tower. Harps will play to you, garlands are hung from the ceilings, nosegays will be presented to the ladies. I declare this retreat open!'

At this the two trumpeters gave another blast, stepped back and opened a 'rock' behind Manning. A brilliant gleam of blue-green light shone out. Simultaneously the servants extinguished their torches. The effect was dramatic. Even Thomas and Sam were silenced. They could hear Manning and William urging people to enter, and the sound of harps gently rippling. They trooped into a large cavern, ablaze with turquoise light from every ledge. At the far end a curtain of water rushed past, very fine and unbroken, disappearing below the rim of the cave onto a smooth slab so that it was almost silent. Baskets of green ferns were hung around the lights to enhance the effect. Green sweet-meats and cordials were laid out on tables of polished stone. The servants wore green garments. It was enchanting, and stunning. People spoke in whispers and marvelled.

'This certainly is beautiful,' Maria confided to Carroll. 'It is fairy-like. The attention to detail is excellent. The curtain of water, perfect.'

The shot seemed to split their skulls. Ears went blank except for the far-off surging of blood. Others lips around them moved, teeth and tongues bared. They must be screaming but silently in a nightmare. There was an explosion of motion in the corner of the chamber and Maria saw fists flying. A woman in front of her looked her full in the face and kept screaming, noiselessly. A great green fish gulping in a green bowl. Manning lay on the floor with a dark stain on his green chest, ragged corners of flesh exposed. The screaming woman was in the way and Maria, hardly thinking, pushed her aside. Faint high sounds were begin-ning to return, pushing through the singing of the blood in her ears. Women squealing, women being ushered away. Men clus-tering round the fallen man, but doing little, stooping, trying to communicate noiselessly as though gulping air. Maria forced her way through them. She was surprised to find Henry already on his knees beside Manning with another man, a stranger she did not know. Henry had rolled up his coat and was cradling Manning's head. In the green light his wet face shone like phosphorescence. His eyelids moved. Henry said something to her, mouthing uselessly.

'I can't hear!' she shouted, but he looked blank, pointing to his ears. She leaned over Manning's body, cupping both hands together, and shouted in his ear. 'Let me look at it! Tear up your shirt!'

Henry still looked at her shaking his head, desperate to understand. She seized his shirt and made tearing motions. He nodded and took it off. The other man followed suit. She pushed back onlookers, waving her hands at them as though dismissing a swarm of flies. They stepped back and stared. Stooping down, she quickly undid the remains of his waistcoat and found that he wore a corset. There was no way she could undo this without turning him over. He was bleeding profusely, the liquid looking black as treacle in the green light. She could see the pistol ball lodged in the centre of the torn black area, half buried, and distorted out of shape. That was good. It had hit waistcoat, corset and ribs at an angle, and appeared to have smashed at least two of the ribs without penetrating further. The hole was jagged but probably not deep. The bleeding must be stopped. Was there a doctor anywhere in the crowd? She had no way of knowing, no way of making herself heard. Perhaps the other man was a doctor?

'Are you a doctor?'

The man looked at her, trying to understand and pointed at his ears. She repeated it slowly in dumb show. He understood but shook his head. She was undecided whether to leave the ball or try to take it out. She had heard it was always better to leave it in. She must take a risk on it.

Making a wad of shirt, they bandaged him with strips that had to be tied individually because they were so short. She could hear some sounds now. Manning was moaning. Henry was shouting.

'That should stop the bleeding!'

It sounded far away, as an echo off a hill beyond a hill.

'We must move him very carefully. Do you understand?'

She enunciated each syllable, pointing at Manning with her

finger as though keeping time. Henry and his helper nodded. She noticed for the first time that the cavern was blue with smoke and smelled of the explosion of the gun. She had not yet had time to wonder who had done it. She was now able to look round for familiar faces.

A man, dressed in hermit's cloak, was pinioned in the corner by John and others. It was what she expected of John. William was hovering around the group, uncertain how to help, for until Manning was dealt with, they stood and watched. A hand on her shoulder came from Thomas, who gently steered her away from Manning. She could hear Henry in a strained, far-off voice, saying that he must be carried to the house. There was confused talk about how this should be done until William, who obviously saw his role as supervisory, produced the practical idea that they should collect the table cloths together and make a litter to be carried by six men. Having produced this, he took no part in the action. His attitude remained that of the artist asking, or indeed ordering his technicians to carry out routine work.

In a short time the carefully prepared banquet was ruined. The beautiful sweetmeats lay scattered on the tables, the green cordials were placed aside, table decorations, centrepieces and flowers ruined. They laid six layers of table cloth upon each other and lifted Manning onto it. The pinioned man, bleeding from the mouth and nose from the fight, watched it all without emotion.

'Who are you?' Men were demanding. The man was ignoring them. Their ears were ringing now but hearing was returning to a more normal volume. Six of the younger men picked up the tablecloths, which were not stiff enough for comfort and pulling as best they could, carried Manning from the cavern into the darkness of the night. The servants in attendance with lit torches marched beside the burden.

'What is your name?' Thomas growled, pushing his way close to the man. 'The constables will be here for you immediately. What sort of devil are you? You have no escape.'

Perhaps it was Thomas's age, or his unimpassioned manner of stating the situation. The man looked at him. 'I am John Smith.' His accent was from the north country.

'You are not John Smith. Be assured, you will be found out. You have shot a good man.'

The hermit's face became suddenly angry. 'He deserves to die! They will hang me. I want to hang for a dead man. I am John Smith and to hell with you all! I am John Smith from Bradford, and I was a weaver by trade. That is all you shall ever know!'

'Not so,' said Thomas curtly, 'you will have much more to say for yourself at trial, and much more with hemp around your neck.'

'You think so?' the man replied. His face was without expression again.

'We'll take him to the house,' said one of the men, and without urging, John Smith stood up and walked forward held by four, including John.

'Look at the scene,' William exclaimed to Maria outside, 'it is more extraordinary than anything I could have designed!'

The calm callousness of his remark stunned Maria. He was watching the two processions with evident delight. The first had the appearance of a cortège, the second was more sinister, for the cloaked hermit looked like a man already on his way to his death.

'This is dreadful for poor Manning, but what a spectacle it makes!' He was talking to himself for Maria had slipped off to take Thomas's arm. Caroline and Sam had joined them.

'Where is Jane?' Caroline asked Henry, who was being draped in a piece of material to replace his shirt.

'I haven't seen her.' He sounded deliberately dismissive. 'I didn't see her come in.'

'She has gone home.' It was Thomas, speaking low.

'We should all go home,' said Henry obliquely. 'When the doctor has arrived and we know the position, we must clear the house. No one can stay here tonight.'

Throughout the gardens and around the water, the servants were extinguishing the lights, moving by the aid of torches. The musicians stumbled through the woods carrying their instruments and complaining that they could not see. One of the servants seemed to be in charge. Under his tabard were tucked two pistols. They would search the whole grotto area. Maria wondered about the other hermits. Williams was remonstrating so

325

loudly that they could still hear him as they walked back to the house. He wanted the lights left on, wanted the scene unchanged, wanted, Maria thought, the ball to go on forever.

The doctor had announced that Manning was not gravely wounded. Although serious, he said, he had an excellent chance of recovery. Two ribs were fractured but he had been struck by the ball at an angle and the corset had done excellent work.

He had made his announcement to a dwindling company from the front steps. Many had already departed out of good or bad manners. Then they took to their carriages for a long ride. The nearest constables had been sent for by a rider. It seemed such an anti-climax, but there was nothing further anyone could usefully do. The doctor was firm that Manning should see no one.

Maria's silence should have warned William, but William was sorry for himself and had been drinking.

'It is amazing how so much that has been carefully created can be spoiled by a madman! In the same way a canvas can be slit by a knife. Beauty, ah, beauty! It is so fragile and easily destroyed.' He prated on in the darkness, Maria only half listening above the clattering and rumble of the wheels. A depression greater than sadness had settled on her.

The extinguishing of the coloured lights haunted her. William's petulant voice, protesting, was the voice of someone she neither knew nor understood. She had been able to accept his childishness in many ways because it represented a harmless, simple part of him. His escapades had seemed foolish but were a fashionable madness. Now he seemed careless of inflicting hurt, wholly selfish and wholly unknown to her. She drew into her corner of the carriage, pulling her blanket up to her chin and stared out at the narrow strip of hedgerow illuminated by the carriage lamps. The night was busy with moths that chased the lights. She watched them, feeling physically sick. They had reached a turning point that had been coming and she could not retreat from it now. In the dark, at this moment, she could brace herself to it.

'Don't you think that man is beautiful?' she asked abruptly, interrupting William who was slow to collect his wits.

'What do you mean?' His tone was aggressive and derisory,

implying she had no right to interrupt his monody on the disaster.

'It's simple enough. Don't you think that man is fragile and can easily be destroyed? Or do you only think that the things made by man are beautiful?'

'What nonsense. What is beautiful about man in the mass? He is dirty, he smells. In the mass they are nothing. It is the ideals of man that are beautiful, and when these ideals are translated by that mystic process into objects, words, music, that is beauty. Is that madman the hermit beautiful? He has destroyed beauty. The garden is ruined. Tainted.'

'What about Walter Manning? Isn't he more important than the garden?' She knew that she had to say it but had not intended to put it so bluntly. She could not see his face in the dark interior, but his words were clear enough.

'He'll recover. I don't believe he fully appreciated the garden anyway. Of course, I am sorry for him and what has happened, but he employed this madman and it is atrocious that five years' work should be destroyed in a moment! He was a man with some ideas, but I have outgrown the Mannings of this world, Maria. Their eyes are like dull pewter plates that need to be regularly polished, for their shine is momentary and soon grows dull! You must see that he bought something beyond his comprehension. What we need are patrons like the Medicis. Visionary scholars, statesmen and poets. Then the achievements are enormous . . .'

Maria's rage was almost as violent as the pistol shot. 'That is atrocious!'

The violence of her feelings shocked William, and his vanity and arrogance covered up for any true feeling that might have been pierced. 'You will not shout at me, Maria. Your behaviour passes all understanding. I said it at the beginning of the evening. Are you determined to wreck it, too?'

'I shall do what I please. Your opinion of yourself has corrupted you, and if you can't see that, then I'm sorry for you. How can you speak of Manning like that? You liked the man. I found him absolutely charming, his appreciation was absolute. No one could have enjoyed your work more. He was full of praise for it and for you, and now he is ill and wounded, all you can think about is yourself. You have already discarded him. I was so ashamed when I heard you trying to have them relight the decorations. It was like some boy who wants his birthday cake lit again and again!'

'I won't answer. Nor will I listen to such . . . abuse.'

'Then if you won't listen, the alternative is silence. You have become famous enough to be arrogant but not good enough to be humble.'

'Be quiet!' William roared so loudly the horses shied. The coachman on the seat could hear every word. 'I will not brawl! You shall have your silence, madam!'

They nursed it like a phial of vitriol.

Caroline, Thomas and John returned with the constraints be-tween them broken down. Thomas had been explaining about his conversation with Jane.

'If I had known this garden party affair would turn out to be so eventful, I should never have come,' he was complaining.

'Battlefields are no different from ordinary pasture,' said John, 'there is no way of knowing.'

Thomas sat in a corner now, covered in a blanket and no longer upright like a chaperon.

'What will Jane do?' asked Caroline. The coach swerved erra-tically and they all jolted and banged against the seats. Thomas muttered under his breath, 'Or Henry for that matter,' and then went on. 'I don't propose to discuss it further, Caroline. I have told Sam about it and we will both give it some thought.' His tone was sharp and final.

John changed the subject. 'I wonder who the man was?'

'Some revolutionary, I don't doubt, as the French call 'em. Some Luddite or Chartist or some such madman. It is all part of a trend!' The coach again jolted heavily. 'A weaver, he said. They are always agitating and making trouble of some sort. They want to change the world by stopping progress.'

'So does the Gothick movement,' said John with malicious amusement.

'By Gee, John, you only say that to upset me! You were always like that and I don't suppose you've changed. They are mad as well. One lot wants things to stand still, the other to turn them back to some time that may or may not have existed. What do they want? Us all in suits of armour, living in castles? It makes things unstable. They none of them care as long as they stop progress. What happens? Investments cannot be trusted. No man's money is safe in the market today. It will bring down the monarchy, you'll see, but I shan't thank the Lord. You shall have a president yet!'

'Then why not pass the reforms instead?' asked Caroline innocently.

Before Thomas could launch into an answer the coach swerved again and a branch thrashed hard against the bodywork with an ominous scrape.

'What was that?' Thomas roared angrily, throwing open the window. 'Morton!' he shouted, leaning out, 'What was that? Are you lost, man?'

'Nothing, sir. A branch.'

'It's scraped the coach. The thing has been leaping about like a stung horse. Are you drunk, Morton?'

'No, sir.'

'Then stop behavin' as though you are!'

'Yes, sir.'

Thomas sat down again, closing the window. 'Where was I?' But they would not let him continue on his favourite theme and after an hour he fell asleep.

Morton, on the driver's seat, was in a sweat that had nothing to do with exertion, but ran down his armpits and back in clammy rivulets, soaking his shirt and then his coat like a man in a fever. He felt very cold. He had continually to drag his attention back to the narrow road. Twice he nearly canted them into a deep ditch and only the other man's frantic nudges enabled him to pull the horses round. The man did not shout or Will would have been in more trouble. He had to think, to have time to know what to do, but he knew there would be little time.

John and Caroline spoke in low voices that could not be heard above the wheels. Thomas was snoring in a relaxed way and they felt safe.

'Neither Henry nor William will put up with me you know,' John was saying. 'They were both at pains to snub me politely. Can you explain that?'

'I think they are both jealous. You are the prodigal returned, whether you like it or not. William does not get on with Father, he never has. Henry has his own troubles, and has no heir. What do you expect if you are taken back into the bosom of the family after all these years away? You know he always favoured you.'

'That's nonsense.'

'No,' insisted Caroline, 'you could not disappoint him because you were always so unexpected. You have even usurped us all with your children!'

'Caroline!'

'Well, you have two. Legitimate heirs to his favourite son.'

'You're teasing me.' John was agitated and answered mechanically. Caroline sensed his awkwardness. 'What's wrong?'

'You are the Inquisition, aren't you, Caroline! A gentle one but persistent.'

'There is something to tell and I know you want to tell it. John, you can't hide it, you are too obvious. Father does not want to know so closes his mind to it, but I do. I know nothing. Are you ready yet?' she asked in mocking echo of his earlier refusal.

'Are you ready yet?' he responded, tense with anxiety.

'Yes. I think I am.'

'They are my children but I was never married.' He blurted it out too loudly, with too much emphasis.

Caroline raised her hand to his lips. 'Hush, you'll wake him. I had already guessed that.'

'You won't tell Thomas?' He was astounded by her calm revelation.

'Certainly not, that is your own affair. It is the rest I want to hear about. Who is this woman? Is she still alive? Why did she leave you, what is it that is eating away at you? You seem always to be looking inside yourself and what you see, you hate.'

In the jolting darkness, John made his first attempt to put into words those emotions that rose like shapeless bubbles of pain.

William could not recollect something that seemed important. He was half asleep and nodded off from time to time. He could hear no sound from Maria and assumed that she had fallen asleep and was grateful for the release. He had rationalized and pushed aside her remarks as being a fit of pique or jealousy or some other unknown female attack, and was smarting with injustice. Yet at the edge of his memory, like the faint after image of light on the eye that has changed all colours to pale grey and is about to fade, something was there that was to do with the hermit and Bradford and weavers. It was something to which he felt he should have a response, but his memory remained inert. It was something to do with prisons. His brain gave up the unequal struggle and he too slept.

Thomas sat in chambers in Two Pump Court. He felt unequal to the task of ploughing through the pile of statements in front of him. Robertson v Macateer, although deserving, was unnecessarily wordy. As a young man he would weigh up how many of the affidavits were substantially perjured and come to the depressing conclusion that one third were, one third might be and one third could be.

Henry v Jane and William v Maria were the cases that chiefly concerned him. He had been alarmed by his seizure in the perfume-garden and felt that it had been a warning. The clock had, as it were, struck the first quarter and he must look to the hour.

They were such a divided family, yet he had done everything that he thought possible to keep them together. He told himself that he had not directly interfered, except perhaps that he had always held Caroline too dear. There was a wild strain in the men that he could not understand. He had not always been sober in his own youth, or continent, but he had not allowed these inclinations to continue into his marriage. Yet by all the material conditions of the world, Henry and William were successful, even celebrated. They could count on their names appearing in the journals whenever they were involved. Thomas was eclipsed by them. It was something that he had craved but now that was gone. Summer was going and life was going. He slept more often now during the day, dropping off without noticing it. He supposed it was a gentle way of nature for easing us into death. He was asleep when the head clerk tapped in vain, then tapped again and entered. Thomas sat up with a start. The sun was bright on the buildings opposite and the window glared unbearably.

'Please pull the curtains. It's too bright.'

'Yes, Mr Kelleway.' The clerk did so, leaving only a small bright gap to illuminate the room.

'What is it?'

'There is a gentleman to see you without appointment on what he says is a matter of personal business. He is from a Mr Masterson and he says it concerns shipping.'

Thomas felt frowzy from sleep, but the announcement made his heart thump uncomfortably. He found that he was clutching it with his right hand. It was a gesture he made too frequently. He must be careful. 'Please show him in. His name?'

'Mr Sears.'

Mr Sears was very hot and sweating and this alarmed Thomas more. He had obviously hurried, if in fact he had not been running. The clerk, although curious, discreetly shut the door and withdrew. He would not dare to listen at a Bencher's door.

'Yes, Mr Sears? I understand you have come from Mr Masterson?'

Mr Sears was blinking and puffing. Having come from the bright sunlight, he found the room almost dark. He was a thinnish young man with a long neck and thin head with fair hair. His hair hung lank with perspiration and his collar was soaked. Thomas vaguely recognized him as a junior from Masterson's office.

'Mr Masterson has sent me with a letter for you, and I am to await your reply.'

'Where is it, then?'

'Oh.' The young man was abashed and fished inside his coat pockets, handing Thomas a sealed letter. Thomas broke open the seal trying to appear calm. The wax crackled all over his desk top like a crushed biscuit.

Thomas Kelleway Esquire.
Dearest sir,

I have just this moment received grave intelligence of our vessel the *Thomas K.* It appears that we must contemplate the possibility that she is a total loss and look rapidly to our insurers. I am sorry that this letter contains such bad news delivered so abruptly and can only apologize, asking that you attend my offices as rapidly as your work permits, in order that we may secure our loss. My news is sound, having come this day from Rhode Island via first ship from that port since the loss was made known in New York.

Believe me, sir, this news brings me no joy as I know it must bring you heavy care. Our insurance in the ship being to the full valued amount of vessel and cargo, we should suffer no substantial loss. I will attend upon you all this day, hoping you find time to contact me direct.

Your obedient servant,

P. Masterson

Thomas read it through twice and struggled to his feet. His damned heart was pumping away and he had to steady himself with both hands flat on the desk. Robertson v Macateer, which had been neatly piled up by the clerk, fell over and slid onto the floor. The young man started over to pick the documents up.

'No, damn it, leave them! It has taken them eight months to get this far. Another day or two will make no difference. We will go immediately. Have you a hackney?'

'No, sir, I ran. I could not find a hackney.'

'Then go and find one, sir. I cannot run that distance!'

Mr Sears darted out. Thomas followed slowly, stooped like a grey heron. The head clerk had never seem him look so grey and concerned.

Masterson rose from behind his mahogany desk as soon as Thomas entered. He stretched out his hand, which Thomas took but was too abstracted to shake.

'Mr Kelleway, you have arrived here with all speed. It is very good of you, please sit down. This chair, the comfortable one. I am sorry to bring you out on such bad news. A very sorry thing.'

'It is devilish news, sir. I hope you can explain the consequences. I have a great deal tied up in it.'

Thomas could not help staring at the picture on the wall behind Masterson's desk, with its ships sinking, guns blazing and sailors clinging to shattered masts and spars. It was singularly inappropriate. Masterson had poured him a very large brandy and was helping himself. Thomas noted that he seemed to be taking it well enough. He had already laid out a sea chart weighed down with tallies to prevent it curling. On this, Thomas could see he had been trying to calculate a ship's position with dividers and rule. When he handed Thomas the brandy, he looked Thomas intensely in the eyes as was his way. Thomas was not sure if it was reassuring or almost too earnest.

'I know all the details, I think, but you must understand that nothing can really be called final. However, I regret that it is certain there's no hope. The master has sent me a letter together with one from the New York agents via the brig *Fair Maid* which put in only this morning, fresh from Rhode Island. I think the best thing would be if I read you this letter. It makes things quite plain.'

Thomas nodded, and drank from his brandy-glass. Masterson was certainly calm. He was treating it as an everyday. He seated himself at his desk, smoothed out the paper and started to read.

P. Masterson Esquire etcetera etcetera.
Sir,

This letter is entrusted to the master of the brig *Fair Maid* with instructions to deliver it to your hands, in which matter he will be rendering good service.

I have to report with deep regret that the gravest circumstance that any master must report has overtaken the ship entrusted to me. The *Thomas K.*, as a result of what I shall describe must be considered by act of wind and wave a total loss, both vessel and burden, having been holed 'twixt wind and water and having no hope of recovery or navigation.

We took cargo at Liverpool and nothing much happened except a succession of heavy gales from the westward, the ship, which was a fine vessel, straining and making much water by the force of them. In consequence of this, the men had much pumping day and night. Our livestock suffered badly and many were injured and died or drowned and had to be put overboard. On July 18th a severe gale blew from the south-west and it was discovered that the ship's main-mast was badly sprung. The gale continuing for twenty-eight hours, our fore-yard and sail were carried away and fore top-sail torn to shreds. At the height of this gale the bowsprit also was discovered to be badly sprung and we were making much water, requiring one pump to be constantly going. She leaked so much and the crew were so fatigued by their efforts to sustain her afloat, that with the injury to her masts and sails she was no longer navigable.

On the 19th, still pumping and able only to hold our helm, another vessel bearing down upon us, we made a signal of distress. This vessel, the brig *Navigator*, undertook to take on board the crew of our ship and this we effected with great difficulty the succeeding day, heavy seas then running and the *Navigator* twice having lost us in the night. The crew were able to transfer only their personal effects due to the heavy seas. The brig *Navigator* also was full laden and could take no cargo. Our animals were all drowned and she was making much water. The cargo being manufactured goods and heavy she was by now very low. We were parted from her by a further strong gale that day and left her awash and without hope. One man of the crew was lost and must be drowned and another two injured. I attach letters to their relatives from the injured men and a letter I have written to the deceased man's next of kin, as I know them to the best of my knowledge, and ask you to see they are forwarded.

Believe me, sir, the *Thomas K.* must be considered a total loss and I have sought this first opportunity to inform you so that you may immediately direct an abandonment to be made to the underwriters. A letter from Townsend and White, your New York agents, accompanies this, giving similar direction. I have tried to give an account of events to the best of my ability, showing that it was an Act of the Almighty and that the crew behaved well in everything possible.

With deepest regret, trusting that nothing I have done will find me wanting.

Your obedient servant,

Cochrane, Master

'The agents direct simply that it is an abandonment and that we charge the underwriters with the burden with all speed.'

Masterson pushed the letter towards Thomas, but Thomas looked at it and away again without attempting to read it. Instead he drank heavily from his brandy-glass. He was aware of a palpitation of his heart, and was trying by concentration to calm himself down. All this might be commonplace to Mr Masterson, but to Thomas Kelleway it was a personal tragedy, not just a business affair. He could remember clearly how he had felt walking the new decks, the smell of wood, rope and pitch, the feel of the thick yellow varnish on the rails. It was as difficult to believe as a death. Masterson was obviously uneasy at Thomas's long silence. He did not understand that the other man was grieving.

'Mr Kelleway, a ship is lost somewhere every day, and often two or three.' Masterson was trying to be reassuring. 'You have only to read the journals. It comes to every owner at some time or another.'

'Like death?'

'It is hardly as serious as that! Good heavens! We must look to Hebson the underwriters. The important thing now is a full recovery. You can't do that with death!' He seemed pleased with this sally. Thomas gave no sign of having heard.

'Are the underwriters subscribed for the full amount?'

'Of course. Three thousand for the vessel and four thousand for the cargo.'

'But the cargo was nearly all in my name! This is an enormous loss, Mr Masterson, not to speak of a fine ship going down. I am stunned. I feel as if I have lost someone of my family. And my loss in it must be four and a half thousand pounds!'

'I think it may be nearer five,' said Masterson quickly.

Thomas glanced at him and shrugged. He was feeling unwell and wished he had not drunk Masterson's inferior brandy. It was turning to gas in his belly and burning him. His heart still thumped alarmingly. He rubbed at his chest with the flat of his right hand.

'Are you all right, Mr Kelleway? Have some more brandy?'

'No, thank you. It hasn't sat well on me.' He took long breaths and puffed them vigorously out. Masterson watched uncomfortably.

'Can I have something else brought in? Tea? Coffee?'

'No, no. I'm all right, just give me a little time.'

He wished the man would stop for a few minutes and let him think. He was newly bereaved and had lost over half the money he possessed into the bargain. Couldn't the fool understand? He found himself fast losing sympathy with Masterson. The man's appearance even irritated him, and all the sailor's trimmings. He remembered that Sam had warned him that shipping was a risky game.

'How do we go about recovery?'

'Leave that to me. I shall direct the abandonment immediately. Your money is safe, but obviously it will take a week or two.'

'What if they can't pay?'

'Hebson's can pay! Their business is enormous. They always pay. I have dealt with them always.'

Thomas wondered what to do. There was nothing he could do that would help. It was the nature of the loss that irked him. There was nothing to see, no remains, nothing tangible. No burial.

Henry's name had climbed three places in gilt script on the black painted board outside his chambers in King's Bench Walk. The death of Mr Agnew and the retirement of Mr Turvey and Mr Thackeray had enabled him to achieve this spurt of advancement. Now Mr Wells was left alone with his carpets and those Mr Agnew had left him, and had no one to vie with. These days, even he was inclined to be friendly with Henry.

Henry's furnishings had much improved, but remained simple. His chairs were comfortable green hide, deep-buttoned and full of boisterous support. From Mr Wells he had purchased a carpet which was in good order, if not of a connoisseur's quality. He did not cultivate dust, and his books and papers were kept rigidly within the bounds of bookcasing and desk pockets. He could not afford the luxury of disorder for he had found himself too busy for pretences.

Corbett's manner towards Mr Kelleway had naturally changed. He sloughed off skins with ease and, he considered, some grace, considering the circumstances.

'Mr Kelleway is a clever man and successful, Mr Jenkins,' he would say in the sanctuary of the clerk's room, 'but he is ungrateful considering as how I put him on his feet. It is always the way, mark you. I have made many men what they are. Do they thank me? Never. They don't want to remember, see! It don't do to look back on how they got there.' Jenkins nodded sagely and forbore to ask Corbett what he had had to do with it. Mr Perrin now had a lot to do with Mr Coke, a situation that was to the benefit of the clerks to a useful sum.

Henry's reputation had grown far beyond that indicated by his modest climb up the name board and although his work was often considered controversial, he was now recognized as an asset to the chambers. His name appeared frequently in the Law Reports. His work stemmed largely from Mr Watson. Today, however, things had gone amiss.

Watson had entered by appointment with the solicitor, Harvey, whom he kept on permanent retainer. Both men were sombre and the greetings were brief and perfunctory. They all knew each other well enough to make nothing of it, but Henry sensed there was more to it than familiarity.

'Well, gentlemen, what have we? I see the "Gorgon" has still got its teeth into the Bishop of Llandaff, but that everyone seems to be at liberty at this moment. It is not Mr Gast, I hope? Or Mr Wade? I see the bazaars are doing well.'

'Yes,' said Watson, still sombre, 'the bazaars are a great success. We now have tailors, shoemakers and carpenters put to work on materials bought out of the funds of our combinations who would otherwise be out of work. We also sell lace and stockings from Leicester, cutlery from Sheffield, flannel from Rochdale, clogs from Kendal. These can all be exchanged, one thing for another, no money being put to use. From Birmingham we have a vast quantity of metal goods and brass ware which has been exchanged for cloth and leather goods from Halifax and Leicester. It is all as Owen stated. The natural standard of human labour is taken as the practical standard of value. Everything may be exchanged according to the labour involved.'

'You will do away with all capital!'

'No. We must have that for materials. What we do away with is profit on a gargantuan scale. All the capital will be communal and used to ensure that all men are able to work.'

'You know, you are very persuasive, Mr Watson. One day you will almost convert me!' said Henry with a laugh.

Watson did not laugh in response. 'No,' he replied with his disconcertingly considered manner, 'you will never be converted because you have never belonged to the artisan class and can never understand. In the end there will be no need for lawyers, and the sooner the better. You are expensive, but you are no more clever with your brains than a master-carpenter with his hands.'

Henry laughed shortly. 'Praise indeed!'

'You don't need praise, Mr Kelleway, you are good at your

job. You should get sufficient satisfaction from it, as the master-carpenter does from fine work. When his work is sold it is never seen by him again but he *knows* it is good, that's all. Why do men who live by their brains insist upon praise as well? They ought to know best whether they are proficient or not. It is a peculiar inversion. Perhaps they are not really sure they have any worth, and there I would agree!'

These brief skirmishes had become a commonplace at their meetings, each party taking them lightly, but somehow Henry felt annoyed by Watson. There was no joviality in him. Even Harvey looked put out at his profession thus being dismissed.

'However,' Watson continued, 'as things are now set up, you are very necessary. We have a bad case, Mr Kelleway. Attempted murder.'

'Oh?' Henry was surprised. Watson's work had never taken him into these realms.

Harvey laid a bundle of papers on Henry's desk. 'I'm afraid this is a *prima facie* case. The accused, Peter Morton, was seized immediately after shooting the man, Sir Walter Manning, with the discharged pistol in his hand. It was in the middle of some celebration and he was seen by many. There can be no doubt about it.'

'Good God!' Henry was amazed. 'I was there!' Harvey was surprised in turn, but not Watson.

'I know you were,' that man observed, 'and your brother John assisted in seizing Peter Morton. Also, Peter Morton's brother is employed by your father Thomas as coachman.'

Henry stared at Watson. It was difficult to grapple with things so near home when so abruptly presented. 'Will Morton?'

'Yes.'

'What do you expect me to be able to do in this man's defence?'

'They will hang him if they can,' said Watson.

'I don't doubt it. What in God's name did he do it for, Mr Watson? This is quite a different animal from anything you have brought me before. I don't know how to respond to it.'

It was Harvey who replied, reading from a sheet of paper. The solicitor was in his mid-thirties and neatly dressed. His accent was Yorkshire, his voice strong, belying his slender build and almost anaemic appearance.

'Peter Morton, formerly a weaver of Bradford in the county of Yorkshire. Employed by the said Sir Walter Manning in the temporary capacity of hermit,' he stopped and gave Henry a sardonic smile that showed little sympathy for the Mannings of the world, 'in his new gardens.'

'As a decoration,' Watson said with contempt, 'to beg, to amuse the guests.'

'Peter Morton, by his own account,' continued Harvey, 'was formerly employed in the work of cotton-weaving in mills owned by the same Sir Walter Manning, an owner on a large scale. The pay and conditions became very bad in the mill, but not as bad as many and for a time the men held their peace. Then Manning decided that there was no profit in it unless he installed power looms. These power looms are machines driven by steam engines, and can be worked by women and boys, so the men must accept whatever wage is offered. The men particularly resent the gig mills and shearing frames, as they call them.

'In July 1817, on the fifth day of the month, a band of men including Peter Morton and his father Josiah, calling themselves followers of a General Ludd, which is a name they all adopt, attacked mills in the Bradford area and many frames were destroyed. The following night, the sixth day of July, about twelve men all masked and armed, came upon the Regent Mill of Sir Walter Manning who had closed the premises securely and had armed his overseers with muskets to resist.

'These men, including the Mortons, approached the mill and informed Manning that they were armed but had no quarrel with any man if they were admitted to the mill, as it was the machinery they wished to destroy. When they received no answer they advanced and were met by a volley of musket shot from the mill. This so incensed them that they loaded up carts with broken timber and pitch, set fire to them and rolled them up to the doors with the intention of igniting them and forcing an entry. Unfortunately they had not allowed for the brisk breeze which fanned the flames. The doors fell and the floors ignited shortly after. The men inside abandoned the mill by swimming the pond. The Luddites did not wish to see the mill reduced as it was their living. They were attempting to pull the carts out of the way when, without warning, one of the walls collapsed under the weight of machinery within. In this collapse four men died horribly. Josiah Morton was one of those trapped under the fallen timbers. Held back by the musket shots fired by Manning's men and the terrible heat, the Luddites were forced to retire leaving the poor man to be consumed.

'Peter Morton insists that Manning was responsible for his father's death. For this reason his followers have sought Manning for a long time, for he immediately left the district, a marked man. They discovered him, but found he took care always to have guards about him. Peter Morton took employ first as an agricultural labourer nearby, then applied for the job of hermit when he heard of it. He states he never had any intention of injuring Manning in any way; that he fired, as he believed, wide of him; that it was his intention to frighten Manning and disgrace him before his new neighbours and friends by exposing his past. It is his very inexperience with firearms that has proved his downfall, for with more skill he would never have discharged the gun to the effect that it had.'

Henry was aware that he was being watched by the other two men. Watson could be affable, but this time was hard-eyed. Harvey he knew well but he realized that he had never really taken stock of him. He concealed himself so successfully behind his clothes and his manner was always correct. However, he too seemed to be playing some other game. Henry did not like the atmosphere any more than he liked the sound of the case.

'That is all very well, Mr Harvey, but I would have thought that if his intention was only to shock and discredit, it would have been sufficient to discharge an unloaded pistol. I cannot see the purpose of firing a ball at the man. Even if he missed Manning he could very well have hit someone else. Your man will have a hard time over that.'

'What do you mean, "your man", Mr Kelleway?' asked Watson mildly. 'He is also your man. We agreed that you would look after our members in trouble.'

Henry fiddled with his pince-nez. He did not have the nerve to put them on to stare at Watson and was aware it would be a futile gesture.

'Mr Watson, you know perfectly well I am in a delicate position. I know this Manning, however slightly, I was present when the incident took place, although I cannot say I saw the shot fired. I did in fact dress Manning's wound. I would seem partisan whatever I said.'

'Yes, Mr Kelleway, but you must ask yourself to whom you would feel partisan.' Henry did not like being pressured. He felt growing anger but contained it. 'We have put a lot of work your way and as a result your name has seldom been out of the Law Reports. It is not too much to say you have made a reputation by us. But this is not defending pamphleteers or even publishers. Are you baulking at it?'

'I see your brother William proposed these hermits should be employed,' interposed Harvey. Henry realized that he was being allowed to see behind the mask. 'I believe that he actually selected Peter Morton. You will remember that it was through your brother William that we first came to you. He was not then one of the pillars of the Royal Academy.'

'Yes, Mr Harvey?' Henry's tone was short and rude.

Harvey replied in his own time, in no hurry. 'We considered that you might think it prudent to conduct the defence, apart from your obligations, for the very reason of such involvement. Otherwise the opposition may try to introduce that William Kelleway was in some way responsible for what happened.'

Henry said nothing. He had learned that at least. He was surprised and angered by the solicitor.

'Was Manning a friend of yours?' asked Watson.

'No.'

'I see. That's all right, then.'

'We believe the case will show wounding by accident, without intent,' continued Mr Harvey. 'Still a serious crime but not, I believe, a capital offence if properly put. You are respected, Mr Kelleway, and will make a good case. We will be grateful. Our man is steady in his innocence.'

Henry had an aversion to the whole affair. He was amazed at the impertinence of the solicitor's innuendo, which was nothing

343

more than a threat, and because of it could only assume the worst about their client. He had not been dictated to in this way before and was not prepared to tolerate it. He found their manner odd, and this confirmed him in his feeling that he should avoid the case. The man must be guilty, and they must know it. They might even support it, and then into what further depths would he wade? He supposed he had always known that it would come to this one day. The insupportable case.

At first he supposed he had identified with them, being himself the victim of a flat purse. But now they needed him, and he did not need them. It was a reality they would not concede, persisting in the belief that he owed them an enduring debt beyond the money they paid for his brains. Harvey's references to William were intolerable and an insult. Let them find someone else, he thought. This innocent shore may be a quicksand.

'Gentlemen, however steady he is, I cannot take the case. I am sorry, but I have been too close to it. You must see that. It will be brought out and will do you no good.'

'But our man is innocent.' Watson was not well pleased. His face had a surly expression. They had not quarrelled before on any matter of importance, but the man showed signs of a bad temper. Henry shrugged. It was the only diplomatic thing he could do. 'Mr Kelleway,' continued Watson grimly, 'I think you must defend our man.'

'I think not.' Henry was convincingly unmoved. They assumed they had him in their pocket, and it irked him. He stood up to give himself the advantage of height. Rather to his surprise, Harvey stood as well. The solicitor was pale and prepared to be unpleasant.

'We did wonder how you reconcile your personal style of life with your work, Mr Kelleway. I think you have just made it plain that you don't.'

'Oh sit down, Harvey!' It was Watson, the weather-beaten squire, trying another tack. 'Mr Harvey becomes too emotional.' Harvey sat, white and angry. 'I have never believed you can force men to do things, Harvey. If Mr Kelleway won't, then that's an end to it. I agree that, Mr Kelleway. But we have worked together over these years with notable success. The man is innocent, and I think the case is a challenge.'

344

'I'm sorry, but I can't take it. I have told you that.'

'Perhaps you are no longer for us, or even impartial? Perhaps you are against us?' said Harvey.

Henry was instantly furious. 'Damn your impertinence, Harvey. Damn your innuendoes. I have stood enough. I will not take this case. It will serve your man no good, nor anyone else!'

'Barristers believe they have the royal command!' shouted Harvey, on his feet again.

'Your behaviour does you no credit, sir, nor our profession. Do not try to dragoon me!'

'But I'm not concerned for credit, Mr Kelleway. Examine your conscience, sir! You have taken enough money from our cause!'

Henry took his time before replying. Harvey knew he had gone too far. 'I do not adopt causes, Mr Harvey. I defend those whom I believe to be in the right, or to have a substantial case. If you thought you had a pioneer then I am sorry to disappoint you. I am a member of the Bar, not a soap-box orator. If you think you can be better served from a soap-box, then I suggest you look elsewhere. Will you please remove yourselves, gentlemen, for I find this situation tedious and distasteful and I prefer not to listen to it in my own rooms. There is nothing useful to discuss.' He automatically did them the courtesy of crossing to the door, which he held open for them. Watson nodded to Harvey to go. As they reached the door, Watson tried again.

'I hope you will reconsider your position, sir. A man's life is at stake. That is what has made Mr Harvey impetuous.'

'Mr Watson, if you had told me five minutes ago that we would part on bitter terms like these, I would not have believed it. However, I am not your servant and you are not my masters and I will not take this case for what I believe are very good reasons. You have not even paused to consider them. You have tried to make me take it. That is not the way I will do business.'

'You are too hasty, sir. I am sure Mr Harvey meant nothing.'

'Mr Harvey has gone too far. However, that has nothing to do with it. I had thought that we had got to know one another and I am shocked to discover that we have not.'

'Very well. No more lawyer's talk.' Watson took the door handle. 'We hope you will reconsider.'

'No, sir, I will not.'

Harvey was about to launch into a harangue but Watson took his arm. 'Say nothing,' he said grimly, 'say nothing.' They left, brushing past Corbett, who looked enquiringly at Henry.

Henry shook his head. 'A case I am better without.' Corbett nodded comprehension and returned to his room. Henry sat down at his desk. He realized he was shaking. He was afraid of Watson, and he hoped he had been right to follow his judgement. It was the end of that line of work. He must build something else up instead. He would see Thomas.

Thomas had gone home. He had seen no point in pretending to work when his mind was so distracted. Crabtree the footman was shocked at his appearance when he arrived in a Hackney coach. His mental struggle seemed to have manifested itself in a physical tussle with his clothing which normally he kept in reasonable control. Thomas was a dishevelled, tired old man, his clothing an empty chrysalis. He walked heavily to the drawing-room and slumped into his armchair without speaking. Crabtree hovered over him dutifully. His concern was real and it must have communicated itself, for Thomas, who sat with closed eyes, opened them suddenly and feebly waved his hand, palm flat, as if dismissing a forceful waiter.

'No, Crabtree. Please don't trouble yourself.'

'Are you all right, sir?'

'All right?' He considered it. 'Yes, I suppose I am all right. I cannot complain – things could be much worse. There's no need for alarm, however. I have had an exhausting and disappointing day. I feel my age.'

Crabtree was at a loss. 'Can I get you anything, sir?'

'No. I think I have got to that stage of life when really there is nothing one can be got. When you are a young man, there is always something that will help, but the devil with old age is that the appetites that distract are dulled. It is, I suppose, a preparation. It concentrates the mind.' Distressed by this gloomy mood, Crabtree could only make a short bow and leave him. Thomas sat and stared at the fireplace. It was dead and black.

In this mood, Caroline first found him. She had called in upon his chambers to be told that he had left for Masterson, and had followed his route, learning the news herself from the old man. She had taken Edward Thomas with her, who was fascinated by everything he saw. He was an alert six-year-old, his bond with his mother very strong, who stood to the side and watched, missing nothing.

'Do you like Mr Masterson?' he asked, as they took their carriage on to Regent Square.

'Not particularly,' replied Caroline, 'why do you ask? Your ears have been flapping too much, Mr Elephant.'

Edward laughed. When he did that, Caroline saw that he had inherited through her the same laugh that John had had as a boy. The laugh that had deserted him so utterly since his return to England. Edward Thomas was dark-haired, with dark brown eyes, quite tall for his age, and wiry. Above all, he was quick with his wits, quick to see a joke, and quick to sum people up. Already she felt she must be careful that he did not become too protective of her. He was intelligent enough to take on that role.

'I'll wager he's never been to sea in his life!'

'Of course he has, he was a captain.'

'In the army, I'll wager!'

'You mustn't keep saying I'll wager! However, you were very polite. I'm glad to see you shook hands politely and kept quiet. I know it was boring.'

'It wasn't boring! It was interesting. He had all those charts, and all those pictures, and besides I liked watching him because I think he is an actor.'

'Edward, you have no way of knowing anything of the sort, and don't say such a thing in front of grandpa!'

Edward grinned and stared out of the window. Yet Caroline felt that the boy had been right. The office was too nautical. She felt sure it was not necessary to dress the place up so. They sat in silence for some time, almost as much like a couple, as mother and son. It was the companionable intelligence of Edward that made it possible. Caroline sometimes felt uneasy about it, feeling that Edward needed the interruption of an adult male. In this John was useful, but because of his family relationship it did not have the same blunt quality of uncaring severance that a strange man could have provided. She shied away from the implications of emotional interruption. They had no part in her life and she must cope with the situation as it was.

Thomas was pleased to see them, but obviously felt disadvantaged. 'If I had known you were coming, I would have had tea prepared!' he kept declaring as though this somehow would make their present problem sink into its proper context. He did not believe that women should talk about business except as table-talk. 'Would Edward like to go out in the garden? I'm sure there is some soft fruit out there he can pick without making himself ill.' Edward patently wanted to stay where he was.

'Mr Elephant has listened to everything so far,' Caroline explained, smiling, 'he will only listen at the door.'

Thomas scowled. 'It's no business to trouble a young boy. What are you bringing him up to be? When I was his age, it was model soldiers and boats, and falling out of trees. He shouldn't trouble his head with this sort of nonsense!'

'It's in his nature.'

'Well, send him out to the kitchen. Mrs Burges will find him something to eat. In competition between stomach and brain, stomach must win.'

So Edward was sent out, and tea was ordered for Thomas and Caroline, although Thomas warned he would not drink it. Burges brought the brandy.

'I know all about it, Father. But how serious is it and how much money is involved?'

'I don't think you should involve yourself. It is my doing and my problem. It will come out all right. Masterson is confident of that. We are fully assured.'

'I think you should rest. Can you give up your cases for a time? Perhaps you could take a few months in the country.'

'What nonsense! Do you want to kill me off? The country is a sort of early grave where the mould sets in prematurely. There is nothing there but fields! I would worry to death in two days. Look at you. Not you personally, but look at the family. We seem to have bred a race that is incapable of looking after both business and family affairs!'

Caroline said nothing, but took his hand. It was old and blue-veined, the skin heavily freckled. Her silence had the desired effect.

'Very well, I have not looked after my affairs any better. You always had the wit to say nothing, Caroline. It is a great gift. It seems to me that we are a microcosm of the state of the country. We are in perpetual disarray.

> Our torments may in length of time
> Become our elements.

So said Milton, and I think they have. I have devoted a considerable part of my life to my family. I don't seek any great virtue from that. It hasn't been any more than any other father. But William! From worse to worse to worse. I could almost stand him when he was unsuccessful and intolerable. With fame he is an ogre. I find myself warming to Maria in a way I could not have believed. She is remarkable. She has worked so hard for him, put her skills in the fire to help him and has turned into a curled darling, a painterly macaroni. Did you see his last things! "Damsels" with mouths the size of raspberries and knights as white as milk, with daubed rocks and Hydras!'

'But he sells them!'

'He believes in them! I must get off this subject, and think about more important matters. What shall I do with this money, Caroline? When Hebson pays up, I shall not put it back in shipping. Nor shall I let Henry get hold of it. I think I shall divide it among you. Edward Thomas is looked after in my will, you need have no fear for that. It is all closing in, you know. I am preparing for it.'

'Quiet, Father, I won't listen to it!'

Caroline was firm and tried to be soothing. However, she knew there was genuine concern in his voice. He was not seeking sympathy, and perhaps it was this that was most impressive. He seemed collapsed and hollow, very unlike the vigorous and irascible man she had buttoned in for the Coronation that now seemed a lifetime away. He was no longer possessive towards her, but seemed more concerned to contain himself, dam up and stop the seepage of his own life.

Henry's arrival interrupted this melancholia, but did nothing to help Thomas's temper. His greeting to Caroline was perfunctory and he looked annoyed that she was there. He had not the grace to conceal it. His enquiries after her health and after

Edward Thomas were dismissive. Caroline made no attempt to move.

'Father, I have come to consult you on a matter of business. I'm sorry to pursue you but it's upset me and I need advice.' He was walking up and down the drawing-room, and Thomas was annoyed by it.

'Business, eh? Can't you sit down, man? Perpetual motion was a folly sought after by alchemists. Have you heard the news?'

Henry was further annoyed at being checked, but sat down on the edge of a chair as though only temporarily perched. 'What news?'

'You don't ask that in a solicitous voice, sir,' said Thomas with some tartness. 'Do you want some tea now you have alighted?'

'No, thank you.' Henry was stony at the rebuke. He assumed his Iron Duke expression, but Thomas was not to be put off.

'I thought you must have heard to hurry here like this. Well, sir, I have had tragic news today that affects us all.' He stopped and let Henry shift and stare. Caroline was aware for the first time of the ticking of a long-case clock.

'What is it?' Henry asked impatiently. Thomas was thinking again of Jane and the perfume garden. Her words had haunted him and he blamed Henry for her sorrows.

'My ship has gone down, sir, with all its burden. A total loss.' Henry was annoyed at this information. He had taken no interest in Thomas's shipping affairs since the launching and had forgotten about them under the pressure of his own work. He tried to grapple with the seriousness of it. It was a disaster he had almost expected and he was indignant at the inopportuneness of it when he had steeled himself to seek advice. 'Well, sir,' continued Thomas, 'have you nothing to say at all?'

'I very much regret you have had such bad news. I hope it was fully assured?'

'Oh yes.' Thomas was determined to plough a way through Henry's censure. 'But does that really matter? She was a beautiful ship. Do you remember how she was at the launch? I look back at that day and I can still see and smell it. You know, it was one of the most satisfying days of my life. I loved that ship like a child. Now it's like having a death in the family.'

'But if she is fully assured, there is no cause for alarm. There will be no financial loss.' Henry knew he was being provocative but he refused to become maudlin over a ship, as his father seemed to wish.

'Devil take it, sir, I don't want to be fobbed off with platitudes, I expected you to be as affected as I am!'

Henry bridled, sitting even straighter. Caroline felt sorry for him because he was not able to understand and had no ability to concede or mollify.

'Father is very upset, Henry. It's very natural. Money seems a poor substitute for a beautiful thing. Don't you feel so?'

Henry was deliberately obtuse. He adopted an air of irritating reason, knowing as he did so that they were heading inevitably for a row. 'Of course it is natural to be upset. But I'm a dull dog of a lawyer. If the money is secured than it can always be translated into another ship. I can't say it felt like a child to me.'

Caroline prayed that Thomas would not make the obvious rejoinder. She caught his eye and gave him a pleading look with a tiny shake of the head. He understood, and changed his tack. Caroline got up and strayed over to the window where she could look out onto the large garden at the rear. Edward Thomas was happily eating raspberries, his mouth, hands and shirt stained bright red. She wished the two men who needed each other so badly would make their peace, but knew it was impossible while Henry was divided from Jane. She wondered what it was that Henry had come to ask about. Both men were so intolerant, and there seemed to be so little time for them to come closer. She had accepted that as a reality. Thomas was looking frail and unwell. As he lay in his chair, his head bobbed and nodded with age, his posture was that of collapse not comfort. Yet there was no respite and she would only wound Thomas if she interfered.

'That is what loneliness is, sir!' Thomas declared. 'Perhaps you should make a note of it because it comes to us all. It is when no one shares your interests or your griefs.'

'It was not my adventure, sir!' Henry protested, 'I always advised against it. You shan't attack me for being indifferent to the personality of a ship.'

'I have not attacked you, sir. I only asked you to show some interest in my grief, sir, some concern!'

The 'sirs' became more and more frequent. Henry sprang to his feet. 'It seems to me, sir, that you and I are too alike to communicate. Perhaps you may like to consider that I came here to consult you with a similar need. As we want the same things, it is inevitable, it seems, that neither of us gets them!'

Mrs Burges was unfortunate enough to enter the room at that moment. She stood stock-still with her tea-tray like an actress who had inadvertently been exposed before her cue. Henry took it as his to walk out.

He had not intended to make for Porchester Terrace, but after his encounter with Thomas is seemed a natural refuge. He recognized the defiance in his action but this only lent more sweetness to the flavour of it. There was a deliberate manipulation about such a re-encounter that appealed to every irresponsible, child-like part of him. The hackney dropped him a hundred yards from the house, and he scrunched along the yellow hoggin road to the open gates, making no attempt at concealment. He felt a delightful excitement in his belly as he pulled at the bell and heard it ringing within the house. He was still partly puzzled by his clash with Thomas but was more deeply resentful. Mulling it over, he was not even clear how it had come about except that Thomas had arrogantly demanded attention for his wretched ship beyond all normal measure. He, in contrast, had asked for help but had been ignored.

The door was opened by the maid who immediately recognized him. The girl's eyes went exaggeratedly round – she was enjoying herself, because it required practice – and she seemed not to know what to do or say. She bobbed a curtsey and Henry took the opportunity to step past her into the chequer-tiled hall.

'Is Mrs Waters in?' It had not occurred to him until that moment that she might not be.

'I don't know, sir, I'll have to see, sir.'

He would have followed her out of sheer impropriety if the maid had not sensed his intention and turned, saying in a shocked voice, 'Oh no, sir! You'll have to wait here, sir!' She looked delighted as she scuttled off. Henry wondered at the rapidity of expressions that flitted across the girl's face. The footman arrived, eyed Henry from a distance and lurked discreetly as though he thought Henry might dash up the stairs or make off with the silver. It enhanced his delightful feeling of guilt.

The maid scuttled back after a pause of about two minutes. 'The mistress says, would you please be seated in the drawing-room. She will join you in a few minutes.' Henry had the impression that the girl would have rolled her eyes and winked if she had had the nerve. The footman stepped forward and opened the door for Henry, closing it firmly behind him. Doors were his job.

The room had changed little. Dried grasses made up for the lack of flowers at this late season. The cases of shell decorations reminded Henry of graveyards, for all their attempt to imitate flowers. He always felt uneasy with them, as he did with stuffed birds and small mammals, each to his improbable branch or log. He noticed a lack of living things in the room and realized that the absence was only noticeable because of the presence of these dead reproductions. Outside, the garden was in autumn motley. The year was slipping by without warning. Ageing.

Mrs Waters entered sooner than he had expected, the footman doing his duties with the door. Henry turned from his contemplation of the garden and immediately walked towards her. They met in the centre of the room as though taking up appointed positions, and there stood looking at each other. Henry took her hand and kissed it. In a light gesture she touched the back of his hand with her left hand. It was a small motion that made him feel a boy. She retained that ability to disconcert with small gesture.

The daylight in the room was not strong, but it was a thousand times less kind than the fluttering light of candles in which they had last met. Henry saw that she had aged. He wondered what she saw in him. He was heavier, his hair more grey. His appraisal seemed to make her uneasy for she immediately moved over to the sofa out of the direct light from the garden.

'This is a surprise, Henry.'

'You did invite me. Remember?'

'Oh, I remember. But I didn't believe you. I don't believe much that men say. Words are the tools of expediency. Deeds count.'

'Not in the law, Helena. Words are deeds.'

'Only if written down or said before witnesses. What about intimate promises between lovers? What does the law make of those? No, the words mean nothing, for you can't bind a heart with paper.'

'Helena!'

'I'm sorry. You must be bored by the law. What sort of world can it be that is divided into the innocent and the guilty!'

'I'm not bored with it. But I have problems.'

Her reaction was acute and immediate. 'But not for me, I hope!' She paused. 'Why have you come?'

Henry felt a terrible disappointment at her response. He wondered if she had anticipated him or whether the words were mere conversation. 'To see you,' he said obliquely.

'To visit me?'

'Of course.'

She was smiling at him. 'And that is all?'

Henry was embarrassed. 'I was promised more,' he said manfully.

Mrs Waters laughed. 'Indeed you were, and you shall have it, but in good time. You are not really so impetuous, Henry. You arrive, no doubt, like a fiery stallion but you aren't good at drawing-room ardour!'

Henry was pink with embarrassment, and angry too. She challenged him to make assertions, then laughed at his ineptness. He thought, unkindly, that a coquette should be a young girl. There was no disguising that youth had left her face forever. Before, it had hovered, an uncertain sweet bird, not sure of the season to depart. Now she was a beautiful woman for her age – the phrase that levels – and the migrant had gone. She was elegantly dressed and Henry at a temporary loss, remarked upon it.

'I don't pride myself on those sort of manners! You won't disconcert me, however. You look beautiful, and I see that your wardrobe has not suffered. Quite charming.'

'It is a sign of age when one's looks and one's wardrobe are linked. Whoever remarks upon a young girl's clothes? Flatter me first, then after an interval compliment my dress.'

'I simply meant that you looked beautiful!' declared Henry hotly. 'Don't make such fun of me.'

'Henry! You are always so easy to tease, and I can't resist. I know it is wicked of me. Please sit down?'

She patted the sofa beside her. Henry obeyed, but felt that it was in answer to a command. She wore the same herbal fragrance, he noted, and felt nostalgia for times past. He could not get away from the feeling that he was irked by her manner. They sat for some time in silence. She put a hand on his arm.

'Relax, Henry. You are sitting there as though you will jump up at any moment. Why are you so edgy? I have missed you, you know. Will you believe that I loved you? Is that a forward thing to say?'

Henry shook his head. He was wondering why he had thought he could find solace here. It seemed to him, remembering Thomas's words, that this was only another form of loneliness. She treated him like a small boy, teased him, promised him things, took from him what she needed but gave nothing of herself but her body. The devil was that he wanted her body as she wanted him, and from it she would find content. He was puzzled. There must be some complexity about her he could not understand.

'Helena, I need to talk to you.'

'The problems?'

'Yes.'

'Let them wait, Henry.' Her hand was withdrawn from his arm. 'Are they the reason for your visit? They were not my terms.'

'Please! Let me just explain. Give me an opinion. I have just refused to defend a man for the Combinations, and it will mean the end of my work for them. They won't forgive me.'

'You know my feelings. You should never have taken up with them in the first place.' She sat coldly upright, and would not look at him. 'No doubt you can consult your legal friends about your future – or your father.'

'He won't listen!'

'Neither will I. Have you considered how insulting I find this?

355

What do you want from me? How do you want me to receive you when you only run to me in trouble? I don't want any man to cry on me. I have given all that up. Can't you learn that, Henry? I am not that sort of woman, nor will you make me into one!' She got up and moved away from him to stare out of the window. 'I thought that I had made it plain before. It was a mistake to see you again. I have done with problems!'

Henry sat silent. He was amazed at the vehemence of her outburst. She continued in a more controlled voice, staring at the autumnal garden.

'You don't understand, poor Henry, do you? If I love you, you will exploit it. I have always known that. You will make a mother of me or a wife. Not in name but in kind. I won't be the sounding board for your unreason and anger and contempt, for that's all it will be. I have had all that before. Love me if you will, Henry, because I need that, but I am selfish beyond your wildest imagination. I want nothing else. I loved you for your vigour and despised you for your dependence. Does that shock you?'

Henry jumped to his feet, a violent man. He took hold of her by the shoulders, turned her and kissed her. He expected her to struggle but instead she went quite limp. He let go of her shoulders. His fingers left red blotches on her skin that would discolour to blue.

'You see,' she said more kindly, 'that solves nothing. You are full of self-pity. So am I. I want a man who will pity me – I have none to give. No compassion, no power to listen, no interest. I am totally selfish, do you understand?'

'No,' said Henry, almost in tears, 'I don't understand you. It seems you brought me here to humiliate me.' She let his response ring like a bell, giving it silence to reverberate.

'Poor Henry, you don't understand. Believe me, I didn't want to hurt you in any way. I could not help myself. I believed that you might have changed and had to find out. I warned you that I am a selfish woman. Will you forgive me?' She tried to kiss him on the forehead, but he pulled away in anger.

'Don't touch me!' he yelled, like a virgin.

'I don't think we should prolong this, do you?' said Mrs

Waters, in command. 'We shall only fight more. It is better that you go hating me. It is more final, and I don't mind.'

Henry managed to compose himself sufficiently to be icily polite. 'I agree that I should go, but I will not hate you. Forgive me for treating you roughly. It was not the act of a gentleman. I fear I was carried away by passion. I had thought it might be welcome!'

'Please go, Henry,' said Helena Waters ignoring his heavy sarcasm. When she finally heard the front door shut, she permitted herself the flood of tears she had been restraining.

Jane was asleep when she was awoken by the noise of Henry stumbling into her dark room. At first she was terrified and screamed, not knowing who it was. Then she was terrified when she found out, but was silent. He smelled strongly of drink and was whispering her name with the lullaby tones of a murderer. She lit a candle, her hands shaking so much that shadows wheeled around the walls. Then she lit an oil lamp, rattling the funnel-glass against the wick.

'Can I sit down?' croaked the figure. As he had already collapsed heavily onto the foot of her bed, it was politeness rather than a question. His collar was loose and his stock undone. He had taken off his coat and his waistcoat was unbuttoned.

Jane wondered what to do next. 'What do you want, sir?' She was surprised at the decisiveness of her voice. It gave her heart.

'I want to speak to you.'

'What about, sir? It is late at night.'

'I don't know. I'm very confused.' He seemed utterly dejected but his manner was in no way a threat.

'You are drunk, sir,' she persisted. 'Will you kindly leave my bedroom.' She hoped that it was the right approach. She had heard that one had to be firm, to dominate quietly, but above all show no fear. She would be resolute .

'But I want to talk to you.'

'Go to your bed, sir. You have been too liberal altogether. Will you please leave my room.'

'Please let me talk to you.'

'Go away!'

The next move must be to rouse the servants. She started to draw up her legs so that she could swing them clear of the sheets and get swiftly to the bell-pull. To her alarm, Henry anticipated this and sat firmly on the blankets, trapping her. She wondered when to start screaming. She was surprised to find that she was reluctant to do so, or unable to. It seemed such an alien and stupid reaction. She looked at him with what she hoped was arrogant coldness and was surprised to see that he looked desolate. Neither hauteur nor dignity even were left. His eyes were rheumy and his body seemed to be a dead weight. She realized that he was maudlin drunk, but had no experience of it herself. It crossed her mind with rogue bitterness that most of her experience was vicarious. He seemed to have deflated to very human proportions and she was suddenly afraid that he might start to weep. She felt uncomfortable panic and excitement as he reached out a hand and stroked her hair. The movement was meant well, but the stroking fingers were jerky and rough.

'Jane, don't look at me like that!' he protested. 'Do I make you so afraid? I suppose you have every right to be afraid. After all, who am I to you?' She shook her head to avoid wounding him with daggers of truth. 'I have discovered something today,' he continued with great profundity, 'loneliness is when no one shares your interests or your griefs.' He paused, ruminating upon his self-pity.

Jane felt an upheaval of rage that made her feel physically sick in her stomach. Her throat constricted as though her will grasped it with strong fingers to throttle down her emotion. Tears started to her eyes yet she neither moved nor made a noise. Henry, she knew, was incapable of ever considering anyone except himself. She thought she had accepted that fact but found it still hurt with terrible freshness. She could not forgive him for it. Perhaps Henry sensed the spasm of tension in her, for he seemed to collect himself, his limbs regaining the balance of a live man.

'Damn it, Jane, I am drunk. I apologize for it. But I am not so very drunk. We have hardly passed a word in years except good morning and good day. What a disaster we have made of things. Is it all my fault?'

His spaniel eyes wanted to be reassured. Hush, my pretty baby, close your pretty eyes. You are too innocent to have faults. A kiss on each lid and the world is right, the sun and the moon rotate again and tomorrow is another day for play, sweet play, all faults washed away. She could not look at him.

'How have you put up with me? God, what a mess. Jane, the Combinations want me to defend that man who shot Manning. He's one of their members, a weaver and Will Morton's brother, but I won't do it.'

'Might that not be dangerous?'

She had not meant to respond but as the conversation had turned to the realms of work and away from pity she felt a curious excitement. She was unable to isolate in herself all the conflicts. She felt perverse gratitude that he had introduced the subject of his work, and pure relief. Relief at making human contact in her isolation. It was, she felt, like finally meeting your enemy face to face after a long waiting and finding he is just another man. The hard lump of hate that she had nurtured in her heart was forgotten. It was the immediacy of survival.

'I suppose that it's professionally dangerous. I relied on them for so much work.' Henry was pensive and almost sober. 'Personally, I don't know. I shall have to be careful.' He thought of the duel about which Jane knew nothing. Now he carried a pistol but knew how useless it would be to him. 'They will hang the man for sure. I tried to tell Father today about Morton, but he wouldn't listen to me. His ship has sunk. The *Thomas K.*'

'Oh, no!'

'It's fully insured, vessel and cargo, so he loses nothing. He's making a fuss about it out of all proportion. Good God, ships sink by the hour!' Poor Thomas, Jane thought. He was so proud of it. She must go and see him. How callous had Henry been? Had he offered any comfort? 'Do you think I was right?' he was saying. 'I cannot believe their story.'

'I don't know their story.'

'No, I'm sorry, you don't. I am confused as to who knows what.' He slurred the words and acknowledged it. 'See, I am not even able to speak clearly. I'm sorry. They say this man Peter Morton – Will Morton's brother – intended only to draw attention to Manning's past. Manning was an Owner and according to their story, a bad one. Peter Morton intended only to frighten, they say. But I asked them why, if that was so, he put a ball in the pistol. You see? The place was crowded and he was sure to hit someone. He could have discharged a blank. I can't go along with it, it doesn't ring true. I think I have had enough of the Combinations. I have sympathy with their cause but I can't support their methods when it comes to this. This is cold-blooded conspiracy to murder, as I see it. What do you think, Jane?'

'I don't know all the facts. I don't think I'm qualified . . .'

'Oh God, Jane!' he interrupted, 'don't say that. Give me an opinion . . .'

She felt him caress her hair as though it might coax it out of her. He was lowering himself on the bed so that he lay half on her, and tried to brush the hair from her face so that he could see her eyes. He smelled strongly of brandy. It was cloying and revolting. She thought back, right back as though through centuries. Gossip round tea-tables. The scandal-water circulating. Women, some of them quite young, who had embarrassed her and themselves as they talked with low voices and bright eyes. The ways of men. Children conceived in drink. Would she shrink from it? She had no idea at that moment if she felt anything for the man who was her husband. She despised his lack of consideration, but his closeness and his hand stroking her hair disturbed her completely. She felt remote from her rational loathings. I will not be barren, she told herself, what is love in that? I look at myself, remotely, from an elevated point of long suffering. I am married to this man in the eyes of the world and want a child. The bright eyes that whispered round the tea-tables had not concerned themselves with love.

'I think you're right,' she said. 'You have made a name with them, but not because of them, as people have tried to say. It is your ability that got them to a position of some legal strength, not their money.'

'Jane . . .' His hand fumbled with the neck-strings of her nightgown.

'Yes, Henry,' she replied and reached behind her neck, untying the string so that it was quite loose and slid down her shoulders. He kissed them tentatively, fearing she would push him away, then ravenously kissed her breasts.

Jane helped him take off his waistcoat and his shirt. Henry floundered about with his trousers, and she buried her head in the pillow so as not to embarrass him. He was awkward, puffing and half-naked, and looked absurd. He was trying to pull off his trousers before his boots but gave up the unequal struggle and made love to her in a tangle of clothing and sheets. Jane was at first astonished by his ferocity, then despite all her doubts and resolves, touched by it. She stroked his head, her own averted from the stink of brandy fumes.

He fell asleep almost immediately, on top of her, and she had to push and heave to extricate herself from the human press. He looked ridiculous stranded on the bed, trousers around his ankles, boots still on and his white buttocks gleaming in the light of the oil lamp. She sat on the chair by her dressing-table, holding her breasts that were sore from his biting and sucking, and wept. She began to shake so much with restraining her sobs that she went through the dressing-room to his room and cried as she had not cried since she was a girl, feeling nothing but overwhelming relief.

Finally she returned and undressed him while he snored, wrapped her body against his and lay awake beside him until dawn. I feel a son, she told herself, I feel a son. It must be, if I feel it like this. It must be a way of knowing. Please God, she prayed, make him still want me, at least until we have a son.

In the morning, as she listened to the first birds and heard early footfalls in the street, she felt him awake and lie still for some time, trying to sense how she was as he could not see her. She moved a hand on his arm to show she was awake.

'Are you angry with me?' he asked like a boy, his face averted.

'No. Why should I be?'

'A thousand reasons.'

She shook her head and he felt her reaction and turned to her. He looked at her, almost shy, looking at her body and breasts, carefully, as though they were of importance to him. He reached out a hand and tentatively touched one nipple with a finger. Jane took his head and pulled his bristled face to her sore breasts. He was quickly aroused again and quickly exhausted. This time Jane too fell asleep, praying God be fruitful, let this seed scatter in my womb, let this sore, sensitive body be such fertile ground that lush water-meadows seem a desert. She hugged her belly. Henry, on the edge of sleep, felt he had found answers, but was perplexed that he could not remember the questions.

12

Hebson stood on no ceremony. Corbett knocked on Thomas's door, but before there was any reply, Hebson took the handle and entered. Corbett made a move to stop him, but was pushed aside by the other man. He shrugged and discreetly hung about in the doorway, knowing that important matters must be coming to a head.

'What's this, sir?' Thomas demanded. He was furious at being interrupted and stared angrily at the wet and steaming figure. It had been drizzling all day and the figure was dripping water all over his carpet. 'I see no one without an appointment and I make no exceptions!' Thomas was still crouched forward as he had been when writing. His stoop was more pronounced than ever and he held a quill pen just before his nose, his head almost on the desk.

'I think you will see me, Mr Kelleway. I do not normally force myself upon people. However, this is urgent.'

Hebson was a man in his fifties, his grey hair and whiskers sparkling with droplets of rain. He had great red jowls like the wattles of a turkey which gave a permanent impression of rage which at the moment was real enough. His hectic colour made Thomas look as though he were embalmed.

'Well, state your business. If you have no excuse, sir, then you must leave. I am busy.'

'My name is Hebson, Mr Kelleway. The name is, I am sure, known to you. I would like a word with you.' Corbett, at the door, was taking it all in.

'Mr Hebson the underwriter. I see. This is a peremptory visit.'

'Mr Kelleway, I have called to see you because of your claim. There may be things you don't understand. May I sit down?'

'The devil there are!'

Thomas waved a hand to a chair. Hebson perched on the edge

and unbuttoned his coat. He was obviously becoming yet more angry at his reception, and took some time to cool down. Looking round, he saw Corbett still standing in the doorway, apparently waiting to be dismissed.

'Do you want your clerk, sir?'

Thomas hesitated. While Corbett remained there, he had not accepted the call. He nodded, tortoise-like, and put down the quill. 'Very well. You may go, Corbett. Shut the door thank you.' Corbett removed himself to the other side where he lingered in the corridor. He knew all about the ship.

'So what are these things, sir, that I don't understand? I understand we have a claim on you for total loss, and can't see much difficulty about that.'

Hebson snorted. His wattles shook. His clothes steamed. He replied with the slow patience of a teacher with a slow-witted pupil. 'I have received a claim on behalf of yourselves, that is Mr Kelleway and Mr Masterson, the assured. I believe that you are an honest man so I have come to see you personally, to find out if you really appreciate what is going on. I am doing this purely because I think you may not fully understand, or may not fully be in possession of the facts. I do not wish to impose, I do not wish to burst in, in fact there is no reason why I should bother, except that, as I say, I think you are an honest man.' His patient tone made Thomas's eyes glitter with suppressed fury. With his bowed head, it seemed that only the desk prevented him from charging headlong.

'You will come to the point, sir! Quickly, sir, or I shall have none of it! Our claim is simple enough as you well know. The ship is lost, and the cargo. You have assured us to cover in full and will do so. There can be no question of anything other than that.'

'Indeed there can, Mr Kelleway. This is a very unpleasant business and I see no point in being anything else but blunt about it. We have no intention of covering you.'

There was a stunned pause. Hebson could hear the drizzle sputtering lightly at the window. He could even hear the flutter of the flames in the fire behind him as they struggled against the damp. Thomas seemed to be having difficulty in getting his breath for he gulped audibly before exploding into words.

'By God, sir, you must! This is outrageous! You hear me, sir, outrageous! What is the meaning of this? Do not forget, sir, that I am a barrister, and be careful what you are about!'

Thomas gasped again for air. He felt fear within him. His heart was thumping, his breath was short, he must try to control his rage. The perfume garden. A maze. The clock has struck once. Here, a new jungle. He must stay calm. He repeated it to himself over and over, but it only made him annoyed.

'My meaning, sir,' Hebson was saying, 'is plain enough to me. Your ship is no more a loss than I am. She is at Rhode Island. I have had intelligence that she arrived there under salvors and was immediately libelled by the Admiralty Court there. Salvaged, sir. In America. I am amazed that Mr Masterson has not seen fit to tell you. I'm sure he knows by now!'

'That's impossible!' Thomas tried to struggle to his feet, but somehow did not seem able to straighten out, and sank back again heavily.

'No, sir. She has been sold, one half going to the salvors, as is customary, and the other half paid into the Court. You have not been kept properly informed. I cannot accept your claim on me.'

'You are a rogue!' Thomas shouted, 'None of that makes one jot of difference even if it be true, and I ain't convinced until I have the papers. What's your purpose, sir? It don't materially alter the case. Take care!'

'That is not the language I expect from you, sir. There is no purpose in this!'

Even in his anger, Thomas knew he had gone too far. He tried to adopt a reasoning tone. 'The abandonment of the ship was complete. The crew was forced to leave for their lives. One man was lost, Mr Hebson. You are saying she was taken by salvors afterwards and that therefore you won't pay. By Gee, sir, it is contrary to the law. You will have to pay.'

Hebson got to his feet, out of all patience with the argument. 'You are wrong, sir. I hoped you would see this more clearly. Your ship awaits recovery from the sale in Rhode Island. As owners it was your duty to exert yourself to recover the ship before she was sold. You had time.'

'I have never heard of it before now!'

'Maybe. But I believe Mr Masterson has.'

'That still alters nothing. She was a total loss at the time of desertion. The crew abandoned the vessel to save their lives. We never obtained any possession of it afterwards. That is a total loss.'

'I am sorry, sir, it is not.'

'You intend to desert our claim, I see that clearly!'

'But you have no claim, Mr Kelleway. Masterson's lack of action has made it so, if you knew nothing. I warn you, sir, we shall reject it in court.' Thomas sat shaking his head as though by doing so he would stop the other man persisting. As soon as he did, he repeated his own point again. 'The desertion of the ship when she is sinking is a total loss in law. You should know it, sir. We as owners lost beneficial use of the vessel. All these other matters of salvors and the like are of no consequence to that main point.'

Hebson in his turn gave a quick shake of the head, his wattles flapping. Thomas was disturbed by the man's assurance. 'No, you are wrong. As a lawyer you should perhaps know it but you do not, I believe, specialize in such matters. Unfortunately, Mr Kelleway, I have to be an expert on cases such as this. It is my business.'

'So you've come here to explain I have no case in law! It's plain what your intention is, sir, and we shall pursue it!'

Thomas wobbled to his feet, his heart jerking irregularly. He could breathe only with difficulty and had a pain like a wound in his chest. He tried to tear at his collar to breathe but buckled in the middle like a hinge and crashed forward onto the table. Hebson rushed to him, trying to pull him up. He looked a terrible mess for he had fallen into his inkstand and was soaked with blood-red and black ink. Hebson could not manage him alone. Thomas slid off the table limply, falling half under it to the floor. The inks, mixed to a damson hue, continued to drip on his clothes. Hebson crossed to the door, opened it quickly and ran into Corbett in the corridor outside.

'Quickly, Mr Kelleway has collapsed!'

'Was that the noise?'

Both men returned to the table, Corbett staring aghast at the mess.

'It's ink, you fool!' snapped Hebson.

'I know,' replied Corbett, 'it's just that our Mr Agnew fell forward into his when he died in just the same way.'

Hebson looked at Corbett suspecting humour, but found none he could recognize. 'He's not dead. Get a doctor.'

Between them they stretched Thomas out on the carpet. Corbett dashed off and reappeared with a bottle of brandy. 'What was it, sir?' he asked innocently. 'Was it bad news?'

'That's none of your affair. Put a cushion beneath his head and get a doctor.'

'Yes, sir. And I'll get the other gentlemen.'

When Thomas was being attended to by an elderly doctor they had found in a nearby inn, Hebson moved to the door.

'Will you be going now, sir?' enquired Corbett slyly.

The doctor had applied a bleeding bowl to Thomas's arm and was cutting rather unsteadily at a vein. Thomas moved and groaned.

'Show me out,' Hebson replied angrily.

'Will you be pursuing the case, sir?'

Hebson again looked at Corbett sharply. 'Your long ears do you no credit, sir. Yes I shall. The suit has been filed.'

'You misunderstand me, Mr Hebson,' said Corbett with monumental dignity, 'I must know, so that I may inform the family. Mr Kelleway's recovery from your tidings may be slow.'

'Thank you, I will let myself out.'

Hebson left with a slightly jerky walk that made his jowls wobble. He put his head down in the drizzle, and stationed himself in a shop doorway in the Strand waiting for the rain to ease. He considered it a very unpleasant business to find that men of the law were often such rogues. But he would show them.

Will Morton had been secretly removing his belongings to the stables over the last two days. He had few possessions but his clothes, and it was difficult to take these out under the eagle eye of Mrs Burges. He had had to wear them, then change in the stables, taking off the second layer and packing them in a leather valise.

Now that valise was soaked black with the drizzle. He had walked out to the stables in his horse-cloak, picked it up and gone. Mrs Burges thought he was grooming the horses. He left no message because he knew it would be obvious why he had fled. As soon as the master found out about his brother he would be dismissed, and he must get clear before the Bow-Street runners found him.

He shook the bag to shed the water off it, but It was becoming heavy and porous. The insistent veil of rain would soak through to his clothes, staining them brown. He tucked it under his cloak, walking awkwardly. His hat brim dripped water onto his nose and down his neck and he inclined his head from time to time to drain the water from it. It was a miserable day and it suited his mood.

People kept off the streets unless they had business. Pedestrians were spattered by the mud from carriages and horses. He was making his way, almost aimlessly, to Bessie Tate. He had no idea what he expected there. Bayliss might find him some refuge, Bessie might give him some comfort. He must find some work for he had no money.

A horse fell in Holborn, bringing down its fellow in harness. Morton found himself drawn by compassion to join the crowd that stared at the steaming beast. It struggled and struggled to rise on its broken leg, although the coachman tried to hold it down. With each effort it screamed with pain. Carriages swept past through the brown river of the street, sending muddy water into the creature's rolling eyes. Its teeth were bared and yellow like a smoker's. Morton could not stand to see the driver struggling alone, and put down his bag in a doorway to help.

'You know what you're doing?' the man was soaked and filthy. From his coach came a string of complaints and enquiries which he ignored.

'I'm a coachman.'

The man looked at Morton's clothes. 'Yes?'

'Yes!'

'Unharness, then. I'll hold its head. The bugger will bring the other one down. Christ, what a day! Listen to them yelling in that coach! You'd think *them* bastards was in pain! Come on, old beast, lie still, lie still . . .'

Will unharnessed the fallen animal. The driver soothed the

animal, unsentimental, not cruel. It was a practical moment. The animal was finished.

'Look at all these sods watching!' the man said. 'Like it, they do. Go away, you idle buggers!' They did not move. The driver took down a horse blanket, and drew a pistol from the wooden box under his seat. He sheltered it with the blanket. 'What are you? Human vultures? Get out of it, if this gun misfires, you'll get your bloody 'eads blown off!' Some moved away, most stayed.

'Are you all right now?' asked Will.

'I'm all right, friend. It's happened before, it'll happen again. Good pickings, mate! I hope I do the same for you if you're ever fixed like this, God forbid!' He shook hands with Will.

'I won't stay, then. I get no pleasure out of seeing him shot.' The man nodded, understanding. 'These buggers will.'

Will raised a hand and waded back to the pavement. He was utterly soaked and filthy. When he got to the doorway, his bag had gone.

'Where's my bag!' he demanded of a man who was obviously the shopkeeper. He had been standing watching the spectacle in rolled sleeves and a waistcoat.

'Your bag? A fellow just went off with it.'

'It was mine!' Morton's plaintive cry fell on deaf ears. The shopkeeper shrugged and never took his eyes off the proceedings. 'What sort of man took it?'

'Never looked. Some fellow. Just said "Ah, my bag!" and was off.'

Morton felt like banging the man's head against his own door-post, but what was the use of it? He shrugged, stared down at his filthy condition and resigned himself to it. The driver had draped the horse blanket over his head and was standing over the beast's head with it to form a screen. It was an act that Morton appreciated. He turned away and started to wade on so that he heard the shot and clatter but could not see the animal's dying spasm.

He came to the Arctic Bear, and it worked on his memory, making him pause. He had change in his pocket that would buy him a drink. There would be a fire and he could try to dry out, if they would let him stay long enough. Dry and with a drink, he felt that his mind would clear of this mush of indecision and uncertainty. He should never have left his bag in a doorway. It was the act of an unthinking fool. It was no way to approach Bayliss or Bessie. He was beginning to doubt if he ought to approach them at all.

The tap-room was hot and humid. The air was blue with smoke so that he caught his breath on it. Men jostled for a place around the fire, their clothes steaming, turning first their buttocks, the tails of their coats lifted, then their trouser legs. Their boots were grey and soggy, but they cracked their soles with the heat. Other men, on more dubious business, rolled dice or played cards to pass the time. They could shear no wool from this flock and were not foolish enough to try.

Will had to push his way towards the counter. He ordered a pint of porter, paid for it, carefully noting his change, and decided he would try to get in by the fire himself. One man had his coat off and was drying it, so why not he? Hats sat in a row on a wooden bench, like targets at a fun-fair. Kerchiefs were being held out to the blaze and steamed like hot flannel. The men were good-natured, and made way for him as best they could. He passed a few words with them on the weather, the condition of his clothes, the filth of the roads, and found the end of a bench he could sit upon. His clothes began to feel uncomfortable as they warmed up, and he unbuttoned his coat and waistcoat. He wondered if he should take off his boots, but thought he could not afford to crack the leather. They must dry on his feet.

At that moment he saw Bessie Tate. He had been aware without noticing that the laughter of women mixed now and then with that of the men. There were always women in the barroom, sitting in the darker corners among the high-backed wooden settles that were secret as small rooms. They might have come in from the street as the weather was terrible, or they might be trading from the inn. He had paid no attention.

He was shocked by her appearance. For several seconds he watched, like a half-wit, because he was not even sure that it was her. He had never seen her powdered and painted. Her pink complexion was white with chalk and she had Punchinello patches of red on her cheeks. Her lips were red with some oxide or dye, her eyebrows almost bald.. Her curls that had been springy as wood-shavings, were pinned up and greasy with pomade. She was in conversation with a man who casually enveloped her in his arm, playing with her shoulders, kissing her neck, while she threw back her head for him. In other dark corners men were entwined with other painted women, hands in clothing, bottles on table, lecherous and laughing, with one eye always on their prize, who in turn had one eye always on their purse. Will got to his feet, oblivious of everything and without thinking. He pushed his way through the solid ranks of men, who glared at him and yielded little ground.

'Bessie!' His tone was shocked and anguished. At close range her appearance was terrible. The flesh of her face, once rounded and plump, had collapsed like an apple attacked from within. The white chalk could not conceal her spotted complexion, or the lip-rouge the chapped corners to her mouth. Her eyes were bloodshot and sunken. She looked up sharply, wondering who interfered, then Will saw her face show horrified recognition and then go blank. She said nothing.

'Bessie! What are you doing?' The question was superfluous. He spoke like a shocked mother finding her daughter *in flagrante*. The man resented it.

'Oy! Push off! What's your friend want, Bessie? Look here, friend, can't you see when you're not welcome?' His arm tightened around Bessie's thin shoulders in a possessive gesture. An animal claiming its kill. Will saw but ignored the man. He gave no sign of having heard what he said.

'What are you doing here?' he repeated.

'Push off, mate, you ain't wanted. Didn't you hear? Don't act deaf, friend, I don't take kindly to it.'

Will stared at Bessie, but Bessie avoided his eyes. She seemed to become limp, as though shrinking from Will's accusation, as a dog shrinks when scolded. Her companion released her shoulder and stood up so that he was between Will and Bessie. He was a rough-looking man, who could have been any sort of artisan, short and thickset. His clothes were shiny with wear and the seams were worn grey in the black cloth of his coat. His face was knobbly and round. His brows and nose were misshapen with scar tissue. A man accustomed to fighting. His fists were clenched and ready. Will would not be warned off. The man had been drinking steadily, for there was a collection of empty pots and bottles on the table. One part of his mind calculated that the alcohol would slow the man down while the other still struggled with the horror of finding Bessie Tate reduced to such a pathetic state.

'I want to speak to Bessie.'

'You can't.'

'I shall.'

'Is that so? I don't take to your patter. Friend!'

As he spat out the last word his fist came up fast and hard at Will's face, but Will was quick and it glanced off his cheek, bruising the bone. Will anticipated the man's next move. As he flung himself forward to butt his head into Will's face, Will brought his fist up hard and short into the pug nose. The man let out a bellow and sat down hard. The whole tap-room was silent. Everyone turned. Will reached out to Bessie.

'Come out of there. I want to talk to you!'

Bessie shook her head and tried to pull away from him. Tears sprang to her eyes. Will had hold of her arm and pulled her from her seat, so that she was beside him at the end of the table. The man grabbed one of Will's legs and twisted it round and up with fierce strength. At the same time he reached out with his free left hand for a bottle on the table. It nearly worked, for it brought Will to his knees, and he only supported himself by grabbing the table. Blood was running down the other man's face from his nose and lip. Will knew he could expect no mercy. He kicked out desperately, hitting the man in the chest. It was enough to prevent him reaching the bottle, and it made him vomit his beer. He was helpless while his stomach contorted and hot flows of black porter vented from his mouth. Will could hear a pot-man shouting. Men running to them. His opponent was bubbling obscenities and retching, choking in the vile fluid, his eyes full of water. Will hit him hard behind the right ear. The man dropped onto his knees with a crash, falling into his own filth. He groaned and bent double, shielding his head from the kicks he expected. He was finished.

Will was abruptly wrenched around by hands from behind and was confronted by a furious man in the white apron of a pot-man. Others pinioned him. The pot-man had a short, heavy truncheon made of dark wood which he waved menacingly in Will's face while he ranted at him, pointing at the man and the mess on the floor. He searched Will's pockets for money while he was held, but finding only pence, stuffed them back in disgust, motioning with his head to the door. Bessie was seized, and he tried to struggle but was held firm. Then he saw with relief that they were both being marched to the door. Faces stared at him, expressionless, curious, laughing and joking. An angry pot-boy came up and shouted at him, making men laugh. The boy would have to clear up the mess. The door was opened, and they were pushed outside, quite gently, perhaps in deference to Bessie. He had expected to be hurled into a puddle. The rain sizzled down on them relentlessly. It devastated her face, leaving cruel marks like wounds as it washed away the powder and rouge in stripes. Her lip-colouring ran down her chin and dropped off, making a stain on her clothes. Will was aware of the ache in his jaw. His hand felt as though it had been tramped by a horse. Bessie was crying, shaking from emotion and the rain and cold. Will took off his soaking coat and draped its heavy weight around her.

'We must get out of the rain. Can we go to your rooms?'

She did not seem to understand, so he bent close to her and repeated the question. She nodded. He put an arm round her, only to guide her, and they started to walk. Will had no idea of the route, but Bessie was sure enough. They ducked into the rookeries where the grey day became black. The water that cascaded from broken gutters was grey with soot. There were no pavements. An occasional plank was laid across deep holes, but otherwise they squelched through stinking filth. The overhanging houses provided shelter from direct rain but the water collected in the centre of the mud alleys and cut a considerable stream, filled with refuse and offal. People were active, for the houses afforded little shelter inside and the rain here was an asset. Men, women and children poked amongst the washed mud for bones, scrap, anything exposed. They would be down the sewers as soon as the flood of water fell. They had no concept of shelter.

They turned into the narrow alley quite suddenly and into the cobbled court. No one had abused them or spat at them. He supposed their condition was much the same as their own. George

Yard. They entered the stair, and without pausing squelched up to the third floor where they stopped outside the door. Bessie had been washed of all artifice. Her lips were blue with cold and dark shadows had gathered in the hollows of her face which looked lean and pinched. Will realized then how emaciated she had become, how necessary had been the powder and colour. Her skin was pitted with using red lead. He did not know what to do next and had not thought about Bayliss. He wondered if he knew, or if in fact he sent her. His anger had not subsided. One brawl had encouraged him and he found that he had no fear of another. He picked up the heavy iron knocker, looking at Bessie, questioning. She had not spoken a word to him so far. She shook her head. Her teeth were chattering and she had difficulty speaking.

'There's no one there.'

She searched about beneath his coat and produced an iron key on a cord which hung about her neck. She gave him his coat so that she could lift it over her head and try to open the door. Her wet clothes clung to her, and again the rain had removed the artifice, this time of dress. She was pathetically thin and her hands shook hopelessly. Will took the key and unlocked the door. He ushered her in, because it seemed as though she might still run away. He remembered the room, but what he remembered was not what he saw now. It had been scrubbed and polished before. Clean, with a fire in the range.

Now it smelled of old food and dirt and was strewn with the litter of carelessness and despair. The bed was tumbled and unmade. He glanced at it once and could not look again. Broken clay pipes lay in the range. Empty bottles stood where they had been put down. The gloomy window supported a spider's web and was thick with grime. The table had remains of a loaf and a dried-out heel of cheese upon it that must have been there for days. Will saw with disgust that vermin had been eating the cheese. The candle had been chewed. Droppings lay everywhere like black rice. There was no fire. An unemptied chamber-pot stood beside the bed. He felt sick at the sight and smell. The place filled him with loathing. He wanted to burn the bed and its uses with it.

He moved away from Bessie. His disgust showed plainly in his

374

face as his eyes wandered about, trying to pick out some saving feature, some sign of care or order, some sign of Bayliss. It was not a room that was being lived in by a man. There were no man's things except the broken pipes and the bottles. No boots, no shirts or clothes, no razor, leather-oil, harness or straps that he would have expected.

'Where's Bayliss?' She did not answer, but started to cry silently again. He shook her violently, not master of himself. 'Where's Bayliss?' His loathing made him vicious and he shook her again as if he could shake her until the filth and immorality dropped from her like caked dirt. She clenched her teeth and refused to say anything. He slapped her meagre face twice, shouting at her, 'Answer me! Answer me!' Red marks stained her pallor vividly as he watched. He was so ashamed of himself that he felt a desire to hit her again.

'He left me,' she said, finding her voice to avoid more pain, but speaking in a grim whisper. She had difficulty controlling her chattering teeth, but Will paid no attention.

'Why?'

'I don't know. Go away. You hate me!'

'Yes, I hate you!'

'Go away!'

'Yes, I'll go away. Look at this place, you whore! Is that why he left you?'

'No!' she spat out, 'I had to do it, Will Morton.' She looked at him with contempt, speaking carefully as though to a simpleton. She controlled the trembling of her jaws and held one hand tight in the other so that only the shaking of her forearms should betray the weakness of her bitter coldness. 'I was starving. I *am* a whore. Go away, don't come here again. Don't hit me because you can't bear to look at me. Sweet Jesus Christ, Will Morton, isn't it enough that I have to do this without you hitting me? You haven't even paid for that! Leave me alone so that I can change my clothes. Do you want me to die of cold? What do you want from me? I ain't your Bessie Tate, she died long ago. I have no name to you. I am a whore and I bring men here if they will buy me a round supper because I would rather live than die. I don't need you, Will Morton. You have no milk of human kindness in your heart. There is more kindness in a man who leaves me an extra penny and treats me to good beef for his pleasure than there is in the whole of you!'

'That's a lie!' Morton was shaken by her contempt for him and by her finding a mature voice he hardly recognized. He had never hit a woman in his life and now he did not recognize the woman he had assaulted. Bessie Tate was gone. She was right. This woman spoke with the strength of experience and conviction. 'I don't have to say it,' he protested unconvincingly, 'you know it.'

'Then go away and prove it. That would be an act of mortal charity, and if you want to help me, don't look round my home like it is a disease but leave a Christian penny to buy food for the pleasure you have had in marking me!'

'I will leave you all the money I have,' said Morton, desperate now to convince her. He put three pennies and a half-penny on the table. 'That's all I have.'

She laughed scornfully.

'It is. I had a bag with some clothes but it was stolen on my way here!'

She laughed again, but enjoying it. 'You are a poor gull, Will Morton. You only survive because you are protected. A servant's life is easy – everything provided. Now what will you do? Why are you running away?'

'My brother is in trouble. He shot a man and they will hang him.'

'And what of that?'

'I gave him my gun.'

'They will never know. Not unless he tells them.'

'He won't tell, but he won't be able to explain it either. It has the maker's mark, so they will find out.'

'And you have three and a half pence! Have you a job?'

'I have no job.'

'Anyway, I don't want to know.' She shivered violently and clutched her bony shoulders in an attempt to control herself.

'Let me light a fire.'

Bessie stared at Morton, surprised. 'No. There is only enough coal for one fire left. I must keep it until it's bitter cold. And it gets marrow cold in here.'

'I'll light it.'

'No!' she shouted, 'I can't go to the coal-hole! That's all I have.'

'I'll get more.'

'Why should you? And how?'

'I don't know.'

'Why don't you go away,' she said in a voice that was almost kind. 'It makes you sick to see me like this. There's nothing here, you know. 'I've changed, found my voice, had to. Lost my looks. Had to. Sold my body. Had to. I'd sell anything. I have to. I've sold my past, my name and my life. There's nothing for you here, Will Morton, except pain, and as you hate me you'll hit me. You can't even afford me, except once!'

Will coloured with rage and embarrassment at her deliberate wounding. She tried to laugh at him to provoke him further but either her heart was no longer in it or she was too cold. Will found that his hand was up and ready to strike her again. He quickly tucked it in his trouser pocket.

'I never knew you were so quick to hit a female. But we all learn something about ourselves, Will, someday. You was quick with that poor cove.'

'Who was he?'

She shrugged. 'We hadn't got to that. Any road, they don't make a habit of telling their names. He said I should call him Jack.'

Will sat down on a dusty wooden chair, holding his head. Bessie ignored him and started to undress. He turned away and hid his head in his hands.

'Don't you want to see? Have a look. Suit yourself, I ain't ashamed of myself, not now. That's the difference between you and me. I can't afford shame no more than fires.'

'I'll make you a fire and get more coal!' He shouted more than he meant because of her taunting. He would have liked to weep but could not.

'How?'

'I'll think of a way.'

'All right,' she said suddenly, rubbing her naked body down with a cloth that might have been any sort of rag, 'make me a fire.' She draped the soaking dress over a piece of cord tied near the range, and changed into an old dark blue dress that she took from under the bed. There was mud around the hem and its skirt was patched with different materials. 'Well, I have some clothes now, you can look without being turned to salt!' Will saw that she was wearing the old dress she had run away in.

He made a fire with some wet kindling from a broken fruit-basket, using straw to start it with his strike-a-light. The coal was poor stuff that had obviously been gleaned from the Thames mud around the coal wharves. Eventually the damp chimney began to draw. The room was cold as a cave and Will was beginning to shiver with it too. The fire seemed magical to him, and Bessie came and stood nearby, so that he moved aside to let her warm her hands. The warmth stilled them. It was the most important thing at that moment. Nothing else mattered. They shared it in quiet, each lost in separate thoughts, staring at the spreading flames.

'I have three and a half pence that will buy us some food and some coal for one evening. If you will let me dry my coat and clothes, I'll go.'

'All right.' She made the bargain eagerly, her face sharper than ever in the light of the flames. 'But give me the money. They will rob you and strip you and make you into pork pies before you have gone ten feet from here. They know me. You see, I'm one of them.'

He looked at her, and thought he could see beyond what he was allowed to see. There was a moment of recognition that was almost illusory. It was like hailing a familiar figure, then when he turns, being confronted by a stranger. His heart ached at the glimpse of this fleeting familiarity. She caught his eye and immediately looked down, fearing his expression. She was warmer now, and rubbed her hands together to break the tension between them.

'If I buy food, I shall have to clean up,' she said quietly, 'so you just sit here and dry out. Don't mind me, I shan't look.'

He looked at her sharply, but she was not mocking him. In fact she hid her face in shadow. The red marks on the side of her face stood out in the firelight. Her eyes would be discoloured in the morning. He felt ashamed, like a boy who has killed something living by accident, wants it to come to life again and is unable to cope with the finality of it.

'I'm sorry I hit you. I didn't . . .'

She shrugged it off. 'Bruises here are common as curses.'

Will took off his wet outer clothes, drying himself with the modesty of a novitiate nun. Bessie cleared the table as best she could, emptied the chamber-pot into the street and went out, returning with a wooden pail of water. She went out again, with a sack around her shoulders, for the food and coals.

Will sat by the fire wrestling with the serpents of contradiction in his mind. Like Laocoon they seemed to be crushing him senseless. When they had eaten the poor food she brought, he slept on the floor by the range as she suggested, because he could think of no other thing to do.

The grey drizzle that turned the city into a field of mire drifted in wreaths about the heights of Highgate, obscuring everything except near trees that seemed to crowd in because of it. It hissed on the leaves of lime and plane and spattered onto the laurels and rhododendrons below. The garden in Southgate Lane was dismal with wet leaves that had already begun to fall. Ferns had turned brown and had collapsed. Bushes hung low. It was no weather for the children.

Caroline had invited John, William and Maria with all their children to join her. She was concerned about John and hoped that company might distract him. He was drinking too much to be left alone in Regent Square with his melancholy. With Thomas at work, he had taken to brooding in the library in front of unread books. Mrs Burges took over Charlie and Nell and played with them in the square, but she was too old for their boisterous games. They had no friends and were delighted to join Edward Thomas and Maria's three children who were squealing and bumping about upstairs.

William, who had accepted the invitation, had not come. Caroline was not surprised and was not upset because she felt that he would have constrained everything with his distance and impatience. It was part of his pose that had become a permanent property. The only loss was that John had no other man to speak to, and unless addressed, lapsed into an uncommunicative silence. She had relented so far as to supply him with the brandy

379

decanter while she and Maria drank tea. A warm fire of good coal gave him a companion, and he stared into its heart as though seeking for consolation there. He was thinking of other fires again, his mind far away on a tortured path of things that might have been, tracing the same worn furrow of reproach.

'What is William doing, then, that he's so busy?' Caroline asked Maria.

Maria seemed to have lost so much of her energy these last few years. She used to be an awesome figure. Caroline was thinking back to that day of Maria's visit and the shameful ignominy of her own feelings and behaviour. Maria had seemed a hurricane of resolve. Now she rarely smiled and seemed weary. She had stopped coaching the children to paint and draw and had retreated to her own occupation of making delicate drawings of plants. She appeared at William's grandiose parties, but said little, knowing they thought her a dull wife and not good enough for him. She didn't care. Their house was unrecognizable now, anyway, only her own working space remaining untouched. She loathed it all.

'William has designed some grand affair for the opening of Hammersmith Bridge on October sixth. The Company has employed him for it. He is painting as well, of course. Something else from Walter Scott!'

'You don't like it?'

'Between ourselves only, no. He can paint much better than that if he tries. It is all too easy. He should look at Turner or Constable.'

'You don't like them do you, Maria?' Caroline was surprised. 'They are all a mad confusion of colour and paint. You can see no detail. I can't tell what they are about!'

Maria smiled slightly. 'What William does is all technique and no art.'

'But he is popular and famous. Look at the prices he can command.'

'He is a safe painter. There is nothing extreme about his work, everything is recognizable, romantically hidden in a sea of umber but struck by the sun. It's not difficult, Caroline, although it is faithless heresy for me to say so. His head is completely turned by success. He is on a money-mill. As long as he keeps tramping round it the gold will fall at his feet. But it is a captive wheel, going nowhere.'

'It makes you unhappy? I mean the type of work he paints.'

'Yes. I think I could stand his manner if I thought it was going somewhere or giving him some satisfaction, but I do believe that is the trouble with it. He *knows* at heart that he gets no satisfaction from it so must pretend that he does, even more. He is convincing himself perpetually and needs me to agree. I'm afraid I fail him miserably there because I cannot.'

'But William is very clever.'

'Yes, he is very clever but he has taken a wrong turning and can't see it. The further you go on, the more difficult it is to make yourself go back. You are always tempted to say that there must be another turning ahead, nearby, and so you go on and on.'

'That is a sad analysis of life,' said John, who had been forgotten in his chair.

'It is trite enough,' replied Maria.

'No, it isn't trite, it's true. The action may be a commonplace, but to observe it isn't.'

'You are not to drink too much, John,' said Caroline. 'Brandy debilitates.'

'Sister, oh sister, leave your little brother alone!' mocked John. 'I don't intend temperance, so shall I try sobriety! Will that do?'

Caroline was annoyed at his tone. It was unkind and produced in her spontaneous distress and alarm. A freed slave cannot bear the sight of shackles. 'You needn't satisfy me. It's your own affair!' she snapped, unable to stop herself from modifying her annoyance by adding, 'You must remember your children now.'

John gave her a wry look, raising his eyebrows and Caroline blushed.

'Well, I'm glad the children are playing so well together,' she covered, 'they should do it more often.'

'Come now, Caroline. You don't think Charlie and Nell get out enough.' He hauled himself upright and poured himself a small brandy, looking quizzically at Caroline who avoided his glance. 'You're right. They don't have much fun. Mrs Burges is a kind woman but she ain't much good at ball games. You should see her run! It's funny how patterns repeat themselves. When I see Charlie in the gardens, I'm reminded of myself as a child.'

'I hope he's not so wild,' said Maria.

'He shows every sign of it!' said John smiling.

'That's the first smile that's cracked your cheeks for weeks,' said Caroline. 'It's good to see it, John.'

John rotated his glass by the short stem. He shrugged. 'I know it is. You're right, I'm a melancholy devil. I don't know how Father puts up with me. I don't even try an occupation.'

'Is it your wife Louise?' asked Caroline. She found it strange that of the three adults in the room, she alone had the energy for concern. Her life had been grinding and sheltered but apart from the lurking fear of Ware making some other attempt on Edward Thomas, she felt unencumbered. John and Maria seemed bowed with experience and worldliness. Like the shrubs in the garden, the rain of events had bowed them low, and threatened to break them.

'Yes,' replied John. How could he explain to them that it was not only Louise, but Louise, Padmavati and himself? They were inextricably entwined so that he was unable to separate one from the other or himself. One was dead, one was perhaps mad. But which one? He had written to Louise at her parents' address, begging them to pass the letter on if they knew her where-abouts. He had received no acknowledgement or reply. He had come to want Louise to the exclusion of reason. His feeling of shame and guilt overwhelmed him. He did not understand it, but it was there, urgent, at his shoulder. Upstairs, there were more happy squeals and thuds from the children. It broke the uneasy silence and they were all grateful for it.

'Shall I go up?' asked Caroline, getting to her feet. She too felt the nervous tension in John. It seemed to stifle him and she wanted the relief.

'No, I'm sure they're all right, Caroline,' said Maria, 'they sound happy, so leave well alone. I'm afraid Aunt Helen won't get much rest.'

'She sleeps fitfully much of the time. She says she enjoys the sound of the children. Age is terrible, isn't it? You are isolated and removed from direct contact with pleasures and must listen to them at a distance. But she seems to find pleasure in it. The appetite shrinks, and a morsel is enough.'

'Now you are being melancholy,' Maria accused.

'No! Aunt Helen is not melancholy. When her energy returns, she is gay, but it burns out more quickly now. She says she has never heard the birds sing so beautifully before, or so enjoyed the sound of horses and people, or the playing of children. But she frets because she can't get out and about any more.'

Madness is deferred death, thought John. He felt that living had come to a halt and that he could see no way forward without Louise. I am bound like a small tree in convolvulus. I must untwine each tendril before I can even find the parent plant.

Dearest Louise, my behaviour was intolerable and you must consider my actions those of a madman. I was driven to them by my inner self which is a dark beast, and by thoughts of my past. I hate these memories and because I hate them I am provoked by them to greater excesses. Do you understand? I beg your forgiveness, if you can forgive me. I miss you beyond sane thought. Please come to England. The children are well but need you. I understand what you did and why and I accept full blame. Dearest Louise, if this letter reaches you, please, please reply. Your life is waiting for you. You must believe that I understand what I have done and shall devote myself to rebuilding our life. Dearest Louise, John.

'John! You must not lapse so into these silences. You don't even hear me.' It was Caroline. John had no idea what she had been saying.

'I'm sorry,' he said.

'Have you any news of Louise? Father said you had written to her, by her parents, and had received no reply, but that was weeks ago.'

'I have still received no reply and I've written again. I shall have to go to Virginia.'

'But what about the children?'

'It's no life for them, searching the country.' He could not tell them of the danger involved.

The afternoon passed sluggishly. Even the bright fire could not lift the atmosphere of introspective gloom. Caroline had tried, but each time the solid ground she thought she had trod on became a morass and she had to retreat.

'How's that poor man, Walter Manning?' she asked Maria, 'We all seem to have forgotten him since that terrible business.'

'I've paid him a visit.' Maria was defensive. 'William doesn't know and I don't propose to tell him. He is recovering well enough, I'm glad to say, but I had to make so many excuses. It was very painful. He is very fond of William and looks to him as a true friend. Naturally he can't understand why William doesn't visit him. He is a lonely man in that big house. The garden is not being properly tended because there is no one to supervise. It was all supposed to be part of William's contract. I have had to make all sorts of excuses about his work, and invent messages that William is supposed to have sent with regards and hopes for recovery. I don't like deceit. I hate it!'

'And why doesn't William come?' demanded John. He found William intensely irritating and his question was rudely put.

Maria coloured. 'William is doing other things.'

'You shouldn't ask so rudely,' interposed Caroline, 'you should know perfectly well that William is not himself.'

'He could write.'

'Like you?' asked Maria. John was angry and would have replied with some provocative remark but Caroline again intervened.

'Please! Can we leave the subject? We're talking ourselves into a gloom and now we're going to quarrel to get out of it. Tell me, Maria, what are your children going to be? We should have a guess. Let's write what we think on a slip of paper, every one of us, and seal the replies in a box. Then, say fifteen years from now, we can all sit here and open it.'

'Pandora's box!' said John. It was intended to be a joke, but provoked a sour silence.

Henry was not accustomed to riding, although he could handle a horse. He wore a heavy cloak that was weighed down like a soaked blanket about him. Both he and the animal were drenched with rain and muddy water. When he slowed down to let the horse walk the long haul up Highgate hill by Green Street, it became a wraith in its own steam.

He had decided he must come himself. It was not the sort of news to deliver by messenger. It was lucky that they were all together, he told himself, or else he would have had to ride to Chelsea, and he was already chafed and sore. The gloomy day seemed appropriate enough. He patted the animal's neck, and it flicked its ears, understanding. The rein was slack so that it could lower its head, puffing. Other horsemen passed downhill, their horses stepping carefully through the cart-furrows where the water ran in brown streams. Each man and horse was a ghost of white vapour, outlines and features invisible. There were no exchanges of greetings. Each man was too absorbed in his own discomfort. He pulled up outside the house and was at a loss where to tie up the horse. He moved the animal on, to tie it under a tree. When he dismounted it shook itself with relief.

Loudon opened the door to his knock. He immediately stood aside upon recognizing Henry.

'It's terrible weather, sir. Let me take your cloak and coat.'

'My horse is under that tree. Is there stabling?'

'There is a stable round the back, sir, down a lane. I'll see to it.'

'Good. I'm afraid there's nothing more you can do for me, Loudon, you will have to take me up as I am.'

'Yes, sir.'

Caroline was already on the landing, having heard the door and voices.

'Who is it?' she called.

'Henry!'

She waited until Henry appeared behind Loudon. His feet squelched in his boots at every step. She sounded alarmed. 'What is it? What's the matter?'

'Who's here with you?'

'Maria and John. Why?'

'Good. I'll explain.' He gave her a perfunctory peck on the cheek and Loudon left them. 'My feet are terrible. I don't want to tramp all over your carpet.'

'Nonsense! Come in by the fire, You're soaked. What is it?'

John and Maria were both on their feet, surprised by his arrival. Henry was not his elegant self. His shirt stuck to him and his trousers sagged in wet folds. John poured a brandy into his glass which he gave to Henry, who drank it gratefully.

'I'm sorry to break in on you like this – especially in this condition – but I had to ride here immediately. I'm afraid that Father is not at all well.'

'How bad is he?' asked John. The women were silent, already thoughtful of action and the complications of their families.

'I'm afraid it appears very bad. He has had a stroke of apoplexy. They are bleeding him, but there is paralysis.'

Caroline began to cry. Maria, able with other people's crises, moved to her and put a hand on her shoulder. 'How did it happen?' she asked.

'In all probability the assurance on the *Thomas K.* will not be paid. The man Masterson has acted very strangely to say the least. That is all I can gather. I have only had a few words with Father, he can only speak with difficulty. Hebson, the underwriter, who subscribed for the full amount for vessel and cargo, called at his chambers this morning. It was too much for him and he collapsed.'

'Why did the man do it?' Caroline was tearful now.

'I think it may have been from good motives, but Father won't believe it. He is convinced that Hebson is running out on him.'

'What do you think?' Maria was very businesslike, partly to stop Caroline from becoming too emotional.

'I think Hebson may have a case, but how strong a one I don't know. I'm no expert on shipping. It all revolves about whether or not we lost the beneficial use of the vessel and I don't even have all the facts. Father is weak but he is determined to defend his claim. After all, if he concedes he loses everything. He is pursuing for total loss. I must do it for him.'

Maria looked at Henry sharply. They all knew of his history of opposition to Thomas's venture. She wondered, cruelly, if he was motivated by money or love. He was being brisk and businesslike, perhaps to cover his emotions. It was possible that the combination of motives would solve things between Henry and Thomas.

'What do you want us to do?' asked Maria .'We must see him. Can we get a carriage in Highgate, Caroline?'

'Wilcox, at the livery stables. Loudon will hire one.'

'Then I think we should leave at once,' said Henry.

'But where is Father?' Caroline was becoming more distraught, 'and I must tell Aunt Helen. She'll have heard you arrive.'

'Caroline, he's in no pain and is quite comfortable in Regent Square. Tell Aunt Helen. The doctor is there, and a nurse.'

'But what about all the children?'

'We shall leave them here,' said Maria firmly. 'They will be quite all right, in fact they will enjoy themselves immensely. Caroline, we will get ready. John, you will have to do what you can for Henry. Perhaps Loudon has a dry shirt. Henry, you must dry your boots!'

She realized that it was the first occasion for a long time that she had been busy on behalf of anyone other than William. She was deeply upset about Thomas but could not deny the relief that activity brought. They had all been shaken out of themselves and she wondered if it might do the same for William.

The yolk-yellow sun shone into the bedroom in Regent Square and fell in a clear swathe on the bed. Caroline wanted to draw the curtain as it was in Thomas's eyes, but he said no, he could feel it warm on his skin. It was exquisite to have feeling for so much of the rest of him no longer seemed to exist. It was not numb, but without any sensation. It did not itch or tingle. Even men who have lost a limb feel it tingle. He lay with his eyes drowned with colour, concentrating on sensation. He studied the inward geometric patterns and looming auroral clouds of afterimage. They played across his brain as bold and as exciting as cumulus over downland. If he squeezed his lids tight, they changed colour and shape, the colours becoming unknown, then grey then black. He could not feel his legs or torso. They felt like a massive weight that restrained him from flying among these inner clouds. His body was an encumbrance. He had no taste for food, his mind had no strength for thought. His inner eye existed above and beyond all these things. The warmth of sun on skin was an ecstasy.

People came and went. They talked to him for a while, but he found answering difficult. It no longer seemed important. There were things to remember, to dwell upon inside his mind that were really important. The children were important. The ship was important. He had been so naïve, so casual on a matter of business which should have had his full attention. If any other man had behaved as he, he would have thought him simple, a flat. He had puzzled it out. The ship was a child of his dotage and he had expected too much of it. It had disappointed him. It could not replace children. These thoughts depressed him and he worried at them like a cat with a frog.

I lost Caroline and launched a ship, he thought, and yet was careless with it. A ship can be made from birth as we want it. What do we put into our ambitions that we don't know? How gullible are we when we are so weakened? We buy and sell, cherish and hate, are astute and stupid according to simple laws of craving, yet remain ignorant of the reasons.

He slept, and was awakened by Caroline calling his name insistently, but gently. The sun had sunk low and was red. The room seemed full of people.

'Who is it?'

'It's Henry, with Maria and John. Sam and Jane are downstairs'.

Thomas struggled to concentrate. He had difficulty in separating their faces.

'Henry, will we lose?'

Henry leaned over him. 'We may. But if we do we shall pursue for partial loss.' He was very firm.

'I don't see we have much chance. I remember it was Mansfield made the ruling in Goss versus someone or other.'

'Withers,' Henry volunteered.

'Yes, that's it. Do you think I have always expected to get more out of life than I put in?'

'I don't know what you're talking about. I'll look after everything. You mustn't worry.'

'But I should have paid more attention. I wanted the money to buy love.' His voice was faint and dry. 'I have only just realized that. All these years I have pretended to you all and to Sam that I wanted you to love one another, but I only wanted you all to love me.'

'Father, that's not so!' Caroline protested. Thomas turned his head towards her, but could not see her face.

'It is. It's what we all want. Tell me what happens.'

388

He was silent and seemed to sleep. They sat by his bed, Caroline holding his hands. When he was breathing deeply and regularly they left quietly to dine downstairs.

Mrs Burges ran into the dining-room at eight o'clock to say that she had gone up with soup but the master had died.

13

The funeral had been a modest affair. Four black horses with black plumes pulled the black lacquer hearse. It's cut-glass windows were draped inside with deep plum velvet, the swathes parted just sufficiently to catch a glimpse of wood and brass handles. Eight carriages followed on a fine autumn day that made every polished surface sparkle and the grass iridescent with lingering dew. In the graveyard the leaves on horse-chestnuts had turned brittle and sear. The silver birches showered the grass with guinea-piece leaves.

Thomas had never expressed any desire to be buried anywhere, so Henry had decided on St James's Chapel off the Hampstead Road. He refused to have him buried in the stinking charnel pit of a City cemetery. But Thomas was a Londoner and it seemed a suitable compromise.

Now they had returned to Regent Square where the house had all its curtains drawn and upper shutters closed. A wreath of laurel tied with black ribbon had been fixed to the door-knocker. Neighbouring houses had their curtains drawn too, out of respect or from show. Dead houses with dead eyes. The weather refused to join in this gloom and the sun was brassy and jolly. Children were forbidden to play in the square. There would be no rattling of sticks down railings. Nannies had a hard time indoors.

Carriages arrived at intervals during the day, slowing from a trot to a walk for the last hundred yards. Discreetly dressed men and veiled women left formal black-edged cards. Burges collected them, offering the family's thanks and assuring them yes, their messages would certainly be passed on. Burges wondered if they ever stopped to consider that he too was a mourner.

Outside, blackbirds were cheerful, turning leaves with passionate vigour. The sky was clear and blue. The undertaker's men chatted in low tones with the coachmen. It was sweltering in thick black clothes. Nature was at odds with the occasion. Inside, the back windows had been thrown open to admit some air, but there was no proper breeze, as decency demanded the front of the house should remain sealed. The family and friends, clothes loosened and hats removed, sat together over refreshments. Mrs Burges, still in her funeral clothes, looked after the ladies. The men helped themselves as Burges was occupied with the door.

The children had all come except Maria's youngest, Jonathan, who would have become restless and cried, and Aunt Helen who had been forbidden to attend. For the other children, it had been their first funeral and they had treated it with natural curiosity that had modified their discovery of the finality of death. It was Edward Thomas who had broken down and cried as the coffin was lowered into the anonymous earth. The other children had stared at him with interest as though trying to understand what they must be missing.

Now they had been urged into the garden with instructions not to get dirty or break the cold frames or the conservatory or the flowers or eat too many apples. Even then the garden was a relief.

'It's like a coffin in there!' Charlie had declared to Henrietta when they were out of hearing.

'I wonder what it's like inside a coffin?' Henrietta pondered. It was something that had been occupying her thoughts ever since she'd seen it lowered into its trim rectangular cleft in the ground.

'You would only find out if you were buried alive,' volunteered Margaret.

'That does happen sometimes.' Charlie was knowledgeable. 'I've heard of it.'

'That's horrible!' bullied Nell. 'You mustn't talk like that.' She was able to control Charlie and knew it, taking pleasure in displaying her powers.

'It's not horrible, it's a fact,' insisted Charlie.

'Facts are often horrible,' Nell pursued. 'It isn't nice to talk about things like that. You wouldn't dare inside.'

Edward Thomas sat apart from the rest on a stone seat. It was very cold. Cold as marble in his imagination. Cold as deep down in the earth with the musty smell of yellow clay that is clean, sticky, and cuts like cheese into slices. Thomas could not be entirely gone. There must be some residual Thomas, a sense of him, the way things were arranged around the house. He wondered if there would be any more visits with his mother or what would happen to the house if there was no one to visit. Mr and Mrs Burges would carry on. When Will Morton had gone so suddenly, Edward Thomas had cried secretly. He could not bear the loss of people. Looking at Charlie, Nell, Henrietta and Margaret, it seemed to him that they had still to comprehend things that he had already discovered. The cold seat was his own penance.

'Come on, Edward!' Charlie hissed, 'we can play at the end of the garden where no one can see us. Mrs Burges will give us some cakes. I've arranged it!'

Edward shook his head. 'Later. I don't want to now.'

'Don't mope!'

'I'm not moping.'

'Well, suit yourself.' Charlie ran off. His black clothes suited his dark hair, eyes and complexion. He was annoyed with Edward but at the same time satisfied that he could show off to all the girls.

Henry stood beside Jane. Maria noticed it immediately and realized the significance, for he had not been in the habit of even such meagre demonstrations of attachment. For instance, William, she thought bitterly, has immediately quit me for John whom he is boring into giving compliments which he shamelessly accepts no matter how unkindly meant. I am accustomed to desertion, she thought, but don't I welcome it to a degree? What can I possibly say to William?

Henry was trying his best to fill the role of host in this hostless house. They all felt the constraint that follows such an event. Each would rather have gone home with his private thoughts, yet felt that some communication was necessary to fill a void. They could not feel that the house was empty of Thomas. They did not talk about the funeral, for that had been discussed in the carriages on the way back.

'Henry, whatever happened about Will Morton the coachman?' asked Maria when Mrs Burges had served tea to the ladies and left the room. Mrs Burges had been weeping and her eyes were bloodshot and her nose red. 'That was a strange affair. We never heard the outcome. Did they discover anything more?'

'No,' said Henry, 'he has gone to earth somewhere. They are certain he was mixed up in the shooting somehow. It was his gun after all and he ran away, and the convicted man is his brother.'

'It must have been very awkward for you.'

'Yes,' said Henry drily.

Jane was more forthcoming. It was a long time since they had heard her volunteer a view. She looked at him before speaking. It was an act of concern. 'Henry has been threatened by these artisans. They seem ungrateful for the work he has done, and the number of men he has saved from prison or even transportation or death. I don't believe they have any gratitude.'

'Oh, I understand it well enough.' Henry seemed quite calm and assured. 'Each case is pressing and desperate, and I have been paid for the past. There can never be any gratitude for the past when each life is as essential a matter as it is in the present. They live all the time for the present.'

'That's a very magnanimous view,' said Maria, 'but what do you really think of it? After all you seemed to be committed to them.'

'Not committed any more than any counsel who believes his client is unjustly handled. I am not compelled to like my clients or believe their ideals. We would be a lean lot if we had to obey those rules!' Henry shrugged. 'I believe they have come to confuse the law with the way the law is administered. If it were administered equally for all men, it would be fair enough. I agree with anyone who says that it isn't. But this last thing was impossible, because it attacked the law itself. I believe the man is guilty.'

'Will he hang?'

'Probably.'

'But how have you been threatened?' asked Maria.

'Oh that's empty nonsense!' said Henry brushing it aside. 'We won't talk about it.'

William was telling John about his grand plan for the opening of Hammersmith Bridge. His enthusiasm was not attractive, because it was strident with demands. 'Don't you think the whole idea is splendid?' he was declaring, pausing like an orator for applause.

'I'm not sure that I do,' replied John coolly. 'I don't really see the need of such a fuss.'

'But it is such a wonderful bridge!' William sounded extremely impatient. 'Surely you have seen it?'

'Yes.'

'Then how can you be so indifferent to it? It is one of the world's marvels! The length of roadway is much greater than the Menai bridge which is five hundred and fifty-three feet. The Hammersmith bridge is six hundred and eighty-eight! Just imagine it.'

'I have seen it.'

'And you have no enthusiasm for it?' Maria was alarmed by William's growing anger.

'I admire it as a piece of engineering. There are greater marvels in the world.'

'Oh, I see! The much-travelled soldier is hard to impress!'

'William, I won't quarrel. I think your arrangements will be a great success.' William was partly mollified. 'William is having bands and fireworks and gondolas full of gondoliers,' explained John to the others, in an obvious and successful attempt to pass William over to them.

'Yes, I have even hired acrobats from the circus who will walk from one side to the other on the cables! Each will have another on his shoulders. I have a thousand other ideas still in my head. I shan't tell you them all!' He waved his finger at them waggishly.

Maria rose. 'Jane, I'd love a stroll round the garden. We can keep an eye on the children.' Jane joined Maria. William gave them the briefest glance of disappointment and continued unabated.

'Mr Gurney's steam carriage is to make the first crossing, followed by displays. What a sight. His great steam beast.'

'But who is the engineer of the bridge?' Maria heard Henry ask, but William continued unhearing.

*

In the garden the two women walked silently for some time, as though testing the quality of it. They did not go to the children, but sat on a bench of wooden slats and cast-iron ends with lion's heads.

'The garden is lovely,' Jane volunteered, like a gambler starting with a small stake.

'Yes, I like autumn colours so much better than summer. Perhaps because they are even more brief. Flowering is so much longer than decay. I suppose that's a cheering thought.' Jane smiled briefly but said nothing. 'I'm sorry I forced you out, Jane, but I can't bear to hear any more of William on the subject of his plans. He's becoming less and less a painter and more a showman. We shall end up a circus.'

Jane looked at the other woman sharply, trying to understand the double meaning in her words. 'He lets his imagination run away with him,' she said politely.

Maria changed the subject too obviously. 'What will be done with the house, I wonder? It means a lot to Caroline.' They looked up at the rear of it, the mellow brickwork glowing in the sun. 'And what about the servants? I feel sorry for them, because nobody considers them. They loved Thomas too but we don't allow them much grief. They lose their future and must find new employment.' Maria fell silent and looked so unhappy that Jane felt she must try to dispel her mood.

'Maria, don't be unhappy. You can't grieve for everyone. And William is just exuberant.' Maria would not look at Jane.

'He's changed. Success means different things to different people, they say. In William it's become a vice. There's no humour in it, no compassion. He argues. His values are too easy. I can't see an end to it.' Jane did not know what she could say to comfort her. Maria walked on as though to give her no chance. 'I suppose it will pass. Here I am talking about sombre autumn with affection! But you, Jane, there's something you're concealing.' She looked at Jane searchingly, and Jane was disconcerted. 'I'm noted for my lack of tact. Why is Henry so diligent? No, not diligent, that's too dutiful. He stands by you in a tender way.'

Jane felt she wanted to tell Maria her news. Her happiness made her less diffident and Maria in this sombre mood seemed more approachable. 'Well, there is a reason,' she replied shyly. 'Henry and I are expecting a child.'

Maria felt a sudden rush of great affection. She put her arms around Jane and kissed her with spontaneous delight. 'That's wonderful!'

Jane was overwhelmed. It seemed that at last she would inherit the affection and attention of the family. She cried, as someone saved. Maria restrained her own tears, not permitting her unhappiness to spoil Jane's moment of triumph. Later they returned to the house arm in arm, Maria steering Jane along the paths strewn with autumn confetti. She would not envy Jane who had had nothing for so long.

Caroline wished she could escape into the garden. Her grief was controlled and private and she wanted peace. She could not bear the carping and snarling that continued between William and John but was afraid to leave them in case it got worse. Neither of them was displaying any respect for the circumstances. William's fluency had turned to sarcasm as John had remained unimpressed. Then as John had become cruelly scornful, William had become childishly angry. Henry tried time and again to quiet them, but they were like two cockerels fighting for supremacy. It made no sense to her.

'Do you think people need these entertainments?' John was asking. 'Or is it just a case of bread and circuses?'

William was patronizing. 'They elevate the imagination. That is commonly one of the features of civilization and of art. Nothing that does that can be dismissed.'

'Oh, no!' John interrupted, holding up a hand like a Roman orator. 'Oh, no! War elevates the imagination.'

'Do you dismiss it?'

'No, but I don't recommend it.'

'Your trouble, John, is that you can't see any work in it. It's a common failing. Even the least event requires planning and thought. The commonalty of people live in a happy belief that these things just happen by some spontaneous process. Or by some divine stroke or miraculous congregation. It all happens through order. You believe in magic!'

'William, this is not the time or place for this sort of conversation,' Henry interrupted severely. 'This is a doctrinaire quarrel.'

'But I am not quarrelling, dear Henry,' returned William, affecting an artificial smile, 'I do, however, object to my work being criticized and dismissed in anticipation!'

Henry held up his hands, palms outwards. 'Pax!' he said. 'Between us all.'

'Pax vobiscum!' returned William churlishly, infuriating John. 'But not for me,' retorted John. 'What stupid vanity it all is, and artifice. You, William, were once a painter. Now you are some sort of organizer for the whims of fashion. You think nothing of me, that's clear, but don't expect me to hold up my hands in "pax"!'

'At least, sir, I work, which is better than living off the family!' shouted William, overstepping the brink.

'Is that better than living off the people?' John demanded, furious. His face was at first white, then flooded with hectic colour. Henry quickly interposed himself between them as it seemed they would fly at each other. They bobbed around him, trying to glare at each other exactly like two fighting-cocks, while Henry weaved about between them. Caroline was begging them to stop it.

'I've been kind to you so far!' John declared furiously, 'But I won't be insulted by a popinjay who lives off the skirts of society. Your greatest pretence is one about which you'll always remain ignorant . . . Get out of the way, Henry!'

'No! This is ridiculous. Stop it.'

'You know nothing about life,' John continued, ignoring him. 'You are such an aesthete that you would faint away at reality. I don't live off you, sir! You couldn't understand my problems if you devoted ten years of study to them! The ploughers ploughed upon my back and made long furrows. That is from Psalms, sir!'

Caroline had jumped to her feet.

'John, please stop, this is dreadful.' She was beginning to cry. 'We have only just buried Father. Our own father! You must stop!' Her tears were more effective than Henry's intervention. John suddenly looked crestfallen, and pulled at his nose. He finally turned his back on William and moved back a pace.

'It's not my fault.'

'Nobody cares about faults!' From Caroline it was a cry of agony.

'This has got to stop!' shouted Henry suddenly and with such unexpected violence and authority that there was immediate silence. 'We are wearing black for mourning. What has got into everyone? What sort of children are we? I hope it's distress, but we have got to find a better expression for it!'

'I'll go,' said John suddenly. 'I'll collect the children.'

'Don't go in anger,' begged Caroline.

'I'm not angry. You don't understand, Caroline, that my real enemy is guilt.' He moved towards the french windows. 'I'll see you when you get home.'

He would not be stopped. William watched him balefully as he collected his reluctant children from the garden, and was rewarded with a curt good-bye. Only to Caroline was he more understanding.

'*You* should understand,' he said, taking her hand in the hall. 'You asked me, if you remember, whether I had anything to tell. I said I wasn't ready. I'm still not ready, that's all. But I shall be, soon.'

Maria and Jane had hurried into the house when Charlie and Nell were abruptly summoned away. They were dismayed at John's white-faced departure. Maria tried to approach him.

'John, please forgive us.'

'I must forgive myself first.'

'No, John. I'm sure it's not like that.'

'And William must forgive himself. There's no place for me, Maria, in civilized company.'

Henry stood with him on the step, when Charlie and Nell had run to the carriage to secure their favourite seats. John was diffident and Henry seemed remote, as if in reaction to his outburst. He had withdrawn to the inner recesses of grief.

'You will come to this opening of William's, won't you?' he asked.

'Must I, do you think?' John sounded half repentant.

'There's no "must". Please, for all our sakes.' It was as though Thomas had for that moment been made reincarnate. John was so surprised that he stared. Henry shifted uncomfortably. The illusion was gone.

'You agree with William, don't you, Henry?' John asked. It was as much to assure himself it was Henry as to elicit an answer.

'No, John. You were cruel to William, but I think you cover your weaknesses by behaving thus. We mustn't quarrel.'

John examined the head of his cane as though he looked for the future in the cut-glass. 'I've no quarrel except with ghosts.'

He turned and walked to the carriage, doffing his hat to Henry as he stepped in. It was a strange gesture, almost loving, and conveying a sense of loneliness. Henry watched them leave, pensively. His inheritance seemed to be upon him quickly and he was baffled by unformed questions.

In the coach, Charlie and Nell were at first outraged at having been dragged away and complained bitterly.

'We had Mrs Burges serving us,' declared Charlie, 'we had three lots of cakes, and lemon sherbet. Why did we have to go? Why were you quarrelling? Now we have to go to Aunt Caroline's which is not nearly so much fun.' John was unimpressed by their precocity. Nell, although saying nothing, was watching, bright as a bird.

'Your Uncle William and I don't get on. It was the right thing to do. He doesn't understand.'

'I don't like Uncle William. He's famous, isn't he?'

'Yes. But that still doesn't mean he understands.'

'I know that. You should hear Margaret and Henrietta.' Nell giggled and John said nothing, not encouraging such a line. People stared at the coach as it passed, because it was still draped with black velour. Other coaches gave way for them.

'Why do we have to stay at Aunt Caroline's?'

'Because it's not proper to stay in Regent Square.'

'Because grandpa died there?'

'Because we would be in the way. Uncle Henry must look after his affairs.'

John stared out at the streets and the faces. The yellow sun never reached them, he thought, although they seemed to strain up like seeds. Instead it glowed around parapets and gables, always out of reach, singeing the tops of autumn trees. The trees reminded him of Virginia and the colours of fall. The pale faces in the street were matched by the pale faces in the dark of the carriage. Charlie and Nell, watching him, wondered why he quarrelled. Pale faces like ghosts. Images tumbled through his mind, prompted by the funeral. Images of clay, black velvet-covered ropes, the irretrievable act of covering. He wondered if he was quite sane. He could not live without knowing about Louise. It was what he had had to discover. It preyed on him, tearing at him, an incubus with different carnal pleasures. He would have to leave the children with Caroline. She would understand. It would only be for a time.

'Edward Thomas is strange,' said a pale face from the dark interior. John had difficulty in bringing his mind into focus again.

'Sit forward, Charlie, I can't see you!' He tried to control a feeling of guilty panic. Charlie's sudden desire for contact made him feel that he had been caught out in a criminal act.

'Edward Thomas is always alone,' continued Charlie, perching on the edge of the buttoned leather seat. 'He says he likes it. You know, when we are doing something or playing he likes to sit and just watch.' He paused in thought. 'What are the Combinations?'

'Why? They're groups of artisans. Some people say they're dangerous.'

'Edward Thomas says that Uncle Henry has betrayed the Combinations. What does that mean?'

'Uncle Henry was to defend them, or rather one of their members against a charge, but he thought that he couldn't. He believed the man was guilty.'

'He says a man will hang because of Uncle Henry.'

'He will hang, anyway, with or without Uncle Henry. He tried to kill another man.'

'What for?'

'Oh, be quiet, Charlie. This isn't the time to try to explain things.' Charlie sighed, and slumped back in his seat.

'He hasn't got a father,' said Nell suddenly, slyly, face hidden, 'like we haven't got a mother.' John ignored her. He must not let them know they had found the agonizing wound. They could only suspect it. 'Margaret asked why we both looked so dark,' she continued, 'she said there must be a lot of sun in Virginia, and was our mother very dark?'

John stared into the sun, blinking off windows. He wiped the multiple images from his eyes, taking care the children should not see.

William and Maria left almost immediately afterwards. Maria thought sourly that William lingered just long enough to establish his superiority over John, dismissing him with tolerant amusement. Henry was not such a fool as to gratify him by paying much attention. Their journey home was noisy with Margaret and Henrietta babbling about everything and pointing excitedly at the sights out of the window. They drove in a circuit that took them through St James's Park, where huge alterations were being made and gangs of men with horses were shifting yellow clay in willow baskets. William was sullenly silent because Maria did not address him but explained what the men were doing to the children. He resented her censure and she suspected he resented the work in the Park because it was not his. The navvies waved to the children in the crêpe-draped coach, and the children waved back. Maria reflected that the children were accustomed to William's estranged mood.

Caroline's homeward trip was a silent and reflective affair. The bond between mother and son allowed much to be unspoken, although their very closeness occasionally worried Caroline. She was still haunted by the recollection of the burden of love she had borne for Thomas. She did not wish it on her own child. Yet Edward Thomas was already a man, she reflected sadly. His childhood had passed as though it had never been. She could see nothing of Charles Ware in him, but realized that her eyes were biased. Their silent communion was delightful, but was a dangerous indulgence. Today, she would let it be, but she reminded herself she must avoid it in the future. The fledgling, she told herself, must be pushed out of the nest for his own good. She wondered what feelings of regret the bird would feel.

Henry and Jane were left to the sad task of shutting doors in renunciation of Thomas's existence. When they had gone from room to room, with no more purpose than to cast a ritual eye over them, they felt that they had been individually sealed as effectively as an Egyptian tomb. It was a final act of putting out the living spirit. They talked to the servants, trying to reassure them of their future. Henry was already considering whether he might move to Regent Square. What had once seemed impossible now seemed almost right. Mrs Burges permitted herself the tears she had restrained for so long and kept apologizing for them, which Henry found embarrassing.

Finally there was nothing more for them to do. Death seemed such a simple tidying-away. Henry and Jane stood in the darkened drawing-room with all its windows and doors now shut and looked at each other for help. The coincidence of their glances was the support they needed. Jane moved over beside him, not yet daring to take his arm.

'There's nothing more we can do now,' she said unnecessarily. Henry understood, for he responded.

'No. The house is asleep. It's as though time has taken a pause, an extended space between tick and tock. It will pass.' They listened to the clock ticking.

'What shall you do about Thomas's affairs?'

'I have still to pursue this wretched business over the ship. We'll never prove anything against Masterson, but if he didn't get half the proceeds from Rhode Island, I'm a Dutchman. We'll get partial loss, I'm sure. How much, I don't know. We'll have to fight for it.'

'And the Combinations?' Jane's voice was full of concern.

Henry was immediate in his reaction. 'I don't respond well to threats. I'll have none of it.'

'People will say you made your name on their backs, then deserted them when you were secure.'

'People *are* saying it. I think I can stand it! It's a lie. Anyway, I must go to Father's chambers and collect his papers. He has all the documents for the case. I'll go to his first and then go on to my own, dining in Hall.'

'Must you?' Henry for once did not resent her question.

'I know, and I'm sorry, but I promised Sam; and as I have to collect the papers I may as well do both. Sam is very upset, and he has no one. No man, I mean,' he added quickly.

'I'll visit him tomorrow,' said Jane, 'tell him that. You're right, you must go now.'

'It won't take very long.' His voice was kindly and she suddenly realized that he was as afraid of her as she of him. It had never seemed possible to her before. 'Things are much better now, aren't they, Jane? I hope so.'

'Yes, they are.'

She took his arm and they stood in this way for some time in the darkening room. She did not dare tell him yet. She felt their new relationship was still too young and that this was a precious gift that could be saved for a short while. She was afraid still that it might not even be welcome. She must be sure.

'You will have to look after everyone, you realize,' she said. 'The rest of the family seem to expect it of you. That's the way it has come out. John is preoccupied and William ... well, does William need explanation?'

Henry nodded. 'It's strange. A few days ago, Father was in command. He and I hardly communicated. We spent so much time quarrelling and misunderstanding each other. I regret that now.'

Jane had no answer, but squeezed his arm. Henry kissed her neck and seemed about to kiss her on the mouth when he said, 'No, not here.' Poor Henry, thought Jane, still bedevilled by the proprieties. The living are more important than the dead. She smiled again, deliberately, and patted his arm.

Later, when the carriages had all drawn away from the railings, lights began to appear in neighbouring houses. Horses and carriages passed at a gallop. The lightless house was no longer of any significance. The black-ribboned wreath would remain, wilting for two weeks. Shutters and curtains would be drawn long before then. The clay heaped over the grave would have settled level.

Crowds had gathered all day on both sides of Hammersmith bridge. The early arrivals stood their ground near the portals and refused to move, staring at the construction in disbelief. Most Londoners had never seen a suspension bridge. Later arrivals pushed forward all day, clogging the approaches and lining the riverside and roads so that only ruthless horsemen could force a way through, whipping at pedestrians and other horses alike.

Those who had expected to walk or ride across it before the

opening were disappointed. The Company had employed a force of hard-muscled navvies and masons to man the barriers at each end. Gentlemen in carriages became florid with anger, demanding to know on which side the celebrations would take place. They were told to stay on the north. Those that had arrived on the south cursed, and flailed their way through the churned-up mud to find a bridge across the river at Vauxhall, Battersea or Putney.

The day was fine with a porcelain-blue sky and high, moving clouds. The river picked up the colour and sparkled as though it were high summer. Flags snapped on their halliards and sailing craft dragged their anchors against wind and tide and had to run up sail and tack for position. Steamers paraded up and down on special excursions, gushing black smoke and whistling and bullying at the sailing boats. Watermen charged iniquitous prices to ferry innocents from the right side to the wrong, then back again.

Later in the day, the mass of common people came to see the free spectacle and ply their trades amongst the crowd. They brought their pie and eel stalls, gin wagons, puppet shows, thieves, card sharps, beggars and acrobats. The Thames mudlarks and coalwhippers took up their station in the mud banks where no one else would go and settled down for the scene. Magsmen had a heyday with thimble and pea and three-card tricks. Professional pugilists offered to knock anyone down for a guinea, and did.

The new bridge was decked with flags along its suspension structure and beneath the deck. Fairy-lights fluttered and flamed in position. It would be dark at five and the bridge was to be opened at six. Tented pavilions had been set along one entire side of the bridge so that the gentlemen and their ladies might dance through the night to bands. An arch of flowers had been erected at each end. Fireworks were concealed in the suspension members and the towers and anchorages were covered with a lattice supporting set-pieces. Within the pavilions, medieval pages and ladies-in-waiting sat with the medieval musicians and jugglers. They were suffering from medieval cold, for it was chill over the water. The sun might be out but the wind belonged to the season.

William was in the thick of it all and enjoying himself immensely. He was dressed like an extravagant courtier and had been rehearsing his gondoliers. The gondolas were pulled up beside a temporary jetty approached by a boarded walk over the yellow site mud. The musicians were dressed in brilliant cloths and carried stringed instruments, mainly mandolins and lutes. They too were flapping at themselves with cold, rubbing their hands and complaining. The gondoliers were an unbeautiful group of watermen dressed for the occasion in pantaloon trousers and slashed doublets. They had been paid well to do it, but still did everything with an air of deep resentment. The foreman appointed to the watermen was having trouble keeping them sober as they had been on the water since early in the day, practising their manoeuvres. The gondolas were their own boats and they had to be rowed as no pole could touch the bottom. William was lecturing them again on the need for utmost precision. They stared at him, slightly glazed and none too steady. One casually urinated in the Thames, having trouble with his pantaloons. William clutched his head in artistic despair.

'Stop the man doing things in the river, Mr Wood!'

'He's got to do it somewhere,' said the foreman reasonably, then remembering his fee, bawled at them sharply. 'All right, you coves! You're being paid for this, so listen to the gentleman, proper like!'

William repeated his instructions yet again. They regarded him with supercilious alertness. They knew what they were supposed to do, had known it all along. They would negotiate their fee on the alleged difficulty.

The grandstands had been erected on each side, adjoining the towers at the north end. They had been filling since mid-afternoon with the families and friends of the Company, the engineer, the builder and others involved. Artisans had been reserved a place on the bare earth bank. A large selection of nobility had been invited by ticket to watch the grand procession and grace the festivities. Their Royal Highnesses the Dukes of Clarence and Sussex were to perform the official opening. The Duke of Wellington, the Marquess of Lansdown, Lords Lyndhurst, Holland, Lowther and Ellenborough had been invited amongst many lesser beings. The grandstands were already well filled and the ladies had dressed with some care for the occasion.

La Belle Assemblée, the tyrant of the dressing classes, had emphasized turban hats decorated with feathers and pale green dresses with white piping. The grandstand crackled with pale green silk. Even Jane and Caroline complied.

Maria was dressed in pale yellow, seamed with brown over white gauze. As she was bereft of her husband, she sat beside Sam who was delighted. Maria was scathing about the ceremony, and about William too. Sam knew he should not encourage her, but she was a better companion than the others who murmured polite nothings among themselves, or talked endlessly about the trouble in Greece, the navy, the Turks and Russians, their servants and their dressmakers.

'Do you know, Sam, he has a special surprise hidden away in one of the tents,' she confided, leaning towards him. 'He is like a schoolboy. Delighted because he has hidden something in the teacher's desk.'

'That's really not fair, ma'am,' said Sam. 'After all, it is his job to amuse. It's not one I should like.' He paused and looked at her slyly. 'Well, come on, ma'am, tell me won't you, or do I have to wait?'

'Should I?' teased Maria. She was trying hard to enjoy herself. It was a frivolous enough affair and she should attach no importance to it, but she had come to hate these public shows. She could see the costume jewellery flashing on William as he moved about below. An actor, a peacock, she thought, without the skill to interpret. He wants to be transformed, he wants to turn the world back to a time that he imagines and that never was.

'Of course you must!' Sam insisted.

'You must promise not to laugh.'

'You have my word.'

Maria leaned closer to him. 'He has four knights in complete armour, with squires all dressed up in the proper fashion and he intends to run a tourney up and down the bridge.'

'A joust, by God!' He immediately looked ashamed of his exclamation, and Maria smiled at his enthusiasm.

'I see he'll please someone.'

'Well, it could be exciting. He's got an imagination.'

'He thought it would bring the King, but we are only to get the heir. He's very disappointed. I think he's lucky to get anyone above Lord Mayor. Poor Wellington! Nothing can happen unless he attends. He has become the state starter, like the man at Newmarket. It is just a bridge, after all.'

Sam was surprised by the acid tone of her voice. 'Maria. That's not like you.'

'Isn't it, Sam? You don't know me, then. I agree it's a fine bridge. William says it is a Gothick bridge although no one understands what he means by that. The bridge across the Hellespont, he says, as it was in Norse legends. He exaggerates everything. I find his brew of the ages very confusing and it is very bad scholarship. He attended that tilting party two months ago given by Viscount Gage at Firle Place near Lewes, and now he declares that it's the new sport of kings.'

'Can't see Georgie doing it,' whispered Sam dryly, 'so fat he'd break the horse!' He slapped his knees and laughed, willing her to join him and discard her acid mood.

Maria realized that as a family they had hardly considered what the loss of Thomas meant to Sam. They had been constant companions, and Sam was not the kind of man to complain or wear his emotions on his sleeve. They had been selfish about their own affairs and inconsiderate. Sam was stubborn. He had never taken a risk in his life, nor complained. The one thing that Maria held against him was his unyielding attitude towards Jane. Yet, when she glanced at Jane now, she wondered if he might have been right by some instinct of fatherhood. Jane sat beside Henry like a bride.

'Why is the King so fat?' asked Henrietta who sat beside her. 'Is it because he eats too much or is it because of ladies?'

Maria raised her eyebrows at Sam, trying to keep a solemn face. Sam gave her a chiding look, as though wagging a finger at her method of upbringing. His faded old eyes twinkled. He liked Henrietta too.

'Hush, Henrietta. You must never ask things like that in public. It's very rude. Especially about the King.'

'Yes, but which is it? I don't understand. I mean about the ladies.'

'That's some children's nonsense,' said Maria firmly.

Margaret, who had been listening carefully as usual, leaned across knowingly. 'It's ladies who get fat, isn't it, not men? But that's from having babies.'

Maria started talking rapidly about fashion and the vogue for Greek-style turban hats, about the death of Canning, about the Emperor of Brazil who was recruiting men in Ireland. Her girls were growing up and she was confused. Sam answered back, enjoying her embarrassment. He was deeply happy because Jane was happy and had told him why. Naturally Jane had not told him that Maria already knew.

Henry and Jane said little. He had not wanted her to come, fearing the occasion would be a strain. She had broken all her resolves and burst into tears when she had finally steeled herself to tell him the news. His solicitous and tender reaction had surprised her. She had not known what to expect and so had imagined all the worst.

He had been subdued these last weeks since Thomas's death, busy with his father's affairs and with Hebson. At times he had seemed preoccupied but his manner had not alarmed her. She knew immediately that this was a different mood from his icy remoteness of the past. It was contemplative, even vulnerable. There was no other woman. She felt able to judge that. He returned from work early and their domestic life was a series of tentative adjustments. Maria was right in her intuitive assessment; it was like being a bride again. They were rearranging their lives in small ways, hesitant in their desire to get them right. It was a remarriage.

'It's getting dark now,' said Henry, 'I wish they'd hurry up. Are you cold?'

'No. I'm warm enough.'

A band had started playing and she watched the flickering fairy-lights in their coloured glass jars. She was remembering Manning's party, and her clash with Thomas. It was a distant hurt that still grieved her. She wished that Thomas could have known and tried to commune with him in her mind, sending a message to him as she remembered him that evening. It was only the cruelty of despair.

Mr Tierney Clarke, the engineer, was becoming anxious. He and Captain Brown, the ironwork contractor from Birmingham, were walking up and down by the parapet, watching the commotion among the craft below. Clarke was soberly dressed and small, with sharp features and a quick manner. Brown was altogether larger and more ebullient. He had dressed to kill and his large bulk bulged to front and rear in his blue tail-coat. The effect was heightened by his tucking both hands under the tails as they walked back and forth. Mr Clarke was almost pallid of complexion. Mr Brown looked as though he had been standing too near his furnaces. They wanted to know what the delay was. Another band started to play at the other end of the bridge and the fitful wind that was stirring made a cacophony of competing sounds.

'The carriages should be here by now,' said Brown for the sixth time in six minutes. Clarke nodded and rocked on his feet. 'What the devil has that Kelleway man got to say about it?' His strong voice and Birmingham accent made heads turn. He lifted his hat to the enquiring faces. The gesture was dismissive rather than polite. 'That was a drop of rain. I swear it was!' he declared, shoving out a large hand, palm upwards. 'That's all we need. Can't we get on with it? Why do we have to wait for the Duke of Clarence?'

'We must wait,' replied Clarke. 'They have got to cross it first. If they get here and find it open, there's no more work for you and me!'

'I suppose not. By God, that *was* a drop of rain. That will be just grand for the fireworks. Why do we have to have all this?'

'Because it is a splendid occasion!' said William, exuding an enthusiasm that hid his own growing panic. The two men turned to him.

'Well, Mr Kelleway, what's the delay?' asked Brown. 'We've been hanging about here long enough! Where's this procession?'

'Delayed,' said William, who had no idea.

'Well, it's not good enough. Look, it's going to rain soon. Everyone will get wet. So much for the dancing!'

'It won't rain,' said William with confidence. To confound him, a scatter of larger drops fell. The engineer looked at the ironmaster. The ironmaster looked grimly at William.

'Look here, Mr Kelleway, what provisions have you made

409

against rain? If we have a pour, it looks to me as though the lot will come down.'

'It's been a perfect day. That's just a passing cloud.'

'Aye? Then where's the stars gone? Or do you save light in London?'

William gave this rude sally a short laugh. He hoped it sounded insulting. The man was insufferable but right. The night was clouding over and the river was dark as tar. He tried to control his panic. Would the pavilions hold? The crowd was noisy and restless. It was time for some diversion.

The Company men were restless too. He could see that the Directors had formed an anxious group at the northern end, by the lamplight shining on their gloss-black top hats. William slunk past keeping close to the parapet and avoided them. It was hardly his fault if the royalty were late. They were droning away to each other like a restless hive. He clumped down the boardwalk and found Wood, the foreman of the gondoliers, who was relaxing with a meat pie and a mug of gin-and-water.

'Get them out on the river. We must give the crowd something. I'll have the bands stopped.'

'It's going to rain.' The man did not even put down his meat pie. William shouted at him with fury, swearing he would get no pay. The man shrugged and called to the watermen to light up the lamps.

The boats were launched, their gunwales laden with coloured lights. It was effective and distracted the crowd who let out a great cheer. Thirty boats moved up and down like soldiers marching and countermarching, merging, parting and turning. In the bow of each boat a long pole had been lashed that jutted out over the water. It was surmounted by a steel spike from which hung a flaming iron brazier stuffed full of rags, tar and oil. These burned with a fierce orange-red glow, and swayed with the motion of the boats. A pall of smoke quickly formed and was lit up by the flames to an incandescent glow. Soon the whole river was covered with orange fog in which men moved with only their heads and shoulders visible and the raging braziers seemed to cruise by themselves. The band stopped and the musicians played. The sound was thin, far off and magical.

In the stands the spectators applauded, chattered and pointed out things to each other. William heard, and was relieved. That, at least, had been a success. What would they do if the Dukes didn't appear? He returned to the bridge feeling he deserved praise, only to see Brown scowling down at the river. He was in no mood for another encounter with the man. He must check that the knights were ready.

They were, and were in extreme discomfort and saying so. The Hon. Peter Jessington and Captain Gage were tired, hot and impatient. They had been imprisoned in their suits of steel for over two hours and were sweating vigorously with the effort of remaining seated. Their two opponents, who were to suffer defeat in the tilting, said less, being only country squires, but swore more to themselves. This was not what they had envisaged.

'Kelleway!' roared Jessington, 'When are we to start? It's getting deuced dark out there and deuced hot inside these coats, ain't it, Gage! How will we see? Where's the royal party?'

'It's all well lit,' said William, 'there are brands at every ten feet. A tilt-yard of fire. It will look splendid.' Jessington was not impressed.

'What happens if it rains? There's been drops.' Jessington was dressed in engraved Milanese armour, inlaid with gilt. It was elaborately fluted and puffed out at the front. The others wore more sombre suits of polished steel. 'At Firle, we didn't have to dress up, Kelleway.'

'But you wanted to,' protested William. 'The yard is covered with sawdust and straw. There's no danger.'

'Damn me, I ain't worried about danger. I wanted to wear armour when I thought it would be in the daytime. I never heard of tilting at night!'

'But it will be magnificent. Everything will sparkle and gleam.' William sounded desperate.

'Well I deuced well hope so,' said Jessington. 'We shall perish soon, shan't we, Gage? Is that the royal party, Kelleway? Have a look and let us know.'

There was a commotion in the distance. Raised voices and a sound of horses. William excused himself and hurried from the tent. The sound had an angry tone and there were no cheers. He walked rapidly back to the north portals with a sickening sense of disaster. The directors of the Company were gathered around a black phaeton bearing the royal arms. There was no Duke of Clarence, no Duke of Sussex, no one but two coachmen and an elderly and distinguished equerry who was having difficulty in making himself understood.

'I could not get through the crowds, gentlemen!' he was shouting. 'You must try to understand that it's not my fault I'm late. The roads are jammed and I have been delayed three hours. The news should have been with you this afternoon. If you will please be quiet, I have a message from the Duke of Clarence.'

The directors were silent. William felt sick. His stomach heaved and he swallowed. The equerry was standing in the phaeton and read from a piece of paper after he had cracked the red seal that held it.

'My lords, ladies and gentlemen, directors of the Hammersmith Bridge Company, I regret to inform you that I have unexpectedly been detained on official business. His Royal Highness the Duke of Sussex is about to leave town this evening for the country and in the circumstances has deemed it advisable not to put himself to the fatigue and trouble of going through the ceremony. We wish the Company every success and hope the ceremony will not be any the less because of our absence. Clarence. Charles Street, Berkeley Square.'

There was immediate uproar and the equerry looked understandably alarmed. The gist of the letter was being shouted back to the stands. The crowd picked up the news, and boos and jeers started. William was at a loss. He wanted to slink away. They must get on with the ceremony at any rate. The equerry was explaining that he also carried letters from Wellington, Lansdown, Lyndhurst, Lowther, Holland, Ellenborough, saying that they had previous engagements which made it impossible for them to attend. The directors were furious, and angry words were spoken about these lords who trailed on the royal coat. William was suddenly grasped by the shoulder by a man in glossy top hat and immaculate dress. He turned, half angry, half fearing some physical assault.

'Ah, Kelleway, I haven't had the pleasure of meeting you for some time. I understand that you are a very busy man, but I would have thought you might have enquired after my health, especially as I paid your bill.'

It was Walter Manning. William stared at him. It was more than he could take in. Large drops of rain began to fall again, plopping noisily on the crowns of their hats. Manning's face seemed more gaunt and he had aged, but his face still glistened in the light of the lamps. His eyes were hard and unfriendly and his manner neither shy nor diffident.

'You remember, Mr Kelleway. I thought you were a different person and that you might convert my view, my scarred eyes. You have converted my gardens but my view is like my wound, overgrown with tissue that is red and ugly. I believe, sir, that you are responsible for all this.'

'You've no reason to talk to me like that!' William was blustering and knew it. 'Nor am I responsible for the whims of royalty.' The eyes that regarded him were scarred with cold contempt.

'I do believe it is going to rain too,' said Manning, not taking his eyes from William's face. 'I think you have a disaster on your hands. Ill conceived, I believe, all of it. I don't expect you will approach the Company to pay for it.' Before William could grapple with the statement he continued. 'You see, I am a director and a large shareholder, and I shall have a say in this mess of yours. I allowed you to be appointed, because I was then convalescing and I thought you were still what you were. Your trouble, sir, is that you have outgrown human feelings like a child outgrows toys, yet you expect the help of others. I don't know you now. I don't believe you know yourself.'

His last words were spoken without anger, and he seemed to expect William to respond with denials but William was too angry and upset to understand Manning's hurt. Manning looked at him silently, hopefully. William responded with stupid rage.

'I won't be spoken to like this. I shall sue the Company if it won't pay. The ceremony will go on.'

Manning abruptly turned away and rejoined the other directors. William should not be allowed to see tears in the scarred eyes.

The downpour was sudden and violent. People on the bridge ran for shelter. The equerry and his carriage were suddenly

413

abandoned, and he shouted to the coachmen to turn about. They cantered off, glad to escape. Immediately the lights on the gondolas started to go out. The thin music stopped and voices could be heard shouting and cursing. The braziers at first hissed, then grew dim, then smouldered. The orange fog on the river disappeared. On the mud banks and the riverside, thousands scrambled towards trees or houses. There was no hope of enough shelter. Pie-stalls were invaded and overturned in the struggle. Quick hands stole what they could and wolfed it in the rain. In a minute the firm mud was a quagmire. The lights on the bridge began to fail as the rain found its way into the coloured glass jars. Workmen rushed about desperately trying to cover the fireworks, but the fuses were already soaked. The night was suddenly black and violent except for the swinging oil-lamps that steamed like stoves.

In the grandstand it seemed safe at first, and the spectators watched with more dismay than alarm. They talked volubly of the terrible disappointment, of the distance they had come and of the terrible journey it would be back home. Young ladies bemoaned the dancing.

'This is an end to it, isn't it?' Jane asked Henry, who nodded.

'I'm afraid so. Look at the mess. I must get you home safely. It will make a terrible journey if it doesn't stop. I don't think we should stay if it does. It will go on too long for you.'

'I'm all right,' she protested. 'Poor William!'

They stared at the tilting-yard. At first it soaked in the rain, then it seemed to rise like a raft, the sawdust and straw following the curve of the roadway, then it broke into a yellow mush that swirled into drains and gullies, blocking everything.

Without warning the grandstand roof started to pour with water. Women screamed and flailed at it, men cursed, beat at it with their hats and apologized for their language. Children screamed but enjoyed it. The boarding of the roof was butted but not tongued together and after its initial resistance it offered no protection at all, the water cascading between the boards as though from a colander. The water was bright pink with dye from the velvet cloth and stained clothing in a moment. The pale green dresses took strange blotched hues of grey and brown. The pandemonium was immediate. Family parties leapt to their feet before they realized they had nowhere to escape to. Their carriages were parked hundreds of yards away across a sea of mud and sawdust. Women burst into tears. Some families started to wade through the mess.

Maria was in tears, too, but for a different reason. She could see William down on the bridge, shouting at men and urging them on, although she had no idea what he was trying to do because of the commotion around her. His vainglorious velvet doublet had collapsed and his bombasted trunkhose hung about his knees in a shapeless roll. He had lost his hat and was spattered with mud and sawdust. She could not bring herself to glory in it. Sam had put his coat around her gallantly and they sat grimly on, determined not to join in the stampede of overdressed women whose clothes now clung immodestly to their breasts. Margaret and Henrietta started to giggle until Sam cowed them with a ferocious scowl. Caroline tried to help, but Sam shook his head and she sat down again, thinking she understood. They must all remain aloof and allow Maria to make of it what she wanted.

John seemed quite abstracted. He did not seem to notice the rain. He too had given his coat, to Caroline. Now he watched the rain, listening to it hissing and thinking of other roofs. Of water dribbling through palm-leaf thatch and making mud-tracks bubble like sulphur springs. He watched distracted women hurrying by for shelter they could not find and thought that they wore too many clothes. A single cloth can be wrung out. He could not imagine these matrons in semi-nakedness with their white skin and overfed bodies. There seemed so much that was ludicrous about this civilized race. Charlie and Nell were cold and wet. They had to shake him to make him realize their condition. It frightened them when he seemed so far away, his thoughts turned upon some inward agony. They all agreed that they must soon try to get to their carriages. The vulgar stampede was almost over.

The knights had been sitting stoically in their pavilion when it collapsed. The velvet was heavy and clinging and they had trouble getting out at all. The grooms in the next pavilion with their horses were in even more trouble for the animals lashed about furiously as the cloth fell on them. Company men tried to disentangle the mess of poles, ropes and cloth to drag the animals clear. They bucked and kicked, finally dragging the whole structure down. Slowly the other pavilions collapsed, deprived of their side support. They lay down in the mud and expired.

Brown the ironmaster cornered William. He was not the kind of man to be put off his purpose by a bit of rain

'Kelleway!' he bawled, 'Kelleway! You had better listen to me, sir!'

William, who was helping the struggling men to restrain a kicking horse, was white with anger and bitter disappointment. Brown was insensitive to anything except his own rage. William had spent days and nights in preparation that was now all ruined. Brown was dealing with a different man, had he known it.

'What do you want, Brown? I'm busy. Lend a hand.'

The knights were staggering heavily along the bridge, still in armour. They could hear the derisive cheers of the wet crowds. The horse pricked up its ears and was distracted. A groom stroked its muzzle and it seemed quieter.

'Damn you, sir, you shan't be too busy for me!' Brown shouted, livid with rage. 'We will sue you for this, because we are certain to be sued. Your tents are no good. They leak, and the dye runs, sir.'

'They're not my tents, damn you, sir!' retorted William, to Brown's astonishment.

'You're responsible, Kelleway. You ruined the opening. You made no provision for rain. And, by God, I'll ruin you.'

'Get out of the way,' said William.

'What, sir?' Brown was incredulous. He had intended to spit on the wilting peacock, but the peacock refused to be spat upon.

'Get out of the way, you fool, there's work to be done. If you can't be useful, be off. Keep your threats.'

'By God, we'll sue. I promise that! Damn your impertinence!'

'Go to hell, sir! And if you step nearer, that horse is liable to put you there.'

Brown looked around him as though for a weapon to launch a physical assault. His face was so red he should have been steaming and breathing fire. He suddenly wheeled about with clenched fists and stormed off along the bridge. William watched him with contempt. He realized he was in no way afraid of the man's bombast. The workmen with him were impressed. They exchanged glances that conveyed approval and surprise.

Brown passed the grandstands, his legs and boots heavy. Beyond this point there was a mêlée of spectators. Some were trying to get away but were unable to move over the clogged ground. All roads from the site were blocked. Carriages had become bogged and gangs of men manhandled them out of mud holes. Other spectators just stood and watched. The poor were no strangers to wet and cold and seemed indifferent to it, laughing and jeering at every mishap. The gin stalls were swamped with trade.

Brown walked right into a pretty young woman, wrapped with a Paisley shawl. She staggered and nearly fell sprawling in the mud. An angry male voice gave an exclamation, and he found himself seized by the shoulder. He turned to find himself staring into the face of a good-looking, well-dressed man of about forty.

'What's your hurry, sir, that you knock over ladies?'

Brown angrily tried to pull away. The pretty young woman took the man's arm.

'It's all right, Tom, I'm sure it was an accident.'

'Damned careless, sir, I call it!' His voice was aggressive and loud.

Brown wanted to find Tierney, he had no time for any more trouble. 'I beg your pardon, madam,' he growled.

The man raised his hat, rather sternly, and let go of Brown's arm. The young woman smiled, and Brown raised his sodden hat, turned and pushed on. He had gone some distance through the confusion of people and vehicles when it struck him as strange that the man had not helped the woman up, but had seized him. He grabbed at his coat pocket, and let out a bellow that turned heads. Wallet, watch and silk handkerchief had all gone. So had his diamond tie-pin.

'What's the matter sir, been forgetful?' Sly faces grinned around him and melted back into the crowd.

Bessie and Will were well clear by now. They had been patient, waiting for a good picking and not taken the first that came along. 'How much?' she asked, holding his arm as they tramped along the river side. They were indistinguishable from the thousands of other couples who were forced to walk because their carriages had sunk in. Will was riffling through the contents inside his own coat pocket.

'Thirty-five at least. My hands are too wet, I can't count them. There may be a fiver in there. Come on, Bess, we'll drink one for poor strung Peter, whose throat they closed for ever.'

'Don't you hate them?'

'Every wallet is a cup of blood from these bastards.'

Henry and Jane had left and John had taken Caroline and all the children. They had talked around Maria's leaving, hesitant and oblique. Sam stayed and sat with her. It was what she wanted. The stands were almost empty. The rain had eased to a persistent drizzle. They had found a dry area.

'You go now,' Maria urged, sounding very unconvincing.

'Nonsense,' said Sam. 'You don't want me to.'

She smiled at him with her mouth, for understanding. 'We must go down and find William, then.'

'Whenever you're ready.'

'I'm ready now.'

They walked down the slippery wooden steps, Maria clutching his arm, more fearful that he might slip than herself. She was full of desperate hope that frightened her with its intensity. They moved along a plank walk towards the dismantled tents. The surface water had drained away, taking the mush of sawdust with it and clearing the crown of the roadway. They were able to walk along this quite easily. The lamps wore haloes that reflected in the river again. Maria had made Sam put his coat on again and relied upon her shawl. Sam's coat was wet through, and she was worried about him. She did not even notice her own condition.

William was sitting under an awning that was still hanging. The tents had been folded up into heaps tied about with their ropes. Men were loading these awkward bundles onto carts. As they lifted them they fell apart and had to be tied and lifted again and again. Nothing could be left for the night or by the morning it would all be stripped by the human jackals who waited in the dark. William looked utterly exhausted and was staring blindly at the ground. His costume, in rags, was unrecognizable. He looked up in absolute surprise when Maria approached. She had never seen his face so drained of energy before.

'Maria! Good God, I thought you'd have gone long ago. You're soaked. Sam, why didn't you take her home?' He struggled to his feet. 'Come under cover. God knows what you'll catch!'

'I wouldn't let Sam take me home,' said Maria, stepping under the awning. She felt terrified because he had changed so much. It was frightening to be confronted with overt weakness even when she had wanted it so much. She must treat it with gentle care. 'William, we'll take you home. The carriage is still there. You've done all you can here.'

He looked around him, reluctant to leave the debris. There was still some desperate hope in him that by remaining it could somehow be resurrected. 'Yes. I suppose I have.'

He let himself be led away. The men still working called out after him.

'Good night, Mr Kelleway!' William stopped and turned, finding it difficult to speak. It was a testimony beyond the florid words of any critic.

'Good night to you all.' He walked on with Maria who fought her tears. 'They've worked hard,' he said, 'they're good men.'

'I think you've worked hard, too,' she said, taking his arm.

14

Court of King's Bench, Westminster. Michaelmas term.
Masterson and Kelleway v. Hebson.

Mr Best was not at all happy. He was a contradictory counsel for he made a habit of saying so yet exuded supreme confidence. His face was the colour of a ripe Worcester and as round, but his eyes were pale grey and shrewd. His white bushy eyebrows were in constant use as he talked. He had taken the brief with some trepidation as it involved a fellow member of the Bar, and particularly as Henry, who was preparing the case for his father, was another considerable ornament of his own profession. It was his diffidence, pessimism and shrewdness that Henry liked. He had seen too many unctuous counsel in action, bolstered by a fat fee and pious hopes. It was his suggestion that they should have the deceptive Mr Best.

'He's nobody's fool,' he had reassured the family, 'he makes a practice of looking hot and confused and has developed it to an art. In that way he is often allowed to continue when other men are brought up short. The judges let him ramble on, and he makes his point against all objections. He can fight a good case.'

'But do we have a chance?' John had persisted, knowing that Henry was being oblique.

Henry's ready response confirmed John's doubts. 'Best will do his best!'

'You won't answer me, will you, Henry!' he accused.

Henry thought for a moment. 'I can't answer you, John. You must not be impatient with the uncertainties of the law. The answer is that I don't really know. We have two good precedents on our side. Whether their Lordships will take the same view or overturn it, I don't know. Nothing is predictable, although everyone wants it so. If I were certain of Masterson I would be a great deal more happy. That man worries me. There are things about his actions that are far from clear. Father seems to have entered into business with him like a child! Clever men can make such foolish arrangements for themselves.' Henry could not suppress the thought that Thomas had always expected to get more out of life than he put into it, in business, and with his children.

The gloomy courtroom was sparsely attended by public ghouls, for it was cold and there were warmer places for the idle to sit. Besides, shipping matters made poor gossip. The law reporters of the daily newspapers acknowledged each other, looked bored and exchanged chat and notes. They adopted poses implying the whole affair was infinitely tedious to them and that they would record it for their readers as a mere kickshaw. It would fill a column or two that no one would read. The court officials went about their business, ignored by these lordly hacks.

Henry was accompanied by John and old Sam Leigh, who had insisted on coming although he was having increasing difficulty with his hearing. They sat behind Best and his solicitor who had laid out their pink-taped papers and were waiting.

Sam had been very affected by what had happened to Thomas. There was little between them in age and he appeared to feel the same chill shadow. He continually blamed himself for not having stopped Thomas from making the investment, but Henry would not let him.

'Sam, you did everything a friend could do to dissuade a friend. Father was always determined. He thought it was a time for shipping, and so it is, but everything has risks.'

'He should never have taken a half-share. I told him to take less. I should have gone with him to this Masterson.'

'Then he would have taken a full share!' Sam paused and nodded to himself.

'Devil take it, I believe you're right. He was a determined man, Henry. If you take after him then you won't go far wrong.'

Henry ignored the contradiction of the statement. 'He was a very determined man.'

He saw Masterson come in at the rear of the room, and hover uncertainly, looking for somewhere to sit that would be safely distant. Sam sensed the tension in Henry and looked round. His rage was immediate.

'There's the rogue! Give me twenty years back and I'd whip him!' He jumped to his feet shaking a fist at Masterson. 'Don't come near here, sir! You are a disease!'

Henry grabbed Sam and pulled him down to his seat. The law reporters buzzed amongst themselves, a malevolent hive, and scratched on their pads of paper.

'Sam, you're a barrister! For God's sake keep quiet!'

'I will keep quiet for so long, sir, but once this business is over, I shall have my own business with that man. He is a villain!'

'It will do positive harm if our party is split. We have got to appear solid,' John intervened.

Sam said nothing, but sat and thought back to a happier day when he had ridden in a carriage to the launch. He had counted the ships in the reach, stopped the carriage to watch the rope-makers. It was a day to dwell upon. He must fall back on memories now, he supposed. Loneliness is bitter aloes, age is wormwood.

Masterson finally sat down not far from them, and Henry, sensible to the politics of the situation, inclined his head to him. To an onlooker it appeared a polite if somewhat formal greeting. The law reporters could make nothing of it.

'John, bid him good day,' hissed Henry. John turned and also inclined his head. Sam would not budge. 'Well, Mr Best, where are their lordships, the King's justices?'

Best turned his head, almost glowing in the gloom. 'They will be at refection, Mr Kelleway, and don't we know it! Thank God we didn't get 'em first day of term. I've seen 'em drink an ink-well!'

Henry laughed, as he was intended to. He felt disorientated in his position as plaintiff. He was beginning to feel the part of a nervous client.

'I am not at all happy,' Best confided, 'by the business of this delay by Masterson. We must put up Cochrane the master and hope his story sticks. What do you say?'

'I'm in your hands, Mr Best. I wouldn't interfere.'

'That's very proper, Mr Kelleway, but I would welcome your opinion. After all, most of my clients ain't got one! Besides, I'm a cautious man, and I know you have a sharp brain. Shan't expect a fee for it, shall you?'

Henry smiled again, impressed at the man's power to make others relax. It was very different from his own politely analytical stalking.

'I think that we are vulnerable. I agree with you that Masterson's story won't hold too well. It must be cemented up solid. I think you're right. Cochrane is all we've got to do it. There can be no doubt that the ship was totally abandoned, but beyond that there is a very grey sea.'

'Then how would you take it?'

'I would establish the abandonment as a fact beyond question. Men's lives come before goods still, even in this day and age. Then we must persist on the loss of beneficial use, which was absolute as from that moment. The ship was never regained thereafter, therefore that she fell into the hands of salvors is beside the point, as they were not acting as our servants nor for our benefit. I think we must stick with that, it is our strong line.'

'Mr Kelleway, I quite agree. I shall go to it.'

Justices Holroyd, Bayley, Park and Filmore made as much of their entrance as the limited audience would permit. The usher banged his staff and they all rose. The justices swayed in unison. Walking with their judicial stoop, they reminded John of a train of camels. They wore black and ermine robes, and full-bottomed wigs and there was much rustling and scraping and scratching as they took their seats. The law reporters stared fixedly at the oak beams of the ceiling until they were permitted to reseat themselves.

'That four's as dry as oakum!' Sam declared to Henry in a voice that carried to the reporters, who sniggered. The judges looked suspiciously around the courtroom for the source of mirth.

Carter was the opposing counsel. His manner was always bullying and abrupt, but he carried weight with those judges that believe the law should be pursued vigorously, much as a fox chased by hounds.

Mr Justice Holroyd addressed the Court. He was thin-featured and narrow-faced so that his wig hung about his face like the ears on a beagle. His brow was similarly wrinkled and he affected an artificial dry cough. However, he came quickly to the point.

'This case is a special case, hem, which has been reserved for the judgement of the Court. There are matters, hem, involved here which are of some difficulty as I understand it. The facts before us do not seem to be in dispute, and I trust this will remain so?'

He looked quizzically at the two counsel. His three fellow judges nodded sagely as though worked by strings and scowled to confirm they had not come here to be trifled with, but wished to get their teeth into a good point of law. Holroyd read out the salient facts and invited Best to begin, concluding with several dry coughs. Best rose quickly and started his exposition. He had been before these men on many occasions, and none of them liked a counsel who dallied with his papers.

'My lords, you have the substance of the plaintiffs' case before you, and his lordship has covered the points at law. I will be brief in my elaboration. There are many matters here beyond dispute. The plaintiffs' ship, a well-found vessel of great value and carrying a valuable mixed cargo of manufactured goods and livestock, met with a disastrous storm. There can be no doubt about the diligence with which the crew exerted themselves to save the ship. Every effort was made to that effect, and for further information I intend to put up her master, Captain Cochrane, so that the Court can justify itself upon that point.'

'What is your purpose in that, Mr Best?' asked Holroyd.

'My lord, as the plaintiffs seek to show total loss, I think it necessary to show that every effort was made and that owing to the storm the beneficial use of the vessel was totally lost.'

'Have you any objection, Mr Carter?'

'No, my lord,' said Carter, quickly. Holroyd merely nodded

'I will not dwell on all the events,' continued Best, 'but suffice to say that on the eighteenth day of July, the mainmast of the ship the *Thomas K.* was discovered to be badly sprung and the gale continuing for twenty-eight hours, the fore-yard and sail were carried away and much other damage done to sail and rigging. The bowsprit was also discovered to be badly sprung at the height of this tempest and she was making so much water that the crew were wholly exhausted in their efforts to save her. At this stage, with the pumps working continuously at all times, the livestock were lost through drowning. Your lordships will be aware how severe the condition of the ship then was.'

It was the turn of their lordships to stare indifferently at the ceiling. The only sound was the mouse-like scratching of the reporters, scribbling in their books.

'On the nineteenth day of July, the ship the *Thomas K.* was so disabled as to be unnavigable and able only to hold her helm. At this time, by God's good grace, the brig *Navigator* came upon her and stood by, without which, I fear, all souls would also have been lost and the tragedy have been yet more terrible.'

He paused for effect, but their lordships were unmoved. Best had not expected otherwise. Justice Bayley pursed his lips and sighed to indicate that he at least was not impressed by such inconsiderable issues.

'The brig *Navigator* was fully laden, but standing by, was able to take on board the crew of the *Thomas K.* with only their personal effects. In this endeavour, one man was unfortunately lost. The decision to abandon was taken only after consultation amongst the master, mate and mariners and for the preservation of their lives. At that time, my lords, the plaintiffs lost the beneficial use of the vessel and never afterwards regained it. The circumstances of the subsequent salvage of the vessel are, in my plaintiffs' submission, irrelevant to that single fact. That salvors were later put on board was wholly unknown to the plaintiffs. The crew that was put on board came from the brig *Navigator* and were never the servants of the assured. Their only object in saving the vessel was the prospect of salvage and they had the entire dominion of the ship until they brought her to Rhode Island, much battered and scarcely afloat. The property was then libelled in the Admiralty Court at that place and was decreed to be sold. The beneficial use of the vessel has never been restored to the assured as a result. They therefore had a right to abandon. The salvage paid was high, being half the value of the ship when sold at Rhode Island and that in itself, I submit, forms a ground for abandonment, as I am sure your lordships will recollect, according to Lord Mansfield in Goss versus Withers.'

Mr Best made a short bow and sat down, out of breath. Their

lordships removed their eyes from the ceiling. Holroyd looked at Carter.

'Mr Carter, have you anything to add, contra?'

Carter got to his feet, bowed to the bench and began in the rasping voice that was part of his armoury. He was tall and commanding despite his ferrety features.

'At this juncture I have nothing to add. I hope to show that the assured allowed the ship to be sold under the decree of the Admiralty Court, which they might have prevented and which was their duty.' He sat down abruptly before he could be stopped or interrupted. Holroyd glared at him but held his peace.

'Mr Best?'

'I will not respond to my learned friend, leaving interpretation to your lordships, but I would now like to call Captain Cochrane and I am happy that my learned friend may direct any questions he wishes to Captain Cochrane as it seems essential to me to establish beyond doubt the circumstances of the ship's abandonment.'

Holroyd nodded, and Captain Cochrane was called with unnecessary vigour from the great hall where he waited. He sported full beard and whiskers and seemed to have been extruded into his clothes which were tight on him as a second skin. He was not a large or heavy man, but extremely muscular, a man who had worked his way up. His face was a weather-beaten red that made everyone else in the room seem ashen. He was nervous in these surroundings, and when put up, his voice was hesitant and he cleared his throat a lot.

'Captain Cochrane,' said Best, 'we are concerned to ask you some details.' Cochrane nodded. 'You were master of the ship the *Thomas K.* at the time of her abandonment on the nineteenth day of July of this year?'

'I was.' Cochrane had grasped the rail of the box, and this seemed to give him familiar comfort.

'In your opinion as master, was the ship capable of being saved?'

'No. She was sinking. We were making water in the holds and could only hold her helm.'

'How did you take the decision to abandon?'

'I ordered the mate and crew to the aft cabin and we discussed her condition. The reports given to me, which I verified with my own eyes, were that if she took a heavy sea astern, she might at any moment founder. She was holed between wind and water, and I took my duty to be the safety of my men.'

'Was the damage such as could have been repaired?'

'There was no opportunity. In such a gale we couldn't get a sheet over the side to patch her, and no work inside would stop the water. With the bowsprit sprung, it would have taken days.'

'Was the gale severe?'

Cochrane seemed to be staring out to sea as he spoke, remembering. 'It was a bad gale, sir, such as you get only once in ten years. A green sea gale with so much cresting of the waves. They were breaking over us, sir, and coming down on her deck. I feared the deck might give next. Although we could hold her helm, without sail we could not run before her.'

'What does that mean?'

'She was wallowing. Being heavy with cargo and water, we could hold her bows into it but could not ride the waves. They washed around us and over us like we were a . . . a whale.'

'Did you expect there to be any chance that the ship would survive when you gave the order to abandon?'

'No, sir, I did not. None at all. My men were lucky to escape with the loss of only one life.'

'How many years experience have you at sea, Captain?'

Cochrane paused and thought. 'Going on for nigh thirty.'

'You did not think at any time that it was possible the ship would survive?'

'No, sir! My duty was to my men at this time. I had discharged my duty to my ship in full! My men were exhausted through pumping. Had they not been so exhausted, we might not have lost one good fellow!' Cochrane was suddenly vehement.

'Quite, Mr Cochrane. I have no more questions.'

Mr Best sat down and Mr Carter rose. He addressed the bench first.

'My lords, I have concurred with my colleague that this witness should be presented, because there are anomalies about this case that must be points of law. I do not propose to question the witness any further on the events leading up to the abandonment, because I do not believe there can be any dispute. My learned colleague will no doubt be returning to Lord Mansfield's decision in Goss v. Withers, where the question of salvage was introduced and was taken of itself to form grounds for abandonment. It is the events subsequent to the abandonment of the vessel that I am concerned with.'

'What is your point, Mr Carter?' asked Holroyd testily. 'The witness is waiting.'

'Very good, my lord.' Carter turned to Cochrane. 'You were, I believe, taken on board the brig *Navigator*, with your crew and their personal effects?'

'I was.'

'But a prize crew was put aboard your ship the *Thomas K.* and succeeded in bringing her to Rhode Island?'

Cochrane shifted his weight on his feet. 'Yes.' It was obviously a matter he found embarrassing. Henry was worried by the signs. Carter was pleased.

'How could it be, Captain, that a mere handful of men could safely bring to port a vessel that you have described as sinking? From your description of her plight I would have thought that impossible.'

Cochrane was gripping the rail of the box hard, and he looked angry. Henry and Best had done all they could to brief the man what to expect, but they knew he had a temper. Henry prayed he would swallow it. Ships' captains are not noted for tolerating questions easily.

'You are not a seaman, sir!'

'You must answer the question, Mr Cochrane,' interrupted Holroyd immediately, 'it is fairly put.'

'The prize crews, sir, are always volunteers.' His 'sirs' were becoming insulting. 'They are men who will risk their lives for the money. They are often lost. I am a captain, a master of a vessel. My duty is in equal parts to the owners and the safety of my crew.'

'Were there no men from the *Thomas K.* who would hazard themselves to form a prize crew as salvors? In that way, could you not have retained possession of the vessel for the owners?'

'My men were exhausted and half-drowned! I should like to see you pump for forty-eight hours. By God, they couldn't climb the companions!'

'Mr Cochrane! If you reply in that vein again, I will hold you in contempt of court!'

Holroyd was angry, wig flapping. Mr Best was on his feet shouting 'My lord! My lord!'

'Sit down, Mr Best. Mr Carter's question was quite properly put. I will not have disorder and blasphemy in this Court. Be warned, Mr Cochrane, that if there is any such outburst again, you will be taken from here to the cells!'

Cochrane was wrestling with a mixture of rage and amazement. Accustomed to command, his opinion of their lordships, the King's justices, was inexpressible. His contempt for Carter was obvious. The suggestion that he, a witness, should be jailed, seemed unbelievable.

'Do you understand, Mr Cochrane?' Holroyd pursued. The other judges sat with pinched lips as though sucking sloes. Cochrane nodded.

'I submit, your lordships,' continued Carter, 'that that was the first opportunity that might have presented itself for retaining possession of the ship. I will now move on to events in Rhode Island. Captain, you knew a crew of salvors had been put on board. What steps did you take when you arrived at New York?'

Cochrane gave the impression of speaking through clenched teeth. 'I informed the owners by the first available ship leaving for England of the loss of my vessel.'

'You have a copy of that letter, labelled document C, my lords,' said Carter, setting them rustling. 'This vessel being the brig *Fair Maid*?'

'Yes.'

'Then you had not heard from Rhode Island that the ship was saved?'

'I had not.'

'You had informed the assured's New York agents of a total loss?'

'I had.'

'Yet neither you nor the New York agents made any enquiry of the Admiralty Court to determine if any application had been made by salvors, or asked to be kept informed.'

'That is not so!'

Mr Best was on his feet objecting. 'My lords, there is before

429

you a document labelled G, which sets out clearly that Mr Cochrane and Townsend and White were informed by the Admiralty Court, to whom they addressed their enquiries, that the ship had been libelled by the salvors in that court at Rhode Island. This is a matter of fact.'

There was more shuffling of papers from the bench. Holroyd looked at Carter, giving a desiccated introductory cough.

'Hem. Mr Carter, this seems to be so.'

'I'm sorry, my lord. I will express myself again. Mr Cochrane made a claim upon the Admiralty Court, as her late master, stating that he acted for the underwriters. It is clear that he did not have their express permission to do so. This claim was known by Townsend and White who could well have intervened on behalf of the assured, as their agents, but did not do so. I put it, therefore, that neither the late master, nor Townsend and White, made any enquiry of the Admiralty Court in a proper capacity on behalf of the assured, although they had every opportunity to do so.'

'We can't answer that,' Henry whispered in Best's ear, 'Mansfield's decision rests on the owners using all means in their power to pay great salvage and not being able to meet it!'

'I know, I know,' returned Best, 'there is something very funny about this business in Rhode Island. We shan't get a decision here except by a miracle.' He sounded upset for once, although his expression seemed bland enough.

'It's what I expected,' said Henry. 'We should never have gone on for total loss. But Father would have insisted.'

'I shall have to say something!' said Best, hoisting himself to his feet. Carter had just sat down, and Cochrane left, looking furious.

'My lords, I submit that notwithstanding what has been said, the difficulty of the assured being such a distance from their ship made the situation impossible for them to act upon. The master acted properly in assuming the situation was that of a total loss and that his duty was to secure the vessel for the underwriters, it no longer being the property of the assured. I am sure no blame attaches to the master for that. I would ask your lordships to consider that the salvage paid was high, being half the value of the vessel, and to consider Lord Mansfield's decision that this itself forms grounds for abandonment.'

He sat down. The judges conferred briefly. Holroyd hemmed twice and spoke.

'It appears to me that at no time was there a loss until the assured allowed the ship to be sold under the decree of the Admiralty Court at Rhode Island which they might through the action of their agents have prevented, and which it was certainly their duty to prevent, by raising money to pay the salvage. Lord Mansfield in his decision says that the right which an owner has to obtain restitution of the ship and cargo, paying great salvage, may be abandoned to the insurers. Counsel have made mention of this. This expression is too general. It must mean such salvage as the assured has no reasonable means of paying, and that they shall have used every means in their power. In this case it would be different if it could be shown that the owners had used every means in their power, their agents being acquainted with the situation. But that is not so. No effort was made to pay the salvage and the ship was therefore sold. I am of the opinion that the assured are not entitled to recover for total loss.'

Bayley merely concurred. Park declared he was of the same opinion.

'The plaintiffs rely upon two circumstances in order to constitute total loss. The first is desertion of the ship, the second the sale. On the first point, the ship was not captured, that is, taken possession of by persons adversely to the owners. It was taken possession of by salvors for the joint benefit of themselves and the owners, had the owners acted properly. The desertion of the crew does not, therefore, amount to total loss. Secondly, the sale must have been found to be necessary and without the fault of the owners. In the case of the sale, there was no intervention, and a ship of great value, three thousand pounds at least, and with a cargo of greater value, was sold for one thousand two hundred pounds. The owners could have acted in time and did not. If they had exerted themselves and had not been able to raise the money, matters would have been different. There is no proof of any such exertion. It is consistent with the meaning of the policy that the assured cannot abandon without having so exerted themselves. On both grounds, therefore, I am of the opinion that judgement must be found for the defendant.'

Filmore concurred. Holroyd nodded, and straightened his papers. 'I find judgement of nonsuit.'

The Court stood as the black and ermine procession swayed back the way it had come. Henry was watching Masterson, determined he should not slip away. Hebson had come from the back of the courtroom and was in animated discussion with Carter. Best folded his papers with a shrug. It was, after all, no surprise. Masterson abruptly turned and left. Henry followed quickly and seized him by the arm outside the Court. Masterson struck away his hand, violently.

'Leave go of me, sir! What do you want? In business we must take these risks!'

'Don't talk to me of risks! Yours is one and a half thousand, and my father's was five and a half. That was well engineered!'

John and Sam had followed Henry out, as discreetly as possible. Any sign of haste might have brought the law reporters after them. John was quickly by Henry, knowing his brother's anger. Masterson tried to walk away.

'We haven't finished yet!' Henry shouted. 'This business killed him.'

'You're mad, sir,' said Masterson. Henry made a grab at him, seizing him from behind with an arm around his throat. John was equally quick and grasped Henry's arm, twisting it away with surprising ease. At this moment Sam came puffing out into the Hall. Heads were turning their way.

'Don't be a fool, Henry,' Sam hissed, 'if anyone is to deal with this rogue, then I shall!' Fearing that Sam would hurl himself at Masterson, John released Henry and grasped Sam firmly by the arm instead.

'Good God!' he scolded, 'what's the matter with you lawyers! What sort of jungle fowl are you? Where's your dry bones, eh? Where's your calm?'

Mr Best, hampered by his full gown and with his wig slightly squint, waddled swiftly past them as though enclosed in a sack. 'Gentlemen, the public! Not here!' His warning was timely for not only were curious spectators beginning to gather about them, but court ushers were sliding quietly from the shadows. 'I think we should quietly leave?'

His calmness was effective, for they all moved with him. The ushers hesitated, then withdrew. The spectators shrugged, looked disappointed and dispersed to find other entertainment. Outside, the yellow afternoon sun made them blink. Henry was already feeling ashamed of his lack of control, but his anger was unabated.

'The effect of daylight and fresh air, I find,' said Mr Best, 'is often to make the rancour of the courtroom seem ridiculous. Don't you find this, Mr Kelleway, Mr Leigh?' He was still moving them along the pavement, away from the entrance to the Hall. 'I find it myself after a particularly trying case, when I could cheerfully murder opposing counsel. I haven't done it yet! Indeed, I wonder if it has ever been done?'

The honest sense of Mr Best was humbling. Henry stopped. He felt calm now.

'Thank you, Mr Best. You have discharged your part of this well and stopped me from some foolishness. The business we have with Masterson doesn't concern you. Perhaps we should discuss later what we do about going for partial loss for the cargo?'

'Certainly, Mr Kelleway. I will wish you all good day, and stay in the fresh air!'

He nodded to them and waddled away in search of a carriage. Masterson glowered at the other three. His beard and whiskers seemed fluffed up like an angry fowl's feathers. He waited for them to begin. It was Sam who spoke.

'You needn't think we shall stop here, sir. We ain't satisfied, I can tell you. The New York agents were under your instructions and we shall want to know what went on.'

'Damn you, sir, that's actionable!'

'I know, sir. Take it. If you have laid off your assurance elsewhere, then be certain we shall find out. Why the devil did your agents not act?'

'The devil with you! How should I know? Have I seen them? I won't be insulted like this.'

'Allow me to say, Mr Masterson,' said Henry very coolly, 'that we are less than satisfied with what has come out so far. We shall proceed for partial loss, but let me tell you that we shall not expect to find that any goods were recovered from the *Thomas K.* and reached Rhode Island. We shall also want to know from Townsend and White why a ship valued at three thousand pounds was auctioned for less than half, and would be obliged to you for an answer. We are also curious as to who purchased the ship, and would be pleased if you would find that out.'

Masterson had gone white with rage, and his fists were clenched. 'What the devil do you accuse me of? Make it plain, so that I can sue! Don't hedge things with your nice legal talk, Kelleway. Assault seems more in your line.'

'You're blustering, sir!' declared Henry. 'I think we will wish you good day.' He turned on his heel and walked away. Sam and John followed suit. They strolled along the pavement a short distance, then stopped to see Masterson striding away in a fury, pushing people aside.

'The thing smells,' said Henry.

'Like a cesspit,' said Sam, 'but there's precious little chance of proving it. I'll wager that cargo was sold in New York and our friend there has had his half of it. Poor Thomas! He would not have been able to stand it.'

After the long day of the trial and with the low aspect of the sun, it seemed to Henry that the day must have already outworn its workings. He was surprised when he entered the chambers in King's Bench Walk to find that the clerks' office was still occupied. It was only early evening.

Corbett, to his irritation, bobbed his head out of the room on hearing the door, then strode into the corridor to accost him. He seemed excited and was flushed.

'Mr Kelleway, sir, can I have a word with you in private?' Henry eyed him suspiciously. He was surprised to see Corbett blush. He had never seen it before and would not have believed it possible. 'It's about Mr Perrin, sir.'

Henry had no inclination to listen to gossip and was annoyed. Corbett understood Henry's reaction, for he continued rapidly.

'He's in trouble, Mr Kelleway, that won't do the chambers any good. In a bad state of affairs. I thought I ought to tell one of the gentlemen and you are the only one except the three juniors and I can't go to them!'

'Come in, then.' He walked into his room followed by Corbett, who stood while Henry took off his coat and settled himself behind his desk. Henry was still unable to decide whether Corbett was distressed or enjoying himself. He delivered himself of the news with tragedian's relish.

'Mr Perrin's been charged with fraud on the Stamp Office in the sum of twenty-five pounds! They have had him down there for two hours today and he is only released on bail.'

'Oh God, not that!'

'I'm afraid so. He is in his room now in a terrible state, which is why I would take the liberty of speaking to you, sir. He went to the Stamp Office for an allowance on a stamp of twenty-five pounds which had been purchased for probate purposes and which he wished to return as useless. Well, the clerks didn't like the look of it, and it was examined further and they say they found marks of ink upon it that had been removed by means of chemicals. Mr Perrin was immediately taken into custody. I have had to find the bail myself, sir, not wishing to leave a gentleman in that state, hoping of course that yourself or some other gentleman will speedily release me from the financial burden, not being a well-off man . . .'

'Yes, of course, Corbett. I'll pay it.' Henry was brief with Corbett's supposed poverty. 'Now what about Perrin?'

'He's in his chambers, sir, and in such a state I don't know what he'll do.'

Henry nodded, sick at heart. 'I shall have a word with him.'

'If you would, Mr Kelleway. I'm sorry to impose on you at a time like this when you are suffering from personal grief, believe me, but they will examine him again tomorrow . . .'

Henry waved him away. 'You go, Corbett. And leave us alone.' Corbett looked offended, but did not respond. He knew what Henry meant.

When Henry knocked on Perrin's door there was no response. He knocked harder so that anyone within must have heard. Perrin suddenly opened the door. For a moment Henry caught sight of his long face deliberately devoid of expression. He looked very grey. Immediately he saw it was Henry, his expression changed. His leg moved forward so that his foot was against the door denying entry. His eyes glittered with anger and quick suspicion.

'What do you want?' His voice was harsh and in no way pathetic.

'I wanted a word with you.'

'What about? We never had anything to say to each other, Kelleway. I'm busy.' He obviously knew. Henry kept his temper at the man's understandable rudeness.

'It's nothing I can discuss out here.'

'Then go away, because I know what it is, damn you!' He tried, very quickly, to shut the door, but Henry prevented him by jamming his boot against it. 'What the devil do you want? Get out or I'll push you out. I'll call Corbett!'

'Shut up, Perrin!' Henry hissed at him. 'I'm trying to help you, you fool.'

'You can't help me, Kelleway, even if you wanted to.' His voice was venomous. 'You never could. You can't help yourself.'

Henry suddenly thrust his weight at the door, unbalanced Perrin and was in, shutting the door behind him with a crash. Perrin, knocked backward, blazed with rage, his fists clenched. He hesitated for a moment, caught between making a physical or verbal attack.

'There must be something,' said Henry pacifically, holding up both hands as though to show he was unarmed, 'surely it was a mistake. They can't be serious.'

Henry was so obviously sincere that Perrin was impressed. He paused, and in that moment of inertia, changed like a chameleon. The hectic colour left his face as quickly as it had flooded it. His crouching stance relaxed, then he seemed to crumple inside the shell of his clothing as though his body had lost substance. He shrugged in resignation, and turned towards the window almost aimlessly, walked there, looked out and turned again, going finally to his desk. He hesitated, as though considering the disadvantages of sitting, then pulled out his chair and sat down.

'You understand I don't want your sympathy, Kelleway? I don't need it. You can't help me. I shall be reported and disbarred.' He looked up at Henry, watching his eyes. 'It's a triumph for you, isn't it. My career, such as it was, over, and you are still on the way up. Ascending to the spectacular income of the Bench, no doubt. You don't seem pleased. I'll be frank about it, I dislike you, Kelleway, but you always knew that. I dislike your arrogance, your privilege in the profession through your father. You came up the same way we all did, buying briefs. I know your scandals and you're no better than I am.

'You took up a cause in which you have no belief because it would make your name and it has. Now you have dropped it because you don't need it and it don't suit what you've planned for yourself. Very good. I would have done the same, but I wouldn't have surrounded myself with pious hypocrisy. You are another Mr Adolphus, but won't admit it. I don't know what you're doing in here. I would understand it if you had come to chew at the body of the fallen. But I don't even know if you have enough human nature in you to do that. Well, Kelleway? There's no way out of this for me because it's true. Now that's privileged information because naturally I have denied it to the Commission, but they'll find out anyway.'

Henry stared at him, amazed at the turn of events. He was stabbed by the other man's criticism and tried to justify himself.

'I did not take up the Combinations without belief. Nor just to feather my nest. Every man is entitled to representation!'

'That's a fine protest. It has a fine sound. But we know, don't we? They pay well. What you don't know is that they came to me instead. No tooting. There's the laugh, Kelleway! I was about to take 'em off you, perfectly fair and square, career assured, and would have made a job of it. But I was broke. Just one more stamp, I thought – it isn't the first I've had to realize – but you wouldn't care about that. I could have lived off the crumbs from your crumbs, I was doing so badly. I couldn't pay my rental. Now it's all gone. They'll have to find someone else. I'm completely vanquished and you're, well, are you triumphant?'

'There's no triumph for me! I won't see a fellow barrister put down.'

'But you will, Kelleway. There's nothing anyone can do to stop it. I could insult you more if I wished, I've nothing to lose, but I won't because I am a man with some scruples. You can reflect on that, when you think back on Perrin. You won't forget it, you know. You never will.'

Henry turned to the door again. 'You're right. I can't help you.'

'Help yourself, Kelleway. You're wasting your time here.'

'What will you do?'

'You don't really care what I'll do, so why pretend? I'll get a job as an accountant and marry a rich shopkeeper's daughter. Will that do? You can have a clear conscience. Watson said you hadn't got one, you know, but I argued the case. I said I knew you must have one to have such a clear good opinion of yourself taking all other factors into account!'

Henry slammed the door behind him and Perrin laughed derisively at the action. After a while Perrin got up and stared out at Temple Gardens. His last privileged view.

Henry walked through the dark stone-flagged courts. Through Figtree Court, Elm Court, Fountain Court and back again through Essex, Brick and Hare Court arriving at the Temple church itself. He kept to the shadows like a felon, for it was dark deep down among the buildings. The oil-lamps on their ornate brackets produced only a local glare. He avoided other men, not wishing to answer questions about Thomas or receive condolences. He could not be polite today.

The stone effigies of mailed knights lay in a row on the floor, surrounded by an iron railing. He supposed he had come there for calm. A verger went about his business, lighting candles, but apart from him, there was no one else in the building. Henry leaned on the rail and contemplated the time-worn figures in such attitudes of discomfort. Did Thomas lie well? He was shocked by the image that floated into his mind. Could he slip in the coffin as they lowered it into the ground? They had held the cords straight enough.

Four of the effigies had crossed legs, looking uncomfortable on the stone floor as though they lay where they had fallen, hand on sword hilt and long shield buckled to the left arm. It was supposed to indicate that they had been on a Crusade. One of the knights' feet rested on a small dragon that held his stirrup, three others rested on small fierce dogs. Every link of their mail was carefully cut. The first Earl of Essex who died in eleven hundred and something and had reduced the eastern counties for King Stephen. A fierce and violent man. He was surrounded by his sons. William Marshal, Earl of Pembroke, who advised King John, and directed the hand that signed Magna Carta. His legs were straight. A sombre mood seeped into Henry. Men of so much power and rough vigour lay unlettered and unremembered except by those Templars who knew. Peaceful-looking men, translated into stone, with smooth unworried features, bland in death. Stone that brings repose. The effigies must have brought comfort to their wives and children. Henry wondered if they had flung themselves upon that stone, and kissed the smooth faces those centuries ago. Thomas had no such memorial, only a slab.

Yet all around him on the walls of the old circular church the stone was in agony. The carved heads on the aisle wall arches grimaced and screamed. Faces full of anguish and fear, carved in the durable material endlessly to endure purgatory. Some had cat-like animals tearing at their ears, others the rolling eyes and drooling jaws of madmen. Why should these men on the floor recline so peacefully? It was a bought thing of rank and wealth. Why had he gravitated to this place of the long-dead? It could not be merely to avoid other barristers. Did he require reassurance or prayer? He pondered upon it, staring into the unseeing eyes of a knight. He was not of a religious inclination yet he felt in need of comfort of the spirit – he hesitated to think of it as comfort of the soul.

Behind him, in the aisle of the long church, other richly decorated effigies proclaimed that after death their occupants had no intention of being forgotten. Henry passed them. Edmund Plowden in gilt and alabaster who built the Middle Temple Hall. A bishop, thought to be Heraclius, Patriarch of Jerusalem, who consecrated the church in 1185. The bishop's feet, too, rested on a dragon as though to remind that these bishops of old were not so different from the mailed knights.

Henry walked down the knave and entered one of Wren's huge high-backed pews. They afforded absolute seclusion. He had failed to bring the papers he had intended to collect and realized that he had fled from Perrin because he was afraid of the man's words. He had no further strength or will to deal with Thomas's affairs or his clerk, with the inevitable questions and commiserations. He was hiding in the dark from the unpleasant probings of his own mind. He kneeled in an attitude of prayer but could not think of anything to say. Questions forced themselves upon him.

Why had he refused to defend the man Morton? Was he convinced that he was really being honest with himself about his motives? Did he believe the case to be indefensible? Had he merely tossed it aside as an episode in his career? Was he influenced by what Mrs Waters had said? He felt guilt at thinking of her in the church, and found himself peering about in the gloom like Caliban searching for his god. Perrin had upset him. Why had he held out the olive branch which had been taken from his naïve hand, snapped and returned with a sneer? Perrin was a fellow barrister in his own chambers, he told himself, and it was his duty, but his thoughts refused to obey his willing. A parallel stream of doubts undermined the structure, wondered why he was producing these excuses. He could make no belated peace with Thomas or himself this way. He rose from his knees feeling a charlatan. It was self-indulgence. He would find more peace at home with Jane. She was to give birth in two months. Henry was proud of her girth. Proud, he realized, as a farmer with a fat pig; he would tell Jane that. He smiled to himself.

His anger with Masterson seemed to have been absorbed into the chill stone of the church. The bland effigies of the knights put anger into perspective. In its place he felt a determination, for the sake of the family as well as for Thomas's wish, to pursue the case for partial loss. It would be a long process, starting all over again with proceedings, but claiming this time for the damage done to the vessel and cargo before she reached Rhode Island. There would be something in it. He might never prove anything against Masterson, but he would accomplish a tying up of ends. The threads of his own life and the threads of Thomas's seemed at last to have converged.

*　　　*　　　*

Williamsburg
James City County
Virginia.

February 1828.

Dear Henry,

I have written separately to Caroline and the children, so this letter is addressed to you only. I know how you feel about me and I don't want you to think of this as a justification. I would rather that you understood, and care nothing about being forgiven.

Caroline will be excellent for Charlie and Nell. They have needed a mother for some time. I was not even a good father. They were afraid of me, for I was often an empty shell. I hope to find their mother now, and think I shall. I never explained to you, but perhaps you guessed like Caroline? I drove their mother to madness. That may confirm in you the worst things you have thought of me, but it is at least honest.

There is still no place for me in civilized company. You cannot know, Henry, what it is like to be haunted by guilt. I am like Macbeth, for what I did was a kind of murder but the victim will not die. My Banquo is maimed and alive. I have done things that only a crazed person would do, or someone so selfish that he forfeits the favour of understanding. That's been my burden and I can't live with it.

I must find the woman. God knows what I shall do then, because again I can't expect forgiveness. Because I destroyed her, I believe I can make her well, even though I know that belief is without any logic. It is an obsession, I know. I have to believe that I can undo my own evil. Surely there is no point in life without that? Perhaps you think me mad. I won't argue, because I don't know.

People here don't recognize me. I have taken pains to alter my manner and appearance. I move about freely and have had news of where she went on leaving here. She is still in Virginia, and I shall set out tomorrow.

I think it was Father's death that was the end for me. He and I never made our peace because I was caught in my lies. It showed me that I should never be rid of them except by taking this action and dealing with it. Even in writing these truths I am concealing more from you than I can ever tell.

I intend to return soon, with the will of God.

John

More About Penguins and Pelicans

Penguinews, which appears every month, contains details of all the new books issued by Penguins as they are published. It is supplemented by our stocklist, which includes almost 5,000 titles.

A specimen copy of *Penguinews* will be sent to you free on request. Please write to Dept EP, Penguin Books Ltd, Harmondsworth, Middlesex, for your copy.

In the U.S.A.: For a complete list of books available from Penguins in the United States write to Dept CS, Penguin Books, 625 Madison Avenue, New York, New York 10022.

In Canada: For a complete list of books available from Penguins in Canada write to Penguin Books Canada Ltd, 2801 John Street, Markham, Ontario L3R 1B4.

In Australia: For a complete list of books available from Penguins in Australia write to the Marketing Department, Penguin Books Australia Ltd, P.O. Box 257, Ringwood, Victoria 3134.

Two magnificent novels from

M. M. Kaye

The Far Pavilions

*'A Gone with the Wind
of the North-West Frontier'* –
The Times

The Far Pavilions is a story about an Englishman –
Ashton Pelham-Martyn – brought up as a Hindu. It is
the story of his passionate, but dangerous, love for Juli,
an Indian princess. It is the story of divided loyalties,
of friendship that endures till death, of high adventure
and of the clash between East and West.

'Magnificent . . . not one of its 950 pages is a page
too much' – *Evening News*

Shadows of the Moon

**India, that vast,
glittering, cruel, mysterious and
sunbaked continent, is captured here
in a spectacular romance by the author
of** The Far Pavilions.

When India bursts into flaming hatreds and bitter
bloodshed during the dark days of the Mutiny,
Captain Alex Randall and his superior's wife, the
lovely, raven-haired Winter de Ballesteros, are thrown
unwillingly together in the struggle for survival.
And, in their love for this torn and bleeding
country, they gradually discover a tender
and passionate love for each other.

Two gripping historical dramas

To the Opera Ball
Sarah Gainham

In the aftermath of the Second World War two women, the younger, Anna, carrying her unborn child, set out in the cruel, unrelenting winter silence to walk across Central Europe. Following in the wake of the Russian and German armies, they endure starvation, degradation and brutal rape ...

Twenty-five years later there is one brief, tender meeting amidst the scented extravagance of an opera ball in Vienna. The man with black eyes is Anna's son; the beautiful girl is the daughter of Monsieur Chavanges, a man who has plans for his only offspring.

'Miss Gainham writes a prose as ... rich as Viennese hot chocolate with cream' – *The Times*

'Fearfully readable' – *The Times Literary Supplement*

'Written outstandingly' – *Financial Times*

From the Broken Tree
Lee Langley

For three generations the family fought to survive.

They withstood the violence and prejudice of the Polish ghetto, they struggled to live in London tenements as grim and pitiless as a Dickens novel, they evaded the dangers of Nazi Germany, to build a position of wealth and security which, in the end, was just as precarious.

For Leah, Manny and Joe, who loved, hated, despaired and strived, the experiences were all different. Only their past and their Jewishness remained the same.

'[It] grabs you from the very beginning and doesn't let go until, with tears in your eyes, you finish' – *She*

'Highly sophisticated, highly civilized and moving' – *Scotsman*

Romance, intrigue, adventure – it's all here in these unputdownable Penguins

Anthony Adverse

Hervey Allen

This book outsold every book in America except the Bible when it was first published: a classic swashbuckler of a historical romance, combining superb narrative with a panoramic sweep of excitement, passion, and a rich feeling for period.

Anthony grows up an orphan in a Europe dominated by Talleyrand, Pitt and Napoleon. As the nations succumb to the tramp of the First Consul's armies, he is propelled into intrigue and adventure that take him to tropical Africa, France, Spain, England and America. And for each of the delicious and voluptuous women he loved and wooed, life was never the same again . . .

The Greenlander

Mark Adlard

Every year the whalers sailed to the northern fishing grounds to confront the sea and ice, and to lock in terrible battle with the leviathans that lurked beneath the waters.

For Arthur Storm, the newest apprentice on the *William Scoresby Senior*, going a-whaling was the fulfilment of every boy's dream. He was to encounter the power of the sea, the ring of the harpoon, the blood, and the bonds – deeper than friendship – forged by the men as they sailed together into the Fishery's worst catastrophe ever.

'A trilogy that leaves one hungry for more' –
Observer

The Crimson Chalice Trilogy

Victor Canning

'Victor Canning is one of the world's finest story tellers'   *Good Housekeeping*

A.D. 450 – and Britain lay wracked by tribal violence and predatory invaders as the Roman presence slipped into oblivion.

Deep in the wilderness and the mists a new force was stirring which was to take the Saxon by the throat and establish the rule of one British overlord. For Arturo, the man chosen by the gods to be king, his Companions and Gwennifer, his golden-tressed, barren queen, were preparing to ride into battle and into our history.

Victor Canning's dramatic and original reconstruction of the Arthurian myth resounds to the clash of arms, to the beat of earth's rhythms and to the truths of flesh and spirit that pass between man and woman.

'A master of his craft' – V. S. Pritchett
'Splendid stuff' – *Yorkshire Post*
'Engrossing' – *Daily Telegraph*